THE SECT

THE SECT

A DETECTIVE RAVN THRILLER

MICHAEL KATZ KREFELD

Translated from Danish by Lindy Falk van Rooyen

Podium

SAGA

EGMONT

Podium

THE SECT

*"Yea, though I walk through the valley of the shadow of death,
I will fear no evil, for thou art with me;
thy rod and thy staff they comfort me."*

Book of Psalms, 23:4

1

He was sitting at the head of the kitchen table. It was mid-October, and in the garden outside, the pruned fruit trees were silhouetted against the evening sky. His son was sitting to his left. The boy had just turned six, and he was trying to impale a chip on his plate with the fork that was clenched in one fist. The other hand rested on a blue toy car with peeling paint on its bonnet. He glanced at his son. The boy had features that reflected his own: a baby hawknose, a mouth that drooped at the corners, and close-set eyes that lent both father and son an eternally pensive expression.

He reached out and stroked the boy's head. The boy let himself be stroked. The chubby cheeks and freckles he had inherited from his mother, who was standing by the stove with her back turned. She fished chips out of the frying pan and dumped them next to the golden-brown Wiener schnitzel on the plate that was within reach on the kitchen counter by the hob.

"Would you like peas as well?" she asked her husband without turning round.

"Yes, please. Just a few," her husband said, laying a serviette on his lap to shield the navy suit trousers from droplets of frying oil. Apart from the shiny black shoes he'd kicked off at the door in favour of a pair of comfy camel-wool slippers, he hadn't had the chance to change after work, so he was still dressed in a pale-blue shirt and navy suit jacket.

"What about you?" he said, turning to his son with a smile. "Would you also like some peas?"

The boy shook his head violently.

"No? But you've always liked peas, right?"

The boy nodded and opened his mouth, which was full of food. "Yes. It's just that . . . they're so hard to eat—"

"We don't talk with a full mouth," he said sternly.

His wife put his plate of food in front of him and sat down with her own plate in her hand. She started squirting ketchup over her chips and fried veal. The bags under her eyes and her chapped lips made her look much older than her thirty-two years. He remembered that the first time they met. It was her smile he had fallen for back then, but she seldom smiled anymore. She was a housewife, stayed home most of the time, and for the life of him, he couldn't fathom why she should be so exhausted all the time. He poured her a glass of juice from the jug standing on the table. She gave him a brief nod of thanks. His son had given up on the chip. The boy was absorbed in vrooming his toy car around the flower-pattern racecourse on the tablecloth—faster and faster, louder and louder, till he took a hairpin bend around his juice glass. Then the boy yawned, open-mouthed, and his car sputtered to a halt.

"We don't play at the dinner table," she said.

"That's all right. Let him play," he said.

A look of surprise came over his wife's face. Understandably, of course, for *he* was the one who made the rules, including the ones pertaining to table manners. "Drink your juice, my boy," he said with a smile.

The boy did as he was told and gulped down his juice at once.

"How was . . . your day?" his wife asked with her mouth full.

"It was fine, thank you."

"Anything special today?"

"No, not really. Same as usual."

"Nothing special at all?" she said.

He put down his knife and fork, picked up the serviette in his lap, and dabbed the corners of his mouth. "Please don't misunderstand me, because I think it's kind of you to ask about my work, but there's really no point, my dear, for if I were to start sharing the content or details of the tasks I performed in the course of my day—any day of the week—you wouldn't begin to understand what I was saying. So, with all respect, having a conversation with you is meaningless."

His wife blinked rapidly, swallowed the food in her mouth in one gulp, and nearly choked on it. "It's . . . it's just that I thought it would be nice to talk . . . We can talk about something else . . ."

"I understand. The *first* bit. Why don't we just enjoy the silence whilst we eat?"

His wife didn't reply and started eating faster, as if she wanted to clear her plate and get dinner over with as fast as possible.

He neither reprimanded nor put her right. Not tonight. He didn't even chide her disgusting table manners. He ate his dinner without another word, looking out over the garden once more. The fruit trees seemed to be staring at him, communicating their own silent rebuke as the low crowns swayed from side to side. There was no wind, yet he felt like they were shaking their heads at him. He was just about to stand up to close the curtains when he was interrupted by the loud clang of his wife's cutlery on her plate.

He turned his head towards her. She was swaying back and forth in her chair, bringing her hand up to her head, breathing heavily. She swallowed rapidly a few times and reached for her glass but merely knocked it over. In a dark-red rivulet, the contents spread over the tablecloth. "I-I'm sor-ry," she stammered. With obvious effort, she raised her head and looked at her son. The boy was slumped over the table. His body motionless, the right hand still clutching the toy car. His mother gasped and turned her head to face her husband.

He returned her gaze as he chewed calmly. "It's all right, dear. Just lie down and sleep now."

His wife stared at him, as if in awe . . . then her gaze shifted to his glass of juice. He had not touched it. "What . . . what have you *done* . . . ?" One arm rose in the air as she tried to get to her feet, but she fell onto the linoleum floor. And she stayed down.

He tilted his head to one side, glancing over the edge of the table, watching his wife as he finished chewing his mouthful of fried veal and peas. Her arm was stretched over her head, as if a swimmer in mid-crawl motion—which was rather ridiculous, he thought, for his wife was not the sporty type, and he doubted very much that a girl like she, who had grown up on a farm deep in provincial Denmark, would ever have learned to swim.

When he had finished his dinner, he pushed his chair back and went over to the bay window. Dusk had long since fallen, and the naked fruit trees had disappeared in the dark, but he drew the curtains anyway. He cleared the table and scraped the leftovers into the dustbin. A few peas escaped from his own plate, and he bent down to pick them up. His son was right; peas *were* a nuisance. He wished they'd had more time together. Perhaps he could've shown him how to *mash* peas with a fork, so you don't run the risk of them scattering all over the place. But their time had run out.

He loaded the dishwasher and turned up the gas under the frying pan. Then he returned to the table and picked up his son. The boy moaned briefly but was sufficiently drugged with morphine. He carried the boy down the long corridor to the boy's bedroom. But he changed his mind; he passed the boy's bedroom and continued to the master bedroom instead. It seemed right, more fitting that they should sleep together in the current circumstances. He deposited the boy in the middle of the double bed and returned to the kitchen.

The frying pan was giving off smoke and the burnt oil stank to high heaven. The next instant, the fumes burst into flames, which licked up the wall behind the hob. With great difficulty, he picked up his wife off the floor—she was a lot heavier than he had imagined. As the flames set the kitchen cupboards alight and spread with explosive speed, he carried her calmly into the master bedroom and laid her next to the boy. He took off their shoes but let them keep their clothes on. He crossed their arms peacefully over their chests.

He sat down on the bed and took off his slippers and socks, flung the suit jacket onto the floor, and lay down next to his wife and son. Then he closed his eyes and tried to breathe normally. He was only partly successful with that. Briefly, he considered whether he should get up and drink a glass of the juice spiked with morphine but rejected that option as cowardly. He deserved to feel the fear of the fire now. He deserved to be conscious the moment he was burnt alive.

Soon he began to cough because of the thick smoke that filtered into the bedroom. He could hear the fire running through the living room, now feeding on the parquet floors and beams in the low ceiling, now eating through the paintings on the walls, including the precious Henry Heerup piece over the fireplace, now transforming his Hornung & Møller grand piano into tinder and ash. Flames like a hoarse whisper spreading down the corridor. And he could feel the glowing heat just behind the wall.

His eyes were closed, but they stung and teared from the smoke that crept down his throat, choking him. There was only one thing he regretted now: the suicide note he had left on his desk at work. At the time, it had felt like the right thing to do, the correct behaviour under the circumstances. Just like proper table manners. There is *always* a right and wrong thing to do in a particular set of circumstances: *Keep your mouth closed when it is full. Lay your family to rest. Cross your arms over your chest. And always mash your unruly peas first.*

There are a set of rules and regulations for everything. More than anyone else, he understood that the world was built on a bedrock of systems.

2

Present time
Christianshavn, August 2014

The radio host, who called himself "Teddy-K," announced that this was going to be the warmest day of the year to date. It was only ten thirty in the morning, and Ravn was inclined to believe what he heard on the radio for a change, even if Teddy-K's high-pitched proclamation didn't strike him as the most reliable source of truth.

Despite having rolled down all the windows in the old Audi, his T-shirt was drenched in sweat. Teddy-K switched to advertisements and Ravn automatically turned down the sound. The car was a loan from his new employer, and he still hadn't figured out how to switch the damn thing off.

Keeping two cars behind, he was following the black Porsche Cayenne that was crawling along with the morning traffic. The driver of the Porsche had also rolled down his windows, blasting his immediate environment with hip-hop music from his radio. Moments later, the Porsche turned onto Uplandsgade and Ravn followed the car into the large car park in front of the supermarket, SuperBest, which was almost empty at this time of day.

Ravn parked the Audi close to the supermarket entrance, just two rows behind the Porsche. He searched for his video camera, which he was certain he'd brought along. "Move over, he said to Møffe, who had been taking a nap on the passenger seat.

Sure enough, Ravn found his camera buried under the bulldog's generous belly and Møffe grumbled at Ravn for the rude interruption.

"Stop complaining, or I'll leave you at home next time," Ravn said, flipping out the camera, which switched on automatically. He raised the screen just above the dashboard, zoomed in on the Porsche, and started filming.

A flabby, bald man in his mid-forties got out of the passenger seat. He was wearing cut-off jeans, a leather jacket with a biker logo on the back, and a white neck brace. The driver's side opened and a large woman with platinum blonde hair stepped out. She had just as many tattoos on her arms as her husband. For a moment, he thought that her face was also tattooed but then realised she had a black eye. Beyond Ravn's earshot, the man yelled something at his wife. The woman gave her husband a dirty look, then she opened the rear door and hauled a boy out of the back seat. The boy looked about ten years old and seemed to have inherited his size and flab from his parents. He was completely absorbed by the tablet in his hands, despite his mother pulling on his arm. The man caught his son's attention, gave him a coin, and pointed in the direction of the shopping trolley bay. The boy made his way over, dragging his heels. By the time he got back with the trolley, his mother looked impatient and snapped at her husband. The man pointed at his neck brace and shrugged. The woman shoved the boy aside and took over the trolley as the family made their way towards the supermarket entrance. Ravn kept filming till the family disappeared inside.

"The time is now"—Ravn checked the digital clock on the dashboard—"is now 10:38 a.m. I have been tailing Carsten Nielsen and his family to . . . SuperBest on Amager. Still no sign that the suspect is simulating his injury."

When Ravn stopped filming and made to get out of the car, Møffe lifted his head and gave him a doleful look.

"You stay here, Møffe. There's a dog treat in it for you if you stay out of trouble till I get back," said Ravn.

Møffe snorted and lowered his head onto the seat again.

Ravn headed for the supermarket entrance with the camera hidden under the hoodie he had slung over his forearm. He doubted that Carsten would be dumb enough to do anything that might reveal in public that the neck injury he had reported to his insurers was fake, but you never knew. Carsten had reported a disability benefit of twenty-five percent, which in hard cash would entitle him to claim 2 million kroner from his accident insurance. He'd bought the policy three weeks before the purported accident. There was only one witness: the man who drove into Carsten. And the sole witness happened to be one of Carsten Nielsen's "brothers" from a local Christianshavn biker club—a man who had successfully cashed in on a similar disability insurance scheme two years ago. Ravn had been on the case for over a week. He needed to find hard evidence today that Carsten—aka "the Rat" to his brothers at the club—was faking his injury. If he didn't, the Rat would win the jackpot.

Ravn entered the supermarket. It was refreshingly cool inside. He grabbed a shopping basket and randomly picked a few items off the shelves as he sauntered down the aisles. When he reached the refrigerated goods section, he spotted Carsten and his family, whose shopping trolley was filled with groceries. Ravn followed them at a safe distance.

The wife was pushing the trolley, and Carsten shuffled after her in his wooden clogs. He looked hot and sweaty and kept tugging on the neck brace, which was clearly bothering him. Every time he looked in a new direction, he had to turn his entire body, which gave his movements a robotic look. When they reached the drinks aisle, Carsten nudged his son on the shoulder and asked him to grab a case of Carlsberg Elephant Extra Strong beer.

"Get it yourself," said the boy without taking his eyes off the tablet in his hands.

Carsten ripped the device out of his son's hands and bent over, his face just millimetres from his son's nose. "Do you wanna lose this piece of shit?! Well, do ya?!" he yelled at the boy.

The boy glanced at the tablet, which was out of reach. Then he turned round and went to the closest stack of beers. With great difficulty, he lifted the top case off the pile. "It's fucking heavy, Dad!"

"I said *Elephant* beer," Carsten replied, pointing out which kind he wanted.

The boy put down the case he had clutched in his arms and traipsed over to find the beer his father had asked for. With the help of his mother, the boy managed to lug the case of Elephant beer into the trolley.

Ravn paused in front of the canned goods, keeping one eye on the family as they continued down the aisle. In his assessment, and compared to other bikers Ravn had met, Carsten's IQ was below average, but he was clever enough not to put his phoney claim at risk. For his own part, Ravn wasn't particularly bothered whether the insurance company would get duped by Carsten or not. The bonus he would receive from the lawyer who'd hired him if he found evidence against Carsten was a nice thought, but that wasn't the reason he wanted to nail this guy. What bothered Ravn most was that the Rat had been giving him the runaround for over a week. And he had an intense dislike for bikers in general. When he was with the Special Crime Ops team at Station City, he'd spent years of his life on these arseholes, and he'd put many of them behind bars. He'd be damned if he was going to let the Rat aka "I-piss-on-everyone-and-beat-my-wife-Carsten" get away with it. He had to come up with a plan that could confirm or deny once and for all whether Carsten was faking his injury or not. Right *now*.

Ravn deposited the shopping basket back on the pile and walked swiftly to the exit. When he came to the car park, he fished a coin out of his jeans pocket and continued to the shopping trolley bay. The trolleys were arranged in two long rows of about ten each under a wooden shelter. He put his hoodie and the video camera on the ground and squeezed in between the two rows of trolleys. When he reached the back of the shelter, he stuck his coin in the slot and freed the first row of trolleys from its lock. Bracing one leg against the back wall, he forced the entire column out of the shelter. With an almighty screech of metal against metal, Ravn pushed the trolleys over to the back end of the Porsche.

In that moment, Carsten and his family came out of the supermarket. Carsten hurried his wife, who was pushing the heavy trolley. Ravn knew it was only a matter of seconds before Carsten would see what he was up to. Putting his back into it, he managed to shove the row of trolleys across the parking bay and block the Porsche's stall. He quickly picked up the hoodie and the camera and returned to his car.

"Hi, Møffe," Ravn said as he slipped into the driver's seat.

Møffe yawned and rolled over, presenting his belly to be scratched, but Ravn didn't have time. He could already hear Carsten's litany of swear words booming over the car park, and he hunkered down in his seat and turned on the video camera. He got Carsten in his sights and zoomed in.

Carsten was pacing back and forth whilst his family looked on in defeat. The row of trolleys stretched from the rear end of the Porsche to the entrance of the wooden shelter, as if a shop assistant had abandoned them. It was impossible to get into the car, never mind drive away.

Carsten commandeered his wife and son to get the trolleys out of the way. They tried pushing, they tried pulling, but no matter how much Carsten kept yelling at them, the wife and son were unable to move them. There was nothing for it; he had to help them. Turning his entire body left, then right, Carsten put one hand on the row of trolleys and tried to help. But it made no difference. The row didn't budge an inch. The wife rolled her eyes, then tapped her watch. Ravn heard her yell something about a manicure appointment. An argument between Carsten and his wife ensued, accompanied by much yelling and shouting and waving of arms. The boy dropped his tablet in the fray, and when he realised that the screen was shattered, he began to cry loudly as well. Carsten, whose face was flushed in rage by this point, tore at the neck brace, which seemed to be choking him. "To hell with the lot of you!" he screamed, and gripped the column of trolleys with both hands.

All the while, Ravn kept the camera lens trained on Carsten with one hand and scratched Møffe's belly with the other. Soon his film was fit for an Oscar. Or, at the very least, a handsome bonus.

3

Ravn's recording from that morning played on the computer screen. Despite its grainy quality and lack of colour contrast, Carsten Nielsen was clearly identifiable on the video. The loosened brace hung around his neck like a baby's bib as he pushed and pulled on the row of trolleys with all his strength.

"It appears he has experienced a miraculous recovery," Advocate Lohman remarked drily. He folded his arms over his large stomach, which stretched his yellow cardigan to breaking point. Lohman, a seasoned lawyer for the past forty years, sat behind a wooden desk in his nicotine-stained office and watched the video sequence unfold before him.

"Yes, Carsten's degree of disability has been reduced to zero percent," said Ravn, who was standing next to Lohman's desk. "You can't complain about that."

"No, not at all. What a stroke of luck for your investigation that those shopping trolleys obstructed Mr. Nielsen's parking bay," Lohman said, pointing at the screen as Carsten finally managed to set the trolleys in motion. The Rat pushed the row away from his car and over to the next parking bay, apparently unperturbed that they now blocked several other cars' exit.

"Yes, sometimes you get lucky," Ravn agreed with a smile, rubbing the bandage on his left forearm.

"So, what happened to your arm?" Lohman asked.

"A little mishap. I stuck my arm too far out the window."

"Out the window?"

"Yes, that comes later," Ravn said, and took a seat in the worn leather chair on the other side of Lohman's desk.

The lawyer sat glued to the screen, watching the scenario play out.

Carsten was yelling at his wife and son. He tried to refasten the neck brace but was too enraged and lacked the patience to get the job done. At last, his wife came over to help him. At this point, Carsten looked in the direction of the Audi and spotted Ravn with his camera. Carsten pointed directly at the lens.

"Shit," Ravn's voice said close to the camera's microphone. Judging from the shaking recording immediately after, Ravn dumped the camera onto the dashboard, and it kept filming on its side as Carsten stormed towards the Audi. The microphone recorded Ravn's swearing as he fumbled loudly with the keys, trying to get them in the ignition. When the car finally started, Carsten took off one of his clogs and torpedoed it directly at the Audi's windscreen, which shattered on impact. There was a high-pitched groan from the gearbox as Ravn tried to find reverse.

"My . . . my car," muttered Lohman, who still had his eyes glued to the screen. "Who the hell does that arsehole think he is?!"

"Had I known that he could throw so well, I would have parked a little further away," Ravn said. "I'll pay for your windscreen."

Lohman glanced at him. "But what happened to your arm?"

"Just keep watching," said Ravn, rotating his good wrist.

Lohman returned his attention to the screen.

Ravn had found reverse and stepped on the accelerator. Carsten's figure became smaller and smaller on the screen, and then you could hear him yell: "Django! Put Django on him!" The son stepped forward and opened the rear hatch and a white pit bull terrier sprang out. The dog set after Ravn and had covered about half the distance between them when Ravn swung the Audi round. The camera shot over to the driver's side of the dashboard and now filmed Ravn, who was struggling to get the car into first gear. He leaned against the door and opened the window because it was almost impossible to see through the shattered windscreen. In that moment, the terrier's jaws appeared in the open window, and the dog latched onto Ravn's forearm. He screamed in pain and tried to shake off the dog whilst the car skidded sideways. Møffe pushed to his feet and gave a series of indignant, asthmatic barks at the terrier, which opened its jaws at the sight of Møffe and tumbled out of view. Ravn put his foot down, and the video camera slid off the dashboard, thudded onto the mat in front of the passenger seat, and the screen went black. Ravn's swearing could still be heard on the microphone.

Lohman switched off the recording and leaned back in his seat. "Have you been to see a doctor about that arm of yours? You ought to get a tetanus shot."

"My arm is fine, thanks," said Ravn.

"We could sue for damages . . . if you like? You were filming on a public road, which is entirely legal."

Ravn shook his head. "Let it go. I would've been just as pissed if I'd discovered someone filming me without my permission. Especially if I stood to lose a couple of million as a result."

"Suit yourself," said Lohman. "Good thing you had Møffe along for the ride. Else you'd still be running around with that pit bull on your arm."

Ravn glanced at Møffe, who was napping at his feet on Lohman's shabby Persian carpet. "Yes. Despite his old age, he's still a good guard dog. And, as I said, I'll pay for your windscreen."

"Forget it," said Lohman. "I write the costs off against expenses. Considering the sum of money we just saved my client, it won't be a problem. Sherry?" He stood up and went to the drinks tray on the round mahogany table in the corner.

"No, thanks."

Lohman poured himself a glass. "You have to allow yourself a few privileges."

"When do you think you could transfer my fee?"

"Have a word with Miss Malling," Lohman said, nodding at the door to his reception. "She'll write you a cheque immediately."

Miss Malling was Lohman's secretary. She had been working for the lawyer since the day he started. Neither of them had ever married, and it was impossible to tell if their relationship was purely professional because they behaved like an old married couple.

"Thank you," said Ravn. He meant it; he could really use the money. He was about to take his leave of the lawyer, but Lohman waved him back into his seat.

"Where's the fire?" Lohman said. "Stay seated. We're far from done, you and I."

Ravn sighed. Lohman no longer appeared in court, preferring to stick to those cases he could settle from behind his desk, which meant that the lawyer seemed to have an insatiable need to hear his own voice. He could talk the hind legs off a donkey. Throughout the summer, which was almost over, Ravn had taken on several surveillance tasks for Lohman, and he'd heard the lawyer's repertoire of success stories in court more than once. "I once had a client who claimed he was insane at the moment he robbed a bank—" Lohman began.

"—the only problem was he'd robbed twenty-eight others before that," Ravn said, cutting him off.

"Ah, have I told you this one before?" Lohman said, and took a sip from his sherry glass, clearly disappointed by Ravn's apparent lack of interest. "Never mind; so where were we?" he said, plopping down into his seat.

"My fee," said Ravn with a conciliatory smile. He didn't have anything against Lohman, but he wasn't in the mood to keep him company today. Besides, he'd worked up a thirst himself; he needed a beer.

"No, we were done talking about your fee. There's a new case we need to discuss. Not quite as much *bite* as the last one," he said, nodding at Ravn's arm in case he hadn't caught the joke. "But there's good money in this one. At least two weeks' work, maybe more."

"Thanks, but I'm not interested."

"How do you know when I haven't told you about the case yet?"

"Because I—"

"The client is a large, renowned Danish electronics company. They've had some stock disappearing from their warehouses overseas. I can't reveal the name of my client, of course, before you agree to take on the assignment, but it sounds like 'bee-n-oh.'" He smiled at Ravn and winked at him, eager to see if he'd understood.

"Lohman, I appreciate the offer, but I'm not interested in this kind of work anymore. It's been fine till now, but . . . this is not what I want to be doing with my time."

"Is it because of the silly injury you've suffered?" Lohman said, pointing at Ravn's bandage.

"Believe me, I've had worse."

"Okay. So, what are you afraid of?" The expression on Lohman's face suggested that he thought this provocation would goad Ravn into accepting the assignment.

Ravn smiled. "I'm not afraid. It's just not for me."

"But this is really no different to what you were doing for the police before, apart from the fact that you're being paid a decent salary."

"On the contrary, it's completely different. Investigation is one thing, spying on other people is something else entirely. I don't want to be a snoop anymore."

"But you're so good at it. Better than any of the investigators I've ever had. I'll admit that when Johnson recommended you, I had my doubts. I hope you won't be offended if I say so."

"Not at all. I wouldn't take for granted anything Johnson recommends. Especially when the recommendation pertains to me."

Lohman raised his glass in a toast. "You're a strange one, you are."

"Regardless of the client, the answer is no, Lohman," Ravn said, pushing to his feet, and Møffe took his cue.

"Think about it," said Lohman. "Young people like you are so impatient nowadays."

"I'm hardly young anymore. And I have thought about it. Take care of yourself, Lohman," Ravn said and made for the door.

"Oh, all right, then I'll have to tell you who the client is, so you know what an exclusive case you're missing." Swirling the sherry in his glass, Lohman took an artistic pause. "You are turning down a case for Bang & Olufsen."

"I figured. And I'm sure they can survive just fine without me," Ravn said with a wave as he walked out the door.

4

The Sea Otter was packed, and from the old Wurlitzer jukebox in the corner, Joe Cocker's raw voice singing "Unchain My Heart" blended in with the chatter of guests. The bar was packed with young people ready for a night out on Christianshavn, whilst the regular patrons were slinging down their beers at the tables, puffing cigarettes that fed the blue mist of tobacco smoke hovering overhead.

Ravn had arrived early and managed to secure a place at the end of the bar. This meant that he had consumed more alcohol than most people in the bar, and he was rather drunk—more so than originally planned. Johnson had been washing and polishing beer glasses all night, whilst the two young bartenders he'd hired could barely keep up with orders from the guests. "What's going on, Johnson? Are all the other bars in Christianshavn on strike?" Ravn said.

Johnson glanced at Ravn and quirked his bushy eyebrows. "You're funny, huh! Don't you know The Sea Otter is the so-called brown gold now," he said, and put down his dishcloth to pour himself a cup of coffee. "Clearly you don't read the local paper." The delicate coffee cup was dwarfed by the barkeep's enormous fingers.

"Nah, Møffe generally rips it to shreds before I get a chance to read it."

Johnson emptied his cup and poured a refill from the flask on the shelf behind him. "The local paper ran a feature on the dive bars in

Christianshavn. Apparently, it's establishments like us—small, quirky, and homely places like The Sea Otter—that are mod again."

Ravn shook his head. "The Sea Otter has never been 'quirky' nor 'modern,'" he said.

Johnson frowned. "If I were the one drinking on tab, I'd start telling the barkeep better jokes."

Ravn downed the remains of his beer and put the empty bottle on the counter between them. "Well then, you'd better get me another one of these."

Johnson took a Hof out of the fridge and popped the cap. "Lohman tells me you quit?"

"In here, gossip flows faster than the water in the canal out there."

"He told me in confidence after his regular game of carom with Victoria the other night."

"He should have concentrated on his game rather than shooting his mouth off," Ravn said, taking a sip from his fresh bottle of beer. "It's not like he was my employer or anything. I just took on a few assignments for him."

"Still. You don't just up and leave a job like that."

"Is that what Lohman said I did? I've just saved his client two million kroner—and almost lost an arm in the process," Ravn added, raising his bandaged arm off the counter.

"No, no, Lohman was happy to have you on the case. And it's a nice bit of business for you as well, I imagine," Johnson remarked in a confidential tone, leaning his massive bulk on the counter. "Apparently, you're even good at it, he said."

Ravn shrugged. "It was a summer holiday job, and summer is almost over."

"Do you have something lined up?"

Ravn shook his head.

"That's what I thought. And that's exactly why you shouldn't have quit. You could have learned something."

"There wasn't much to learn. It was a snooping job. A monkey with a camera could have done it."

Johnson shrugged. "It's not as if you have a helluva lot of options."

"I get by," said Ravn. He couldn't figure out if Johnson's concern was aimed at him, or Lohman, or some question of personal pride. It was Johnson who'd recommended him to Lohman, after all. All he knew about the two dinosaurs' relationship other than Lohman's patronage and a regular game of billiards was that, back in the day, the lawyer had supported Johnson both legally and financially to buy The Sea Otter. Lohman had a modest share in the pub, and in age-old Christianshavner circles, they were considered blood brothers.

A girl in a white vest top squeezed to the front of the counter next to Ravn. She grinned at Johnson to get his attention and ordered a round of beers. Feigning a nonchalant air, she puffed her fringe out of her eyes. Ravn tried not to stare down her cleavage, but she caught him looking.

"Camilla," she said, offering Ravn her hand in greeting.

Ravn took it. *She is much too young*, he thought.

"Want to join us for a game of pool?"

"Pool? Thanks, Carina, but I'm afraid I'm a little too drunk to play pool."

"*Camilla*," she said, giving him a playful clap on the shoulder.

"Sorry, but it was so close."

"Afraid to lose?" she said with a flirty smile. Johnson put her order on the counter, and she paid for the beers.

"No. I might do something really stupid."

Camilla gave him another smile and gathered up the five beer bottles with both hands. "Come over to our table if you change your mind," she said. The next moment, she disappeared in the crowd, but he saw her resurface at one of the tables near the jukebox.

"As I said: Lignite is in vogue," Johnson observed drily. "Even an old codger like you has a modest chance of getting laid," said Johnson. "She seemed cute."

"You mean young. Are you also trying to hook me up now?"

"Good lord, no," Johnson snorted. "You're on your own *there*, my friend." He picked up the next beer glass and started polishing furiously, ignoring the throng of thirsty guests vying for his attention at the counter. "By the way, you know Robert, right?"

"Name doesn't ring a bell."

"Of course, you know him: Robert. He comes in now and again. The boxer. From the Swedish Sports Club. We used to spar together, years ago. Hits hard as a hammer. Or rather, he used to—back then."

"Sounds like a deadbeat. So, what about him?"

"He works as a security guard now, has his own business with a few employees. I could ask if he needs another man . . . I'm sure he could use an ex-cop like you."

Ravn put down his Hof and stared at Johnson.

"A security guard! Seriously? Are you suggesting I should patrol the mall in a suit and tie, with a little shield on my shirtsleeve?"

"Why not? There's nothing wrong with being a security guard. Robert also does night shifts. That could be something for you—so you don't end up insulting anyone."

Ravn shook his head in disbelief. "Johnson, can we agree on something? From now on, you don't have to provide any more job opportunities. I'm just fine without your interference, thank you very much." He stuck his hand in his pocket, extracted a 500-kroner note, and put it on the counter.

"You can settle your tab tomorrow."

"That's all right, I'll do it now."

Johnson shrugged and took the money. Moments later, he returned with the change. "Go straight home now, will ya?"

"We'll see."

5

Ravn tugged on Møffe's leash as he crossed the Town Hall Square and shimmied past the stream of tourists outside the main entrance to Tivoli. In the old garden on his way over from Christianshavn, he had watched the midnight fireworks light up the sky in bursts of colour. The walk had done him good. He was no longer drunk—or rather, he was probably still drunk, albeit relatively clear-headed, simply cruising along with the buzz—and although it was almost twelve thirty on a school night, the street was filled with people who didn't want this summer evening to end either.

He tried to convince himself that this was just a brisk walk before bed. But he knew damn well where the booze was taking him. He was heading back to the old hood, Vesterbro, where his former workplace, Station City, rose as a fort in the middle of the enemy's territory. Back then, when he was the second-in-command of Crime Ops, he knew every alley and every back street, the cellars and brothels and drug dens. He knew the pushers and hookers on a first-name basis—at least those who managed to stay alive long enough to become legends on the streets. But it wasn't nostalgia pulling him back to Vesterbro; it was something much more dangerous, something hidden deep in his soul. Eva's unsolved case haunted him, especially when he was pissed.

With Møffe by his side, he stole into the shadows of a dark courtyard off Colbjørnsensgade. The street was deserted. In the last half hour, only two prostitutes and their clients had come past. But Ravn was watching the abandoned hairdresser's salon right across the road. Behind the dirty windowpanes and yellowish curtains, a light was still burning. The flickering blue shadows of a television screen. For the past ten years—ever since the hairdresser has declared bankruptcy—the location had officially been registered as the property of a cultural association: a club and meeting place for people from the former Soviet states, created to maintain common cultural ties and strive for better living conditions for the Slavic minority in the neighbourhood. The club even received an annual grant from the government's cultural fund and a modest subsidy to pay the rent. Unofficially, it was a gambling club, run by a gangster called Andrej Kaminsky.

Kaminsky was a savvy businessman who had attracted the big names in international gambling circles to Copenhagen. Most of these gamblers were dangerous men who placed their bets with blood money. The success of Kaminsky's club was based on his uncanny ability to keep the authorities from interfering with his business, not least his reputation for knowing how to deal with bad losers who were kicked out of his tournaments; he spared their lives and served them a plate of his infamous beetroot soup instead. And, for his trouble, Kaminsky kept two percent of the winnings.

The door opened and two young men came out. They made their way down the street in a cloud of cigarette smoke and Russian words Ravn didn't understand. Experience told him that they were small fry; the louder they were and the more they tried to appear cool, the lower they were in the hierarchy. Regardless of whether they were bikers, members of a foreign gang, or the Baltic Mafia, his judgement on this point never failed. It was the other guys, the ones who quietly stole away in the corner, that you had to watch out for. Those men were dangerous.

The two Slavic pups hadn't closed the door properly and a wedge of light spilled onto the pavement. It was impossible for Ravn to see what was going on inside, how many men there were, or if Kaminsky was present at all. And yet the open door beckoned. The situation reminded him of the moment when the Special Ops team was finally given the order to storm a location. It was a tremendous rush unparalleled by anything else he had experienced. A liberation after several days' patience and expectation. It was both a physical and mental state. As if the team were a single being, a combined force that kicked the door in and pinned the dealers to the ground before they could dispose of the evidence. You felt like the king of the mountain when those fellas were lying face-down in the dust with their hands cuffed behind their backs, whilst you and your team confiscated their dope. And the more narcotics you found, the longer these criminals would spend behind bars. Which is exactly where he wanted to put Kaminsky: behind bars. For the simple reason that if anyone knew something about Eva's case, he did.

As if drawn by the open door, he stepped out of the shadows in the courtyard. But he only got as far as the sidewalk before a hand grabbed onto his collar and hauled him up against the wall. Møffe strained against his leash and growled viciously.

"Control your mutt, Ravn, or it will get a kick in the liver."

Ravn tightened his grip on the leash, holding Møffe back. He hushed Møffe, and the dog quietened down a little.

"What the hell are you doing here?" said Dennis Melby, staring at Ravn.

"Taking an evening stroll. And you?"

Melby shook his head. "You're interfering in a police operation. I could cite you for obstruction."

"This is a public road," Ravn said, staring back at the cop. Dennis Melby seemed even bigger and broader than he remembered; he looked like a bloated frog. Ravn couldn't stand the bastard. Never could. "I see you're still taking your vitamins."

"What the fuck has that got to do with you?!"

"Best you get a couple more from the pushers over at Maria Church whilst you still can."

Melby put his right hand on Ravn's throat and squeezed. "You're a bum, Ravn, always have been. Even when you were on the team."

"Let . . . go of me. Before this . . . ends badly for you."

Melby grinned at him. "Go back to your shitty island with all the other losers, you got that?"

Ravn freed his arm and grabbed onto Melby's balls. "I said let go of me."

When he tightened his fist, Melby grimaced in pain, but he didn't let go, merely shifted his thumb to Ravn's Adam's apple. "I could . . . also let the dog . . . take over . . . chew on your balls . . ."

Melby glanced down at Møffe, who was growling at him again, straining at the leash Ravn held in his free hand.

"Cut that out!" a voice called in a hoarse whisper from the other end of the courtyard.

Ravn and Melby turned their heads in the direction of the figure that emerged from the dark.

"I said stop, both of you!" Mikkel said in his thick countryside accent.

Ravn and Melby did as he asked, and Ravn gasped for breath. "You look . . . like shit, Mikkel," Ravn choked out.

It was true. Obviously suffering from sleep deprivation, Ravn's former partner was unshaven with dark rings under his eyes. "What the hell are you guys thinking?! You want to risk exposing an operation for the sake of a pissing contest?"

Melby pulled down the crotch of his jeans and winced. "I merely asked this civilian to keep moving. He declined."

"Shut it, Dennis. You'd better go wait for me in the car," said Mikkel.

Ravn watched Melby lope down Colbjørnsensgade. "All those steroids have fried his brain," he said.

"You're one to talk."

Ravn shrugged. "I get by. What are you doing here?"

"That's my question for you."

"As I said to the steroid junkie: I'm taking an evening stroll."

"You've been standing in this courtyard for over an hour."

"Nah, half an hour, maybe, because I needed to lie down for a while."

Mikkel looked at him patiently. "We are close to nailing Kaminsky."

"You promised to keep me informed, Mikkel. Have you forgotten that?"

Mikkel held his hand over the microphone of his headset, which was dangling from his left ear. "Lower your voice, would you," he said, doing the same. "The last six months' surveillance of the club has confirmed our suspicions that—apart from the illegal gambling operations—Kaminsky is involved in the drug trade, human trafficking, and fraud on a grand scale."

"None of which interests me. You promised that if any information about Eva's case came up, I would be the first to know."

Mikkel looked away. "I know. And I stand by my promise. But nothing has come up yet. With respect, Ravn, your case is not a high priority compared to everything else that Kaminsky is implicated in. And we don't even know for sure if Kaminsky was involved in Eva's murder at all."

"Which is exactly what we could ask him."

Ravn tried to brush past Mikkel, but his ex-partner put a hand on his chest and gave him a gentle shove. "Ravn, don't be a fool, you're drunk as a skunk. I promised to help you, and I will. But these things take time. You know that better than anyone."

Ravn stared at his feet. All at once, he felt utterly exhausted, and he could feel a hangover approaching.

"Are you okay? Do you need money?" Mikkel started going through his pockets.

"No!" snapped Ravn. "Just get Kaminsky to talk. You owe me," he added, pointing a finger at his face.

Mikkel nodded. "You will be the first to know if he talks."

It was time to go home. Ravn pulled on Møffe's leash, and the dog stood up reluctantly. Then he turned on his heel and walked away from Mikkel.

"Ravn," Mikkel called after him, and Ravn looked over his shoulder.

"If you want a piece of advice: I think it's time to move on."

"I didn't ask for your advice."

"Still . . ."

"Do you know what day it is tomorrow?"

Mikkel shook his head.

"Three years since Eva was murdered."

6

Whatever you do, don't go into the living room . . .

Eva put her keys in the lock and let herself in. She was talking on her mobile phone, which was cradled between her ear and her shoulder, as she pushed open the door with her elbow. Walking down the corridor, she had her laptop bag slung over her shoulder, her coat in one hand, and a shopping bag and a bunch of tulips in the other. "Hi, my love, it's me. I'm home. I'm hoping we can have dinner together tonight. I've been to Brugsen, and I've got us a bottle of vino. Send me a message when you get a moment. Kiss, kiss, hopefully see you later."

She dumped everything on the kitchen table and ended the call, then put her phone down on the counter and went back down the corridor to close the front door.

Whatever you do, don't go into the living room . . .

Eva glanced at herself in the mirror on the wall in the entrance. Her face was damp with sweat, and the dark stains under the armpits of her white shirt were testimony to the hectic day at work behind her. She undid the top buttons and pulled the tails of her shirt free from the belt of her skirt. She kicked off her court shoes and padded barefoot into the kitchen. Once she had unpacked and put away the groceries, she poured herself a glass of rosé and flipped through the post. Apart from bills, she found an invitation to the christening of her friend Lillian's child. Eva smiled at the picture of the baby with a wide, toothless grin on the front of the card. She fixed the card to the fridge with a magnet, between the menu from Era Ora, where they had gone out for dinner on her birthday, and a picture of the two of them on *Bianca*'s deck.

Whatever you do, don't go into the living room . . .

Eva picked up her coat from the kitchen table and went into the bedroom to hang it up in the wardrobe. Then she made their bed and picked up his T-shirt, bringing it to her nose and inhaling deeply. After a moment, she folded it neatly and laid it on his pillow. She yawned and went back into the kitchen. Sipping her glass of wine, she arranged the tulips in a vase. One of them was already drooping, and she plucked it from the vase and threw it in the bin under the sink.

Whatever you do, don't go into the living room . . .

Eva picked up the vase and was about to make her way into the living room when her mobile phone vibrated on the kitchen table. It was a message from him: "Busy. Will try to get home in time. Just start without me!"

She replied with a heart emoji, put down the phone, and went to the living room with her flowers.

Whatever you do, don't go into the living room . . . Whatever you do, don't go into the living room . . .

Whatever you do, don't go into the living room . . . Whatever you do, don't go into the living room . . .

The sun poured through the windows and the living room was steaming hot. Eva sidestepped the glass table in front of the sofa and placed her flowers on the windowsill. She moved around the knick-knacks on the sill until she was satisfied with the arrangement. Then she opened the windows and secured each one on its hasp. There was a brisk wind outside, and she enjoyed the fresh air on her face as she took in the view over the embankment. The trees bowed graciously in the wind, the sun's rays reflected on the surface of the canal beyond. She closed her eyes and took a deep breath. At the sound of creaking floorboards behind her, she opened her eyes and turned her head . . .

The silver candlestick hit her cranium with a sickening sound. Eva's legs gave way and she crashed onto the glass coffee table, which shattered under her weight. She slid onto the floorboards beside the sofa.

The sun seemed to shimmer with renewed strength in a myriad of brilliant shards of glass. Blood seeped out of the open wound at the base of her skull. Eva stared up at the ceiling, and the fingers of her left hand trembled, as if playing scales on a piano. Air bubbles appeared in the spit at one corner of her mouth. She sighed one last time, and then she was still.

The dark figure in the room was wearing a baseball cap and black rubber gloves. He threw down the candlestick and bent down to check Eva's pulse with two fingers on her neck. When he found none, he wrung Eva's Rolex off her wrist and stuck it in his pocket. Then he stood up and walked calmly into the kitchen. He unzipped her laptop bag, found her wallet and computer, and put them in the empty shopping bag that Eva had left on the table. Then he made for the front door. In the entrance, he paused briefly by the mirror.

Show me your face . . . just a glimpse . . . just for a second . . . show me . . . show me your face . . .

The man pulled the baseball cap down over his eyes and disappeared out the door.

"Show me who you are!" Ravn screamed and started awake. He bolted upright and banged his head on the ceiling. He sat gasping for breath for a moment, till he realised he was on board *Bianca*.

"You all right, Ravn?" Eduardo's voice called from his ketch moored next door

Ravn looked up through the open hatch above the bed. The stars were out. "Yeah, no worries, I'm fine," he said. "Get some sleep, Eduardo."

"Okay, good night, then," Eduardo mumbled, still half-asleep.

Ravn glanced at the display of his mobile phone. It was four thirty in the morning. He hadn't slept for more than an hour or two, but he knew it would be impossible to get back to sleep. He swung his legs over the side of the bunk, wrapped his duvet around him, and went into the main cabin, where Møffe was sleeping. He continued out onto the rear deck and sat down in one of his plastic chairs by the railing. The canal was quiet in the early hours. Other than the single carpenter's van that crossed the bridge to Christianshavn Square, the canal and embankment were quiet as a churchyard. It was the precious hour when the pubs were closed for the night and the rest of the neighbourhood was still fast asleep, the time when you had it all to yourself.

Bianca rolled ever so slightly on the water, rocking him gently in his chair. He thought about his nightmare. It was always the same; every time, he tried to warn her and prevent the inevitable. The details reflected what was revealed by the police investigation—Eva's actions before she died, the items the killer stole—but the sight of her body he saw with his own eyes when he and Møffe came home and found her dead on the living room floor.

Sometimes he caught a glimpse of the killer's face, but it was always in the shape of his own, and he knew why, of course—you didn't have to be a psychologist to understand the guilt he still felt. *He should have been there.* At the very least, he had to find out who her killer was. No more than a hapless thief who Eva chanced upon in the act. Evidence suggested the perpetrator was connected to the Baltic Mafia and, in all likelihood, fled the country immediately after. On the bare bones of the police report, Ravn and Mikkel constructed the theory that Kaminsky may have information on the gang members who were operating in Christianshavn at the time. Watching the still waters, Ravn realised how flimsy that theory was, how desperately he had clung to the hope of solving her case. It was pathetic. Just as pathetic as he was sobbing like a child, slouched in his duvet in a white plastic chair.

7

The sun was baking hot over the Church of Our Saviour's graveyard, and in the stagnant air inside the red-brick walls, the long gravel paths appeared to hover just above the ground. In the distance, Ravn could hear the traffic on Amagerbrogade, which flanked the south side of the cemetery and actually belonged to his local parish on Christianshavn. It was a so-called "out-lying" graveyard that was established in the wake of the cholera epidemic in eighteen hundred and something. It was the kind of local history that Eva would share with him on their walks. As a rule, he merely nodded in reply—only half-listening as usual—constantly distracted by some or other case at work.

Ravn crouched on his haunches by the black gravestone and removed the wilted bouquet and remains of the tea light he had brought the last time he visited her grave. His guilty conscience reminded him that his last visit was around Christmas. He would have liked to come more often, but he hated coming here because it encapsulated everything that Eva wasn't. Her grave was a bitter reminder of the injustice of it all, the fact that she was lying here, under the ground, rather than walking around Amagerbrogade—with him.

"Did you know that this churchyard was established during the cholera epidemic in Copenhagen in the late nineteenth century?" Victoria asked. She was standing above Ravn, her wild bush of curly grey hair, as if electrified, silhouetted against the pale-blue sky behind her.

"Is that so?" Ravn said, depositing the wilted flowers and tea light into the plastic bag he'd brought along.

Victoria exhaled a cloud of smoke. "Yes. In 1853, it was prohibited to bury the dead inside the city walls. Lucky for me."

"How so?"

"Because if they had, my bookshop would not have been right by the church today."

Ravn nodded. Victoria's shop was only a stone's throw from the Church of Our Saviour, where Eva's funeral had taken place.

He looked up at Victoria. As always, she was dressed from top to toe in a smart tweed suit, looking for all the world like a member of some bygone Christianshavner nobility. "You must be hot as hell in that suit."

"There's no excuse for sloppy attire."

"You're one of a kind, Victoria."

"I should hope so. I don't care for copies. Only originals. Which is why I loved Eva's company so much."

Ravn stood up and brushed his hands on the thighs of his jeans. "Thank you for coming with me. You didn't have to do that."

"Don't mention it. Although this place does give me the creeps. You should have spread her ashes from the Øresund Bridge instead."

"Is that allowed?"

Victoria shrugged. "You should have done it either way."

They stared at the gravestone in silence together. Ravn regretted the pansies now, and he considered removing them. Victoria's bouquet, on the other hand, was beautiful—simple and discreet, just like Eva would have liked it. "There are so many things we didn't get to do together," he muttered.

"Don't you think it's time you stopped beating yourself up about that?"

"I should have seen it coming, Victoria."

"No. What you need to do is move on. Eva would have said the same."

"I ought to remove those ridiculous flowers. They look like shit," Ravn said, pointing at his pansies.

"Indeed. An unfortunate choice, my friend."

Ravn bent down and picked up the pot of flowers.

"I mean it, Victoria. It's not just a question of guilt; I should have seen it coming. I've worked for the police my entire professional life. I've witnessed firsthand what hideous things people can do to one another. I know violence, I've stood eye to eye with murderers and rapists, I've seen their mutilated victims, and I know the stats. I had all the knowledge I needed to predict something like this happening, Victoria. So why didn't I install an alarm? Why did I leave Eva home alone so often? Why didn't I investigate the activities and movements of the gangs working our neighbourhood in the weeks up to the attack? I'm trained to recognise all the signs, and yet I was completely unprepared."

"Still sounds exactly like guilt to me."

"No. Not guilt alone," said Ravn firmly. His throat was painfully dry. "It's a question of being able to sense evil. Know when it is underway; see where it will strike. Why was I blind to it in the place that mattered most?" He looked Victoria directly in the eye. "It's just like that old saying: The Devil's greatest strength is his ability to pass unseen amongst us."

Victoria shivered and looked over her shoulder. "Ravn, you're scaring me."

"I was just trying to make a point."

"That's all fine and well. But what do you say we get out of here?"

They walked down the narrow path that was flanked with gravestones on either side. By the gate at the end of the path, the sexton was raking the gravel in a cloud of dust. Victoria lit a cigarette and exhaled a stream of smoke from the corner of her mouth. "You know I play a game of carom with Lohman every Wednesday, right?"

"I suppose you're going to say it was a dumb idea to quit working for him?"

Victoria shrugged.

"Don't bother. Johnson's already been there."

"But you're so good at—"

"At snooping in other's people's business, I know. Everyone keeps telling me so, but it's not what I want to do, so some or other insurance company can save a buck or confirm to a miserable person that their partner has cheated on them. I'd rather clean toilets if I have to."

"Well, toilet cleaners are a dying breed," Victoria quipped. "I hear what you're saying. But there are other options."

"But that was the only kind of work that Lohman had to offer."

"So forget Lohman. Start your own business."

"My own business?" Ravn stopped in his tracks and stared at her. "And what do you propose I do? Open a bookshop like you, or a pub like Johnson?"

Victoria burst out laughing. "No, of course not. You don't have the social skills for that, Ravn. You'd scare away your customers within a week. No, I'm saying, why don't you establish yourself as an investigator?"

"You mean . . ." He was reluctant to say it out loud. "Private . . . detective?"

"Exactly."

"And how would that come about?"

"Like you open any other business," Victoria said. "You come up with a name, get yourself registered with a VAT number and everything, rent an office space, and start rustling up clients."

"Great, thanks, but *how*?"

"How would I know? It's not my field. Research what your competitors are doing, put out advertisements on the internet, or in the local papers. When I gave up my job as a teacher, I was also clueless, but I figured it out along the way."

Ravn smiled. "It's not a terrible idea, actually . . . It's just that—"

"Think about it. I can help you with the administrative side of things to get you up and running."

As they came past the gravedigger, Ravn dumped the pansies and the plastic bag on his wheelbarrow and held the gate for Victoria to exit onto Amagerbrogade.

8

That afternoon, Ravn decided to do some work on *Bianca*. Crouched in the engine room, the sweat was pouring down his brow, and he wiped his forehead with his arm, which was just as covered in grime and engine oil as the rest of his naked torso. In the last three hours, he had cleaned *Bianca*'s hydraulic cooling system, from the pumps to the actual heat exchanger that had been clogged with slag and algae. It had taken six litres of petrol system cleaner to get through the entire system, and now the chambers were all spick and span. But the fumes had given him a pounding headache. The heat and his failure to hydrate sufficiently along the way made the headache worse. He was hopeful that his efforts would stop the motor from overheating and cutting out. As soon as he'd fastened the last bolt on the exchanger, he stuck his head through the open hatch and looked out.

Clad in shorts and a spiffy hat, Eduardo was standing at the railing of his boat, charming two girls who were drinking rosé whilst catching a tan on the embankment. The girls were laughing at something Eduardo had said, and Ravn could see that his friend's Mediterranean good looks and Spanish accent were working their magic as usual.

"You think you could tear yourself away for a moment?" Ravn yelled from the engine room.

Eduardo reluctantly turned to face Ravn.

"Would you mind popping over and starting the engine for me?"

"Right now?" said Eduardo.

"No, when winter comes."

Eduardo gave him a dirty look. Instead of coming aboard, he leaned over and stuck his arm through the side window of *Bianca*'s cabin, where he was just able to reach the ignition. "Ready?" he yelled back.

"Fire her up!"

Eduardo turned the key in the ignition, and a few clicking sounds came from the engine.

"I think it needs to warm up first," Ravn said. He explained to Eduardo that he had to turn the ignition halfway and then wait a moment before turning the last bit. Eduardo gave it a few seconds and then tried again. When nothing happened on the second try either, he withdrew his arm from the window. "Sorry, Ravn, it's not working."

"I said twenty seconds."

"No, you did not."

"Just try again, please."

Eduardo took a deep breath. Then he stuck his arm through the window again and turned the ignition halfway. Demonstrably looking at his watch, he counted twenty seconds.

In that moment, Ravn's mobile phone vibrated in his pocket. He wiped his fingers on a cloth and fished out his phone.

"Ravn, I'm glad I caught you," Lohman's voice said on the other end of the line.

"I don't have time to talk, Lohman," Ravn said.

"Always so subservient on the phone," Lohman remarked drily. "But I'm sure you'll be interested when I tell you what I've got for you."

"If it's about that B&O job, I'm still not interested. Have a nice day."

"It's not B&O. This is much more interesting. An exciting case for a large and important company."

"Lohman, it's good of you to think of me, but I'm not interested in the type of work—"

"Just wait and hear what they want. We can have a meeting where—"

Bianca's engine roared to life. Eduardo gave Ravn a thumbs up. He bent down and pulled the throttle cable, injecting fuel steadily till she was idling nice and smooth. As soon as Ravn was satisfied the saltwater pump was drawing seawater into the filter properly, he crawled out of the cramped space and sat on the edge of the hatch with his bare feet on the gently vibrating engine block. "Lohman?" he said into the receiver of his phone, but the lawyer had hung up in the meantime.

"So it's running at last," said Eduardo, jumping onto the deck behind him.

"Yup." Ravn smiled. "What happened to your girlfriends?"

"They found other company," he said, jerking his thumb over his shoulder where the girls were engaged in conversation with two young men their own age. "*Dios mios*, for the life of me I cannot understand what they see in those two pups."

"Aren't you ever gonna get too old for that?"

"I don't understand the question."

Ravn shook his head. At that moment, the engine sputtered and died.

"Fuck," said Ravn, throwing down the dirty cloth in his hand.

"Maybe it's time to get a professional to take a look at it," Eduardo said.

"I did. They said there was no point trying to fix it. That I'd be better off buying a new one," Ravn said, meeting Eduardo's gaze.

"Sounds sensible to me. I mean, when did you last actually sail *Bianca*?"

Ravn shrugged, but he knew the answer: a month before Eva's death.

"The mechanic is right," said Eduardo. "That motor's in a sorry state."

"Probably, but I don't have the money to replace it. I can barely afford to keep her docked here."

Eduardo looked at him. "Are you in arrears with your harbour dues?"

"I've had other priorities," Ravn said, getting to his feet.

"Ravn, *mi amigo*, you can't get behind with that kind of thing. They'll confiscate her if you don't pay your dues. Preben is an evil man."

Ravn smiled. You could call their harbour master, Preben Larsen, many things, but *evil* wasn't one of them. At worst, Preben was probably still bitter after he was fired from Burmeister & Wein when the shipyard closed what seemed like a lifetime ago, and he took it out on his environment, including people who didn't pay their dues on time or failed to observe the harbour regulations to a tee.

"Either way, Preben would have a hard time removing *Bianca* from the quay in her current state."

"Do you want to borrow some money?"

"I'd rather die."

It was long after midnight, and Ravn found himself more than a little drunk in a chair at the entrance to The Sea Otter, stroking Møffe's coat as the dog lay asleep at his feet. The festive atmosphere at the pub had spilled onto the street and along the canal, and people had plonked themselves down on the embankment with their drinks, laughing and chatting with their friends. Inside, Barry White and other disco hits were being played on repeat on the jukebox as a group of women sang along off-key, which was somehow comforting. Eduardo appeared in the doorway with three shot glasses in each hand. He took a seat next to Ravn and handed him half the glasses. "What are we celebrating?" asked Ravn.

"The dead," said Eduardo. "It's an old Spanish tradition. We honour those we love with a toast, or applause. Today, we drink in her honour."

"You remembered the date?"

"Of course. Eva was one of a kind."

Ravn nodded and sniffed the contents of the shot glasses. Brandy, a cheap one that Eduardo had somehow convinced Johnson to buy. But the thought behind it and the alcohol percentage was entirely in order. "*Salud*, my friend."

"*Salud, mi amigo.*"

9

Ravn stretched his stiff limbs and opened his eyes. He was sitting on his white plastic chair on *Bianca*'s rear deck, and the morning sunshine was inhumanly bright. He fumbled for his sunglasses in the breast pocket of his shirt. It felt as if the sun were burning through his eyeballs and frying whatever remained of his brain. He couldn't remember what time he and Møffe had come home, and how that had happened. *Wait . . .* now he remembered . . . *He and Eduardo had drunk to Eva's honour.* For his own part, Ravn felt more dead than alive. He ran his tongue along his chapped lips and looked around for something to drink within reach, but all he could see on deck were empty beer bottles and an upturned coffee cup. Getting up and going into the cabin for some water was asking too much. All he wanted to do was close his eyes and sleep it off till next summer.

A harbour tour passed on the canal. He could hear the tourists' cameras clicking away, and the guide with routine monotone informing the passengers about ". . . the old shipyard that has now been converted into exclusive condominiums . . ." As Ravn shifted in his chair, trying to find a comfy position for his head, he noticed the immovable figure sitting on the embankment, watching him. It was a woman.

"Good morning," she said.

The woman looked to be in her mid-thirties and was dressed in a dark suit made of soft material and a T-shirt. Her hair was scraped back into a ponytail, enhancing the angular features of her face. And she was wearing sensible shoes, Ravn noticed. Had she been a little taller, his best bet would have been that she was a bodyguard for the Danish secret service. That said, she had to be privately employed, even though her entire aura screamed COP from a mile off.

"Mornin'," he muttered.

"Late night, I see. There's nothing worse than waking up with a hangover on a stinking hot summer's day. You might want to turn over because you're pretty burnt on one side," she said matter-of-factly, pointing to the left side of his face.

He wasn't sure if she was taking the mick—but within the space of two minutes, she had managed to piss him off. "Is there something I can do for you?"

Without warning, she threw a 500ml bottle of water straight at his head. He caught it in time. *Good throw*, he thought. Like a professional handball player.

"Thank you," he said, and unscrewed the lid.

"Nice . . . or rather, interesting boat you got there. Grand Banks?"

He nodded.

"Hmm. A classic. But you ought to do something about the teak on your deck—seems to be some rot in places. Does she have a name, your boat?" She leaned to one side and checked out the stern. "Bii-aan-ca," she said in an exaggerated singsong voice. "Of course, no other name would do."

Ravn emptied the water bottle, returned the lid, and put it down on the deck next to him. "And you are?"

She didn't reply and looked at Møffe instead. "English bulldog? What's his name? Does he bite?"

"Only strangers. Listen, if there's nothing I can do for you, I'll say thank you very much for the water, and goodbye." He raised the bottle in a toast and turned his back, hoping he would shortly hear her feet retreat up the quay. But he wasn't that lucky.

"I've never met a private detective before. Nor, for that matter, a man who lives on a boat. I'm not sure that's interesting or just desperate, Ravn."

Ravn sighed, turned his head towards her, and tipped his sunglasses. The woman hadn't budged an inch and she was still staring at him. If she wasn't a cop now, she'd been one at some stage in her life—he was convinced of that now. "I'm sure you didn't come here for a chat about my boat or my dog, so what do you want?"

The woman launched herself off the embankment and dropped the one and a half metres down onto the deck. Møffe stood up and started to bark, but she kept walking straight towards him. "Shhh, give me your paw; there's a good boy," she said, taking a dog biscuit out of her pocket and giving it to him. "Are we good now?" She patted him on the head, and Møffe seemed pacified.

Ravn raised his eyebrows at his dog, then looked at the woman. "You're well prepared," he said.

She smiled and stuck out her hand. "Katrine," she said. The firm handshake didn't surprise him. "I work for Mesmer Resources," she said, presenting him with her business card, which Ravn didn't accept.

"Did Advocate Lohman send you?" Ravn shook his head. "I'm sorry, I don't work for him anymore, and besides, I'm not a private detective."

"Lohman mentioned that you were treading water," she said. She cast a glance round the boat and into the cabin, which was in a frightful state of disarray. "I can see what he means."

"Great, so I assume you'll be on your way . . . Katrine." He let his sunglasses fall back into place.

"Although Lohman did say you're so talented. So good at what you do." Her tone suggested she was referring to a child or a dog, but Ravn refused to let her rile him. "My boss, Ferdinand Mesmer, would like to meet you." She let her business card drop into Ravn's lap. It looked professional and discreet, blue with a logo at the top. "He would like to discuss an important matter with you, face-to-face."

"Still not interested."

"He pays well."

"So did Lohman. I refused. Tell your boss that I'm not interested in spying on other people." He extended the blue business card towards her, but she didn't take it.

"I'm aware of Lohman's rate. We're in a different bracket. And I can assure you we're not involved in 'spying on other people.' This is a serious case."

"What's it about?"

"Take the meeting, and Ferdinand Mesmer will give you all the details."

"So you're just the . . . office messenger?"

He could see he'd delivered a blow to her vanity, and the satisfaction took the edge off his hangover.

"Shall we say tomorrow at ten? If that's not too early for you? The address is on the card."

They were interrupted by the telltale sound of wooden clogs on the quay above, a sound that Ravn knew only too well. The next moment, Preben appeared. Despite the heat, he was wearing his Burmeister & Wain windbreaker as usual.

"Hey, Preben," Ravn said without looking in his direction.

"Well, yes . . ." the harbour master said, put out that Ravn was not alone. "Will you be in later, Ravn?"

Ravn raised his arms in the air in reply. *Where else would he be?*

Without further comment, Preben turned on his heel and left as quickly as he'd come.

Ravn sighed. "What did you say your boss was called . . . Frederik?"

"Ferdinand . . . Mesmer."

"Right. Tell Ferdinand that I'll meet with him, but I cannot promise him anything."

"Excellent."

"And I'll need four thousand eight hundred and fifty kroner in advance."

Katrine raised her eyebrows. "To come to a meeting? You want to charge us for taking a job interview?"

Ravn shrugged. "Call it whatever you want. But you're welcome to round up to five thousand."

Katrine shook her head and was about to take back the business card Ravn waved in the air, but something changed her mind.

"Can I count on you being there tomorrow as agreed?"

"Of course. I'm a professional."

She made no comment on that but stuck her hand in her pocket, brought out a wad of banknotes, and counted out 5,000 kroner. He had to admit, he liked her style—first water, then dog treats, then a stack of ready cash. He wondered what kind of weapon she'd be packing under her suit. A baton, knuckle-dusters? Something like that? He wondered what this guy Ferdinand Mesmer wanted with him if he already had this woman on his payroll.

Either way, he'd managed to buy himself—and *Bianca*—some time with respect to the harbour master.

10

The offices of Mesmer Resources were at the end of Nicolai Eigt-veds Gade, in the last block of Henning Larsen's famous office complex—six rectangular monoliths of glass and steel slotted into the harbour landscape near Knippelsbro Bridge. As such, Mesmer's firm rubbed shoulders with others in shipping, offshore mining, and the financial sector. Ravn had never liked these black buildings whose imposing end walls were reflected on the water. At least they were an outer bastion of Christianshavn, so they needn't taint the rest of the neighbourhood.

He entered the rotating door into the entrance hall and made his way up to Reception, where a woman with cherry-red lips and nails to match gave him the once-over. "Can I help you?" she said automatically.

Her eyes wandered from his T-shirt, over his worn chinos, down to his Converse, and settled on Møffe, whose tongue was hanging out of his mouth. "You cannot take it with you," she said, waving the point of her pen at the dog as she glared at Ravn.

"I have an appointment with Ferdinand Mesmer."

"Yes," she said, without checking the register. "But you can't take *it* with you in here. We have a dog's corner outside."

Ravn glanced at her nametag. ". . . Sabina, would you be so kind as to relay the message to Ferdinand Mesmer that Thomas Ravnsholdt was here to see him? Have a nice day," he said, and turned on his heel, making for the rotating door he had just entered before the receptionist could utter a response.

He heard his name resound in the hollow entrance hall. Casting a glance over his shoulder, he saw Katrine walking briskly over to him.

"Good to see you," she said with a cool smile when she reached him. "Where are you going?"

"Your receptionist refused to let us in."

"Good heavens. Follow me," she said, cordially showing Ravn and Møffe back to the receptionist.

"Let's get Mr. Ravnsholdt and his dog entered in the register," Katrine said to the receptionist in an unmistakable tone of authority.

A tight smile on her red lips, Sabina opened the register and pointed to the columns where Ravn was invited to enter his name, signature, and exact time of arrival.

"You'll need to sign this as well," said Katrine. She took a document from her inside jacket pocket, unfolded it on the counter, and pushed it over to him.

"What's this?" Ravn said.

"A confidentiality agreement confirming that everything you hear at your meeting with Ferdinand Mesmer will not be disclosed to third parties. Just a formality. Standard procedure."

"Would it not be more standard for Mesmer to stick to subjects that tolerate the light of day?"

Katrine had a retort on the tip of her tongue, but apparently she decided to let it go whilst he signed the agreement.

Katrine escorted Ravn and Møffe to the elevators on the opposite end of the hall. It was unbearably hot in the glass building, and the doors to the conference rooms they passed along the way were wide open. Inside, people were sitting in their shirtsleeves, sweating, as they listened to lectures or participated in some kind of conference, as far as he could glean. The last time he'd listened to a lecture was in the police academy, and he still developed a tic whenever he thought about it.

"What kind of business is Mesmer in, exactly?"

They stepped into the elevator. Katrine scanned her ID card and pressed the button for the top floor. "We teach."

"Teach what?"

"Leadership strategies. Mesmer Resources is one of the leading firms in the sector."

"Sounds like a profitable business."

"Last year we had a turnover of eight hundred million kroner."

The elevator set into motion. When they reached the top floor, he hadn't the slightest clue what Mesmer could possibly need him for.

11

Katrine showed him to Ferdinand Mesmer's office. The door was open, and she invited him to go inside and wait for Mesmer, who was on his way up. Ravn took a look round the moment she left. Cold steel. An impersonal style that matched the general atmosphere of Mesmer's domicile, and expensive designer furniture that would emanate success and exclusivity the moment you stepped through the door. A calculated choice, Ravn thought. If you excluded the large painting mounted on the end wall, there were no personal effects in the room at all. Ravn couldn't remember the name of the artist, but he recognised the characteristically sombre motif that depicted deformed bodies amongst shocking-yellow lemons. It was the kind of art that Eva used to like. One time, she dragged him to the Louisiana Museum north of Copenhagen to see an exhibition of this particular artist's work. Ravn reckoned the exemplar on Mesmer's wall would go for at least 2 million kroner. He walked over to the glass wall that lined one side of the office and looked down over the large conference hall below. People were streaming out of the meeting rooms and gathering round the high tables where water and coffee had been provided for the delegates. It was like looking into a swirling water well of brilliant blue and white shirts.

"I've always been fascinated by the sight myself," a voice behind Ravn said. "So much energy and lust for knowledge gathered in *one* place."

Ravn turned round and regarded Ferdinand Mesmer carefully. The director of Mesmer Resources was almost a head taller than Ravn. He had a full beard that was silver-grey, but his muscular torso and tanned face gave him an aura of vitality that belied his seventy years of age. Mesmer dabbed the sweat off his brow with a paper serviette, apparently bothered by the heat in his dark suit and black shirt.

"Bloody hot, isn't it? Of all the days for our air conditioning system to give up the ghost," Mesmer said, smiling at Ravn. "We have one hundred and fifty delegates from Novo Nordisk and Danske Bank down there. The poor sods are drenched in sweat already, and they've got another six hours of lectures ahead of them. Won't you take a seat?" he said, pointing at the sofa, and dropped into a chair opposite it. Mesmer kept looking at him intensely, and Ravn had the acute sense he was being measured up.

"Thank you for taking the time to come meet me. My friend Lohman praised your investigative talents highly."

"Katrine tells me that you offer seminars on . . . management?" Ravn said, turning the conversation away from himself.

"In Scandinavia, we are the biggest player in the field. We teach approximately ten thousand leaders and management professionals a year."

"Impress—"

"We're the best at what we do," he said, cutting Ravn off. "We maintain a score of more than ninety-five percent on customer satisfaction and loyalty ratings. Our seminars present a unique personality type and management strategy system that has a far more effective configuration than JTI, Belbin, Myers-Briggs, and DISC."

"Okay," said Ravn. He didn't have a clue what Mesmer was talking about. "So what kind of case would you like me to investigate?"

"You cut to the chase," Mesmer said with a smile. "I like that. You must be a GC man, a Gamma-Centurion."

"Well, I have no idea what that is, so you'll have to explain it to me."

"You're right." Mesmer smiled easily. "It's not fair of me to categorise you two minutes after we've met, but I'm usually pretty good at reading people on a first impression. If I'm not terribly mistaken, you're the observant type: methodical, practically oriented, innovative with a strong sense of justice, not afraid to cross swords with your opponents."

"No, you're not mistaken. Although I imagine that ninety-nine percent of investigators could match that description."

"Exactly, a sceptical mind to boot," said Mesmer, dabbing his forehead with another paper serviette. "Have you ever considered taking a personality test?"

Ravn held Mesmer's gaze. It was not the first time someone had asked him that question. The last was a Scientologist on Vesterbro Square. He'd responded by waving his police badge under the guy's nose. "No," he replied to Mesmer.

"Training an individual's ability for self-insight is one of our greatest priorities," Mesmer said evenly. "We employ the best business and sports psychologists in the country."

"Good for you," Ravn said. In the aftermath of Eva's death, he was called in for a "psychological evaluation." At that time, he was a complete mess and took out his anger and frustration on everyone around him, including a couple of Slavic thieves that he and Mikkel had picked up on a hunch. Mikkel had had to intervene before Ravn beat the shit out of the guy he was "questioning." The subsequent session with the police staff psychologist wasn't helpful, in his opinion. "I have no intention of taking a test now if that's what you're suggesting," he said to Mesmer.

"Not at all. We're just talking here," Mesmer replied. "Lohman mentioned that you used to work for a special unit in the police force?"

"Yes. At Station City. For six years. I worked in various task forces, primarily focussed on biker gangs and drug trafficking."

"Sounds exciting—and dangerous, I would imagine."

"Sometimes, yes."

"But you quit. Why, if I may ask? Did it all get too much for you?"

"Personal reasons," Ravn said, shifting in his seat. "Mesmer, what exactly is the nature of the case you want me to look into for you?"

"We'll get to that in a moment," Mesmer said evenly. "I've paid for your time today, after all," he added with a smile. "So, tell me. What do you think of Mesmer Resources?" he added, raising his arms in a sweeping gesture that encompassed the room.

"I'm not familiar with your industry, so I have no opinion about it."

"But when you were employed by the police, surely you must have experienced reforms that were implemented to . . . streamline the force, for example?"

Ravn shrugged. "I don't remember. Apart from the new Police Reform Act a couple of years ago, of course. After the new measures were implemented, half the force was consumed by stress, whilst the other half ran around not knowing what to do."

"Yes, the public sector is far behind the private sector on that score. So what is your first impression of my house? How do we present ourselves?"

"Surely, it's irrelevant what *I* think. Clearly, I'm not in your target group."

"Indulge me. I'd appreciate your honest opinion—precisely because you're *outside* our target group, looking in, as it were. Come on, don't be shy. I can handle it."

"Okay," Ravn said, taking a look around for a moment. "I think you spend a lot of time and effort on trying to make your business look exclusive: You run your shop from a top-notch location, you have designer furniture and expensive paintings on the walls that are intended to dazzle your management delegates who come here to learn a bunch of buzzwords that they can rattle off and force down their employees' throats so they'll work even harder—if for nothing else, then for the sake of being able to pay the bill that you're going to send them afterwards."

Mesmer laughed heartily. "I honestly hope we can achieve a little more than that. But your analysis is sharp; I'll give you that. Do you know how I formulate a first impression?"

"By asking a lot of questions, like you're doing right now—and sending folks on a lot of courses."

"No. By giving them the coffee test."

"Yet another clever acronym?"

"No, no, it's not an acronym," said Mesmer seriously. "The 'coffee test' is my own way of evaluating a company. In a country with an annual consumption of 7.3 million cups of coffee, the test is an excellent indicator of social intelligence, as well as the interaction among employees, which give me a clear first impression of a company's structure. It's quite simple, I assure you. Let me explain: The first time I meet with a potential client, I ask for a cup of coffee. Considering that eighty-five percent of the adult population drinks coffee, this request should hardly come as a surprise. And yet, it's astonishing in how many cases this simple request can knock a department sideways. All other important tasks are swept aside in favour of answering the frantic question: *Who* should fetch the cup of coffee for their guest? Or, if a cup isn't immediately available, *who* shall be the one to brew a fresh cup? Their reaction tells me something about the hierarchy of the organisation, or whether there is one at all. After this, I make a note of a series of indicators: the attitude of the person who brings me the coffee; whether the order is cast into the room, which means that several employees might engage in the task simultaneously; how long it takes for the coffee to arrive. These are small things that reveal the efficiency of a particular department. And then, the *quality* of the coffee is important: If I am served the last bitter dregs in the coffeepot, it indicates a lack of respect for your customers and, as such, a lack of care in the day-to-day management of a firm. As a rule, large companies in the medical or tech industries have a thermos placed on the table when you arrive—clearly, they think in terms of quantity rather than quality. Law firms and accounting firms generally use Scanomat coffee machines—an effective but uninspired choice. Most marketing and architect firms have aluminium coffee capsules. The architects always apologise for using this unsustainable, climate *un*friendly option—so why do they keep using the capsules?" His little lecture apparently over, Mesmer scoffed and leaned back in his chair.

"Interesting," Ravn said with as much patience as he could muster. "You haven't offered me a cup of coffee . . . yet," he added with a smile.

"You don't seem like the coffee-drinking type. I doubt you drink coffee, especially when you're working." Mesmer narrowed his eyes. "But in the mornings, you like to drink a cup of Nescafé—two teaspoons and a generous helping of sugar—that you enjoy on the rear deck with Møffe," he added, looking at the dog at Ravn's feet. "Ain't that right, Møffe?"

Ravn wasn't smiling anymore. "I have asked you *twice*—but you haven't answered my question: Why do you want to hire me? Has someone dipped into the office supplies for personal use?"

Ferdinand Mesmer threw the soggy serviette in his hand onto the table. "I want you to look for my son," he said gravely.

"Your son?"

Mesmer nodded.

"When did you last see him?"

Even though they were alone, Mesmer looked over his shoulder and lowered his voice. "It's been quite a few years now."

"Are the police involved?"

"No, no, a crime has not been committed. I just want to find him."

"How old is your son?"

"Um, he . . . he must be forty-seven or forty-eight by now."

"And you think he may be in danger?"

"For obvious reasons, I'm not sure if he is, but I don't think so. At least, I hope he isn't . . ."

"When exactly was the last time you saw him?"

"It's . . . it's been more than ten years," Mesmer said. "We had an argument, and after that . . . we haven't spoken again . . ." His gaze dropped to his feet.

"I'm very sorry, Mr. Mesmer, but this is not my line of work."

Mesmer's head jerked up in surprise. "But you're a private detective, are you not?"

"Not really. I don't know what Lohman told you, or what impression you received, but—"

"But you found that girl, the prostitute who was kidnapped in Sweden. And not so long ago, you helped the German police track down a bookkeeper."

"He was an accountant, but apart from that, you're quite well informed."

"My headhunters know how to do their research. So why don't you want to take on this case? I can assure you that your fee will be generous, and I will be deeply grateful to you."

"Because your son doesn't appear to be in danger. I'm sure you can find someone else with much more experience than I have to help you— someone from your own organisation, perhaps."

Ferdinand Mesmer shook his head. "So you're saying this case is too banal for you?" he said, sounding hurt rather than offended.

Ravn shrugged. "I'm just saying that this isn't my field of work."

"But I believe that if anyone understands the pain of uncertainty, it's you. How it eats you up alive if you don't get the answers you're looking for . . . especially when it concerns the people you love most . . ."

Ravn was beginning to understand just how thoroughly Mesmer's headhunters had conducted their research. He pushed to his feet. "Thank you, it has been an interesting meeting. I hope you find your son."

Mesmer stood up as well. "I can only ask that you will think this over before you make your final decision. It would mean the world to me if you would take on this case. And . . . I'm not the worst person in the world to have as a friend."

Ravn shook Ferdinand Mesmer's hand, which had a rough and gnarled surface. When he let go, he couldn't help glancing at it and saw that it was deformed; the skin and flesh of his fingers were a web of knotty scar tissue, and only the thumb was free. It looked like a third-degree burn. Ravn could only imagine how painful that must have been.

12

After the meeting with Ferdinand Mesmer, Ravn walked down Wilder-sgade in the direction of Torvegade. Even though it was the hottest time of the day, it was a relief to get out of Mesmer's melting pot of an office building, and he didn't envy the delegates who had to listen to lectures in there for the rest of the day. Ravn couldn't shake off the meeting. Mesmer had gotten under his skin. It was as if the old man could see his soul. He hadn't said much, but Ravn felt exposed. Robbed of something. He'd felt something similar after the meeting with the police psychologist. He still remembered the suffocating room, the intimate questions, the unbearable weight of grief. He'd had his walls up, of course, and was entirely focussed on being declared fit to continue service—and it had worked—but the fact that he had a breakdown and was loath to request sick leave of his own accord ten days later was another story. Besides, he was curious to know what had caused the rift between Ferdinand Mesmer and his son—he didn't regret turning down the job, he just wished he'd asked for more information about the case. In that moment, Ravn's phone rang, interrupting his thoughts.

"Have you heard?" Eduardo asked breathlessly on the other end of the line.

"Heard what?"

"It's all over the news."

"What is?" Ravn asked, stopping in his tracks. He pulled on Møffe's leash and made the dog sit at his feet.

"The shooting, in the middle of Copenhagen. The police have raided that Russian club on Colbjørnsensgade."

"Kaminsky's place was raided? When?"

"This morning. There was a shootout between the police and Kaminsky's men. The news also reported an exchange of gunfire on Istedgade nearby."

"Any fatalities?"

"They've only mentioned eight to ten wounded."

"Are you home or at the office?"

"Home."

Five minutes later, Ravn hopped onto the deck of Eduardo's ketch with Møffe in his arms. He could hear the news through the open hatch. Eduardo was in his cabin, wearing a pair of shorts, and he was glued to the screen. A blonde girl Ravn hadn't seen before was standing in the kitchen. "Would you like a cup of tea?" she asked, bending over to pat Møffe.

Ravn declined the offer of tea. "Have they provided any more information on the wounded?" he asked Eduardo, removing the stack of books on the sofa so he could take a seat next to his friend.

"Not just the wounded. They now say that three people have been killed, including a police officer," Eduardo replied without taking his eyes from the screen.

"Fuck," said Ravn. The news was broadcasting directly from Colbjørnsensgade. The police had cordoned off the area. Men in battle gear were patrolling the street with machine guns. In the background you could see Kaminsky's club. The front window was shattered, and the door had been broken down.

"Have you made enquiries at the paper?" asked Ravn.

"Yes, but they don't know more than what has already been announced on TV2 News."

Ravn took out his phone and dialled Mikkel's number but was instantly directed to answerphone. He didn't leave a message and called Mikkel's home number instead. The phone rang for a long time until it was finally answered by one of Mikkel's twins. "Wrong number, sorry," Ravn muttered into the phone and hung up.

"They're starting to bring folks out now," said Eduardo, pointing at the screen. The broadcast zoomed in on the doorway of the club, and two paramedics emerged with a stretcher. There was a glimpse of the injured man.

Ravn jumped to his feet. "It's Mikkel!"

"Are you sure?"

"Ninety-nine percent sure. Didn't you see him?"

Eduardo shook his head. "It's too hard to tell . . ."

Another paramedic appeared in the doorway with a stretcher. This time it was a policeman in battle gear who was carried out onto the street.

"Can you look after Møffe for me?"

"Of course," said Eduardo. "Where are you going?"

"To Rigshospitalet. I'm certain that's where they'll take him."

"I'm coming with you."

"Not if you're thinking about writing an article about this."

"Take it easy, *amigo*. I write the business column. How come you always forget that?"

"Because I know you. Can I still leave Møffe here?" he said, glancing over his shoulder. Møffe was lying on his back with his paws in the air, having his belly stroked by the blonde.

"Of course. Your dog is in good hands. *Mi casa es* Møffe's *casa*," Eduardo said, pulling a T-shirt over his head.

13

Ravn and Eduardo got out of the taxi in front of the hospital and walked past the news teams' vans that were parked close to the main entrance. The crowd was held back by a few uniformed police. Eduardo greeted his colleagues from the paper and asked if there was any news, but they simply shook their heads.

They stood with the press for a while. Ravn tried to reach Mikkel on his mobile number again, but he wasn't picking up. "There's no point in us standing here," Ravn said, drawing Eduardo away from the crowd.

"What do you suggest?" Eduardo said.

"Let's see if we can get in the main building via A&E," Ravn said in a lowered voice.

They crossed the car park, went round the back of the main hospital buildings, and continued down Juliane Maries Vej. Ravn paused behind a balustrade where they had a clear view of the emergency bay in front of the A&E reception area. Two ambulances had just pulled up to the entrance, escorted by several police cars and motorcycles that parked just behind the open doors.

"See anyone you know?" Eduardo asked.

"No. But even if I did, the police won't let us in."

"But couldn't you ask them for news about Mikkel?"

Ravn shook his head. "I don't think that would help." He scanned the reception area. "Perhaps it's a good idea if we split up. Why don't you go back to the main entrance and call me if there's any news."

"Okay. Where are you going?"

"I'm going to see if I can find a way into A&E."

Ravn continued down the corridor of the oncology department. An elderly gentleman in a wheelchair stared vacantly at him as he passed. The automatic doors at the end opened and two nurses came towards him. They returned his cordial greeting and kept walking past. He hated hospitals, most of all the chemical smell that assaulted your nostrils—no matter where you happened to be in the building.

He had reached the main building and here the ward had the feel of an airport terminal with patients, next of kin, and hospital staff hurrying from one corridor to the next, as if passengers late for their planes.

Ravn glanced up at the signboards to the A&E department and was directed to the elevators at the end of the corridor. He was certain the police would station a guard at the entrance to A&E and he would need an excuse to pass through. A doctor's coat would be useful, but he doubted he would find one lying around in one of the other departments. At that moment, he noticed one of the cleaning staff with her trolley outside the men's toilets. The woman's white coat was draped over the trolley as she tore a fresh plastic bag free from the roll. The minute she disappeared into the toilets, Ravn walked over briskly and borrowed her trolley. As he pushed it towards the elevators, he put on the woman's white coat and a blue hairnet that he found in her pocket.

In the elevator to the A&E on the ground floor, he cast a glance at himself in the mirror. Apart from the woman's picture ID on the breast pocket of the coat, his disguise was just fine. When the elevator doors opened, he flipped the ID so it faced inwards and pushed the trolley out into the corridor. At the other end, two police officers in battle gear were talking by the swing-door entrance to A&E. Their backs were turned, and Ravn knew that getting past them without having to identify himself was a question of timing. At that moment, the doors opened, and a porter came out, pushing an empty gurney before him. Ravn took his cue, and the moment the porter presented his ID to the guards, he pushed the trolley into the doorway, waving the woman's ID in one hand. "Could you guys make a little room, please?" he said to the police officers. "We're terribly busy today, thank you."

They automatically stepped back to the wall to let Ravn and the porter pass through in opposite directions.

The atmosphere in the A&E ward was chaotic. Paramedics burst through the doors with injured people from the shooting and medical staff were attending to them immediately, calling instructions to one another. There was blood on the floor, along the walls, and even on the ceiling. In the rooms alongside the corridor, Ravn could hear the injured moaning. There were too many police officers watching, and he couldn't slip into the rooms unnoticed to look for Mikkel, so he continued down the corridor with his trolley. He came past two injured men who were handcuffed to their gurneys. The door into the room at the other end of the ward was ajar, and Ravn recognised the man lying on the bed with a drip overhead. Leaving the cleaning lady's trolley outside, he pushed the door open quietly.

Ravn skirted the large pool of blood on the floor and went up to the bed where Mikkel lay. His chest and left shoulder were thoroughly bandaged, and he was pale as a ghost. "Mikkel?"

Mikkel opened his eyes slowly and turned his head to Ravn. His gaze was blurred, as if heavily medicated, and he sent Ravn a peaceful smile. "What's with the get-up, man? You look . . . like shit," Mikkel mumbled.

"Speak for yourself," said Ravn, taking off the blue hairnet. "Are you okay?" he said, glancing at the pool of blood.

"It's not mine," Mikkel replied. "*Bandit* blood. I don't think he made it."

"Where were you hit?"

"Left side, by the clavicle, two shots, three centimetres from the heart. The doctor says it was my lucky day, even though it doesn't feel like it right now . . . hurts like hell."

"What about Dorthe, does she know?"

"She's on her way. She's just taking the girls to the neighbour's."

"Is there anything I can do for you?"

"Get me some water?"

Ravn picked up the water bottle from the bedside table and put the straw to his lips.

"What the hell happened, Mikkel?"

Mikkel drank some water before he replied. "They put up a fight."

"I figured as much. Were you outnumbered?"

Mikkel nodded. "At first, everything went according to plan. All the criminals lay on the floor, but then . . ." He waved, indicating that he needed more water.

"But then what?"

Once Mikkel had taken a few sips, he continued. "We advanced to the back room. The big players were there . . . They'd obviously been at the table all night. Kaminsky was calmly stirring his soup at the stove . . . He refused to lie down with the others. René, a new man, went over to make him—"

"That's against standard procedure."

"I know, as I said . . . he's new . . . pretty keen . . . so he goes over to Kaminsky . . . He was quick . . . Before we could react, Kaminsky grabbed René's gun . . . He was the first one to go down. Kaminsky executed him with a shot under his chin. I froze, everyone froze, which is probably what Kaminsky wanted because then all hell broke loose . . . More criminals arrived . . . The ones we had ordered to the floor got up and retaliated . . . It was madness. People were mowed down at close range. A bloodbath . . ." Mikkel closed his eyes, and the tears ran silently down his cheeks.

Ravn squeezed his hand. He desperately wanted to know if Kaminsky had survived, but he couldn't bring himself to ask. Not whilst Mikkel was crying. Ravn had never seen his partner like this. Then he was distracted by the tumult out in the corridor. A police officer yelled for back-up. Ravn cast a look over his shoulder and saw several men run past the open door. In between the shouts of the police, a string of Russian curses. Ravn went to the door and looked out.

At the other end of the corridor, three police officers had a man on the floor who looked as if he'd been dipped in a cauldron of blood. His clothes were in tatters, and despite being outnumbered three to one, he tossed his wild mane of blood-splattered hair and beard as he fought off the men. The police officers struggled to get the man's hands behind his back so they could cuff him. At last, a doctor intervened with an injection that he smartly jabbed into the man's right buttock. The effect was immediate; the man's body went slack. He lowered his head and snorted violently, spraying blood from his nose and the corners of his mouth. The police officers hastened to cuff his hands behind his back.

Despite the bloody state of the madman's face, Ravn recognised him: It was Andrej Kaminsky.

14

It was early evening and The Sea Otter's patrons were lounging on chairs just outside the door, watching the sunset over the canal. Inside, Ravn was propping up the bar with Eduardo and Victoria. Eduardo leaned over the counter and turned the fan, directing a jet of cool air at his face.

"Hands off," said Johnson, swivelling the fan back in his own direction. "I bought that for the staff!"

"But it's ridiculously hot in here," Eduardo moaned.

"I thought you loved the heat."

"If I liked sweating, I'd have stayed in Málaga," said Eduardo, returning to his barstool. "So Mikkel's going to be okay," he said to Ravn.

"I think so, but it will take a while before he can return to work."

"He was lucky," said Eduardo. "Apart from the new guy who was killed, two other men in his team are seriously wounded."

Ravn nodded.

"So what happens now with the case against Kaminsky?"

"As long as Mikkel is out of action, everyone else in the department will want a piece of the cake because Kaminsky has caught the attention of the media. They'll be standing in line, waiting to talk to him," Ravn said, and took a swig of beer.

"The news reported that a hundred kilos of hash and three kilos of cocaine were found at the club, as well as a stash of contraband in a house out back," Johnson added.

"Do you think he'll talk?" asked Victoria.

"I doubt it," said Ravn. "Because he has nothing to gain if he does."

"You don't think he can make a deal?"

Ravn shook his head. "All the circumstantial evidence points against him. And the prosecution is hardly inclined to do a police murderer any favours."

"It's simply too hot in here," Eduardo said. He picked up his beer, and demonstrably fanning his face, he went outside to get some air.

Victoria rolled herself a cigarette and looked at Ravn. "Are you up for a game of carom?"

"Not today," Ravn said.

"Not even if I give you a ten-point head start?"

"Thanks, I'm not in the mood for a game, Victoria." Ravn ordered another round instead—a Hof for himself and a sherry for Victoria.

Victoria drew on her cigarette and blew out a cloud of smoke. "They'll put him behind bars for eternity, Ravn. That ought to be enough."

Ravn bit his lip. "He wasn't the one who murdered Eva. Her murderer is still out there, Victoria."

"But you said yourself that Kaminsky is behind the murder. So his capture lends some form of justice to the case."

"Perhaps. Either way, Kaminsky is beyond my reach now."

"What about that job interview you had?" Johnson asked, trying to lift the mood more than anything else. "Eduardo told me you had a meeting with some bigshot."

Ravn nodded and rested his gaze on Møffe, who was sleeping on the floor under his barstool.

"And? What was it about?" Johnson insisted.

"I'm not at liberty to say," said Ravn with a smile. "They made me sign a non-disclosure agreement before the meeting even started."

"Hmm. Sounds important," said Johnson.

"It was an interesting place. Very hush-hush. They earn a fortune lecturing business folks on leadership. All that efficacy and performance bullshit."

"God help us," Johnson scoffed. "But I hope they pay well?"

"They would, had I accepted their offer, but I didn't."

"You didn't . . . what?!" Johnson gave him a look from his boxer days, the one that used to annihilate his opponent in the ring.

"I turned it down . . . I said I needed to think about it," Ravn lied.

"Unless they asked you to kill someone, what the hell is there to think about?! You're up to your eyeballs in debt, Ravn. You owe money to every man and his dog."

"It's not that bad," Ravn said with a laugh.

"Two thousand three hundred and fifty kroner for this month alone," Johnson said, glancing at his tab in the little black notebook lying open on the counter. "Excluding this evening's entertainment. Have you even paid your harbour dues?"

"Of course I have," Ravn said, offended. "And I told them I'd think about it!"

Victoria emptied her sherry glass. "I think I'll call it a night. I have a job to do in the morning," she said, patting Ravn affectionately on the shoulder in parting.

"See? You could learn something from that, Ravn," Johnson muttered.

Ravn made no reply. He glanced around the bar. Apart from a guy who had fallen asleep at a table in the back corner, only Ravn and Johnson remained. The barkeep brought his coffee cup to his mouth and took a sip as he flipped through the daily news.

"You've never offered me a cup of coffee," Ravn said.

"Excuse me?" Johnson said, looking up from his paper.

"A coffee. Could I have a cup, please?"

"Is there something wrong with your beer?"

"Not at all. I'd just like a cup of coffee."

"But you *never* drink coffee."

"A change is as good as a holiday, they say."

"Not in here," said Johnson, putting down his cup. "If you want a cup of coffee, you can head off into the kitchen and make it yourself."

So much for Mesmer's coffee test, thought Ravn.

15

At quarter to nine the next morning, a fresh group of delegates were drinking coffee in the glass-and-steel conference hall of Mesmer Resources. The first lecture would be given by Mesmer himself, and he enjoyed the view from his office before turning his attention to Ravn, who had taken a seat opposite his desk. "I can offer you an advance of fifty thousand kroner to find my son."

Ravn made no reply. Merely followed Ferdinand Mesmer with his eyes as he sat down heavily behind his desk.

"But I will expect a swift result," Mesmer continued, drumming the fingers of his left hand whilst the other was motionless on the desk. "Shall we say within a week?"

Ravn nodded and tried to hide his surprise. Before the meeting, he had calculated an hourly rate based on the fee he had charged Lohman: 50k for a week's work far exceeded his expectations.

"I'll do the best I can to expedite matters," he said, "but I can't promise you anything."

He took out his notebook and the Mesmer Resources ballpoint pen that he'd pocketed earlier—after signing yet another non-disclosure agreement. He'd brought along the notebook because he'd felt somewhat empty-handed when he left the boat that morning. Turning to a blank page, he noticed that the last time he'd used it was when he'd bought spare parts at Lynette's Boat Service. He'd made a note of various oils and filters he'd needed, as well as a life jacket for Møffe—which he'd never used.

"Your son, Jacob," Ravn said, forcing himself to focus on the present. "I need some details about him. The more you can tell me, the better."

Mesmer didn't reply, merely stared at Ravn expectantly.

"You said your son is about forty-eight years old. When is his birthday, exactly? A social security number would also be useful."

Mesmer still made no reply and just kept staring at him.

"If you have an address, even if it's just a city or a neighbourhood, it would help," Ravn said, and gave Mesmer a smile, which his new client didn't return. "A photograph would also be useful if you have one?"

Mesmer glanced at his watch.

"I'd also like to know who has had contact with your son. Family status, friends, and colleagues, even if it's from several years back, and if we could make a list, then—"

"Are you a religious man, Ravn?" Mesmer interrupted him, but at least it was a verbal response of some kind.

"Religious? No, not really. Why?"

"Nor am I," Mesmer said. "I've always regarded religious people with some scepticism. In my opinion, religion is more often than not some kind of crutch, or way to compensate for something—most of all, a lack of belief in yourself."

"Possibly," Ravn said diplomatically. "But, returning to—"

"Jacob was—*is*—deeply religious. A kind of fundamental Christian, I think it's called. His religiosity is one of the reasons why we lost contact. It's not that I didn't respect his beliefs—that is his own choice, of course—but Jacob turned his back on us, his own family."

"And this happened . . . ten years ago, as you mentioned the first time we met?"

"The actual blow-up between us was ten years ago, yes, but the tension between us had existed for a long time." Mesmer stared into space. "Jacob had always had a troubled mind. He was very introverted. There were long periods of depression, despite the efforts of his mother and me. This continued into adulthood. Jacob always made things difficult for himself, an outsider who tended to isolate himself from others."

"Had he always been a religious person?"

Mesmer gave Ravn a look of disgust. "No. He only 'found Jesus' after his breakdown," he said sarcastically. "At that time, he became a member of some kind of Baptist church and started attending the sermons of some or other evangelist preacher. At first, we thought it was just a whim, a delayed teenage rebellion—I even blamed myself for his actions . . ." Mesmer said, pointing to his chest with his scarred hand. "And we tried to help him as best we could."

"In what way?"

"Well, in the way that parents generally do: We tried to talk to him, appeal to his common sense, and point out what this was doing to him. How much he was hurting those around him with this kind of behaviour."

"But he was a grown man at this point, right?"

"What difference does that make?" Mesmer scoffed. "Your responsibility as a parent never ends."

"Of course not," Ravn said.

"Unfortunately, Jacob broke off all contact with us after that. He said that there wasn't 'space' in his life for anything or anyone other than God. He was 'obliged to follow his calling,' as he put it. My wife, his mother, never got a chance to see him again. Cancer took her life a few years ago."

"I'm sorry for your loss," said Ravn. "Is Jacob still a member of the Baptist congregation you mentioned?"

"We found out through other channels that Jacob fell out with that preacher and became a self-proclaimed evangelist himself—with great success, apparently." Mesmer shook his head. "Apparently, my son has the gift of persuasion."

"Does he preach in any specific church, or a fixed location?"

Mesmer looked past Ravn at Katrine, who had quietly entered the room and taken a seat on the sofa. Ravn heard her stand up and, the next moment, she was at his side with a faded yellow file in her hand. She put the file in front of him. A CD-ROM was attached to the file with an elastic band. "What's this?" Ravn asked.

"The first investigator's report," Katrine said.

Ravn looked up at Mesmer in surprise. "Someone was on the case before me?"

Mesmer looked at his watch and stood up. "No. The report is several years old and stems from an earlier investigation."

"An investigation into the activities of your son?"

Ferdinand Mesmer buttoned his navy suit jacket and stroked his beard. "Into the activities of God's Chosen, the sect that my son leads."

The name sounded familiar to Ravn, but he couldn't remember in what context.

"The press had a field day. They accused the sect of all sorts of illicit activities, including brainwashing and asset stripping," Mesmer said.

"Rings a bell. I think I read something about it in the papers."

"You and the rest of the country. That was the reason why I decided to start my own investigation. So I could figure out . . . what was going on."

"For your son's sake?"

"For the entire family's sake."

"And was there any substance to the rumours and accusations against the sect?" Ravn asked, glancing at the file.

"It doesn't matter anymore," said Mesmer. "I would just like you to find Jacob. Discreetly, of course. I don't want anyone to know you're looking for him, not even Jacob. No one likes to feel as if they're being watched."

Ravn nodded.

"Now, if you would excuse me, my delegates are waiting," Mesmer said, heading for the door. "I'm sure you'll find in the file whatever you need to know about my son's contacts and activities. Katrine will take care of the practicalities regarding your fee, et cetera." With a brief farewell, he stepped out the office and was gone before Ravn could reply.

Katrine took a seat on the edge of her boss's desk and folded her arms in her lap. "Do you have a bank account number for me so we can transfer your fee?"

"Yes, I . . ." Ravn patted down his pockets, only to find that he'd left his wallet on board *Bianca*. "Can we sort that out later?"

"Of course. It's your money."

He glanced at the file. "There's something I don't understand."

"Yes?"

"If someone had investigated Jacob before, why don't you just contact him again? Surely, he'd have some idea where Jacob might be?"

"I believe Ferdinand Mesmer was not very happy with the previous investigator's work and did not wish to use him again. Luckily for you, right?"

Ravn regarded her evenly. "He could have just asked you."

"*You* are the private detective, Ravn, not me," she said, smiling like the Cheshire cat. "The question is how good you are at your job. We're waiting in anticipation to find out." Another smile, before she pushed off the edge of the desk, indicating that the meeting was over.

She escorted him in the elevator to the ground floor. When they walked past the open door to the conference hall, Ravn caught a glimpse of Ferdinand Mesmer at the podium. He had removed his jacket and was talking to his audience energetically, his arms raised to the sky.

16

Ravn was sitting in his shorts on *Bianca*'s rear deck. He had retreated to the little shade that the cabin cast on deck, but he was still uncomfortably hot and considered taking a dip in the canal. Instead of the dip, he decided to take a look at the file that Mesmer had given him. A case number was printed in large font on the cover, as well as the name of the investigating agency: BC CONSULTING V/BENJAMIN CLAUSEN with an address on Amager.

Ravn skimmed the contents, including the investigator's report consisting of several loose sheets of paper, and between a thin stack of black-and-white photographs, he found a dog-eared pamphlet: JESUS LOVES YOU was printed on the front leaf above a drawing of a crown of thorns on a cross. He put down the photos and the pamphlet and began reading the report. It reminded him of the countless reports he'd written when he was on the police force. He'd always hated this part of the job, and as a rule, he'd palmed them off on Mikkel.

However, contrary to his own and his colleagues' reports, Benjamin Clausen appeared to have taken great care with his choice of words. But it was extremely verbose, with the result that even the simplest surveillance, like meeting two women dealing out pamphlets on Christianshavn Square, was unnecessarily long-winded. There were details describing the women's clothing, how many pamphlets they distributed, when they took breaks—even the people who accepted the pamphlets. It appeared that Benjamin had ignored the most important rule for writing reports: KEEP IT SIMPLE.

Ravn continued to the next page, which described day two of the surveillance: Benjamin had engaged in conversation with the two women and accepted a pamphlet on God's Chosen. The two women, who were called Amalie and Lisa, were described as *pretty, groomed, and articulate, but not from Copenhagen*—he did not say where they *did* come from.

Ravn skipped a large part of the text and read the final lines on the page where Benjamin was invited to a Bible meeting the following day. The next two pages of the report were about this meeting. The description of the attendees alone filled an entire page. The people were *common folk from all walks of life*, and Benjamin included a comment on the preacher's sermon and the congregation, which, in his opinion, *seemed quite obsessed with the work of the Devil and his many forms, and how we need to ward off his evil with prayer. The preacher reminds us over and over that we are all sinners, but that God will forgive us.*

Apparently, Jacob Mesmer had not attended the meeting, and Benjamin wrote that he'd asked Lisa where the leader was. Lisa reportedly replied that their Master had been waylaid, but that he would be attending the next meeting. After the meeting, Lisa invited Benjamin to come and meet the Master and—in the same sentence—requested a donation to the movement. In the margin, Benjamin had made a note of claiming the 200 kroner as a business expense.

It appeared from the next two pages of the report that Benjamin attended the aforementioned Bible meeting, which turned out to be a marathon arrangement that lasted the entire evening and well into the early hours of the morning. The location was packed, and a few prominent people were present, including an ex-professional football player and popular television host, although Ravn had never heard of him. In the final paragraph, Benjamin noted that Jacob Mesmer had not arrived, and he asked Lisa about her Master once more. Apparently, several members of the congregation became suspicious of his motives and directly asked Benjamin why he was so keen to see Jacob Mesmer. By his own account *maintaining the façade*, Benjamin declared that he had a burning desire to hear Jacob Mesmer preach, and the congregation was *satisfied with his explanation.* Benjamin was told that the Master was on a mission abroad but would soon return to preach for them. He reports that there was a *mildly paranoid* atmosphere at the meeting, probably because of the negative press that the movement and Jacob Mesmer in particular had received.

Ravn turned to the last page, which contained Benjamin's conclusion:

CONCLUSION

The movement known as God's Chosen was founded in 2001 by their leader, Jacob Mesmer. The "Master," as he is called, has a bachelor's degree in theology from the Danish Bible Institute, and has subsequently been awarded an honorary doctorate from the River Bible Institute. God's Chosen is an ecumenical and evangelist organisation, which has its theological roots in Christian religious belief. The movement preaches the Word of God and helps the weakest members of society.

BC Consulting has not found substantiation for the allegations that the media has brought against the movement. These allegations include "brainwashing," oppression, and humiliation of its members. On the contrary, all activities of the movement appear to take place on a voluntary basis. With respect to allegations of tax avoidance, BC Consulting has not been able to obtain insight into the accounting books, etc., but all donations made to the organisation, including my own, were accepted upon the due issuance of an invoice, and presumably brought to bear in the organisation's official balance sheets. Despite repeated attempts, it has not been possible to meet Jacob Mesmer personally. However, based on the character reports given by his close colleagues and friends in the organisation, it must be assumed that media allegations regarding abuse of power and psychological instability are fallacious. Therefore, BC Consulting concludes that the movement known as God's Chosen is an organisation based on sound Christian values, dedicated to improving the conditions of the needy and less fortunate members of society.

Benjamin Clausen, Senior Investigator
BC Consulting

"Holy shit, what a load of crap," Ravn muttered to himself as he slapped the covers of the file shut. On the canal, a large speedboat slid past. Three beefed-up blokes with identical sunglasses and beer cans in their hands nodded in time to the music pumping from a ghetto blaster as they continued to the bridge.

Ravn was appalled by the report's lack of quality. If Benjamin Clausen had been a doctor, he would be dismissed as a quack, and it didn't surprise him that Mesmer had chosen to find someone else for the job. At the very least, Clausen was an amateur who had no idea what he was doing; there was no factual basis for his conclusions. He wondered how a man like Ferdinand Mesmer had come into contact with BC Consulting in the first place, but he guessed it was probably through Lohman. He picked up the pamphlet. Some of the black-and-white photos were taken of the two women dealing them out on Christianshavn Square.

"*Groomed and articulate*," Ravn muttered to himself, shaking his head in disbelief.

The remainder of the photographs were taken at the Bible meetings, including several portraits of one of the women. Ravn paged through the pamphlet instead. He noticed that Benjamin had copied the part that described God's Chosen in glorious terms, including their leader's mission and background, directly into the introduction of his report. Ravn wondered what the CD-ROM contained. Probably more photographs. *Or perhaps recordings of a sermon?* He needed to find out what it was, but he no longer owned a computer, so it would have to wait until he could borrow Eduardo's laptop.

Ravn stood up and went to the railing. He stared out over the canal. For all his meticulous detail, Benjamin had forgotten to include the most important information: *contact* details. Not even the sect's address or telephone number was included.

He saw no other alternative than to contact Benjamin Clausen directly and question him about the first investigation of Jacob Mesmer.

17

Ravn went into the cabin to fetch his iPhone. He took a bottle of water from the fridge and went back on deck. As he passed Møffe in his basket, the dog looked up at him with his tongue lolling out of his mouth. Ravn smiled and dialled the number Benjamin had printed on the cover of the file, but an automated voice told him that the number was no longer in use. He ended the call and rang up telephone enquiries instead. Unfortunately, no information was listed for Benjamin Clausen at the address he provided.

Considering BC Consulting's lack of professionalism, it wouldn't be surprising if the business had gone under in the interim, Ravn reckoned. To be sure, he checked BC Consulting's homepage but found no useful information on Benjamin there either. He googled "God's Chosen" on his phone, which gave thousands of general biblical hits and references. There were many articles about the movement itself, but they didn't bring him any closer to the whereabouts of Jacob Mesmer, and Ravn was well aware that he was much better at looking for people in the real world than cyberspace. His digital skills were rather limited; in truth, nonexistent. He recalled the time he tried to order a takeaway on the internet for himself and Eva. After struggling through the online menu and various pop-ups for an hour, he gave up, and the two of them had popped down to Café Wilders for a late dinner instead.

Operating on the assumption that Lohman had facilitated the contact between Benjamin and Ferdinand Mesmer, Ravn called up the lawyer's office. Moments later, he had Miss Malling on the other end of the line. "No, you can't speak with him," she said, vaguely annoyed as usual. "I'm afraid Advocate Lohman is in a meeting."

"Could you ask him to call me as soon as he's done?" said Ravn.

"I'm terribly sorry, but the meeting is out of town, so it won't be before tomorrow. What did you say your name was again?"

"It's Ravn," he said. Miss Malling voiced no recognition. "Thomas Ravnsholdt," he added with a sigh. "I was in your office to wrap up a case less than a week ago."

"Oh, it's *you*," Miss Malling said, the vague annoyance in her voice switching to patent dislike.

"Forget it, I'll find Lohman myself," he said, and ended the call.

Ravn was pretty sure that "out of town" in Lohman's book could be no further than The Sea Otter around the corner from his office. And it was Wednesday. It might be swelteringly hot, but Ravn would bet his life that he'd find Victoria and Lohman in the billiards room for their weekly game of carom. He snatched his T-shirt from the back of his plastic deck chair and pulled it over his head. "Let's go, Møffe," he said, slapping his thigh.

Møffe stretched lazily, then got to his feet reluctantly and came over.

There was a thick pall of tobacco smoke in the billiards room at The Sea Otter, and it was impressive that Victoria and Lohman could play at all with such poor visibility. A home-rolled Petterøe in the corner of her mouth, Victoria had her eyes trained on the table, considering her strategy as she chalked the end of her cue. She nodded at Ravn briefly in greeting.

Ravn took a seat next to Lohman, who was watching the table with a similar intense concentration, his cue in one hand and one of his signature Manne cheroots in the other. "Lohman, I have—"

Lohman raised his cigar hand. "Ssshh, not now, Ravn."

Victoria leaned over the table and took her shot. An expert curve ball that bounced off one side, then another, before hitting its target with a satisfying click.

"Bravo!" said Lohman.

Victoria nodded and walked round the table to set up her next shot.

"Lohman, I just need to ask you if—"

The lawyer turned to him irritably. "We're in the middle of a game, Ravn. Surely you can see that?" he said, waving his hand in a gesture to signal in no uncertain terms that he wished Ravn would piss off.

Ravn chose to stay. He leaned back in his chair and crossed his arms over his chest, determined to wait—which he did for at least an hour, whilst Victoria and Lohman completed their game. At last, Lohman set up for his decisive shot. His cheroot stump in the corner of his mouth, Lohman leaned over the table with a frown on his face. The shot started out fine but missed its target by millimetres.

"Bloody hell!" Lohman muttered, spilling ash onto his shirt.

Victoria smiled sweetly and shook his hand. She was playing it down, but Ravn could see that she was thrilled with her victory. Lohman reached for his wallet in his back pocket and pulled out two 100-kroner notes. "You're ruining me. You do know that, don't you?" he said to Victoria.

"That would be a shame," said Victoria, stuffing the money into the pocket of her tweed waistcoat.

"It's *his* fault," said Lohman, pointing at Ravn. "He ruined my concentration. What's so important that you felt the need to interrupt me?"

Ravn smiled sweetly. "Benjamin Clausen," he said.

Lohman returned the cue to the stand in the corner and came over to Ravn. "Benjamin Clausen?" he snapped, and puffed on his cheroot. "Doesn't ring a bell. One of my clients?"

"No, a private detective. Former detective, I believe, as his number is no longer valid."

Lohman exhaled smoke. "Ah, that guy . . ."

"He worked on a case for Ferdinand Mesmer, so I thought you—"

"He wasn't much good. He was very friendly and all, but . . ." Lohman shook his head.

"Do you know how I can get hold of him?"

"No idea, I haven't seen him in years. I only used him once."

"But . . . didn't you recommend him to Ferdinand Mesmer?"

Lohman emptied his glass of sherry and nodded. "Yes, I . . . no . . . it was the other way around," he said. "Yes, now I remember. Mesmer was the one who found him. And I used his services, once, after that, and it didn't work out well. Benjamin Clausen . . . strange fellow, frail, a little shaky if you know what I mean . . ." he added, tapping his temple with his left index finger.

"Do you have his contact details?"

"We might have an invoice from him on file, but if his business has closed, then it doesn't help you, does it?"

It was after midnight by the time Ravn returned to *Bianca*. He was starting to think Johnson had covered the barstools at The Sea Otter with Velcro; he had no intention of hanging around, but somehow he did, even though the pub was dead. To be fair, he had been waiting for Eduardo so he could ask for help with Benjamin's CD-ROM, but the Spaniard never arrived. The moaning coming from the open hatch on the ketch provided the plausible explanation.

Ravn carried Møffe on board and put him down on the rear deck. He knew he wouldn't be able to sleep until Eduardo and his guest were done, so he sat down on his chair and looked out over the dark waters of the canal. All evening, he'd been mulling over Benjamin's sloppy report, which didn't provide any indication as to where Jacob Mesmer could be. He could, of course, go over to Christianshavn Square tomorrow and see if any of his *disciples* were there, trying to attract new members into the fold. But it had been more than two years since Benjamin photographed them over there. For his own part, he had never seen these women on the square before, and he passed through every day.

He took another look at the report. The only trail he had was the Danish Bible Institute, where Jacob had reportedly received his education. It was years ago, but it was possible that the institute had an address for Jacob Mesmer on file, which might point him in the right direction. He googled the Bible Institute on his phone and found an address on Leifsgade, which was within walking distance of *Bianca*. He would go there tomorrow.

Next door, the evening seemed to have reached its climax—as half of Christianshavn could not fail to notice.

18

The elevator was out of order, and Ravn had to take the stairs to the sixth floor, where the Danish Bible Institute had their premises. The institute was the only occupant in the entire office building, and the place seemed deserted.

He was quite out of breath when he reached the top floor. The receptionist was an elderly lady with thick glasses. She squinted at Ravn when he paused in the doorway, and gave him a measured greeting from behind her desk. Ravn nodded in reply and looked out over the enormous roof terrace, where the students were eating their lunch at long tables in the sun. "What a fantastic view you have," he said.

"Thank you. What can I do for you?" said the receptionist.

"My name is Thomas Ravnsholdt. I'm here to enquire about one of your students, Jacob Mesmer. I'm trying to find an address or a telephone number for him."

"A student enrolled in one of our courses?" she said, frowning at him.

"No, a *former* student, and it's quite a long time ago."

"I'm afraid that kind of information is confidential."

Ravn leaned on the counter between them. "Yes, I understand. That's why I am here in person, to ask for your help. I'm here on behalf of the student's father. Unfortunately, they've lost contact with each other."

She nodded thoughtfully. "So . . . this is a *family* request?"

Ravn did his level best to look as pious as he could. "Exactly. Jacob is . . . his father's prodigal son . . ." He couldn't remember the details of the parable, exactly, but he knew it had something to do with a father who forgives his long-lost son. *Close enough*, he thought.

The receptionist brought her hand to the little gold cross that lay at the throat of her white cowl-neck blouse. "Well, I . . . you had better have a word with the rector."

She stood up and went onto the terrace. A few moments later, she returned, accompanied by a middle-aged man with a suntanned face and a receding hairline. "Poul," the man said, extending his hand as the receptionist hovered on the threshold.

"Forgive me for interrupting your breakfast, Poul," Ravn said to the rector, who was the spitting image of his carpentry teacher back in high school, and he couldn't help smiling at the memory.

"No problem," said Poul, returning Ravn's smile. "Karen tells me you're looking for one of our former students?"

Ravn nodded and repeated what he'd said to the receptionist—minus the reference to the prodigal son, that is.

"Well, you look like a reliable fellow," said Poul amiably, "so I think we can find a way to be helpful." Poul took a seat on the receptionist's chair and logged into her computer. "Let's see what we have. What did you say the student's name was?"

"Jacob . . . Mesmer."

"Oh . . . yes," Poul said. "I remember him well."

"Okay," said Ravn, impressed that the rector could recall a particular student's name after so many years.

Poul did a quick search in the institute's records. "I'm sorry. It appears that it's too long ago, and we no longer have Jacob's details on file."

"Perhaps you have a physical archive that we could check?"

"I'm afraid not," Poul replied. "When we moved out here a few years ago, we took the opportunity to throw away what we didn't need." He stood up and came round to the other side of the counter. "When the case was running in the press, we got a lot of calls from journalists looking for information on him."

"What kind of information, exactly?"

"Oh, you know, the usual . . . what kind of student he was, if he'd got into trouble at the school . . ." Poul shook his head with a smile.

"Is that why you remember him? Because of the media coverage?"

Poul shrugged. "Not only because of that," he said. "Jacob was a good pupil. Very dedicated and enthusiastic, always looking out for the younger members in the class—I don't care what the press wrote and said about him afterwards."

"Do you know if any of the students or other teachers kept in touch with Jacob?" Ravn asked, glancing at the students sitting on the terrace.

"I doubt it. And I'm the only one of his teachers who's still working here."

"And you wouldn't happen to have the contact details of any of his former classmates who might know where he is?"

"I'm sorry, no," Poul said, and he looked as if he meant it. "Jacob was not the kind of fellow who hung out with a lot of friends. Please don't misunderstand me; he was well-liked by everyone here at the school. He was passionate about his studies with a natural talent for attracting co-students and outsiders alike, especially at Bible meetings, collections, and missionary trips. But he was more reserved at social arrangements, which might have had something to do with the fact that he was much older than the other students."

"Do you know anything about the church he joined?"

"Yes, it was a Baptist church, but I think Jacob soon realised that he could serve God better by creating his own movement—or becoming a preacher himself," Poul added with a smile.

"In what way?" Ravn said, returning the smile.

"Well, I don't want to speak badly of anyone. But I think it's fair to say that Jacob wanted to be a leader more than anything else—*more* than he wanted to serve God, as such. He had quite a significant *superbia*."

"A super . . . what?"

"*Superbia*, the first of the seven deadly sins. You can call it 'arrogance' in layman's terms. I often asked him to work on this aspect of his personality . . . but apart from that, he was a good person. Please give him my regards when you find him."

"I will. Thank you for your time," said Ravn, shaking Poul's hand.

When he was on his way to the door, Poul called after him and he turned round.

"I'm not sure if it's useful, but I remember that a few years after he left the institute, I received an invitation to a Bible meeting that he'd arranged. It was held here somewhere, on Amager—"

"A location for God's Chosen?"

"Yes, that was it . . . God's Chosen . . . that's what Jacob called his movement." The rector smiled again. "But no, I don't know where Jacob preached. It was in one of the churches, but I couldn't make it, and I can't remember in which church on Amager the meeting was held."

19

When Ravn returned to *Bianca*, he found Eduardo alone on the deck of his ketch, sunbathing with his laptop open in front of him. Ravn stood on the embankment, deliberately blocking his friend's sun. Eduardo glanced up briefly whilst his fingers danced over the keyboard. "What's up, *amigo*?"

"Late night?"

Eduardo shrugged. "They're going to kill me, *las señoritas*. They hinder my work—this article was due two days ago."

"Poor baby," said Ravn. "I need your help."

"Not now, Ravn. You don't know how much weight is resting on my shoulders," Eduardo said. His fingers paused for a moment.

"Sounds hard."

"Do you have any idea how hard it is to write responsible journalism in the current climate in the industry? We've got pressure from all sides, battling to protect our freedom of expression!"

"Not really, no. So what's your article about, then?"

"How public transport in Copenhagen has been pushed to the right by members of the City Council."

"But we've always driven on the right-hand side of the road."

"*Politically*—the *political* right, Ravn!" Eduardo said in exasperation.

Ravn raised his fist in a mock-revolutionary salute. "Okay, *Che*, take it easy," he said. "Just pop over when you're done. And bring your laptop with you. Can it read CD-ROMs?"

"See you later, Ravn," Eduardo muttered, returning his attention to the screen.

An hour and a half later, when the sun was at its zenith, Eduardo knocked on his open cabin door. Ravn was busy making lunch for Møffe—cm-thick cubes of white bread with liver pate. It was the only thing that Møffe would eat. He put the bowl on the floor for Møffe and invited Eduardo into the shade. "Did you remember to bring your computer?" Ravn said.

Eduardo nodded, put the laptop on the coffee table, and took a seat on the sofa. "So what do you need my computer for?"

Ravn picked up the CD-ROM and his own plate of sandwiches, sat down next to Eduardo, and handed him the disc.

"What is it?" Eduardo asked. "Music?"

"If so, choir music. It came with the investigator's report I received from Ferdinand Mesmer."

"How's the case going? Any progress?"

"Still waiting for a breakthrough, let's put it that way."

Eduardo put the CD in the drive, which immediately began to hum. Then a series of text and image files popped up on the screen. "It's data files," Eduardo said, shaking his head. "Why didn't they save them on a USB stick? That would have been a lot more practical."

Ravn shrugged. "Can you open the files?"

Eduardo clicked on the top icon, and the first file opened. "Goodness me," he said, scrolling down. "It's an entire novel." The first file was more than fifty pages long, and the CD contained another ten files. "I wonder if the other files are just as large." He clicked on a few more and discovered that they had at least as many pages as the first.

Ravn sighed and moved Eduardo's computer onto his lap so he could take a better look. "It's gonna take me years to get through all this paperwork."

Eduardo laughed.

Ravn began reading. "Hmm. It seems to be some kind of logbook," he said in surprise. "Written by Benjamin Clausen, the first investigator hired by Mesmer."

"How did Mesmer get hold of it?"

"I have no idea."

"And why did he give it you? It doesn't make any sense."

"Just a second," Ravn mumbled, reading through the introductory text. When he'd read the first page, he leaned back on the sofa and looked at Eduardo. "You're right, this is very strange. About a month after the first investigation into God's Chosen, Ferdinand Mesmer hired Benjamin Clausen again."

"What's strange about that?"

"Because the first investigation was amateurish. Why would Mesmer hire him again? For whatever reason, Mesmer hired Benjamin to investigate God's Chosen a second time—undercover, this time. Apparently, Benjamin was instructed to infiltrate the congregation and report his observations directly to Ferdinand Mesmer." Ravn looked down at the screen. "Benjamin writes: *Agreed with the client that BC Consulting will not draw any conclusions, merely record information on a daily basis and provide the same to the client for his own purposes. The scope of the assignment will be 24/7 surveillance for a period of three months from today's date.* Benjamin also notes that if and when he should meet Jacob Mesmer, he is instructed to give a detailed description of Jacob's physical and psychological state."

"Good lord, this Ferdinand Mesmer guy sounds like quite a control freak," Eduardo said. "It must have cost him a fortune to employ Benjamin for such a long time."

"I'm sure you're right," said Ravn. "Mesmer paid me fifty k for one week's work—I can just imagine what he paid for three whole months, full-time . . ."

"Fifty thousand kroner . . . Congratulations, my friend . . ."

"Yeah, thanks."

"But you don't look happy."

"I'm just wondering what, exactly, motivated Mesmer to hire Benjamin a second time. Was it purely concern for his son after all the accusations made in the press, or something else . . .?"

"You think Mesmer might be looking for something?"

"Maybe. I'll have to read through all these files to find out," Ravn said with a sigh.

Eduardo looked out of the cabin window thoughtfully. "It would also clarify your own assignment . . ."

"What do you mean?"

"I mean, why did he hire you to find his son three years *after* Benjamin's assignment? Is he still just a concerned parent? Or does he have some other interest in God's Chosen?"

Ravn nodded. He'd already asked himself the same question, even though Mesmer had seemed sincere and concerned for his son at their first meeting. He appeared genuinely upset, even bereaved over the loss of his son. On the other hand, Ravn knew that grief had a way of transforming into other passionate emotions.

Obsession, hate . . . revenge.

20

Eduardo had printed out the first two files for Ravn. So far, the report was almost 150 pages long, and Eduardo had only stopped printing because he'd run out of ink. He promised to print out the rest as soon as he got to work. Ravn didn't have his own computer, which would have spared Eduardo the trouble, but he actually preferred to underline the important sections on a hard copy, especially the details of those people who'd had direct contact with Jacob Mesmer.

Hiring Benjamin to infiltrate God's Chosen was a smart move by Ferdinand Mesmer. Benjamin's diary and report had given Ravn some insight into the nature of Jacob Mesmer's organisation, which was founded on a strict hierarchy. Only God stood above the teachers, or "Elders," and the "Aspirants," as the newbies were called, knew their place at the bottom of the hierarchy.

Benjamin was enrolled in a course called Introduction to the Holy Spirit. He'd paid 15,000 kroner for the privilege with the possibility of advancement to the next level if he passed the exam upon completion of the first five weeks of instruction. Benjamin noted, however, that none of the Aspirants had failed the exam to date, nor was it clear what kind of "education" their teachers would provide—other than how to become a "prophet of the gospel," which would enable them to instruct the new Aspirants at one of the organisation's many centres across the country, or, if they excelled in their work, they could partake in evangelical missions abroad, exactly like their "Master," Jacob Mesmer.

The course consisted of daily Bible studies, in which the teachers explained their interpretation of the various allegories in the New Testament. In his logbook, Benjamin wrote that the instruction reminded him of confirmation classes back when he was a teenager, albeit more intense, and his classmates were more engaged in the subject. He also mentioned the cover story he had prepared in the event that anyone would ask questions about his background, but fortunately he was never called upon to rely on it, because their church encouraged Aspirants to withdraw from their former lives. It was believed that the past had no significance for their future journey to God. The teachers emphasised that the less contact you had with your past—including your family and friends outside the church—the better, and the Aspirants were instructed to nurture contact with members of the congregation only, so that they could concentrate on accepting the facilitation of God's grace and wisdom.

After the first week, each of the candidates was allocated a mentor. Benjamin was assigned to Lisa's mentorship, and Ravn had a sense that Benjamin's tone became more poetic whenever she was described in the report.

Apart from the instruction, the pupils in the course participated in the church's charitable service, in which they provided food and shelter for homeless people, accompanied by hymns and a few readings from the Bible—usually about abstinence. It irked Ravn that Benjamin never noted *where* these services took place.

The physical work that the Aspirants performed could also be cleaning or shopping for one of the teachers, thereby allowing the latter to devote more time to their theological studies and missionary work. *All members of God's Chosen serve God—some of us harder than others*, Benjamin wrote, after he had spent most of his day cleaning out the cellar of one of his Elders.

Honestly, Ravn thought Benjamin's willingness to work for these people was somewhat ridiculous. But he admired his colleague's dedication to the job, regardless of the menial tasks he was forced to undertake, especially after an unpleasant episode on Christianshavn Square. In an attempt to recruit new members, Benjamin and Lisa had gone to the square to distribute pamphlets. The only people who took any notice of them that day were a couple of drunks who became abusive and cast an empty beer bottle at them. Benjamin was struck on the back, and they fled in a hurry. That night, Lisa asked the congregation to pray for the drunks. The Elders decided to cease missionary work in the square and concentrate their efforts on other neighbourhoods instead.

Benjamin and Lisa were allocated the old embassy quarter in Øster-bro, and Lisa had high expectations for their work in this area. Unfortu-nately, they had no success. And although the denizens of Østerbro were not physically abusive, their verbal insults were just as harsh as those they had received from the drunkards in Christianshavn Square. Housewives, students, and pensioners alike freely expressed their disdain for the Word of God and their church's missionary work. In Benjamin's own words, they *were unable to distribute many pamphlets in that time*. Ravn could read between the lines that Benjamin was worried about Lisa, who he believed was fragile and vulnerable to all the unpleasantries they were exposed to on a daily basis, despite her strong faith in God.

Ravn knew from experience that you should never get too close or personally involved with the people you were watching because it mud-died the waters and clouded your judgement; you began to doubt whose side you were on.

Ravn had lost track of how long he had been reading. It was dark out-side, and his body was aching from sitting in the same position for so long. Apart from the water lapping against *Bianca*'s hull, all was quiet on the canal. He found Benjamin's report an interesting read, as if it were a good novel that gradually revealed the sympathetic character of the protagonist. He flipped ahead through the remaining printouts, eager to see if Jacob Mesmer's name came up. He didn't find any references to the Master, but another paragraph caught his attention: Benjamin joined a team of Aspirants who had been given the task to fetch some cardboard boxes from Maria Church. The boxes contained office sup-plies, books, and crockery that belonged to the congregation, which had used the church for sermons before God's Chosen had its own premises.

Benjamin described how they had sung hymns as they moved the boxes to Belgiensgade.

If he was not mistaken, Belgiensgade was right next to Amager Centre, which was only a few kilometres away from Christianshavn. He felt a surge of excitement. This was a good lead, and hopefully he wouldn't have to plough through the rest of Benjamin's report after all.

21

Compared to the other geographically named roads on Amager, Belgiensgade was relatively short. It was no more than a 500-metre stretch between Amagerbrogade and the private properties, warehouses and a row of residential blocks that were obviously overdue for renovation on Reberbanegade. Møffe was straining at his leash, sniffing at everything that came past as they made their way down the road. Ravn tried to hold him back but decided to give up the fight and let Møffe scuttle on ahead.

Benjamin had not mentioned a street number in his report, but Ravn figured all he had to do was look for a building that was relatively detached from its surroundings, with room for thirty-odd people. Logically, this excluded the residential blocks, so he concentrated his search on the palatial villas on the right-hand side of the road, checking the names on the postboxes in the front gardens as he passed. He found no indication that any of the houses belonged to Jacob Mesmer's church. A few low-ceilinged workshops came up on his left, and he went round the back to see if there was a building hidden from the road, but only found a locked garage complex. He returned to the road, and Møffe came up to him, wagging his tail.

Ravn wondered whether Benjamin had meant *near* Belgiensgade? He considered checking some of the streets branching off Belgiensgade, or simply waiting for Eduardo to deliver the remainder of the printouts, which may provide him with a specific address. He turned round and walked back up the road the way he had come, but stopped when he reached a green fence covered in graffiti. A bush of some sort grew along the top of the fence and obscured his view of the property that lay behind it. When he had come past before, he had assumed that the grounds belonged to the house alongside, but now he noticed that the fence divided two lots. Standing on his toes, he could just see over the top and discovered the remains of a collapsed red-brick building that was overgrown with dense shrubbery, tall grass, and two large trees that had toppled onto the grass.

"Sit, and stay here," Ravn said to Møffe.

Smacking his underbite, Møffe reluctantly did as he was told and gave his master a disgruntled look for good measure. Ravn replied with a look in kind, then entered the neighbouring lot.

Ravn walked along the green fence, searching for a gap in the bushes where he could climb over. Once he was on the other side, he looked round and found a narrow passage that led past the clump of thorn bushes and one of the toppled trees, which took up most of the front garden. Only the end wall and the chimney of the red-brick house were still standing. The remainder of the original building appeared to have been destroyed by fire, and Ravn carefully picked his way through the rubble, piles of bricks, and charcoal. Discarded pizza boxes and empty bottles indicated that the ruin had been used as a refuge, probably local teenagers or various homeless people. He sat down on his haunches and arbitrarily picked up a brick or two, but there were no immediate signs that could identify the former occupants of the house.

He gave up the search a few minutes later and clambered back over the rubble. Standing in the front garden, he dried the sweat off his brow and looked round. He noticed something white in the branches of the toppled tree. Wrangling his arm in amongst the thorn bushes, his fingertips could just reach the piece of paper flapping in the wind. He retrieved the paper, but his arm caught on the thorn bushes in the process. Once he had dabbed the bleeding scratches on his T-shirt, he looked at the piece of paper. It was frayed and partially disintegrated by wind and weather, but at the top, he could make out a few letters printed in red ink:

GOD's . . . He could guess the rest. It was here the church had its premises, until a fire forced them to leave.

Ravn climbed back over the wooden fence and returned to Belgiensgade. He spotted Møffe standing on the pavement in front of the closest residential block. Resting his front paws against the wall, Møffe was snatching up biscuits that an elderly woman dropped out of her kitchen window on the ground floor. Ravn went over and greeted the woman.

"Is this your dog?" she asked in a throaty voice.

"Yes," said Ravn. "His name is Møffe."

"Møffe likes vanilla cookies, I see," said the woman. "And they're the good ones—from Aldi."

"Yup, they must be," said Ravn. "He's usually quite a fussy eater. But sometimes it helps when the company is good. It soothes his sensitive stomach," he added with a smile.

The woman blushed and tossed a few more biscuits down to Møffe. "So, that will have to do, my friend," she said fondly. "You don't want to get as chubby as I am." She brushed the crumbs off her fingers. "Did you hurt yourself?" she asked, pointing at Ravn's bloody arm.

"No, it's just a scratch. I got caught on a thorn branch over there," Ravn replied, pointing at the wooden fence.

"Aha. Are you one of them?" the woman said with a frown.

"One of who?"

"You know, those weird church folk . . . some kind of sect," she said.

"Nope, I was just taking a look round. Do you know what happened over there?"

"The place burnt down. Years ago."

"Really? Sounds dramatic . . ."

"Yes, it was. Firefighters, ambulances, and police officers all over the place . . . I was terrified that the fire would spread, but luckily the guys from the fire department got it under control."

"I can imagine. Good thing they managed to douse the flames in time. Did anyone get hurt?"

The woman nodded and lit the cheroot stump that rested in the ashtray on the windowsill. "Yes, the firefighters hauled several people out of the burning building. And one person died in the blaze. It was all over the papers. *Amager Bladet* wrote a feature too," she said, raising her painted eyebrows.

"Did they find out what caused the fire?"

"There were so many rumours going about. Some said it was arson. Set alight on purpose . . ."

"By whom?"

"I don't know," said the woman, shaking her head gravely. "Someone who'd had enough of them, probably. There was always such a palaver going on over there. Helluva racket. If it wasn't the choir singing, it was all that yelling and shouting from those homeless bums they invited over for a meal on a regular basis."

"Ever go over there yourself to take a look?"

"No bloody way," said the woman. "I've got better things to do with my time."

"Do you know what happened to the congregation, where they moved to back then?"

"Nah, no idea. But they could jolly well have cleaned up after themselves. It's one helluva mess."

22

As soon as Ravn had thanked the woman for the chat, not least the biscuits for Møffe, the two of them made their way towards Amagerbrogade. He sent Eduardo a message to find out when he would be back from the office. He hoped there was some record in Benjamin's logbook of the fire because he needed to find out who had died during the incident, so he could exclude the possibility that it was Jacob Mesmer. Soon after, Eduardo replied that he would be home with the printouts later that afternoon.

Ravn and Møffe continued along Amagerbrogade, where the midday heat was a test of the drivers' patience. He reckoned the fire would have been sufficiently spectacular to be remembered by the journalist who reported it to *Amager Bladet*. He paused his walk to google the number for the newspaper, and moments later, he asked the receptionist on the other end of the line to refer him to the news desk.

"Just a moment," said the receptionist, and put him on hold.

Ravn waited on the line for almost five minutes, tapping his foot on the pavement. When at last a journalist answered the phone in a very tired voice, he explained that he was looking for the journalist who had reported on a fire on Belgiensgade three years ago. "It involved a Christian movement. Does that ring a bell?"

"Yeah, I remember the incident well," said the journalist, yawning audibly. "But I think the fire occurred on Frankrigsgade, isn't that right?"

"No, it was on Belgiensgade. The movement was called God's Chosen."

"I didn't cover the story. I remember the fire though. The name of the movement doesn't ring a bell, but you can ring my colleague Tage when he gets back from holiday," the journalist said with a chortle.

Ravn ignored the lame joke. "Do you have back issues with the story that I could read?"

"Not anymore. But you could try contacting the main library in Tårnby. I think they keep archives on local history in a central database."

"Do you know if they have back issues of *Amager Bladet*?"

"I should think so, yes."

The moment he ended the call, Ravn hailed a taxi. In the back seat, he checked that he had remembered to bring his wallet. If he'd been alone, he would have taken the bus. Møffe had always hated public transport, but the dog absolutely adored riding in a car, and he was resting his head on the open window, watching the cyclists as they whizzed past.

Ten minutes later, they pulled up in front of the main entrance to the library on Kamillevej, and Ravn paid the driver. He put Møffe on his leash as they entered the library and headed for the information desk.

The friendly librarian, a thin woman with a huge amber stone in a locket strung around her neck, confirmed that the journalist was quite correct. "We have a large archive on local history," she said. "Including the Communes of Amager, Ullerup, Tømmerup, Maglebylille, and the island Saltholm," she added with obvious pride in her voice. "Our archive includes everything from church registers, photography, cassettes, paintings, maps, local literature, firm records, to articles of association, architectural drawings, magazines, *and* local newspapers—"

"—including *Amager Bladet*," Ravn said, interrupting her list.

"Of course," she said, unperturbed. "You can look through the back issues archived in the cellar, or view them on microfilm if you prefer," she said, tucking a stray lock of hair behind her ear.

"Well, in that case, I'll take the microfilm version," Ravn said with a smile.

The librarian blushed and made a little snort of laughter. "The microfilm version it is, then."

* * *

Five minutes later, Ravn was seated in front of the monitor that the friendly librarian had referred him to on the top floor, waiting for her to return from the cellar with the microfilm archive of *Amager Bladet*. Apart from an old married couple, Ravn was alone in the large room with light flooding through the windows. The couple were scribbling in their respective notepads as they pored over a church register spread out on the conference table before them, as if their enthusiasm for genealogy were a newfound Olympic discipline.

Carrying a box in her arms, the librarian returned and came over to Ravn. The box contained a microfilm archive of the weekly issues of *Amager Bladet* from 2011 to 2013. The librarian put the first microfilm spool into the device and patiently demonstrated to Ravn how to view and exchange spools. He thanked the librarian for her help and began searching for news of the fire.

The microfilms were like one long narrative of recent history unfolding on Amager. There were articles on shops opening their doors for business while others announced bankruptcy and bargain basement sales; articles on some local politicians who broke their promises; articles on other politicians who were voted back into power; articles on problems with social care measures; talented local sportsmen and women who'd made their neighbourhood proud; pets that had gone missing, and pets that were happily reunited with their owners. But the front page articles were always presented in dramatic fashion and were usually about the imminent closure or bankruptcy of a business or one social institution or another that would have to close down due to lack of government funds. Once in a while, a crime would be reported, usually involving some con artist or another.

Once he had worked his way through all the issues published in 2011, Ravn was sure that an article about a deathly fire would be given priority. Twenty minutes later, his presumption was confirmed: FREE CHURCH IN FLAMES was written in red caps on the third page of the issue he was reading, followed by a photograph of firefighters with hoses trained on the burning building. Ravn read that the fire was reported at 10:30 p.m. It was presumably caused by a cigarette that initially set alight a sofa and quickly spread through the building. The police had not yet identified the man who was killed in the blaze. The congregation that was holding a church service in the room next door only discovered the fire too late, and by the time the fire department arrived, the house could no longer be saved. Another photograph showed two firemen carrying a person out of the building on a stretcher. The caption reported that several members of the congregation were taken to hospital for observation due to smoke inhalation. The police presumed it was an accident, but the test results from forensics to confirm the cause of the fire and the identity of the person killed were expected before the week was out.

Ravn spooled the film forwards, eager to read the next issue to find out what happened, but unfortunately, he'd reached the end of the reel. "Shit," he said involuntarily. The two family-tree enthusiasts at the table gave him disapproving glances and he waved his hand in apology before inserting the next reel into the device.

He found the brief follow-up report he was looking for on the second-last page of the issue, just above the wedding announcements and congratulations: The fire department confirmed that an unattended cigarette was the cause of the fire. The deceased was identified as the fifty-seven-year-old Ove Nielsen, a homeless person who had participated in the church service next door. The police had interviewed a few people present on the property, and the case was closed.

Ravn scrolled on to the following few months' issues to see if any forwarding address for the church congregation was mentioned, but in vain. He was about to turn off the device when a photograph he had just scanned over caught his attention. He scrolled back until the black-and-white photograph reappeared on the screen. The picture was taken just outside the entrance of the Church of Our Saviour, where a large crowd had gathered. In the middle of the photo, Ravn identified himself coming out of the church. Johnson was next to him, with Eva's father and her brother just behind them, as they bore Eva's coffin out to the hearse, which was just visible in the bottom left of the frame.

Ravn swallowed hard. His memory of the day of the funeral was a haze. Many people who wanted to pay their last respects, people he had never met. The community mourned the tragic loss of the young defence attorney, the champion of the needy, who was murdered while her boy-friend, a police officer, was protecting their city. It was the kind of story that broke the hearts of *Amager Bladet*'s readers—and shattered his own. Once again.

He had to get out of there. *Immediately.*

Ravn stood up and stumbled blindly towards the door. *This was a mistake*, he thought. *The entire investigation was a mistake. There was only one case he was interested in. Eva's case. And it was going to follow him to the grave.*

He needed a drink. *Now.*

23

Ravn kept a safe distance from the embankment as he walked down Overgaden Neden Vandet on his way home. He managed to spot *Bianca*'s mast and the little lantern and radar hub at the top that served as a point of orientation—as it had done so many times before when he was blind drunk. This time, he had avoided The Sea Otter, not least the prying eyes of Johnson. Instead, he'd done a pub crawl of Christianshavn, starting at Kanalbodega, then Eiffel Bar and Skipperkroen, after which he couldn't remember the pub's names anymore, but at least no one knew him, and he could drink in peace.

When he reached *Bianca* at last, he sat down on the quay with his back leaning against a bollard. Møffe came to greet him and hopped onto his lap. After a few minutes, Ravn struggled to his feet, and with one arm around his dog and the other hand clinging to the railing, he managed to get them both aboard without mishap.

"That's gotta be tricky," a voice in the dark observed.

Ravn put Møffe down on the deck carefully and squinted at the figure that was leaning against the railing a few feet away from him. Møffe wagged his tail and waddled over to Katrine. She didn't have any dog biscuits with her this time, however, so he slipped back into the cabin behind Ravn instead.

"You're . . . working late," Ravn said, trying his best not to slur.

"Yup."

"So, what are you doing here?" Ravn said, leaning against the side of the cabin to keep his balance.

Katrine came a few steps closer. "I was in the neighbourhood. Thought I'd pop in and see how far you've come with the investigation. Decided to wait for you."

"Well, do take a sssheat," Ravn said, waving an arm in the direction of his white plastic chairs. He immediately regretted the motion, which made his body pitch to the side.

Katrine made no move to accept his insincere invitation. She fixed her eyes on him with an arrogant smile on her lips. "Your neighbour was here, the journalist, right? He dropped off a stack of papers for you."

Ravn turned his head and, through the cabin window, caught a glimpse of the pile of printouts on the kitchen counter. "Fabulous. Did he try to pick you up?"

"Not that I'm aware of."

"No . . . well, you're not his type anyway. He likes sssweet, romantic girls . . ."

That smile of hers was stuck to her lips. "How far have you come with the case?"

"I believe I have until Monday. There's still time."

"Something tells me you haven't even started, even though we've agreed to pay you generously for your time."

"I'm on it."

"Do you have an address for Jacob Mesmer?"

"Yes, I did, as a matter of fact, but the place was burnt down."

"Well, at least you managed to get that far. I mean, a current address."

Ravn's legs caved a little and he steadied himself with a hand on the railing. "Why is Mesmer looking for his son?"

"Mr. Mesmer has already explained. He wants to be reunited with Jacob."

"Yes. But why? Your boss doesn't strike me as the sentimental type if you ask me."

"I'm not asking. When can we expect to have a concrete location on Jacob?"

Ravn shrugged. "If you already knew that the house on Amager burnt down, why didn't you tell me about it?"

Katrine sighed. "Focus on the task at hand, Ravn, instead of speculating on things that have nothing to do with the case. It's very simple: Find Jacob. And get drunk when you've done your job, not before."

"I'm done. Right now. I quit," Ravn said, sliding past Katrine and sitting down heavily in one of his plastic chairs.

"Is that the alcohol talking?"

"No. The host. You don't even have to pay me for the time I've spent on it so far. Just leave."

"I have to say, I'm impressed," Katrine said, walking over to him.

"I don't think I want to know why," Ravn said, staring at his feet.

"For lasting so long," she said. "Two whole days without quitting. That's a miracle, especially for people of your kind."

"And what kind is that?"

"Losers like you, of course. What else?"

"You're funny. If that's what Mesmer is paying you for, you're worth every penny."

"Ferdinand Mesmer pays me for my advice, amongst other things. My recommendation to him was to stay as far away from you as possible."

"In that case, he doesn't always take your advice. Why is that? Doesn't he trust you?"

"Unfortunately, Ferdinand Mesmer tends to have a bleeding heart, especially when it comes to hopeless cases. Including his son."

Ravn looked up and studied her face as best he could. "What do you know about Jacob Mesmer?"

"No more than you can read in Benjamin Clausen's report."

"But I've already quit. Did you forget?"

Katrine ignored the question. "Jacob Mesmer deserted his father, and his excuse was God. What's *yours*?"

"Probably none quite as good as God."

"No. It's probably the same bad excuse that you use every time."

"Oh yeah, what's that?"

"Your dead wife."

Ravn clenched his jaw. "Stop now, while you still can, Katrine," he said.

"Why should I? It's the truth, isn't it? You use her as your excuse every time things get too hard for you—"

"I said stop. NOW."

"Amazing what the dead have to take the blame for, isn't it?" she said, clicking her tongue.

Ravn sprang out of his chair before she could react. He put one hand round her throat and shoved her backwards three paces until her back came against the cabin door, slamming it shut. "I never got the chance to marry her," he snarled. "Mention her name again and I'll beat the shit out of you—and I don't care if you're a woman."

The second before it hit him on the temple, Ravn heard the whoosh of the telescope baton that Katrine engaged with a single flip of her wrist. He blacked out and crashed onto the deck. The next blow hit him on the kneecap, and he screamed in pain.

"If you ever touch me again . . . it will be the last thing you do in your miserable life," she choked out, and brought her free hand to her throat. "If you insist on quitting now, I need you to return the report and whatever else your friend has printed out. And I need it now."

"F-fuck you, Katrine," Ravn stammered, holding on to his aching knee. She landed the blow with clinical precision, and he knew it was impossible for him to put any weight on it. "You've shattered my knee."

"Put some ice on it. You'll be able to walk again tomorrow," she said coldly. "The report. Give it to me. Right now." She snapped the baton shut and returned it to the inner pocket of her suit jacket.

"Get off my boat. And don't come back."

"Can I take it you're still on the case, then?"

Ravn nodded.

Katrine extended her hand to help him up, but he ignored her. "Are you still here?" he said through gritted teeth. Moments later he heard Katrine clambering over the railing. "Pick up the speed, Ravn, will you?" she called down to him. Then her footsteps faded on the cobblestones along the embankment.

Ravn rolled onto his back on the deck and stared up at the stars. His knee was still throbbing and already swollen. He'd never taken a hit from a woman. The meanest bikers, thugs, and psychopaths by the dozen. *But a woman? Never.* He would never admit out loud, but he was a little impressed. From the first moment he saw her, he knew she would be armed, of course, but her choice of weapon surprised him. A telescope baton required experience and finesse, and obviously, she had both, not to mention explosive reactions to boot. Katrine was an extremely dangerous and fascinating acquaintance, which didn't make her any less attractive.

24

When Ravn woke up the next morning, he could barely put his weight on his knee. Hopping on one leg, he did his best to prepare breakfast for himself and Møffe without falling over. He regretted going straight to bed and not taking Katrine's advice to put ice on it immediately. His knee was so swollen it looked as if he had a tennis ball under the skin. The only consolation was that the pain in his knee distracted him from his hangover, which pounded in his head like distant thunder. He was about to switch off the radio when Huey Lewis and the News came on with the old hit "I Want a New Drug." He turned up the volume instead and hummed along with the tune. It was boiling hot in his cabin, so he went out onto the rear deck with a cup of coffee and the printouts that Eduardo had delivered the night before. He would have liked to thank his friend for the trouble but judging from the closed cabin door of the ketch, Eduardo had already left for work.

Ravn skimmed through the papers, looking for the date, but it seemed Benjamin had forgotten to record the time and date of his observations halfway through his logbook, or perhaps he no longer thought it was important. Then he sat down to read more carefully.

Towards the end of the logbook in particular, Benjamin's observations seemed to become increasingly random, and then the text took a manic turn. In some places, the writing made no sense at all, and the style was far removed from the sober and objective reporting at the beginning.

The logbook now had the character of subjective observations on life, interpretations of the gospel, Purgatory, and Judgement Day, especially the latter:

There will be signs in the sun and moon and stars. On earth, people will be filled with fear and confusion over the tumultuous, angry seas. Humankind will fear for their lives and the fate of the world as the power of Heaven is unleashed. And then they will see the Son of God descend in a cloud, bringing with Him the power and glory of God.

Benjamin praised the Lord, God's Chosen, and, not least, hailed Jacob Mesmer as the true leader of mankind.

Glory to the Lord! Joy to the world that we may follow Him. We give humble thanks to the gift that He has given us. We bow before our shepherd. Thank you, Jehovah, for bringing Jacob Mesmer to us, our guide to Gethsemane. We rejoice in the Lord. Hallelujah! We thank him for being God's Chosen One.

Ravn found it hard to imagine that this was written by the same person who had started the report. He wondered what had changed Benjamin's outlook so radically. *What had he experienced in the interim?* The change was disturbing, even creepy.

Turning back to the middle of the report, Ravn traced the last time Benjamin had recorded a date to a month or two before the date of the fire. At this point, the text was still precise and objective reporting. Benjamin observed that, as the weeks passed, the pupils got to know one another on a personal level. Even though the Elders had specifically emphasised that the lives they led *before* entering the church was irrelevant, the Aspirants shared confidences and personal details as they cleaned up, worked in the garden, or prepared meals together, and Benjamin began recording information about his classmates. He noted that some of the younger girls came from stable Christian homes, and it seemed as if they had joined God's Chosen to rebel against their parents. Others came from similar evangelical movements, but they were looking for *inspiration* rather than escape, or they were keen to come into contact with Jacob Mesmer. Benjamin described some of the Aspirants as *refugees*: people who had fled from violent partners, physical abuse, or suffered from psychological illnesses. A guy called Patrick was a typical example. Patrick was a soldier who had lost one of his legs in the war in

Afghanistan and returned to Denmark after his service with a severe case of PTSD. Patrick told Benjamin that he had found Jesus on the S-train platform at Dyssegård Station—just before he was about to throw himself in front of the oncoming train to Høje Taastrup: *"It was Jesus who kicked the legs–both my own and the aluminium one–out from under me, and I fell over before I could jump in front of the train,"* he told Benjamin. *"Jesus kicks your butt, you understand, my friend?"*

Benjamin also wrote about his mentor, the woman called Lisa. It appeared that after the unpleasant incidents they had shared in Christianshavn Square and in Østerbro, Lisa had taken to confiding in Benjamin. She had told him about her confinement in the psychiatric ward at Nordvang; she had shown him the white scars on the insides of her wrists and forearms. *A map of the nightmare of my childhood*, as Lisa called it. But she had abandoned blades and pills in favour of a new life with Jesus.

According to Benjamin's report, Lisa and some of the others had begun to question Benjamin about his past. He wrote that he tried to deflect, replying vaguely that his past had been difficult, but luckily he had found his way to Jesus. He noted that Patrick in particular was insistent, and he feared that the veteran had shared his suspicions about Benjamin with the Elders, several of whom had started asking questions about his past, as well as his motives for wanting to join God's Chosen. Benjamin had remained strong but recorded that it was increasingly difficult tomaintain the façade. Not only because of his fear of being discovered, but also because he felt like a *jerk*—the same word that Lisa had used to describe her ex-boyfriend who had cheated on her and used her bank card without permission.

The Elders became more paranoid after the press again started criticising God's Chosen in the newspapers. Benjamin did not mention a name but described how he had witnessed a heated discussion between two teachers and a journalist on the premises when he had arrived at the gate on his bicycle early one morning. The journalist and a photographer had been waiting in the front garden, and repeatedly asked the teachers whether the pupils were there on a voluntary basis. *Did the teachers have any comment on allegations of brainwashing? Where was their mysterious leader, Jacob Mesmer?*

In the end, the journalist and the photographer were kicked off the property. Benjamin reported that the negative press had resulted in loss of members, both in Belgiensgade and other centres across the country. The former football player whom he had seen at one of the first meetings was one of the people who'd deserted the movement. He too had mouthed off in the press, calling the movement a *sect* and Jacob Mesmer *a dangerous charlatan who exploits weak and vulnerable people in our society.* That night, they prayed for the football player's soul, *for he knows not what he has done.*

Benjamin also reported that two centres in Jutland and Fyn had closed down. At this time, the first rumours of Jacob Mesmer's return began to buzz in the congregation. Soon after, the Elders announced that the Master would come to their church in Belgiensgade, and everyone was given jubilant instructions to prepare for his return. The atmosphere was euphoric amongst the Aspirants in particular, and their discussions in class were not so much about the gospel as the return of Jacob Mesmer. Lisa in particular livened up in anticipation of his arrival, and Benjamin reported that she had taken the lead in the choir and chosen which hymns they should practise for his welcome, and two days later, she coloured her hair and pitched up with a new hairstyle. Ravn could sense an undertone of jealousy in Benjamin's otherwise neutral observations:

Jacob Mesmer arrived today. In the back seat of a black Audi. He has quite a muscular build. White shirt and trousers. Smiles a great deal. Shook everyone's hand as if we were diplomats in his service. He has a firm handshake, his teeth as brilliant white as his shirt. "May the Lord bless you, my brothers and sisters, on this glorious day," he said in greeting. These were his first words. Everyone ecstatic for his mere presence. Many people wept for joy. Tove, one of the Aspirants, threw herself at his feet, but Jacob helped her up and hugged her instead. People on the other side of the street stared at us through their windows, not entirely sure what all the fuss was about or who this man was exactly, but they hadn't seen anything yet . . .

Ravn took a break and reached for his coffee cup. In the background, the news came on the radio. He was only half-listening as he watched two women paddle past in a kayak. They were both in exceptionally good physical shape, he noted, and wondered whether it was time he pulled himself together and did something about his own dismal lack of form. As the radio news wrapped up, the host announced that the funeral of Officer René Mørck, who was killed in action during a police raid of a club in the city, would be held at Holmen's Church at 2 p.m., and a large crowd of politicians and members of the community who wished to pay their last respects were therefore expected in the area. The weather report followed—more sun, even more heat, and a prohibition on swimming in the Øresund due to an unusual increase in algae in the water.

Holmen's Church lay just on the other side of Knippelsbro Bridge, less than fifteen minutes' walk from *Bianca*'s berth on the canal, and Ravn considered whether he should go to René Mørck's funeral. He knew nothing about the officer, apart from how Mikkel had described him: the new man, who had made a single dumb mistake with Kaminsky and paid for it with his life. *A hard fate to bear*, Ravn thought. He wondered whether some people are simply tainted with "black luck," as if their fate were sealed. *Like Eva's, perhaps, the moment she stepped into their flat? She was in the wrong place at the wrong time. Perhaps the earth needed a quantum of evil in order to keep turning? A vent for the madness in the world. God venting his hangover?*

Ravn stood up, gathered the printouts, and returned to the relative shade of his cabin. He put the papers down on the kitchen counter. Benjamin's report about the resurrection of Jacob Mesmer would have to wait. He needed to check on someone else.

25

The turnout on the square in front of Holmen's Church was even larger than Ravn had expected. At the fringe of the crowd, with Møffe by his side, he watched the police officers in gala dress flow through the doors, as if a continuous dark-blue wave. The State funeral service for René Mørck appeared to have brought the force together—old rivalries between the departments set aside, at least for today. Once the uniformed police had entered the church, the plainclothes filed through the doors, including curious members of the community and ex-cops paying their last respects. Ravn had no intention of attending the service. Truth be told, it reminded him painfully of Eva's funeral—as he knew it would— so he remained standing at a distance amongst the posse of press, photographers, and the occasional flock of tourists that pushed past on the sidewalk.

Before Ravn knew it, the church bells had begun to toll, and the heavy doors opened once more. The swarm of photographers surrounded the hearse that had pulled up to the entrance in the interim, and the moment the pallbearers emerged with the white coffin on their shoulders, they started to click their cameras furiously. And once again, Ravn was transported back in time to Eva's funeral . . .

The uniformed officers had filled the square in front of the church. Ravn spotted Mikkel standing in a group with Melby, Chief Inspector Brask, and a few other colleagues he knew from Station City. The moment Mikkel caught sight of Ravn, he excused himself from the group and came over. Brask and Melby looked up, but neither bothered to make a gesture of greeting in Ravn's direction.

"How you doing?" Ravn asked, nodding at the white sling Mikkel had over his shoulder.

"Great . . . good, I guess."

"Are you back at work?"

"Basically: at my desk, typing with one finger," Mikkel replied drily, demonstrating the restricted movement of his sling arm.

"So, nothing's changed, then," Ravn quipped.

Mikkel smiled. The hearse passed them and drove out the gates and onto the road. They both looked up and followed its motion with their eyes.

"It was a beautiful ceremony," said Mikkel. "Even Brask said something sensible."

"Definitely," Ravn said.

Mikkel's gaze met his. "You weren't inside, were you?"

Ravn looked out over the square at the large church door. "I was there in spirit," he said. "It's good to see you back on your feet."

"Thank you. So . . . why did you come?"

"To make sure you're okay. I thought you'd be here."

"Well . . . I'm no longer working on the Kaminsky case if that's what you want to ask me," Mikkel said with an awkward smile.

"No contact with him at all?"

"Ravn, you know how it is," said Mikkel. "Kaminsky is locked in a maximum-security prison cell at police headquarters, and only a select few on the force have been given access to him. I'm not on the list."

"But surely Station City will be allowed to question him at some point?"

"I doubt it. Once the Homicide Unit, the Mobile Crime Squad, and the guys from Intelligence are done interrogating him, a long list of other European police authorities, including the German police and the Swedish Security Service, will be badgering us to hand him over . . ."

"What about Brask? Surely he can get a piece of the pie for our team?"

"Keep your voice down a bit," Mikkel said, casting a glance over his shoulder.

"But we can't just let Kaminsky get away, Mikkel!"

"*We?* The last time I checked, you were no longer working for Station City, Ravn."

"You know what I mean, Mikkel."

"The bottom line is that Kaminsky is behind bars—for good. I'll bet they've already prepped Palle Sørensen's old cell for him."

"We had a deal, Mikkel. You promised to find out if Kaminsky had information on Eva's murderer."

"What do you want me to do, Ravn?" Mikkel said in a harsh whisper. "This case is over my head. There's nothing more I can do." His gaze dropped to his feet. "To be honest, I need to put the Kaminsky case behind me, Ravn. Dorthe is beside herself with worry. She wants me to quit, for heaven's sake."

"And? Are you going to?"

Mikkel met his gaze again. "No. But I want to move on. I don't want to dwell on the fact that it could have been me in that coffin today. Surely you can understand that, Ravn?"

Ravn nodded. "Of course I can," he said. "Take care of yourself, Mikkel," he added tonelessly, and tugged on Møffe's leash.

"Ravn, wait," said Mikkel, resting a hand on Ravn's forearm. "There is one thing: We've obtained some information on the location of Kaminsky's contraband."

"What kind of contraband?"

"Mostly drugs and money. Occasionally, weapons. But recently we discovered three containers filled with stolen goods that have been sent to HQ for registration."

"And?"

"And . . . I know it's unlikely, but perhaps some of Eva's stolen effects will turn up in one of the containers."

"And in that case, it would indicate that Kaminsky knew about the burglary . . ."

"Exactly," Mikkel said. "But whether we ever get a chance to talk to Kaminsky is another story altogether . . ."

It was a long shot, Ravn thought. *Why would Kaminsky still be in possession of stolen goods more than three years after the burglary? But it was still better than nothing. Better than yet another funeral service.* Ravn nodded thoughtfully to himself. "When will you know?" he said to Mikkel.

"I'll call you in the next couple of days. I promise," Mikkel said.

26

Ravn had lit an oil lamp and hung it up on the beam above *Bianca*'s rear deck. The warm light was bright enough to read the rest of the report under the stars, and the fumes emitted by burning oil kept the mosquitoes at bay.

According to Benjamin's report, Jacob Mesmer had moved into the premises on Belgiensgade. Here, a few of the Elders, two instructors, and a small group of Aspirants lived together in some sort of communal residence. In the cellar, the instructors had private rooms, and the Aspirants had bunkbeds in a large sleeping room at the back. On the first floor, the Master had his own quarters, including a bedroom, a bathroom, and a study. It was here he read the Scriptures, prepared his sermons, and did research for his next book—the third in a series of theological texts. When the Master withdrew to his quarters after mealtimes, he required everyone to be quiet in the house. Naturally, the other members of the community were still expected to meet their obligations, but these had to be performed in absolute silence.

Benjamin described Jacob as *energetic* and *forever smiling* in his dealings with everyone in the congregation, but observed that beneath it all, the Master seemed exhausted, as if he had taken the forced closure of the centres in Jutland and Fyn personally, and the constant pressure and scrutiny of the media had taken its toll. However, his exhaustion seemed to disappear when he delivered his sermons at the Bible meetings in the evenings. And his mere presence attracted members from far and wide, who came to hear him preach and pray for them. According to Benjamin, there was nothing the Master could not fix or heal, no demon he could not drive away. In just one evening, the Master had managed to fix a member's iPhone, straightened a woman's left leg that was three centimetres shorter than the right, and expelled a demon from a young man who was incapacitated from the waist down.

As a rule, Benjamin reported events objectively, so it was hard for Ravn to judge whether he also believed in Jacob Mesmer's powers. Sometimes, Benjamin's tone was unabashedly positive with respect to Jacob, and he clearly resented the bad publicity of the press, which he believed was unjustified and consistently distorted the truth. But Benjamin also pointed out that the Bible meetings had an economic purpose in addition to praising the Lord. On several occasions, he had overheard Jacob yelling at the Elders when the meetings had not yielded sufficient donations, in the Master's opinion. *"It wears on my soul!"* he shouted one night. *"I'm trying to get the Word of God to as many people as possible! All you lot have to do is reach out and collect the donations–and yet you fail me! Is your faith so weak? Do you no longer believe in me? In the teachings of the gospel?"* Jacob went on in a rage.

Ravn was interrupted by the sound of someone boarding *Bianca* at the bow. He half-turned in his chair and saw Eduardo making his way over to the rear deck.

"I have some news," Eduardo said, out of breath.

"Okay. Would you like to sit down?" Ravn said, pulling up the second chair for his friend, and Eduardo plopped into it gratefully. "Glass of wine?" Ravn said, leaning forward to extract a glass and the bottle from his minibar.

"Since when do you drink wine?" Eduardo said.

"Since I ran out of beer."

Eduardo took the bottle and read the label. "Good heavens, a Reserva?"

"What did you want to tell me?"

"Momentito." Eduardo poured himself a glass and tasted the wine. "ARRGH . . . this wine is corked, Ravn," he said, pulling a face. "How long have you had this bottle?"

"No idea. I can't remember buying it, in fact. Perhaps it came with the boat?" Ravn shrugged and finished his glass. "Isn't this how red wine is supposed to taste?"

Eduardo shook his head in resignation. "One day I'm going to teach you how to appreciate a decent bottle of wine, *amigo.*"

"Are you going to tell me why you came over or what?"

"Yes. Today, as I was working on an article about the sale of State property, I came across the news of an imminent merger of two corporate giants."

"What a crazy day you must have had," Ravn said lazily.

Eduardo ignored the jibe. "Wait till you hear what companies are planning to merge: none other than Mesmer Resources and SIALA Industries."

"Okay, and?"

"And, when that happens, the combined corporation will be bigger than McKinsey. They'll be able to dominate—no, create—a de facto monopoly in the implementation of management strategies in the public sector."

Ravn sipped his wine. Now that Eduardo had mentioned it, he noticed that the wine wasn't great. He put the glass down on the deck, wishing Eduardo had kept his mouth shut. "How's that for a coup?"

"Amazing," Ravn said.

"You couldn't care less, could you?"

"Honestly, no, not in the least. I don't work for Mesmer Resources; I work for Ferdinand Mesmer in his *personal* capacity. He's looking for his son. That's all."

"Do you even know what Mesmer Resources does?"

"Of course I do. Courses . . . leadership seminars and stuff . . . for big business, which, according to you, is getting even bigger, apparently . . ."

Eduardo leaned forward in his chair. "I've dug a little deeper into what they offer their clients," he said seriously.

"Okay. Find anything interesting?"

"The foundation of their classification into personality 'types'— Mesmer's entire management philosophy—stems from a patented system that he calls the 'Mesmogramme.'"

"The Mesmogramme," Ravn snorted. "Not exactly a quantum leap for his marketing department to come up with that one . . ."

"Well, no . . . but guess who actually developed the system?"

"I don't know. Ferdinand Mesmer?"

"Guess again." Eduardo smiled.

Ravn stared at Eduardo for a moment. "It wasn't his son, was it?"

"*Correcto.* Jacob Mesmer."

"Are you saying that Jacob worked for the company before he found God?"

"I'm saying *more* than that. It appears that Jacob Mesmer has joint ownership of the patent to the system at the core of his father's business, which is about to go from being a million-kroner firm to a billion-kroner conglomerate . . ."

"Wow, I didn't see that one coming," Ravn said, scratching his beard. "So it appears that Ferdinand Mesmer has a bigger stake in finding his son than we first imagined . . ."

"Perhaps you ought to back out of this assignment while you still can, Ravn."

"And why would I do that?"

"Because you don't want to get caught between these sharks. It could be dangerous."

Ravn laughed out loud. "Is that the friendly socialist warning me about the ruthlessness of the big bad capitalist pigs?"

"I mean it, Ravn," Eduardo said, dead serious. "This is not just about money; it's about power, *comprende*? There's a lot at stake for these people."

"Eduardo, I'm not afraid of Ferdinand Mesmer and his corporate cronies."

"Well, perhaps you should be. Case in point: What, exactly, happened to that detective who wrote the report?"

"What do you mean?"

"Where is he?"

"I have no idea. I haven't been able to track him down. But I'm sure he's fine, wherever he is."

"Let's hope so. For his sake. But why all the secrecy surrounding this investigation?"

"It's the nature of the management psychology business, isn't it?"

"*Is* it? If Ferdinand Mesmer was merely interested in handling this case quietly and discreetly, he could have put his lawyers on the case. And I'm not talking about Lohman. I mean the big-time lawyers who can come up with an airtight agreement . . . So why did Mesmer ask *you* to investigate instead?"

"I have no idea."

"No, you don't. That's my point. And what do you think is going to happen once you've delivered an address for Jacob Mesmer?"

"For heaven's sake, Eduardo, you're making me paranoid. Right now, the only problem I have is that the man's son seems to have disappeared without a trace," Ravn said, trying to smile, even though he had to admit that Eduardo had a point: Ferdinand Mesmer's motives were ambiguous, at best. "Okay, I'll talk to him before I continue with the case."

"If I were you, I'd drop it, Ravn. Right now. Just tell them you can't find the son and keep the money."

"That's not the way I work, Eduardo."

"It's your call, of course. But whatever you do, be careful, *amigo*." Eduardo stood up and yawned. "I'll see you in the morning."

"Thanks for coming over, Eduardo," Ravn called after him as Eduardo hopped back onto his own boat.

Ravn stared out over the canal, mulling over Eduardo's warning. His thoughts strayed to the fire at the building on Belgiensgade, and the severe scars on Ferdinand Mesmer's hand. He had no idea what the one thing had to do with the other, but the detail was disturbing. He thought about Katrine's comment when he asked her why her boss had not simply handed the case over to her: "*You* are the private detective," she said.

If Katrine was right about that, what was *her* role, exactly? Was *she* the one who would be ordered to finish off the job when Jacob resurfaced?

27

Ferdinand Mesmer's secretary opened the door for Ravn and stepped back in her high heels to let him pass into the office. Mesmer was seated behind his desk, reading through some papers. Without looking up, he made a listless hand gesture for Ravn to take a seat in front of the desk. Katrine was sitting on the sofa with a cup of coffee in her hand and a kitten-sweet smile on her lips. "How's the knee?" she said with mock innocence.

Ravn did not return her smile. He walked past her and remained standing in front of the desk. Mesmer looked up and pointed to the seat again. "Sit down," he said unequivocally.

Ravn relented and took a seat.

"Do you have Jacob's address for me?" Mesmer asked impatiently.

Ravn shook his head slowly.

"I see. Do you have any idea where he could be?" said Mesmer.

"Not that either."

"Have you at least read the report?"

Ravn shook his head again. "Not to the end."

"So why are we having this meeting?"

"Because you owe me an explanation."

"*Owe* you an explanation?" Mesmer sat back in his chair and frowned. "An explanation for what?"

"The real reason you are looking for your son."

"I've already explained that to you."

"No, you fed me a pack of lies about wanting to reconcile with your son."

Mesmer blinked his eyes rapidly, taken aback. "Excuse me?"

"This is not the time to play the concerned father, Mesmer; this is where you tell me about the upcoming merger between Mesmer Resources and SIALA Industries."

There was a pause as Mesmer gave Ravn a hard stare. "What about it?" he said. "We have received an interesting offer from a former competitor. We are currently negotiating a deal. You can read all about the details in *Børsen*, which published an article on the deal last week. I honestly don't know why you are so angry, or why you believe I've lied to you . . ."

"It's what you *didn't* say that concerns me. Why didn't you tell me that Jacob used to work for Mesmer Resources at our first meeting?"

"I didn't think it was relevant. I still don't."

"If you want me to continue my investigation, you're going to tell me what Jacob was working on and, not least, why you need to get hold of him now."

Ferdinand Mesmer looked at him as if he were a naughty child. "All right, what do you want to know?"

"For starters: Was Jacob the one who developed the Mesmogramme?"

A muscle contracted at the corner of Mesmer's right eye. He bowed his head and stared at the papers in front of him vacantly. "It's not that simple. Contrary to what you obviously believe, I *am* concerned about my son. But there are indeed several aspects to this case."

"So tell me the truth."

Mesmer shook his head slowly. "The truth . . . the truth is that I took Jacob into the firm . . . after he dropped out of his psychology studies. Back then, the firm consisted only of myself and a handful of consultants. We did the same kind of work we are doing now, albeit on a smaller scale, and our business was based on other firms' systems—"

"Fast-forward to where Jacob started working for you. Did you present seminars together?"

"No, not at all. Jacob was in no condition to do something like that . . . My son was suffering from a severe depression . . . He was taking a great deal of medication. His mental condition was the reason he dropped out of university."

"Okay. So what did he do for the firm?"

"In the first instance, he was appointed as my personal assistant. He took care of the practical arrangements for the seminars . . . he made copies of study materials, checked that the equipment was working properly, brought in the chairs, that kind of thing."

"I was told that Jacob did a little more than that for Mesmer Resources . . ."

"Well, yes, eventually . . . he got better, and his health improved. He started taking an active interest in the business. After about a year, he started studying the various methods that we used. At first, he assisted the consultants, then he started teaching himself, and after a few years, he became one of our best consultants."

"What about the system you were developing? The Mesmogramme?"

"The Mesmogramme was Jacob's idea. None of us saw it coming—no one knew what he'd been developing after hours. It was little more than a diagram that he presented at first, but even at this primitive stage, we could see that he was on to something exceptional. He had simplified the thought processes we were using and created a more sophisticated profiling system. Jacob laid the foundation for an advanced typology that could create better results in *half* the time. Not only that, but his design also had an unlimited potential for further development. In addition to leadership and management strategies, his system could be implemented in the fields of psychology, and all levels of tuition in the education sector."

"So, in effect, you owe all this to Jacob?" Ravn said, looking around the room.

"That would be an overstatement. Jacob's idea was revolutionary, but it was just an *idea*. It took us seven years to *develop* it in consultation with the brightest business psychologists, human resources consultants, and leading experts in the field who had formerly worked for the likes of McKinsey and Microsoft. We conducted intensive test-training groups and invested almost thirty million kroner to develop the patented design. And we are still continuously investing large sums of money to maintain the system to this day. Due to the hard work and dedication of our staff, the Mesmogramme has become a highly renowned brand. It's an ongoing battle to maintain our success and the merger will help us to reach our goals."

"So why did Jacob leave?"

Mesmer shrugged. "Jacob has a habit of withdrawing into himself—or distancing himself physically from his family."

"Something must have triggered him."

"As I said, it was no mean task to put his idea into operation. And Jacob was working around the clock to make it happen. I don't know . . . perhaps he buckled under the pressure? In any event, he became increasingly difficult to work with. He fired competent members of our staff if they contradicted him; he treated our partners with disrespect, not to mention our investors. I think in the end, he simply gave up."

"In what way?"

"He stopped coming to work, simply bailed on us—and we had our hands full repairing the damage, smoothing things over with our investors and saving the project from disaster. Relations between Jacob and I had been strained for a long time. We argued constantly, and he decided to leave the firm. He wanted no part of the Mesmogramme project." Mesmer sighed heavily before he continued. "He turned his back on his family. We didn't see or hear from him for many years. Then he resurfaced in the guise of the evangelist priest," Mesmer said in disgust.

"Had Jacob always been religious?"

"No. On the contrary, he had always been extremely pragmatic and concrete. He believed all religion was banal or superstitious."

"So what made him change his mind?"

"Bad company, perhaps?" Mesmer said. "Your guess is as good as mine."

"Okay. So, apart from your fatherly concern, why do you need to find Jacob?"

The look on Mesmer's face revealed that he didn't appreciate Ravn's tone, but he replied calmly. "Jacob disappeared without warning, from one day to the next, and he might have cut all personal ties with his family, but the legal ones remained intact . . ."

"And you need his signature in order to close the merger deal?"

"I need Jacob to officially surrender his rights of ownership in Mesmer Resources—with due compensation, of course, as long as he steps down. Which is why I would like you to give him this contract for his signature, when you find him." With his fire-scarred hand, Mesmer pushed the manila envelope across the desk to Ravn.

Ravn looked at the envelope but made no move to pick it up. It had been lying on Mesmer's desk all this time, as if he had known the outcome of the meeting before it had started. "I said I would find your son because I thought it meant something to you personally, not because Jacob was good for your business."

"It *does* mean something to me. More than you will ever know. I apologise if you feel as if I have misled you. It was never my intention to do so. I want to find Jacob and reconcile with him, but I *also* have a responsibility towards my family. As well as everyone who works for me—everyone who will reap the future benefits of the system we have created." Mesmer leaned forward. "And I would be happy to raise your fee to compensate for the misunderstanding."

"That's not how I work."

"As you wish." Mesmer smiled at Ravn. "Then I will assume that you are back on the job."

28

After the meeting, Ravn walked home along Strandgade with the manila envelope tucked under his arm, mulling over the meeting. There were plenty of private detectives who would give their right arm for such a lucrative assignment—professional investigators with a lot more experience and much less attitude than he had. And yet, despite his deliberate provocations, Mesmer still wanted him on the job. *Why?* Ravn suspected that there was a great deal that Mesmer was not telling him about the break with his son. *Family skeletons in the Mesmers' closet that were yet to tumble out?*

The envelope was thick, so the contract must be long and detailed. He had to admit that Mesmer knew how to play people. When he'd set out that morning, he'd thought the assignment consisted of finding an address, but now it had morphed into something a lot more complicated. And apparently, he'd been promoted: Now he'd been entrusted with the delivery of an important package. And he needed more information to do this.

Ravn fished his phone out of his pocket and called Victoria's number.

"Hi, Ravn," she said, sounding out of breath on the other end of the line.

"What are you doing?"

"Unpacking books and placing them on the shelves. They arrived this morning, six boxes that I acquired from a deceased's estate."

"Right. When you have time, could you check if you have something for me in the business section?"

"Sorry, I don't have any more copies of *What Can I Be When I Grow Up?*"

"Very funny. Can you find out if you have anything on management strategy according to the Mesmogramme system?"

"Mesmogramme? Do you mean like 'Mesmer,' the guy you're working for?"

"Exactly."

"I thought you were just looking for Mesmer's son."

"Right you are again."

"Isn't it strange to investigate your employer?"

"Not in this case. Do you think you can find something for me?"

"If I can, it's going to cost you a bag of cinnamon rolls."

Ravn thanked Victoria and ended the call. He could have asked Mesmer for the information on the Mesmogramme or bought one of the many books that were displayed in the company's reception area, but he preferred to do this part of his investigation without the knowledge of his employer.

When he returned to *Bianca*, he settled down on the rear deck to read the last part of Benjamin's report: The introductory course was almost over. Most of Benjamin's classmates had taken the exam and all of them had passed—only one of them had decided not to continue and pay the requisite 15,000 kroner to be enrolled in the next level. For his own part, Benjamin noted that he wished to remain with God's Chosen after he had taken the exam. Because Mesmer had paid for the course, he felt obliged to continue with the logbook, even though it made him feel *lousy*. Ravn wondered whether this was why Benjamin again pointed out that the criticism of the press was unjustified and unreasonable. He emphasised that the church's intentions were charitable and their wish to support the needy in society was commendable. He also deeply regretted his initial harsh judgement of Jacob Mesmer. He was ashamed that he had unjustifiably accused Jacob of having an economic motive for the Bible meetings. Benjamin realised that he had been wrong about the Master, who was entirely dedicated to his work, and he vowed to do everything in his power to correct the wrongs that he and others had committed against Jacob Mesmer. Now that the Bible meetings were a success and the congregation on Belgiensgade was growing, they were determined to maintain their progress.

It was also apparent from this part of the report that Lisa had moved in with the new recruits in the cellar on Belgiensgade. Benjamin wrote that he had helped her move. And he made a nametag specially for her locker by burning her name into a little wooden sign with a flower etched above it: *Lisa Brask*. Ravn wrote down her name in his notebook. If all else failed, he could track her down and question her about the church.

Towards the end of the report, Benjamin confessed he would have liked to live with the others in Belgiensgade. He was reluctant to go back to his own flat in the evenings. He added, on an equally emotional note, that the three months he had spent with God's Chosen had been a gift from Heaven, and he thanked Ferdinand Mesmer for indirectly granting him this opportunity, even though he found it difficult to keep writing the logbook now that he knew the truth. *I think you can be proud of your son, sir,* Benjamin wrote simply at the bottom of the page.

Ravn smiled. It seemed as if Mesmer's private detective had not only changed sides but found love as well, which paved the way for a happy ending to the investigation. He was about to get up and fetch the final pages of the report in his cabin when his mobile phone rang.

"You are welcome to pop in with cinnamon rolls, Ravn," Victoria said on the other end of the line.

"Have you found something on the Mesmogramme?"

"I found more than that."

"Oh yeah, what's that, then?"

"Cinnamon rolls, Ravn—and I mean the *good* ones from Lagkagehuset!"

The smell of freshly ground coffee filled Ravn's nostrils when he entered Victoria's bookshop. He found her behind her shopkeeper's counter, sorting through a large cardboard box of books. The weather hardly invited customers indoors, and apart from an elderly man skimming the Young Adult Fiction shelf in the rear, the bookshop was empty.

"Do you have any Salinger books?" the man asked.

"I don't think so. Folks have started hoarding the classics."

"The bloody youth of today," the man muttered, returning to his search.

Victoria nodded at the man and turned to Ravn and his brown paper bag from the bakery. She waved him closer, and Ravn put the bag on the counter. Victoria's eyes lit up. She brushed off her hands on the trousers of her tweed suit and reached for the coffee cups on the shelf behind her.

"So, where are the books you found for me?" Ravn said without preamble.

Victoria poured coffee from the French press into two mugs. "Are you blind? The books are right in front of you," she said, nodding at the pile on the corner of her desk.

Ravn picked up the top book on the pile and read the title out loud. "'*The Mesmogramme: Success Breeds Success*.'" He put the book down and skimmed through the others. *Mesmogramme for Personal Development*; *Mesmogramme for the Leaders of the Future*; *The Mesmogramme: Your Successful Business Partner*.

"Only the first book cites Jacob Mesmer as the author. Why is that?" Ravn asked.

"That's not unusual," said Victoria. "The authors of the other books are probably people who have studied the Mesmogramme and certified themselves as experts on the topic. In exchange for granting a large percentage of their royalties to Mesmer, they apply the philosophy to a different field. I see this happening all the time, whether it's management strategies or the latest diet that is sold using the name of a successful brand," Victoria said. She ripped open the bag and took out one of the cinnamon rolls.

"Have you read any of these books?" asked Ravn.

"I have better things to do with my time," Victoria said with her mouth full. "If you've read one of these management books, you've read them all."

A shout of joy came from the elderly man at the back of the shop. He stuck his head round the side of the Young Adult Fiction shelf, triumphantly waving a tattered edition of *Nine Stories* in the air. "Look what I found hiding on the shelf," he said. "Good ol' JD."

"Congratulations on the find," Victoria said with a smile.

The man nodded and returned to his search.

Ravn sipped his coffee. "Thank you for taking the time to find these for me, Victoria," he said. "I think I'll take the one that Jacob Mesmer wrote."

"That's not the only one I found written by him," Victoria said with a sneaky smile.

"What do you mean?"

"It's a different genre but the same author," Victoria said. She bent down to retrieve the book she had kept under the counter and put it on the desk in front of Ravn.

Ravn looked at the slim volume with an interesting black ink drawing of a burning tree on a grey cover: *Textbook on Modern Exorcism* by Pastor Jacob Mesmer.

"How much do you actually know about Jacob Mesmer and that sect of his?" Victoria asked.

Ravn stared at the tree on the cover, speechless.

29

Victoria had her full attention on the cinnamon rolls, and Ravn picked up Jacob Mesmer's book on exorcism. There was a portrait of the author on the front flap. He was wearing an unbuttoned white shirt and looked like a younger version of his father without a beard, his gaze deep and trained directly at the beholder. Jacob Mesmer wrote in his foreword that he hoped his book could make a positive contribution to the fight against Satan, and he pointed out that, historically, there had always been a fight between good and evil, and that every religion—whether it was Islam, Judaism, Hinduism, or Christianity—had its own methods to expel evil. Furthermore, the author claimed that even modern science acknowledged demonic possession of the soul, although it was simply classified as something else, such as "mania," "hysteria," or "depression" in the field of psychiatry, for instance. However, he pointed out that only the Christian faith had the power to expel demons effectively, and therefore it was important to study the doctrine of exorcism. Finally, the author warned that an unskilled approach could exacerbate the possessed's condition and even transfer the demon to the person who attempted to perform the exorcism. He concluded his foreword with a Bible citation:

Then Jesus asked him, "What is your name?"
"My name is Legion," he replied, "for we are many."
The Gospel of Mark, 5:9

Ravn turned the page and skimmed the contents. Divided into chapters, the book contained a historical overview with case studies; a list and classification of demons and their nature; several chapters on how one became possessed; a selection of prayers and chants to expel demons; a list of useful relics and amulets; and finally, a detailed methodology of the various phases of exorcism that could range from a single session to a "battle that could take years," as Pastor Mesmer put it.

Ravn shook his head in disbelief as he read.

"So, any wiser for it?" Victoria asked, putting the last chunk of cinnamon roll in her mouth.

"Not really. But I have to admit that Jacob Mesmer is full of surprises. The practise of exorcism is quite a leap from business psychology," Ravn said. He referred to one of the final chapters. "It says here that you can pray with a person to find out if their soul is impure, and then perform an initial expulsion to determine the nature of the demon, and the degree of possession."

Ravn looked at Victoria. "Benjamin wrote in his logbook that they always ended their Bible evenings with prayer, but he made no mention of exorcism rituals."

"Perhaps Benjamin didn't know the full extent and nature of their activities," Victoria said, looking at him with a grave expression on her face. "And it doesn't sound healthy or harmless. I think the sooner you find Jacob Mesmer, the better, Ravn. Before someone gets hurt."

Ravn deliberately chose not to tell Victoria about the contract he had promised to deliver to Jacob. "What do I owe you for the books?" he said instead, sliding the book on exorcism into the front pocket of his hoodie.

"The cinnamon rolls cover it," Victoria said.

Ravn nodded in thanks and made for the door.

"Don't you want to take these books on management with you as well?"

"To hell with them," Ravn said. "Or . . . you know what I mean. See you soon, Victoria."

Back on *Bianca*, Ravn concentrated on reading the last part of Benjamin's report—or rather, the last part of his objective reporting, before he started to digress into long Bible citations and ecstatic praise of God's Chosen. A growing sense of unease and concern crept up on Ravn as he read, and he wondered what could have caused the radical change in Benjamin.

THIS IS MY FINAL REPORT

I passed my examination today. Lisa and the others have given me their well wishes and blessings for the future. Even the Master came by the classroom to congratulate me, called me an "Evangelist of the People" . . . he made a speech, praised my progress, and said he had great expectations for my future. I am proud and humbled all at once, and I feel wretched about betraying everyone here, and therefore this is my LAST report to you, Mr. Mesmer.

Ravn read on about the dinner that was held in his honour. Everyone had asked Benjamin whether he intended to enrol in the next course. According to Benjamin, the others applied kind yet firm pressure on him to advance to the next level, but he merely replied that he had not yet decided what he wanted to do. After the dinner, everyone settled down in front of the open fireplace in the living room, and they prayed and sang hymns together. At one point, Lisa had reached out spontaneously and squeezed his hand. She whispered in his ear that she was proud of him for passing his exam, and even received such high praise from the Master himself. When the others began to withdraw to their rooms, Lisa asked him to stay behind for a moment, and they sat by the fire and talked, deep into the night. At first, they spoke about the evening hymns, many of which Lisa had composed. Later, they spoke about God's Chosen, and how grateful they both were that Jacob had come into their lives. Lisa also spoke about the other members of the church. She said that she felt as if she had found a new family with God's Chosen. Then she confided some of the terrible things that had happened in her childhood. Benjamin noted in parentheses that he would not betray her confidence in his report, but sufficed to say that the things Lisa had experienced were *absolutely awful.* Lisa had thanked him again for his support the time they were harassed in Christianshavn, and they laughed about the experiences they'd shared on missions in the neighbourhoods of Copenhagen.

She confessed that she had never experienced so much support from another man in her life, and therefore she hoped that he would consider advancing to the next level, so they would not be forced to part company. Benjamin told her that he was considering moving into the church as well, and asked if she thought this was a good idea. In reply, she gave him a big hug, and he noticed that there were tears in her eyes. Lisa said that Jacob would have to give his permission, and that it probably depended on whether he intended to continue with the second part of his course. Benjamin jokingly replied that he would take the second, third, or umpteenth course if he had to! Lisa laughed out loud and said it was wonderful to meet someone she could rely on. Her words stung, and Benjamin wrote that this was the moment he realised he had to tell Lisa the truth. He was terrified of how she would react, but took comfort in the fact that, from the beginning, the Elders had emphasised that their lives before turning to God were irrelevant. All that mattered was that you dedicated your life to God and God's Chosen in the future.

Ravn took a break and looked out over the canal. He was taken aback by Benjamin's intimate report to his employer, as if he were following a twelve-step plan like Alcoholics Anonymous, determined to acknowledge his actions to everyone. Ravn doubted Ferdinand Mesmer would appreciate the gesture, to put it mildly. Especially after he read the next page:

Today I confided in Lisa. I told her about my past life as a private detective and confessed that I joined the church on assignment from a client. Naturally, I did not reveal the identity of my client—and I have no intention of doing so, sir. I hope you can understand, Mr. Mesmer, that I need to tell Lisa the truth, so that I can begin this new, glorious epoch of my life with a clean slate. I have faithfully reported the activities of God's Chosen and your son, and acquitted my assignment as agreed. As such, I believe that any further investigation would be pointless, and I kindly request that you donate the balance of my fee to God's Chosen. I will send you my invoice shortly.

Ravn wondered why Mesmer had not told him that Benjamin had changed sides—that he was "converted" by the church—and that *this* was the real reason the first investigation into God's Chosen was abandoned.

Katrine had merely said that her boss was "dissatisfied" with the quality of Benjamin's work, and that this was why Mesmer had decided to hire Ravn to investigate instead. Perhaps Mesmer had taken Benjamin's conversion as a personal insult, even if the detective had completed his report faithfully? Ravn was intrigued and eagerly turned to the next page to see what happened, but nothing could have prepared him for what he found there. Cold shivers crept down his spine.

30

"I DON'T KNOW WHAT TO DO OTHER THAN WRITE TO YOU AGAIN, MR. MESMER, AND APPEAL FOR YOUR HELP. NOTHING HAS GONE AS PLANNED. I AM WAITING FOR JACOB, DAMN JACOB . . ."

Ravn skimmed the email, hoping the date would appear at the top of the printout, but the header, address, and other identifying details had been removed. Then he began to read Benjamin's desperate appeal to Ferdinand Mesmer:

I'm terrified. Literally shaking with fear. Everything is in chaos. I don't know what is happening. The Elders panicked. The séance got out of control. The exorcism was . . . I don't know what to call it other than . . . HORRIBLE. Jacob. I am waiting for Jacob to come and fetch me. I'm in the sleeping quarters in the cellar. But I should probably start at the beginning, to help you understand . . . Lisa . . . I trusted her . . . After our talk by the fireplace, I gathered my courage and told her I had a big secret to confess. She was supportive and listened. I thought she understood, and I made her promise not to tell anyone. Just like I would never tell anyone what she confided in me. I thought our secrets would remain between us and God alone: "Your secrets are safe with me." That's what she said! So I told her everything about my background and my profession as a private detective.

At first, she seemed pleasantly surprised. She said it was refreshing to meet someone like me. But then I told her about my investigation. That I had been reporting to someone else about the church's activities. She fell silent. Then asked who had hired me. But of course I revealed nothing about you. Lisa asked whether I had reported on her as well. I said that I had only shared details that she could be proud of–her singing, her dedication to help the needy, her tireless work for the church and the community. I assured her once again that I would never betray her confidence, and I hoped that she felt the same way. She said that she did. And then we prayed together. For me. For all the wrongs I had done. I thought that everything was going to be okay, and when we parted, I felt as if our bond was stronger than ever. That we were equals before God.

BUT I WAS WRONG. I WAS TERRIBLY MISTAKEN.

In the afternoon, when I was weeding the herb garden behind the house, I was called inside by one of the Elders. I thought they wanted to confirm my application for the advanced course (I had already paid for it), but the moment I came into the hall, I knew something was wrong. All the Elders were waiting for me: Åse, Reikendorf, Birgitte, Samuel, Karl-Emil, and Jacob, of course. Lisa was sitting next to him, staring at her feet. She didn't look up once. I knew immediately that she had told them. They asked me to take a seat on the chair that had been placed in the middle of the room, facing them. When I sat down, Jacob stood up and addressed me on behalf of the Elders. He said that Lisa had come to him and reported what I had done. He asked what I had to say in my defence.

I repeated everything I had said to Lisa. It was a relief to confess the truth, even if Åse was crossing herself the entire time I was talking. Jacob quietly asked who had commissioned the investigation. He wasn't even angry. So I told him it was you, his father, who had requested the report. Jacob asked me to bring it to him. I did as he asked, and showed him my tablet, which contained all my notes, emails, and daily logbook to you. I realise that this was a breach of our agreement, Mr. Mesmer. But you must understand that I had betrayed Jacob and God's Chosen before I betrayed you, and I believe it was all I could do, sir. I sincerely hope you can understand my predicament.

Jacob started to read. And he didn't stop until he had read every single note and comment I had written. It got dark outside, while the rest of us sat in silence, waiting. Just like Lisa, I stared at the ground most of the time. Occasionally, I caught the gaze of one of the other Elders. Their eyes were filled with judgement, disapproval, and reproach.

At last, Jacob stopped reading. He thanked me, and even smiled when he returned my tablet. Then he addressed everyone in the room. He said that a demon had invaded our church. The ugliest demon in existence. Everyone agreed, even Lisa nodded. He turned to the Elders and asked for their counsel. Even though they were in agreement, everyone seemed to talk at once. Their answer was to pray for my forlorn soul. Then I would be excommunicated. Åse added that my tablet ought to be confiscated and destroyed.

Jacob thanked the Elders for their insightful answers but announced that he disagreed. Pointing at me, he said that when I came to God's Chosen, I was full of demons; I was consumed with sin. My profession alone was a sin. My work for Ferdinand Mesmer was in league with the Devil, he said. But during my time with the church, I had shown genuine and heartfelt repentance. And this was proof that even the worst kind of sinner can be saved. Instead of judging me, they ought to fall on their knees and thank God for the wonder he has performed on me; they ought to repent for their pride.

Åse was the first one to drop to her knees. She bowed her head in shame. The others followed and prayed to God for forgiveness. Jacob blessed them, resting his hand on their heads in turn. Then he gave me a bear hug and said he could only imagine how arduous my journey to God must have been. He said I had shown great courage. The same courage of the Israelites who had followed Moses across the Sinai desert. But then he turned to the others and said that we were not out of danger. That an ugly demon was still amongst us, the demon that had shown itself in Lisa's gossip-mongering and betrayal of her mentee's confidence.

The Elders nodded as one, but Lisa looked at Jacob in horror. She tried to explain herself. Implored Jacob to understand that it was never her intention to gossip; she merely wished to express her loyalty to the church and felt obliged to inform her Elders about my investigation of God's Chosen. Jacob interrupted her plea with a citation from the Book of Proverbs, 11:13: "A gossip betrays a confidence, but a trustworthy person keeps a secret." *Then he laid a curse upon her.*

Lisa was beside herself, of course. She begged Jacob not to do this to her. He said she only had herself to blame. Lisa begged him for forgiveness, but Jacob was unmoved. Then Lisa replied with her own citation from Proverbs, 11:9: "With their mouths the godless destroy their neighbours, but through knowledge the righteous escape." *Jacob looked at her thoughtfully for a moment. Then he asked Lisa whether she wished to escape from the demon's power. "Yes!" Lisa cried. She begged Jacob to free her from the demon that was feeding on her mind. Once more, Jacob asked the Elders for their counsel on whether an exorcism ought to be performed on Lisa.*

Everyone replied YES.

At first, I was relieved. I thought that once we had prayed for Lisa, and spoken in tongues, Lisa would be free. And we could all start over.

I MADE A TERRIBLE MISTAKE.

The next moment, Jacob instructed Åse and Birgitte to take Lisa downstairs to the furnace room and get her ready. Then he turned to me: "We need your help with the exorcism of our sister Lisa. Are you ready to annihilate the demon in our midst, Brother Benjamin?"

31

A grunt nearby made Ravn start in fright. He looked down and saw that Møffe had sat down next to him. The dog looked at him with an expression at once disgruntled and reproachful, and Ravn realised it was long past their regular evening walk. "Can't you see I'm working here, Møffe?" he said.

Møffe grunted again, this time with a loud snort and another doleful stare. Ravn knew that he would have no peace until the dog had his way, and if he put off their walk for much longer, he'd simply shit on the deck. That damn dog had him over a barrel.

"All right, all right, let's go, then," Ravn said with a sigh.

Moments later, the two of them were walking along the canal towards Christianshavn Square, in perhaps the shortest evening dog walk in history. Møffe barely had a chance to finish his pee before Ravn hauled the dog back down the embankment, oblivious to the shouts of laughter outside the Canal Bodega, which, more often than not, had had the irresistible charm to pull him inside for a pint or two.

When they got back to *Bianca* five minutes later, Ravn sat down in his chair and picked up Benjamin's report immediately.

I DIDN'T KNOW THERE WAS A FURNACE ROOM IN THE CELLAR—OR EVEN WHAT A "FURNACE ROOM" WAS—I WISH I HAD NEVER FOUND OUT!

Holding a silver crucifix in one hand and a Bible in the other, Jacob took the lead. The other Elders followed at his heels, chanting a Latin verse that I hadn't heard before. Samuel was carrying the old chalice Jacob used in his sermons and a carafe of water. Confused, I felt as if I'd stumbled into the murky scene of an old horror movie. It only got worse when we arrived in the "furnace room."

Lisa was lying on a bare wooden pallet in the far corner, stripped to her underwear with thick leather straps secured around her wrists and ankles. The room was hot as an oven. But Lisa's body was shivering, as if she were freezing cold. Jacob and the others began to recite our credo and the others followed suit. He took two old coins from the pocket of his robe and placed one on each of Lisa's eyes. Taking our cue from Jacob, the rest of us kneeled around the pallet, chanting the credo of God's Chosen over and over, louder and louder. Lisa began to cry.

I don't know how long we prayed for her, but my mouth was bone dry when at last Jacob stood up. He poured some of the water into the chalice. "Drink this holy water, demon," *he said, bringing the chalice to Lisa's lips. She drank the "holy water" greedily. Then the ceremony took another unpleasant turn. While we continued to pray, Lisa's character began to change. She began to scream and yell in an unintelligible language, spitting at us in rage. In the end, her body convulsed, and she spewed a greenish transparent liquid like stomach acid. Jacob handed me a rag to mop it up. Then he gave her more holy water.*

The holy water provoked the demon once again, and Lisa tried to expel it from her mouth. Straining against the leather straps, she retched again. Her wrists and ankles were chafed and bleeding. The demon inside her kept screaming at us. It was horrible. She looked terrified. She seemed to fear Jacob more than anything else, begging him not to take her soul. Her body convulsed again, and she bit her tongue. There was a lot of blood coming out of her mouth. It took Karl-Emil, Samuel, and Reikendorf to hold her down, as we forced a rag into her mouth to stem the blood and keep her snapping jaws apart.

Jacob turned to me and said that the demon was about to come out. And because I was a novice, I had to leave the room, so that the demon would not be transferred and possess my soul instead. He told me to drink the holy water. Then he crossed himself and uttered a prayer before sending me away.

Now I am in the sleeping hall. In the semi-darkness. Further down the corridor in the cellar. I'm sitting here alone, writing to you. I can still hear Lisa howling. As if she were a dog getting a beating. Some of the Aspirants are out in the corridor, comforting one another. Everyone is scared to death. I feel as if I'm going to throw up, just like Lisa. I'm dizzy and my stomach is churning.

Struggling to write. Cannot think. Scared. The demons. Am I in their world now? Sending this email now. Before it's too late, Mr. Mesmer . . . no, it's already too late . . .

The next three pages were blank, and nothing was recorded about either the conclusion of the ceremony or the outcome of Lisa's exorcism in the final pages. After the gap, Benjamin launched into the final part that Ravn had skimmed earlier, which read like an extended glorification of God, God's Chosen, and Jacob, who was now routinely referred to as the Shepherd or the Master.

Ravn put down the last stack of pages on his spare plastic chair and looked out over the canal. He wondered whether the orchestration of the ritual was Jacob's way of sending his father a message through Benjamin Clausen. A demonstration of power, perhaps? Jacob's need to show his ability to manipulate and convert Benjamin into one of his own obedient servants? *If that was what Jacob intended, his mind was very twisted,* Ravn thought. *And sick.* And if that was the case, how had Ferdinand Mesmer responded? Many things had happened in the interim: Benjamin had disappeared; the church on Belgiensgade had burnt down; God's Chosen had gone underground and Jacob Mesmer himself had disappeared; most recently, there was the rising success of Mesmer Resources and the prospective multi-million-kroner deal that depended on his son's signature . . . but the question that bothered Ravn most at this point was this: *Why had Mesmer kept all this information from him?* It was clear to Ravn now that he was merely a pawn in some or other grand scheme for Ferdinand Mesmer's own purposes—and he didn't like being used.

Finding Jacob was no longer his primary concern. Ravn was much more concerned about his predecessor on this job. Before he did anything else, he had to find Benjamin Clausen.

32

The caretaker's name was Folmer, and his overalls were freshly ironed, Ravn noticed, as he led him down the stairs and unlocked the cellar store on Lysefjordsgade. Apparently, after BC Consulting had vacated the premises, the cellar had been converted into a common bicycle garage for the residents. Folmer flipped on the light switch by the door and turned to face Ravn. "This is where Benjamin used to keep his offices. But, as I explained to you on the phone, all his stuff was moved out," he said, the fluorescent light reflecting in his thick glasses.

"For how long did he rent this place?"

"Three or four years, perhaps a little longer. He did a couple of other things before he became a private detective."

"Such as?"

"Bookkeeping, websites, something to do with IT. But he had the most success with his work as a PI. Are you also a detective?"

"Something like that."

"Ha! The detective looking for the missing detective," Folmer said with a snort of laughter. "Don't get me wrong, I liked Benjamin. He actually helped me out once."

"How's that?"

Folmer adjusted his glasses, which had slipped onto the tip of his nose, then he looked around, as if to satisfy himself that they were alone. "My ex-wife liked to eat 'foreign foods' and Benjamin found out who the cook was, if you get my drift . . ."

Ravn said that he did and smiled at Folmer sympathetically. "And when was the last time you saw Benjamin?"

"A few years ago," said Folmer. "When he quit the property. He was jumpy and irritable, as I recall. You know, sad and a bit short-tempered. Back then, I thought it was because he'd gone bust. That kind of thing is always tough on a guy . . ."

"So you're sure he didn't just move his business to a different location?"

Folmer nodded. "He didn't have much stuff. What little he had he took to the dump. All he left behind were the cardboard boxes containing his paperwork. He was supposed to pick them up the next day, but he never showed."

"So what happened to the cardboard boxes? Did they get tossed?"

"Come with me. I'll show you," said Folmer.

Ravn and the caretaker returned through the cellar and proceeded along a narrow corridor that was lined with the residents' private storage rooms. When they came to the last red door on the corridor, Folmer stopped and took out his large bunch of keys. It took him a while to find the right key, but at last he opened the door. "As I said, I liked Benjamin," said Folmer. "So I stored his stuff for him."

Ravn peeked inside the room that looked like a broom cupboard and saw that it was stuffed with all sorts of paraphernalia.

"Can you believe the stuff that people leave behind when they move?" Folmer said, shaking his head. He picked up a blonde wig from the nearest shelf.

"Were you and Benjamin good friends?"

"We weren't close, but I knew his mother in the ol' days. She used to live on Gullandsgade. A tough lady. Jehovah's Witness or something like that . . ."

"Was Benjamin also a Jehovah's Witness?"

Folmer shook his head. "No, but his mother was very religious. I'm not sure if Benjamin was religious or not, but he was a nice kid, always helping out folks here in the neighbourhood. Good manners, but a little shy and awkward. I think his mother gave him a hard time. When he finally moved out of her place, he only got as far as the flat just below hers . . ."

"Okay. Do you know if he still lives there?"

"No, he doesn't. He got tired of living there pretty quick. He spent most of his time down here, when he wasn't off investigating something or other."

"Did Benjamin ever mention a movement called God's Chosen?"

"Not as far as I can remember." Folmer's phone rang, and he took it out of his breast pocket. "Benjamin's stuff is in those two cardboard boxes in the corner. You can take a look if you like," he said, stepping out into the corridor to take the call.

"Thank you," Ravn said. He squeezed past the other boxes and personal effects and sat on his haunches by the two boxes that Folmer had pointed out. Most of the contents of the first box appeared to be invoices, old tax declarations, and their supporting documents. He pulled the second box closer and opened it. Inside he found an old passport photo and more files containing invoices and various addenda. The invoices were all addressed to the current address on Lysefjordsgade. There was nothing to indicate Benjamin's new address. Ravn went through a few receipts that Benjamin had stapled together.

Folmer appeared in the doorway. "I'm afraid I need to get moving."

"Of course," said Ravn, pushing to his feet. He looked at the last receipt in the pile; it was from Interflora for flowers delivered to the Psychiatric Centre on Amager. "You mentioned that Benjamin's mother lived nearby. Do you know where she is now?"

"In the cemetery. She died a few years ago. Why?"

Ravn shook his head and returned the bundle of receipts to the box.

"Please give Benjamin my regards when you see him," said Folmer as he locked the door behind them.

"I will," said Ravn.

They walked through the cellar and made their way to the exit. When they reached the gate back on Lysefjordsgade, Folmer smiled at Ravn. "By the way, a couple of years ago, a young woman came round asking questions. It was just after Benjamin closed his business."

"Was her name Lisa?"

"I can't remember her name, I'm afraid. She was petite and sporty, slim body like girls have these days. Dark hair. She smiled all the time, but there was no warmth in it. She was very insistent. Does that sound like Lisa?"

"Not really, no, but thanks for telling me."

After Folmer had gone on his way, Ravn wondered if the insistent woman had been Katrine, looking for Benjamin after Lisa's exorcism on Belgiensgade. Did Ferdinand Mesmer send her to try to find Benjamin? But the question that intrigued him most was who Benjamin had sent flowers to at Amager Psychiatric Centre.

Ravn had a pretty good hunch who it could be, but he hoped he was wrong.

33

Møffe was waiting for him on the boat, wagging his stubby tail. Ravn leapt onto *Bianca*'s deck, bent down to pat the dog, and stroked his massive head. Møffe immediately sprang up against Ravn's knees, and he grabbed the dog's paws with both hands, swinging them back and forth as if he were a child on the playground. Møffe loved it when he did that.

On the way back from Lysefjordsgade, Ravn had tried to figure out how to confirm his hunch that the flowers sent to Amager Psychiatric Centre were meant for Lisa. If he was right, the hospital would probably still have her contact details. It struck him how much easier it had been to track people down when he had been working for the police—which gave him an idea. He fished his phone out of his pocket and googled the Psychiatric Centre's reception desk. Two minutes later, he placed the call.

"Amager Psychiatric Centre," a slightly nasal voice said on the other end of the line.

"Thomas Ravnsholdt, Station City, ma'am," Ravn said. "We're looking for the contact details of a former patient of yours."

"Why do you need this information?" the day shift nurse asked.

"It concerns a missing person's investigation, a Ms. Lisa Brask, who appears to have been committed to your hospital about two years ago . . . I don't have her national ID number to hand . . ."

"Where did you say you were calling from?"

"Station City on Halmtorvet, Crime Ops," Ravn said patiently.

"In that case, I'm sure you're well aware of the proper procedure, Mr. . . .? We can't disclose any information on former or current patients without a formal request in writing."

"I understand," said Ravn. "But I need this information to continue my investigation. Are you sure you can't do a quick search for me in your files?"

"I'm afraid that's out of the question. What did you say your name was, Mr. . . . ?"

Ravn ended the call. He must be out of practice, he thought in frustration, if he couldn't even charm an identification number out of a nurse. In the good ol' days, he and Mikkel had managed to extract highly confidential information from mean bastards and drug dealers alike. In the cabin, he removed the seat cushions of the sofa and extracted one of his black sports bags from the storage compartment underneath, where he had stored most of his clothing. He rummaged through his shirts, socks, and spare trousers until he found the white envelope containing his personal papers, including his official police ID. He opened the laminated badge and stared at the photograph inside. The picture was taken what felt like a lifetime ago. He was clean-shaven with short hair and dressed in a uniform shirt and tie—every mother-in-law's dream—and the picture was a far cry from what he looked like today. It was just after he had qualified and been assigned to the force. Back then, he had shared every other newly qualified rookie's dream: He had believed that they could make a difference or, at the very least, make a contribution to a safer society for everyone. He had believed in justice, in right and wrong, and that—as a rule—good would prevail over evil. There were no grey zones back then. Now he knew better.

The idealistic picture depressed him, and he slipped the badge back into his pocket. He was supposed to hand it in the day he went on sick leave, of course. He wasn't sure why, exactly, but he lied to Brask and said that he'd lost his ID. Perhaps it was the copper in him who refused to let go? he thought.

34

Darkness had fallen over Amager Fælled, stretching like a dark ocean under the monorail overpass and the soundless metro train. As soon as the train stopped at Sundby Station and the doors slipped open, Ravn stepped out of the first car. He walked through the dark station building and continued down Digevej, following the psychiatric hospital's cement-grey buildings towards the main entrance. As he approached Reception, Ravn could see that a male night shift nurse was sitting in a reinforced glass cage, eating a sandwich that was wrapped in tin foil at his desk. Ravn sighed with relief. He'd gambled on the likelihood that the woman he'd spoken to on the phone earlier would no longer be on duty. Plus the fact that there would probably be less staff to deal with in the graveyard shift. Ravn pushed the buzzer next to the door. The young guy in the glass cage started at the sound and cast a glance over his shoulder. Then he saw Ravn, put aside his sandwich, and stood up. Brushing off the crumbs on his hands on his white coat, he came over to the door.

"Police," said Ravn, slapping his ID against the glass partition.

The guy opened the door and invited him inside. "What can I do for you, officer?" he said with a smile. He looked relatively young, and Ravn reckoned he was probably a medical student, moonlighting at the hospital to make ends meet.

Ravn glanced at his name badge. "Well, Shahid . . . the thing is . . . I could really use your help with an investigation I'm working on," he said, putting an arm around the guy's shoulder and gently nudging him towards the reception desk.

"A case? Something that's going on here?" said Shahid.

"Partly, yes. It concerns a former patient. We're afraid that she's a victim of identity theft . . ."

"Oooh, that's not good. The same thing happened to my uncle," Shahid said, taking a seat behind the counter. "It was an uphill battle to get his money back from the bank—all bankers are complete bastards, I tell you."

"Isn't that the truth," Ravn said, returning Shahid's smile. "Do you think you could take a quick look for me? See if you've got a current address registered to her name on file? That would be great."

Shahid shook his head. "I don't know . . . you're asking for confidential details . . . Perhaps you could come back tomorrow and talk to one of the permanent staff instead? I'm sure they'd have more information than I do."

"Shahid, I'm afraid I need the information right now. The *bandits* never sleep . . . The sooner the two of us close this case, the better. I promise this won't be traced back to you. In fact, I wasn't here," Ravn said, winking at him. "What do you say, do you think you could help me out here, *amigo*?"

Shahid looked around quickly. "Okay, give me a name, and I'll check to see if we have it on file," he said, his hands poised over his keyboard.

"Her name is Lisa Brask."

Shahid's fingers froze in the air, and he looked up at Ravn. "But . . . but I know her . . ."

"Great, do you have her address?"

"No . . . I mean she's here . . ."

"Lisa Brask is . . . is still here? Are you sure?"

"Yes, definitely. We have thirty-five patients committed on a permanent basis, and Lisa is the one who has been here the longest. 'Sleeping Beauty,' we call her," Shahid said, and cast his eyes down. "Well, it's a silly nickname . . . and I'm not the one who came up with it—"

"Can I see her?" Ravn said, cutting him off.

"Now?" said Shahid, casting a glance at his watch.

"Yes, *now*. So I can confirm her identity." He could hear how hollow his words sounded, but Ravn kept staring directly into Shahid's eyes. "*Now*, Shahid. This is important."

Shahid sighed heavily, the expression on his face of a man being led to the gallows. "It's this way," he said at last.

Ravn followed Shahid down the dark corridor that led to the permanent patients' ward. When they reached the end of the corridor, Shahid tapped a code into the panel on the wall, and the heavy automatic doors opened with a faint whooshing sound. "This is totally against the rules, man," he said.

"It's okay, Shahid, I've just gotta check it's her. In five minutes flat, you can return to your sandwich."

"*Totally* against the rules," Shahid repeated as he stopped in front of the door leading to the first room. He opened it carefully, they slipped inside, and Ravn could just make out the contours of the person lying in the bed.

"Her face is hard to miss," said Shahid. "That much is certain."

They went closer to the bed, and Shahid switched on the lamp by the wall. "As I said before, the nickname is a bad joke."

Ravn involuntarily took a step back. "What . . . what happened to her face?"

"Caustic soda."

The grey skin on the lower part of the woman's face was hideously disfigured by knotty scar tissue that spread down her neck. Her lips were eaten away, and her toothless mouth was a gaping hole. Most of her nose was gone, which gave her face a reptilian expression, in stark contrast to her long, beautiful blonde hair.

"Who . . . how did this happen?"

"She drank caustic soda. Suicide attempt, apparently. We usually see this kind of scarring in children who accidently drink drain cleaner. But, as I said, in Lisa's case it was attempted suicide."

"Who brought her in?"

"I have no idea. It happened before I started working here."

"Let me see her medical chart, Shahid."

"But—"

Ravn looked at him sharply, and Shahid nodded dutifully.

"I'll be back in just a moment," he said.

When Shahid was gone, Ravn took Lisa's hand and gave it a gentle squeeze. "Lisa," he said. "Lisa . . ."

A weak gurgling sound came from her throat as Lisa slowly started to wake up.

"Lisa, can you hear me?" Ravn whispered. "I need to talk to you."

Lisa opened her eyes and stared vacantly at the ceiling. Ravn squeezed her hand again, and she turned her head towards him.

"My name is Thomas Ravnsholdt. I am—"

Lisa made a gasping sound and snatched her hand away in fright.

"It's okay, Lisa, I'm not going to hurt you. I'm here to help you."

She looked at Ravn for a long time, as if she were trying to recognise him.

"How did this happen, Lisa? Did it happen while you were with God's Chosen?"

Lisa started to mumble incoherently, and spittle trickled from the corners of her mouth.

"Was it Jacob? Did Jacob Mesmer do this to you?"

"Ben . . . min . . . Ben . . . min . . . Ben . . . ja . . . min . . ."

"Did Benjamin do this?"

"Ben . . . min . . ."

"Do you know where he is? Do you know where I can find Benjamin?"

Clearly affected by drugs and medication, Lisa closed her eyes and fell asleep again.

Ravn took her hand again and shook it gently until she opened her eyes once more. "What about Jacob?" He heard the automatic doors whoosh open, and soon after, footsteps coming closer. "Where is Jacob Mesmer, Lisa?"

Her eyes focussed briefly, and she began to mumble something. "Messssssssmer . . ." she whispered through her destroyed mouth.

"What is going on here?"

Ravn looked over his shoulder. Shahid had returned with the medical chart and a bulky man who was obviously a doctor, even if he looked more like a heavyweight boxer.

"Get . . . mann . . ." Lisa said. "Get . . . mann . . ."

"Thomas Ravnsholdt, Station City," Ravn said to the doctor, then turned his attention back to Lisa. "What did you say?"

"Get . . . mann . . ."

"Can I see some ID?" the doctor barked.

"Yes, of course," Ravn said irritably. He flashed his ID and turned back to Lisa. "Lisa, please repeat that, I can't understand what you're saying . . ."

"Get . . . mann . . . Get . . . mann . . . Get . . . mann . . ." she said, louder and louder. "Get . . . mann . . . Get . . . mann . . ." Lisa kept mumbling, as if she had fallen into a trance.

"Step away from the patient," the doctor said, laying his hand on Ravn's shoulder. Then he turned his attention to Lisa and tried to calm her down by tucking the duvet around her. "There you go, my friend," he said. "Now you can go back to sleep."

Lisa gripped Ravn's sleeve and tried to pull him closer. "Get . . . mann . . . Get . . . mann . . . Get . . . mann . . ." she said, again and again.

Ravn took the chart from Shahid and started skimming the pages. At the top of the first page was a short description of the injuries caused by ingesting caustic soda, as well as the operative procedures performed at Rigshospitalet. Thereafter, she was transferred directly to Amager Psychiatric Centre, where she had been ever since. Her medical history referred to multiple suicide attempts. A list of prescribed medication.

Ravn flipped through the file as fast as he could, looking for Lisa's next of kin, but couldn't see anyone listed. "Does she have a guardian, Shahid? Who visits her?"

"I've never seen anyone visit her . . ." Shahid said, and looked at his superior.

The doctor spun round to face Ravn. "Get out," he said, snatching the medical chart from his hands.

"Hey, take it easy, doc, I'm just trying to find out who did this to her," Ravn said.

"*She* did this to herself, okay? There's no question about that, do you understand?"

"Understood," said Ravn, raising his hands in a conciliatory gesture. He let them fall to his sides and tried to appeal to the doctor's sense of justice instead. "I'm looking for two people: a Benjamin Clausen and a Jacob Mesmer. Do you know if either of these people have tried to contact her?"

The doctor ignored his questions and bodily escorted Ravn and Shahid out of the room. "As Shahid already said—when he broke his oath of silence—no one has come to visit her in all the time that this patient has been here."

Five minutes later, Ravn found himself shown to the door—with a promise from the bulky doctor that he'd be reported to the police in the morning. He was pretty sure it was an empty threat though, because if his visit became public, it would be the night-shift staff who would have hell to pay, rather than a renegade cop.

Ravn was shaken by the extent of Lisa's hideous injuries. He could really use a drink, but unfortunately, there wasn't a pub anywhere near the Psychiatric Centre.

35

Ravn was sitting on the windowsill of Eduardo's office at *Information*, a room that was as claustrophobic as a prison cell. Stacks of newspapers and files were scattered everywhere, and the shelf along one wall was so stuffed with books it might have toppled onto the desk at any moment. A framed original poster from the film *Belle du Jour*, featuring a semi-naked Catherine Deneuve, was the only decoration on the walls. Eduardo came in, holding two steaming cups of coffee. The minute he crossed the threshold, Eduardo kicked the door closed on the lively discussion in the large editorial office next door.

"So, you believe this is a case for the police because a crime has been committed?" Eduardo gave Ravn one of the cups and sat down on his well-worn desk chair.

"Yes," Ravn said, "I think it's likely that Lisa was injured in the exorcism that Benjamin describes in his report, but obviously that's between you and me." He sipped his coffee while Eduardo paged through Jacob Mesmer's book on exorcism. "Can you see any reference to the use of caustic soda in the ritual?" he asked Eduardo.

"No, not at all," said Eduardo. "What about Benjamin's report? Does he mention anything about using caustic soda?"

"No. He only mentions water. 'Holy water' is reportedly the only thing that Jacob Mesmer gave her during the ritual. But Benjamin wasn't present during the last part."

Eduardo nodded and put the book down on his desk.

"What did the doctor at the psychiatric hospital have to say?"

"He said it was a suicide attempt. In fact, he was very specific about that, and his opinion accords with what is written in her medical chart."

"They *showed* you her medical chart?" Eduardo said, raising his eyebrows.

"Not voluntarily," said Ravn. "But I managed to see that she'd been committed to psych hospitals before, in connection with previous suicide attempts."

"If that's true, it's not unreasonable to deduce that Lisa could have taken the caustic soda herself."

"I guess not, but . . ."

"You're not convinced?"

Ravn shrugged. "I have a hunch that it wasn't another suicide attempt."

"Your sixth sense?" Eduardo smiled.

"It's more than that. According to Benjamin's report, Lisa told him that she was a 'cutter' in her teenage years. And her suicide attempts—at least those that were registered in her medical chart—were either done with sleeping pills or cutting her wrists."

"I think I can see where you're going with this. Drinking caustic soda doesn't accord with her medical history."

"Exactly."

"So you suspect someone else did this to her?"

"It's certainly justifiable to confront Jacob Mesmer and Benjamin with this possibility."

"Do you have any leads on their whereabouts?"

"The trail ends in a fire at the movement's last-known premises on Belgiensgade. And I have no idea where they have moved to."

"Have you checked the ministry's database?"

"Which ministry? And what database?"

"The Ministry of Church Affairs has a database on religious communities registered in Denmark," Eduardo said, logging in to his computer.

Ravn came over to Eduardo's side of the desk and peered over his shoulder.

"Here it is," Eduardo said, moments later. The ministry's homepage had come up on the screen, listing all the religious institutions that were registered in Denmark. "The list is subdivided according to religious orientation," said Eduardo, clicking on the link labelled CHRISTIAN.

The list of Christian organisations was longer than they had both expected; it spread over six screens. Luckily, it was alphabetical, so they could quickly find their way to God's Chosen under the subtitle EVANGELICAL.

"Belgiensgade is listed as their last-known address," said Eduardo, pointing at the screen.

"So, it probably hasn't been updated," said Ravn, scratching his beard. "Can we call the ministry and ask?"

"We could, but it's the church organisations themselves who are responsible for keeping the ministry up to date, so I don't think calling them will do us any good. At the end of the day, the whole point of registering your details with the ministry is to qualify for their financial support," said Eduardo. "So if they are still active, this ought to be enough motivation for Jacob to keep the ministry informed."

Ravn insisted that they call the ministry anyway and make some enquiries. So Eduardo found the number on their homepage and gave the ministry a call. It took him fifteen minutes on the phone to get through to someone who could answer his question.

"I'm terribly sorry," said the office assistant, who was on speakerphone. "But that is the only address we have registered for God's Chosen."

"Okay. Do you have a telephone number or an email address?" Eduardo asked.

"Neither, sorry."

"Okay. Do you know if they have disbanded?"

"Not according to our list, but it often happens that the organisation dissolves, ceases to exist, or disbands before we are informed and deregister them accordingly."

Eduardo thanked the office assistant for her help and ended the call.

"So much for the Ministry of Church Affairs," said Ravn.

"Come with me, I have another idea," Eduardo said, and stood up. "Perhaps Kjeld can help."

"And 'Kjeld' is?"

"An institution here at *Information*. He's the one who wrote our articles on the palaver surrounding Faderhuset and the eviction of the squatters who took over Ungdomshuset. He's also spent a lot of time and energy on investigating splinter groups within the Jehovah's Witnesses and the radicalisation of Islam in prisons."

"Okay, but I wouldn't want him to write about any of this," said Ravn with concern.

"Don't worry, Kjeld cannot be coaxed to his keyboard unless it's a big story. We'll keep this one in the family," Eduardo said, patting Ravn on the shoulder.

Ravn wasn't sure he wanted to be included in *Information*'s "family," but as long as news of his investigation didn't leave Kjeld's office, he was willing to give it a try.

Moments later, they knocked on the door of Kjeld's office, which lay on the far side of the editorial desk.

"Come in," a rusty voice said.

Eduardo and Ravn entered the office, which was even smaller than Eduardo's and enveloped in a thick haze. At the overfilled desk by the window sat an elderly man in a lumberjack shirt and red braces.

"It smells like a Turkish bazaar in here," said Eduardo. "Are you seriously smoking a bong at your desk, Kjeld?"

"Don't be ridiculous, Eduardo. It's an e-cigarette," Kjeld replied, and coughed. "It's good . . . apple flavoured."

"Either way, the boss will blow a fuse if she catches you smoking," Eduardo said, waving his hand in front of his face in an attempt to clear the haze. "You know perfectly well that we've issued a zero-tolerance policy with respect to smoking on the premises."

"But this is *vapour*, not smoke. And besides, I issued a veto at that meeting; everyone knows that. So, what do you want, Eduardo, other than spreading negative energy?" He leaned back in his chair, which protested loudly under the lumberjack's weight.

"We're trying to track down a sect that appears to have splintered from the evangelical movement. The church goes by the name God's Chosen."

"God's Chosen . . . hmm . . ."

"There was a fire on—" Ravn added.

"Amager, yes, I remember," Kjeld said. "A few years ago. So, what are they up to now?"

"We can't find out where the group has moved to since," said Eduardo. "Do you know what happened to them?"

"Weeelll," Kjeld said, puffing on his e-cigarette. "I think they disbanded after that incident on Amager."

"But are you sure?"

"Hmm . . ." Kjeld scratched his scalp thoughtfully. "Have you tried the Ministry of Church Affairs website?"

"They've only got the old address listed, and they couldn't tell for sure whether the group still exists."

Kjeld nodded and exhaled a cloud of vapour. "It's starting to ring a bell. I remember that I considered doing a piece on the former national football player who was a member . . . the left-back . . . What was his name again . . . Lars? . . . Lasse? . . . Lennart?"

"Did you talk to him?"

"No, he left the church before I got a chance, so the story was dead in the water. It was before the fire too."

"Do you think they shut up shop?"

"Possibly. Many groups of their kind did so at the time. Faderhuset and Evangelists for Now, to name the most prominent examples that disintegrated and flew up to Heaven," he said, raising his arms in the air with a chuckle.

They thanked Kjeld for his help and returned to Eduardo's office.

"What about Mikkel?" Eduardo asked. "Why don't you ask him to search the national registration database?"

"He can only do that if both Jacob Mesmer and Benjamin Clausen have officially been registered as missing persons."

"Sure. I meant *un*officially."

"I don't have their national identification numbers. Besides, I promised him that last time was the *last* time."

In truth, Ravn didn't have too many qualms about that, but he preferred to reserve his ex-partner's assistance for Eva's case. Which reminded him; Mikkel had not come back to him about when they could check out Kaminsky's contraband, as promised.

Eduardo sat down at his desk and picked up Jacob Mesmer's book again. "It takes a lot to force caustic soda down someone's throat," he said.

"Not if you have the help of several others, or your victim is tied down, like Lisa was."

"No, I meant *psychologically*."

Ravn shrugged. "I've seen people capable of doing worse, so nothing really surprises me anymore. But I'll admit that you've got to be pretty sick in the head to do something like that to another person."

Eduardo put the book down again. Ravn picked it up and was about to pop it back into his pocket when he noticed the name of the publisher on the bottom of the first page. He ran his finger over the name. "Gethsemane. The same name that Benjamin mentioned in his report as the place where Jacob would lead them all to."

"Gethsemane was the garden where Jesus bathed with his disciples the evening before his crucifixion."

Ravn quirked his eyebrows.

"What? No need to look so bloody surprised. I went to Sunday school."

"Really?"

"Of course. All Spanish children do. But tell me why you think this place is significant?"

"I got no more than a few words out of Lisa, but I think that was one of them."

"Why would she mention it?"

"I have no idea. But it clearly upset her, and she kept repeating it."

"Do you think it has something to do with the publisher?" Eduardo asked.

Ravn nodded. "Something tells me that either it is Jacob's own publisher or that of God's Chosen. Could you take a look if it still exists?"

Eduardo turned to his computer and googled the publisher. There were no hits. "We could try the national business registry."

He found the relevant website and tapped in the name "Gethsemane." A long list of businesses with that name were registered. Eduardo leaned closer to his monitor. "All these firms belong to the same three co-owners: Jacob Mesmer and two others."

Ravn came round to his side of the desk to take a look. "Holy shit. God's Chosen owns more firms than Scientology does!"

"Indeed. Take that, L. Ron Hubbard," said Eduardo with a smile. "Apart from the publisher, they also own . . . inter alia . . . a building maintenance firm, an agricultural firm, a cleaning firm, and an agency that designs webpages."

"Do you have a list of addresses for these firms?"

"Give me a minute," said Eduardo, clicking on the first link.

"Looks like the building maintenance firm closed down several years ago."

"What about the others?"

"The same goes for the web designer and . . . the cleaning firm." He clicked on the next few links. "And the publisher doesn't exist anymore either."

"What about the agricultural one?"

" Yup, looks like it still exists."

"Okay. So what's their address?" Ravn asked, trying to follow on the screen.

"They appear to be operating from an address on the island of Lolland. Shall I write down the address and telephone number for you?" said Eduardo.

"Yeah, that would be great, thanks."

Eduardo noted the details on a yellow Post-it and gave it to Ravn. "So, are you planning to give them a call?"

"I think I'll hold off for a bit."

"You're not thinking of going down there, are you?"

Ravn shook his head, thinking so hard he could almost hear the wheels turning.

"So . . . what's your plan?"

"I can't help thinking that Ferdinand Mesmer has known all along where his son is."

Eduardo leaned back in his chair and stared at Ravn in surprise. "But then why would he go to so much trouble to get you to find him?"

"Because he likes to control people."

"But it would have been so much easier just to give you the address from the beginning."

"Yes, it would, but Ferdinand Mesmer is not the kind of man who takes the easy route."

"What could his motive be?"

"He wanted to show me what his son was capable of first, before I met him . . ."

"But why?"

Ravn shook his head. "I'm not sure. Maybe . . . so I wouldn't change sides, like Benjamin did. Or he has some other, entirely hidden agenda."

Eduardo looked at him with a worried expression on his face. "As I said before, Ravn: I think you should stay the hell away from this one."

"It's too late now."

"So what are you going to do?"

"First, I'm going to have a chat with the Devil himself," Ravn said, popping Jacob Mesmer's book back into his pocket.

36

Ravn leaned up against the pillar in the parking garage under Mesmer Resources. The garage was pleasantly cool in a blue gleam from the plethora of pipes and technical installations in the ceiling. Soft tones flowed from the loudspeakers. It was the kind of music intended to create a false sense of security, so the cellar wouldn't seem so oppressive. Ferdinand Mesmer's parking bay was empty, and his nameplate stood out from the other bays occupied with exclusive automobiles, which indicated that business was obviously going well. A few hours ago, the receptionist upstairs told Ravn that Ferdinand Mesmer was at a meeting in town, but that he was expected to return later that day. Ravn had declined to wait. And it suited him to confront Mesmer here, away from his office—and Katrine, his orderly.

Ravn waited for another half hour before he heard a car come down the ramp to the parking deck. The headlights of a large black Mercedes S swept over the lane, its twelve-cylinder engine thundering. Mesmer was seated behind the wheel, and he swung the car deftly into his parking bay. Ravn crossed the lane and stood behind the car when Mesmer got out.

"Nice car," said Ravn.

Mesmer started in surprise. "I . . . I've been waiting for an update from you," he said, locking his car with a click on the keys. He was clearly uncomfortable with the situation.

"Why didn't you give me Jacob's address from the beginning?"

"Why . . . don't we go up to my office and talk there?"

"Did you know how seriously Lisa Brask was injured? Have you seen her yourself?"

"Lisa Brask? The woman whom Benjamin writes about in his report?"

"Stop playing the fool. You know perfectly well who I mean."

"I don't deny that. My brain just needed to kick in," Mesmer said. He laid his soft leather satchel on the roof of the Mercedes. "I know that she was committed to a psychiatric hospital, badly disfigured."

"And what about Benjamin Clausen's disappearance? Do you know what has happened to him?"

"We . . . looked for him . . . a short time after he had completed his task."

"You mean after he joined Jacob's congregation and started sending you praises of the Lord instead of reports on your son?"

"Yes, I was worried about him, so I initiated an investigation into his whereabouts."

"I know that Katrine went to check out Benjamin's former office. Did she find out where he moved to?"

"I'm afraid the trail ended there."

"Why did you choose Benjamin in the first place?"

Mesmer shrugged. "I think his agency was listed first in the telephone book."

"Bullshit. Benjamin was hand-picked for the job, just like I was—to follow in his footsteps."

"Where are you going with this?"

"You knew his background, and probably also knew that he was brought up in a strict Christian home. Did that make him particularly well suited for the job?"

Mesmer narrowed his eyes. "You are better at this than I thought. I admit that I knew about Benjamin's background. I thought it could give him the necessary point of departure for a thorough investigation . . ."

"You mean to work undercover?"

Mesmer nodded. "But I wasn't prepared for the eventuality that Benjamin might regain his faith in God. My son can be convincing, apparently."

"Is Benjamin still with Jacob?"

"I don't know any more than you do about what has happened to him. But it appears he is still with Jacob's church, yes."

"Unless he has suffered the same fate as Lisa?"

Mesmer looked away and reached for the satchel on the roof of his car.

"What do you know about the fire on Belgiensgade?" Ravn nodded at Mesmer's disfigured hand, which was resting on the satchel.

Mesmer smiled fleetingly. "No more than what was reported in the newspapers back then. You don't think I had something to do with that, do you?" He stretched the hand towards Ravn. In the strange light in the cellar, it seemed even more deformed, almost like a hoof. "This injury is an old one, I can assure you of that," he added with another sad smile. "Do you have any other questions you would like answered?"

"I haven't even got started. What about your son's publications?"

"I assume the ones that aren't about the Mesmogramme?"

"Yes."

"I was shaken when I discovered he had published a book on exorcism. It seemed absurd. And I realised I had to find out what his sect was all about, exactly. I needed to know what he was mixed up in."

"Are you also investigating the other businesses that belong to your son?"

"Of course. It's strange that they've all gone bust, considering the fact that most of their employees worked without pay, and that all the proceeds went to God's Chosen. But I guess that's exactly what bad press can do to a company."

"What about the agricultural business? I assume that this is where the congregation is located?"

Mesmer sighed. "Dust to dust . . ."

"Is that supposed to be a *joke*?" Ravn said.

"More of an ironic observation. The agricultural firm cultivates mushrooms."

"Really?"

Mesmer nodded.

Ravn leaned against the Mercedes. "If you knew all this, why didn't you just send Katrine to Lolland with the contract?"

"Because I need to find out if my son is *completely* irrational."

"Surely, Katrine could be the judge of that?"

"I wanted someone who could judge the situation from the outside. A fresh perspective. Someone with your skills."

"If you suspected your son or someone else in his movement had committed a crime, you could have gone to the police."

"We both know that there is very little the police can do."

"*Do* we? I think the only reason you didn't report to the police is the negative press it would have caused your company. Not to mention the potential jeopardy of your deal with—"

"You misjudge me. I don't wish to cover anything up, including my son's actions, if it turns out he had something to do with Benjamin's disappearance, Lisa's hospitalisation, or other grievous matters. This is the reason I contacted you, Ravn. To bring all these things to light."

"And get the deal signed."

"That too, yes."

"But why would he sign it if there is so much bad blood between you?"

"Because Jacob needs money. The farm on Lolland is deep in debt. If my information is correct, their agricultural production has been stopped altogether. In order to save what is left of his congregation, the deal is a viable solution to his financial problems. A divine intervention, if you like," he added.

Ravn pushed off the Mercedes. "And you win, I assume?"

"No, I've already *lost*," said Mesmer. "I blame myself for allowing things to come this far. That I wasn't a better father to Jacob. He didn't have an easy childhood. There are many things I regret."

"Save your excuses for someone who cares."

Mesmer shrugged. "I expect neither your understanding, nor your sympathy. Both of which are irrelevant. Can I assume that you are still on the case?"

Ravn made no reply, merely turned on his heel and left him standing there. He was tired of the old man.

"Can I?!" Mesmer called after him.

His voice reverberated in the empty cellar as the soft music from the loudspeakers played on.

37

It was just after midnight, but the air was still warm. Ravn and Eduardo were seated on the deck of the ketch with their feet in the water, drinking a beer. Laughter and cheers came from the nearest pub, where the guests had spilled onto the embankment to hold their own party. Ravn had told Eduardo about his meeting with Mesmer. He trusted that man less every time he laid eyes on him.

"He's exceedingly manipulative. I've never seen anything like it before. It's as if he tells a sliver of the truth only to build a pack of lies," Ravn said, and took a sip from the bottle.

"So why are you going to Lolland? Why don't you just let that woman Katrine deliver the stupid bloody contract?"

"Because I need to find out who did that to Lisa."

Eduardo stared into the water. "I still think you should drop it. Don't go, Ravn."

Eduardo looked genuinely sad, and Ravn gave him a friendly nudge with his shoulder. "Are you starting to worry about me, my friend?"

"I have a bad feeling about this."

"I'm going to Lolland, Eduardo. The worst thing that can happen is that I die of boredom before I get to the mushroom farm. Who the hell cultivates mushrooms anyway?"

"Still . . ." Eduardo slumped forwards, his face like someone at their best friend's funeral.

"What are you not telling me, Eduardo?"

Eduardo sighed. "After you left, Kjeld stopped by my office."

"The guy with the bong and red braces?"

"E-cigarettes—but that's beside the point. I told Kjeld about the farm, and this reminded him about a story that a colleague once told him."

"What story?"

"When the hype around God's Chosen was at its highest, the farm was used as a rehabilitation camp . . ."

"And?"

"Perhaps *rehabilitation* is not the right word . . . it was more like a reform school. Yes, that's what he said. Like a Soviet gulag or a labour camp."

"Okay. So who attended these 'camps'?"

"Those members of the congregation who had expressed criticism of the church, or simply not performed sufficiently well in the interests of the movement. Sometimes they were people who had attended seminars but could not pay the course fees. Kjeld says that it appears as if Jacob Mesmer was inspired by Scientology's Rehabilitation Project Force camps.

"I don't have a clue what that is, but . . . why didn't the members simply refuse?"

"Because it was a choice between attending the reform camp or excommunication from the church."

"Does Kjeld know what happened in the camps?"

"Hard physical labour and Bible training. Kjeld said that one of his colleague's sources, who had left the group, reported that all interns wore boiler suits, were completely isolated from society, and even subjected to corporal punishment if they didn't follow the rules to a tee."

"And what about now that everything is being shut down?"

"Kjeld didn't say anything about that—but that's exactly my point: Who knows what the hell is going on there? I doubt very much that things have changed for the better under the current circumstances . . ."

Ravn emptied his beer and stood up. "I think I'll have a much better idea of what is going on once I've been down there."

"You're still going?"

"Yup." He put his beer down in the cockpit. "Thanks for the beer."

* * *

Ravn walked along the embankment to *Bianca*'s aft deck. It surprised him that Møffe hadn't come to meet him, as he usually did. He called the dog as he clambered down onto the deck. Then he heard the characteristic chomping sounds, and he caught a glimpse of Møffe and a dark figure feeding him dog biscuits by the railing.

"He's not much of a guard dog, is he?" said Katrine.

"I haven't told him to go for you . . . yet," Ravn replied, coming closer.

Katrine smiled and brushed her hands off on her black vest top.

"How long have you been here?"

"You mean how much of the conversation with your friend did I overhear?"

"That's another way of putting it."

"Enough for me to know that I'm glad I don't subscribe to his newspaper."

"I never realised you read the newspapers."

"I never realised you scared so easily."

"Then you weren't listening properly. It takes more than a fanatical sect to make me shake in my boots. So why are you here?"

"I was in the neighbourhood."

"Then you must be working late again."

"Who says I'm working?" Her unwavering gaze was provocative. She took a step closer. Close enough for him to catch a whiff of perfume and sweat.

"Who are you?" he asked, holding her gaze.

"Someone who helps to arrange things."

"Is that all?"

"Usually, it's more than enough." She took another step forward and surprised him by putting her arms around his shoulders and pressing her body against his.

"Where did you serve before, Katrine? Which unit?"

Katrine kissed him in reply, and Ravn returned her kiss, biting her bottom lip and tongue gently.

"You mean, whether we belong to the same sect?" she said, smiling up at him.

"And what kind of sect would that be?" he said, drawing her towards the open cabin door.

"The blue-shirts. Who else?"

He smiled and quickly pulled his T-shirt up over his head, exposing his naked chest. "Right now, you're wearing far too many clothes, Katrine."

He took her hand and led her into the cabin, where they tore at belts and zippers. She tossed her shirt, and he helped her out of the rest of her clothing and nudged her back against the bed. "You're too petite to be a bodyguard, so I'm thinking former secret service. Am I right?" He lay down on top of her, caressed her taut and muscular body that felt so warm under his.

"I don't talk about the past," she said, pulling him closer. Katrine kissed him greedily, then spread her thighs so he could thrust inside her. "It is only the present that interests me . . . and . . . perhaps a little of what the future might bring."

He took her deep and slow and let himself be swallowed by the moment, their rocking motion almost matching the lapping sound of the water against the hull.

Afterwards, they lay together in silence, staring up at the night sky that shimmered through the open hatch in the ceiling. All was quiet outside, and it seemed as if the city had gone to sleep. "So what does the future bring?"

"What?" She turned her head towards him.

"You said you were interested in what the future brings."

"I said 'a little' interested."

"So what do you see?"

She propped herself up on one elbow and caressed his chest.

"It's not so much about seeing the future than it is about being prepared. Accepting whatever comes . . ."

"Sounds philosophical."

"Common sense, actually." She patted his chest and got out of the bed.

Ravn watched her gather her scattered clothing from the floor. She looked beautiful in the moonlight, but he knew he was going to regret this when he woke up early in the morning. A moral hangover that would arise as sure as amen in a church, his eternal sense of guilt for a woman who was long since dead.

"Was this Mesmer's idea?"

"If that's what you think, you don't know me at all." She put on her underwear and vest top. "It's more of a bad habit that I have . . ."

"And what habit is that?"

"Falling for the wrong man." She put on her shoes. Blew him a kiss. "Take care of yourself, Ravn," she said, and disappeared out the door.

He listened to her footsteps slowly fade on the cobblestones along the embankment. *Falling* was a good description for what had just happened. He knew this feeling all too well, when his thirst got the better of him. And she still hadn't revealed where the hell she came from. In his world, that only made her more intriguing.

38

"You're going *where?*" Victoria looked at Ravn in disbelief.

He took a bite of one of the cinnamon rolls he routinely brought along when he had a favour to ask. "Lolland," he repeated with a full mouth.

Victoria smoothed down the folds of her tweed trousers. "You do realise that there's nothing but country bumpkins down there," she said smilingly, and helped herself to another cinnamon roll.

"I thought your prejudices were reserved for Swedes and Germans, Victoria."

"They're not prejudices; they're experiences gathered over a lifetime. I'm not saying you won't find any nice people on the southern isles; I'm just saying that I'm yet to meet any myself . . ."

"And when did you last venture beyond the greater Copenhagen area?"

She arched her eyebrows and gave him an indignant look. "I often venture beyond the city limits to buy books, but I don't mind admitting that I don't like to travel. Especially not to the beet farmers down south. Why in the world would you want to go there?"

"To check something out," he said evasively. He was not keen to mention the contract he needed to deliver. "I think Benjamin is held up there somewhere with Jacob Mesmer and his disciples."

"You're going to visit that exorcist?"

Ravn nodded.

"Nothing good will come of it." She dipped her cinnamon roll in her coffee and took another bite. "So what have you come here to borrow this time? A road map?"

"Sure, if you have one, but it's a little more than that . . ."

"What's that? I don't think I have any more books by that guy. And besides, you never remembered to take along the books I found on the Mesmogramme, or whatever it was called."

"I don't want to borrow any more books."

"What then?"

Ravn took a sip of coffee.

"You're not getting any money out of me."

"I don't need cash either."

"Well, what is it, then?"

"Your car," he said, and looked away.

Victoria stopped, swallowed the last of her mouthful, put her coffee on her desk, and stared at him for a full minute. "You'd like to borrow *Wilma?*"

"I didn't know your car had a name. But yes. Can I?"

"Can't you borrow a car from Ferdinand Mesmer?"

"No, unfortunately not."

"Okay, then . . . what about Lohman's Audi? You've been cruising around in that tub all summer."

"Yes, but that was when I was working for Lohman." Ravn failed to mention that he still hadn't paid for the windscreen that Carsten smashed when he had the biker under surveillance. "It would be a really big help, Victoria."

"They must have public transport that can take you down there."

"The farm is far away from everything. I promise I'll take good care of your car . . . of Wilma. I'll be back tonight, before it's dark."

Victoria stared at him as if he'd lost his mind. "You can't take Møffe with you. I don't want dog hair and gob everywhere."

He was about to argue that Møffe neither gobbed nor shed hairs, but he reckoned it was probably best to choose his battles carefully. "Don't worry, Møffe will stay home with Eduardo."

Victoria dug in her pockets and brought out a key on a keyring, a large silver *W*. "Okay," she said. "You can borrow her just this one time. But if you get as much as a scratch on her, we're enemies for life. For life, Ravn. You understand?"

Ravn snatched the key from her with a smile.

Ten minutes later, Ravn was sitting behind the wheel of Victoria's red Volvo Duett P 201 station wagon from 1966. Victoria had her head halfway through the open passenger window, watching him, as he tried to get the car in gear. The gearbox groaned when he finally managed to find first.

"Do not go over eighty kilometres an hour. And keep your eye on the temperature gauge. It can't go over eighty-five. And stay away from field tracks, so you don't get any gravel chinks on her body."

"I'll be careful, I promise," Ravn said, revving the engine. "See you later."

"Disengage the handbrake!" she yelled so loud he almost went deaf in one ear.

He disengaged the handbrake and the car rolled down Dronningensgade towards the intersection at Torvegade. In the rearview mirror, he could see Victoria keeping an eagle eye on him, and he looked forward to getting round the corner, beyond her sight.

39

The old Blaupunkt radio snatched the occasional local station as Ravn headed south along the E47 in the direction of Lolland. Occasionally, the radio emitted more atmospheric noise than music, but right now, just south of Præstø, he could hear Johnny Cash's "Walk the Line" clearly and turned up the volume. Since hitting the highway, he'd kept the needle on 100km/h, which was enough to avoid being overtaken by trucks but well over Victoria's speed limit. The Volvo seemed to be coping just fine, however, and Ravn kept an eye on the temperature gauge. Even though the car was noisy and stank of exhaust fumes, it was a pleasure to drive, not least because other drivers obviously thought it charming, giving him a thumbs up when he passed.

Twenty minutes later, he crossed the Kalve Strait and looked over the clear blue sea towards Masnedø, which shimmered in the heat as he drove over the first Farø bridge. Years ago, he and Eva had planned to sail *Bianca* to the southern isles, docking at the small, idyllic ports along the way. Actually, it had been Eva's idea, after she'd seen the old tubs tethered in Nyhavn, selling fresh fruit from Fejø island. Eva loved the idea of sailing down there to fetch apples, but—like so much else—they never managed to realise that dream before she died. Ravn reckoned his fee for the Mesmer case would enable him to repair *Bianca*'s engine, so he could fetch Eva's apples. The thought of honouring her memory in this way made him smile.

As he made his way across Falster, the sky became increasingly darker. When he rolled down his window, the air was thick with the promise of thunder. He hoped to reach the mushroom farm in about a half hour, before the heavens opened. The radio signal died when he drove through the Guldborgsund tunnel between Falster and Lolland, and instead his ears registered a hacking sound to the engine's whine that wasn't healthy, so he automatically slowed down. The oil pressure and temperature gauge showed no cause for alarm, however, so everything ought to be in order.

Moments later, he emerged on Lolland and, as if on cue, the first burst of thunder roared in the distance. He hadn't thought of checking the weather forecast before leaving home, and now he wasn't looking forward to the prospect of driving the Volvo back to Zealand in dark, stormy weather. The next instant, a loud bang came from the engine, and the bonnet exuded a white cloud of smoke that obscured his vision. Ravn slammed on the brakes instinctively, and the car swerved. He took his foot off the pedal and turned the wheel hard in the opposite direction, only to have the car swerve into the oncoming lane. He yanked on the wheel again in a desperate attempt to correct his course, which brought him skidding onto the verge on the right. Seconds later, the car landed in the ditch, and Ravn banged his head hard on the wheel as the car hit bottom.

When Ravn put a hand to his head, he realised his forehead was bleeding. He pushed the door open with his shoulder and tumbled out of the car. Smoke was still coming from the bonnet, and he could hear the glowing hot engine block hissing.

"You've got to be fucking kidding me," he mumbled.

He crawled slowly out of the ditch and pulled himself onto the verge. He sat here for a while, staring at the car. Luckily, the ditch was a relatively soft landing, and only the front fender was slightly bent. But he was dreading the damage that the engine must have suffered. There was no point in trying to start the car because it was impossible for him to get it out of the ditch on his own anyway. He peered down the deserted country road. In the distance, the asphalt drew dark with rain that began to fall, permeating the air with its metallic smell. He needed to get hold of a towing vehicle that could pull the Volvo out of the ditch and, in the worst-case scenario, tow the car to a workshop. He hoped the damage would not be too bad, so that Victoria didn't have to know about his little accident.

It took three hours for the towing vehicle to arrive. In the interim, he'd taken shelter from the rain in the Volvo's boot. As he clambered out the back, he realised that a local haulage contractor was providing the "towing service." His company slogan, "Dan—the Man with a Van," was written on the battered door of the truck's cab.

"Whoa, don't you have any brakes, mate?" said Dan the Man. He was dressed in black and looked like a good-natured biker.

"Sure I do. But the car got the skids. Something popped in the engine, and all of a sudden, there was smoke everywhere."

"Yeah. Well, it can happen to anyone."

"Sounds like you know what's wrong?" Ravn said expectantly.

"Sorry. No clue. I only tow," said the man, pulling on a pair of work gloves. But I can get you to a garage. It's a fine car." He connected the Volvo to the winch and hauled it out of the ditch without any problems. Once the car was back on the road, Ravn tried to start the engine. It spluttered as if it would spit out all its cylinders through the exhaust pipe, so he turned it off quickly.

"Best you get a mechanic to take a look. My brother's pretty good at that sort of thing," said the man.

"As long as he is fast."

Inside the dilapidated garage, there was a strong smell of diesel oil. Spare parts, dissembled engine blocks, and gearboxes were scattered around the grease pit where Wilma was hoisted on the lift. Dan the Man's twin brother was bent over the hood, checking out the Volvo's engine. Ravn stood next to him, shifting his feet, occasionally casting an impatient glance at the time on his iPhone. If he could sort out the car quickly, he would still be able to reach Jacob Mesmer before dark. The farm was only a few kilometres away from the garage. "So, can you fix it?" he asked.

The mechanic mumbled under his breath as he worked.

"It would mean a great deal to me if we could get the car fixed before dark," Ravn tried again.

A few more minutes passed before the mechanic pulled his head out from under the hood and gave Ravn a dull stare. "Yeah, it's a long way to walk to Copenhagen . . ."

"Exactly," said Ravn, biting his lip. "So, can you fix it?"

"Didn't you keep your eye on the temperature gauge at all? You have to watch it like a hawk when you're driving such an old car. Anything less amounts to sabotage."

"Of course I checked the gauge. Every ten minutes. And I didn't drive over eighty. Not much, anyway."

"Well, the engine doesn't get cooked on its own, does it?"

Ravn swallowed hard. "The engine is . . . cooked?"

The mechanic wiped his hands on his overalls. "Not completely, but the radiator has blown."

"Okay. But you have one in stock, right? I'll pay you whatever it takes to get it fixed."

"In stock?" The man laughed incredulously. "This kind of radiator isn't produced anymore, Mr. Copenhagen."

"But . . . but what can we do, then?"

"We'll have to get hold of the scrap dealer in Nakskov and ask if he has anything we can use. But it won't be before tomorrow afternoon."

"Tomorrow? But I need the car now! Can't you give the man a call?"

"I could. But they've all gone home by now, so there's no point. You should have checked the water, then you wouldn't be in this spot right now. The good thing is that you'll probably remember to do so next time. If you give me your number, I'll call you when I have news."

Ravn leaned against the wall, exhausted. Above his head, Samantha Fox looked down at him from a faded calendar from the mid-eighties. He gave the mechanic his number. "Is there a hotel nearby?"

"You can try the B&B a little further down the road. But they only take cash."

Ravn walked out of the open gates of the garage and began walking down the deserted main road of Søllested, his mobile phone in one hand and the manila envelope in the other. The rain had stopped, and the last rays of the sun cut through the black clouds in the sky. In the far distance, the thunder was still rumbling. He sent a text message to Victoria, regretting that he couldn't bring back her car tonight because, unfortunately, he'd been delayed and would need to spend the night. She called him back the next minute. He chose not to take the call. It was hard enough to lie to her in a text message.

40

Ravn found the B&B on a small farm in the outskirts of Søllested. He walked into the courtyard, past a large lorry, and continued towards the front door. When he knocked, a dog barked loudly inside. A moment later, a scrawny man appeared in the doorway, one leg blocking the path of a large sheepdog.

"Yes?" said the man.

"I'm looking for a place to spend the night. Do you have any vacancies?"

The man looked him up and down. "As a rule, we only take in folks we know."

"I'm happy to pay you in advance."

"That's all right. Are you alone?"

Ravn spun once on the spot to show the man that he was. "Yup, it's just me," he said, smiling. "My car broke down. They're fixing it for me over at the gar—"

"One must help your fellow men," the man said, cutting Ravn off. "Stay!" he yelled at the dog, giving it a hefty shove with his knee so it would stay inside.

Ravn followed the man around the house to the annex, where he was invited to take a look at the small room to let. The furnishings consisted of two single beds and an armchair squashed up in one corner. Despite the window being ajar, there was a palpable smell of mould.

Once Ravn had seen the room, they stepped back into the short corridor, and the man showed him the shared bathroom opposite the room.

"So, that's what we've got," the man said, planting his hands on his hips.

"It's perfect, thank you. How much do you charge?"

"Two hundred kroner a night. We can settle the bill when you leave," the scrawny man said, handing him a key.

"Is it possible to get something to eat?"

"Yes. Breakfast. We're a bed and breakfast, after all."

Ravn nodded. "That you are," he said to the man, who was already on his way out the door.

When the man had gone, Ravn sidled over to the window and opened it wide. He looked out over the fields where combine harvesters were forging their way through high rows of wheat. If the weather held, they would probably work all night, Ravn thought, and the chance of getting some sleep was slim. His stomach grumbled. Søllested was barely a two-horse town, but even here there ought to be a place where you could get something in your belly—hopefully, washed down with an ice-cold beer. He buried the envelope under the mattress. It was hardly an ingenious hiding place, but the risk someone would break in and search the room was close to zero.

At the other end of the main road lay the Søllested Pub. On the yard outside, people were eating their dinner at long wooden benches that were arranged under coloured fairy lights strung between pillars. A pleasant whiff of fried onions wafted over from the grill, where two teenage boys in basketball caps and identical aprons were turning sausages and hamburger patties on an iron grid. Ravn took a seat with the locals at one of the long tables and tucked into his food. When he stood up to get himself another beer, he offered to buy a round for the three other men sharing the table. When he returned with four beers shortly afterwards, they raised their glasses in a toast and fell into conversation easily.

All three men were locals. The two guys sitting opposite him had to bring in the rest of the crop after dinner. The one seated next to Ravn was a long-distance truck driver called Arne, who said he was headed to France in the morning.

"Yeah, it's pretty clear from your accent that you're not from around here," Arne said. "So what brings you to the southern isles, Thomas?"

"I'm checking out some properties," said Ravn. "But my car broke down."

"Hah, someone looking to move here," said Arne. "Usually it's the other way round. The entire community is falling apart. Young folks leave to get a higher education when they finish school, and they don't come back." He took off his John Deere cap and brushed a hand through his thin hair. "That's the way things are headed," he said with a sigh, and slapped the cap back on his head.

"I heard a couple Copenhageners bought a farm near here. But it was a few years ago . . ."

All three men looked at him and shook their heads in turn.

"Near Søllested?" said Arne. "I never heard anything about it. Where, exactly?"

"Perhaps I'm wrong," said Ravn, taking a sip of his beer. "It could've been someplace else on Lolland. They cultivate mushrooms or something. Some or other movement, I think," he added with a shrug.

"You mean those sect people?"

Ravn nodded. "Yeah. I think it was a church of some kind."

"The farm is over by Dannemare," said the bulky man sitting opposite Ravn. "It's not far from here," he added, jerking his thumb over his shoulder.

"Ah, I see. Are they still there?"

Arne nodded. "I think so, but they keep to themselves. I've seen a couple once in a while when they come to the supermarket. They're a sorry-looking bunch if you ask me."

"Sorry-looking? How so?"

"Thin as rakes, they are. Sickly bunch. If they'd been animals, someone would have put them down ages ago."

The men laughed in unison. Ravn did not join in.

"And I don't think there's much farming going on either, to be honest," said Arne.

"Nae, it takes more than faith in God to work the land; it takes hard work. Speaking of which," the big man said, looking up at the sky, "I'd better get back on it." He stood up and his pal followed suit. They waved goodbye and wished Ravn and Arne a good evening before heading back to the field.

Arne offered to buy a round and went to the bar to get more beer.

Ravn took the opportunity to survey the crowd unobtrusively. More people had arrived, and the talk around the tables was lively. The cosy atmosphere reminded him of The Sea Otter, and it struck him that every town—regardless of where it lay—always had its own watering hole where folks came to unwind after a long day.

"I overheard you guys talking," said an obviously very drunk man who was swaying on his feet in front of Ravn, a bottle of beer clutched in one hand. "About those people on 'The Farm.'"

"Oh, yeah? What have you heard?" Ravn replied with a smile.

"They're . . . they're stir-fucking-crazy, I'm telling you. I've got a sister. She went over there once for a ssshervice. It's a madhouse, I tell ya. They . . ." His legs nearly caved under him, and he rested a hand on the table to catch his balance. "They don't pray to *God* . . . you understan' what I'm sayin'?"

"Nope . . . not really, no."

The man leaned his full weight on Ravn's shoulder and looked at him as if through a haze. "They . . . talk to the Devil. Pray to Lucifer, you understand?"

Arne returned with their beers. He put them down on the table, grabbed the drunk man firmly by the collar, and pulled him off Ravn. "Bong-Ole, I think it's time you went home to bed."

"*Ja, ja,*" the man mumbled, teetering a few steps backwards and just managing to regain his balance in the process. "I'm on my way now. One for the road?"

"Go home. Now," said Arne.

"Remember what I said." Ole pointed at Ravn. "The Devil himself."

Arne took his seat next to Ravn and put the beer in front of him. "Don't worry about him. Over the last twenty years, Bong-Ole has probably stewed most of his brain cells in hash and alcohol, but he's quite harmless."

Ravn nodded. As he watched the man sway down the road, an old adage sprang to mind:

To know the truth about everything, listen to drunkards, children, idiots, and women . . . he thought, raising a toast in thanks to Bong-Ole of Søllested.

41

Ravn woke up in the uncomfortable bed whose mattress was much too soft and opened his eyes in a haze of sleep. It took him a moment before he realised that he was in the rented room on Lolland. The sun streamed through the thin curtains, and despite the early hour, the room was already hot. The drone of the combine harvesters in the field outside his window had woken him. They'd probably been at it all night. He stood up, drew the curtains, and threw open the windows in an attempt to get a little air into the room. The combine harvesters and the blue tractor were heading for the far end of the field, and it appeared as if the men were almost finished bringing in the harvest. The naked, stubbly field was bathed in warm morning sunlight.

Ravn decided to skip the breakfast part of the B&B, and ten minutes later, he was dressed and trudging over the farmyard, heading into town. He noticed that his host was standing at the window in the main house, watching him go. From Søllested, it was only a five- or six-kilometre walk to Jacob Mesmer's farm, so he reckoned he could use the time waiting for the Volvo to wrap up the delivery of the contract.

Ravn made a pit stop at the bakery, where he bought a couple of hot rolls with butter and cheese from the girl behind the counter. He ate his breakfast on the go, following the country road to Nakskov, which would lead him to Gethsemane. Before long, he was on the edge of town. The road was deserted, and the wheat fields were an undulating sea of green dappled with the shade of clouds floating overhead. It was a breathtaking view.

After walking for about forty minutes, Ravn came to a high whitewashed wall behind a row of old oak trees. The entrance was a black wrought-iron gate. On the wall next to the gate, the word **GETHSEMANE** was painted in large, curling black letters with a quote from the Book of Psalms just below:

Even though I walk through the darkest valley,
I will fear no evil, for you are with me;
your rod and your staff, they comfort me.

Ravn pressed the button on the intercom that was mounted on the wall beside the quote. There was no answer. He tried three or four times, to no avail. He looked up. Rolls of barbed wire were fixed to the top of the wall, so he decided to follow the wall, which ran in the gap between the farm and the tall rows of wheat. A little further ahead, between the high trees inside the complex, he spotted a surveillance camera. He wondered whether the wall was intended to keep strangers *out* or keep people *in?*

He decided to return to the gate and try the intercom again. Still no one answered. There was a slot for post in the gate, and he reckoned he could simply slip the envelope through the slot and be done with it. This might complete his job for Ferdinand Mesmer, but delivering the contract was not the only reason he had come all this way. He took a step back and looked up at the high gate. *You'll just have to scale it and search the grounds,* he told himself. Using the postbox slot as a foothold, he clambered up the gate.

At the top, he peered over the wall. There was nothing to see but a charming driveway flanked by oak trees that made a bend about one hundred metres ahead. He was about to pull himself over the top when he heard a partially muffled siren behind him. Ravn looked over his shoulder. *Yup, he'd been caught in the act.*

Ravn jumped down from the gate and walked towards the dusty four-wheel-drive police car that was parked on the other side of the road. The policeman sitting at the wheel was wearing sunglasses and one arm was resting on his rolled-down window. He waved Ravn over lazily.

Not sure what to expect, Ravn crossed the road and walked over to the policeman.

With the back of his hand, the stocky, sunburned police officer wiped away the sweat clinging to his broad sideburns. "You might have had an envelope clenched between your teeth moments ago, but you don't look like a postman," he drawled.

Ravn sent the officer a smile and shrugged. "The buzzer isn't working, so I thought I'd just take a peek over the gate to see if anyone was home."

"I see. And do you have any ID on you?"

Ravn patted down his pockets and took out his wallet. He handed the officer his driver's licence.

"You're a long way from home, Thomas. I can tell that from your dialect," the officer said, checking the back of his license. "What brings you to the neighbourhood?"

"I'm here to deliver this," Ravn said, waving the envelope.

"There's a postbox in the gate," the officer pointed out. "Why don't you use it?"

"This is an important document that needs to be delivered to Jacob Mesmer personally," Ravn said. "Do you know if he's here?"

The officer tipped his sunglasses and regarded Ravn over the rim. "A document? With all respect, you don't look like a government official or a lawyer, so who are you, Thomas Ravnsholdt from Copenhagen?"

"'Ravn' is just fine. That's what everyone calls me," he said with an easy smile. "I work for a lawyer in the city."

The officer returned Ravn's driver's license. "Are you a private detective?"

Ravn shrugged. "More like a . . . consultant," he said. "A freelancer."

"Freeee . . . lancer, that sounds mighty fine," said the officer.

Ravn regretted his word choice instantly. "I used to work for the police. Station City, on Halmtorvet."

The officer took off his sunglasses. "I was with the Store Kongensgade Station when I was a rookie," he said, shaking his head. "Fine folks, every one of them, but it wasn't a party."

"When was that?"

"Back in '93."

"So you were there," Ravn smiled sympathetically, "during the raids, back then."

The officer nodded and a grave expression came over his face. "Yup, got myself a little souvenir from the May 18th demonstrations." He turned his head to the side, revealing an ugly scar by his right temple. "The bricks shattered my helmet. I was hospitalised for a month."

"Close call. But at the end of the day, sounds like you were lucky," said Ravn.

The officer nodded and put his sunglasses on again. "Did you walk all the way from Copenhagen?"

"Hardly. My car is at the garage in Søllested."

"Hop in," the officer said, nodding to his passenger seat.

"I'd really like to get these papers delivered."

"Maybe you should try calling for an appointment first. It's going to rain soon."

Ravn looked up at the sky. There wasn't a cloud in sight. "Really? How can you tell?"

"Really," said the officer, pointing at the passenger seat again.

Ravn walked round to the passenger side. He knew this was classic police protocol. The officer had no intention of letting him trespass on the property, and he would have to come back later.

With the wind streaming through their rolled-down windows, Ravn and the officer drove back to Søllested.

"So, how long have you been working down here?" Ravn asked.

"Twenty years. Celebrated my anniversary last June," said the officer. "Much too long."

"So you know the area pretty well?"

The officer nodded. "We've got more people leaving than arriving, but we've got plenty to do. The rich municipalities over on Zealand treat us like a dump for social misfits—Lolland is the end of the road for people who nobody wants on their doorstep."

"What kinds of cases do you see here most?"

"Breaking and entering, drug trafficking, a lot of domestic violence, a murder once in a while." The officer smiled at Ravn. "We definitely work for our pay cheques over here. I can promise you that."

"I don't doubt that for a second," Ravn said quickly. "What about God's Chosen? Do you have anything on them?"

"God's *who?*"

"The people from the farm . . . Gethsemane," Ravn said, jerking his thumb over his shoulder.

"Ah, so that's what they call it," the officer said with a chuckle. "Those folks keep to themselves."

"Behind barbed wire and surveillance cameras?"

"Down here, folks like to be left in peace. Which is well within their rights."

"Of course," said Ravn. "But the rumours about that movement are quite disturbing."

"Rumours spread fast in a small community. Folks don't have much else to do than gossip about their neighbours."

"Well, the same rumours about them have travelled all the way over the bridges to Zealand. Have you ever been to the farm yourself?"

"I never talk about my work—not even with the wife back home."

Ravn shrugged and changed tack. "Of course. I meant in your private capacity. 'Bible meetings,' I think they call them. Singing and prayers, a little exorcism on the side . . ."

The officer laughed. "No, I can't say I have, although it sounds entertaining."

"And you've never met Jacob Mesmer either? *Privately*, I mean."

"You're quite the chatterbox, aren't you? A real Copenhagener . . ."

"Actually, I'm from Christianshavn, but yeah, folks from the Copenhagen canals can talk too. So what's this guy Mesmer like?"

The officer slowed down and stopped at the intersection with the main road. "Where did you say your car is parked?" he asked.

"At the garage on the other side of town," said Ravn. "But I doubt it will be ready yet. Do you think you could give me a lift to the B&B instead? It's right over—"

"I know where it is," the officer said, taking a left onto the main road.

A few minutes later, they pulled over to the side of the road in front of the B&B. "I hope you manage to deliver your envelope—in a proper fashion, got it?"

Ravn nodded. "Of course. I'll get an appointment before I go over there again. Thanks for the lift," Ravn said, opening the passenger door.

"They're quiet folks. God-fearing people. When they moved to our neighbourhood, they tried to recruit every man and his dog for their church. But they had about as much success with that as they did with their mushroom farming. So now they keep to themselves. Don't cause any trouble. That's what a provincial officer like myself appreciates most," he said, pointing a thumb at himself.

"Do you know if Jacob Mesmer is on the farm? It's really important that I deliver the envelope to him personally."

"I haven't seen him in a long time. But there's a good chance he's there. Why don't you ask your host?"

"Does he know Jacob Mesmer?" Ravn said in surprise.

"Yes. Ejner is the only one in town who they managed to recruit. It probably wasn't too hard though; Ejner has always had a particular interest in Heaven. First, it was Jehovah's Witnesses, then Inner Mission, and now God's Chosen . . ."

"So you knew what they were called?" Ravn said with a wink.

"I know everyone around here, Ravn. And they know me. You have a good day, now."

42

The moment Ravn crossed the farmyard, his mobile phone vibrated in his pocket. Victoria had written him a message. In all caps: "WHEN WILL YOU BE BACK??? I NEED WILMA NOW!!"

"Soon as I can. I'm sorry," Ravn replied.

He hoped the mechanic would have the Volvo repaired the same day so he could give it back to Victoria by nightfall, and he reminded himself *never* to borrow Wilma again. He saw that Ejner was on his lawn behind the fence around the main house, so instead of heading for the annex, Ravn took the path along the hedge instead. Ejner was feeding the seven or eight rabbits that were hopping about on the lawn in front of their wooden stalls. Ravn walked up to the low wire fence and put his hands in his pockets casually. "Nice rabbits. What breed are they?"

"Do you know anything about rabbits?"

"Not the slightest thing."

"Chaudry rabbits," said Ejner, without looking up at Ravn.

"They look . . . sweet."

"They don't cause any trouble," Ejner said with a shrug. "And there's nothing wrong with their meat."

"You eat them?"

Ejner looked at him as if he were an idiot. "Of course. Why else would I breed them?"

Ravn felt a surge of dislike for this shabby man with his stained trousers, but he tried to check his feelings and smiled at Ejner instead. "Good point. Your local police officer gave me a lift home."

"Yes. I saw you guys arrive."

"I went to visit Gethsemane."

Ejner stopped sprinkling rabbit food on the lawn and looked up at him with interest.

"He said you know the place well."

"Who did?"

"The police officer."

"Oh, him," Ejner said, casting his eyes down.

"Who did you think I meant?"

Ejner didn't reply and kept his eyes trained on the rabbits, which had gathered round his feet.

"He said you know Jacob Mesmer. Is that right?"

"Why do you ask?"

"Because I'm here to see Jacob."

"Many people come here for that reason. Did you see him?"

"Nobody answered when I rang the buzzer at the gate."

"In that case, you probably weren't welcome," Ejner scoffed. "Not everyone is—even though Gethsemane is supposed to be a house of God . . ."

Ravn stepped over the fence and walked over to Ejner. The rabbits immediately hopped into the safety of their stall. "I need to talk to Jacob Mesmer. When did you last see him?"

"A long time ago. What do you want with the Master?"

"I . . . want to listen to him, hear the Master's message. I was a member of the church on Belgiensgade."

"Before the fire?"

"Yes. With Benjamin and Lisa and the others."

"I never made it over there myself, so I don't know them. But I've heard about the church on Belgiensgade on Amager."

"It was a blessed place," Ravn said in what he hoped was a sufficiently pious tone.

Ejner wiped his mouth with the back of his hand. "There's a Bible meeting the day after tomorrow."

"At Gethsemane?"

"Yes."

"And Jacob . . . the Master will be there?"

Ejner frowned. "Yes, of course. Who else would initiate the exorcism rituals?"

"Yes, who else. Do you have a number?"

"A number? What for?"

"A telephone number . . . the Master's number . . ."

Ejner blinked rapidly. From experience, Ravn knew that this usually meant a person's brain was busy concocting a lie. "I . . . no, I don't have his number . . . I'm not even sure he has a telephone."

"Okay, thanks, Ejner," Ravn said, clapping him on the shoulder. Then he turned round and stepped over the wire fence again.

"But if they . . . know you from Belgiensgade . . . why didn't they let you in today?"

Ravn shrugged and cast a glance over his shoulder at Ejner. "Maybe they weren't up yet," he said with a crooked smile.

From his window, Ravn watched Ejner on the lawn with the rabbits. He was talking into his mobile phone, gesticulating with his entire body. Ravn did not know who Ejner was talking to, but he had a pretty good guess what the conversation was about—and it definitely wasn't about rabbits. He took his phone out of his pocket and rang the garage to find out when he could pick up the Volvo.

"This afternoon," the mechanic promised.

43

It was already quarter past two when Ravn drove along the same country road he had walked early that morning. It hadn't been possible to get a new radiator from Nakskov, so the mechanic had fixed the old one, a fine job that was only noticeable if you looked closely. With a little luck, he needn't tell Victoria about his little mishap, he thought. And the bill for the repairs was far below what he might have paid for the same job in Copenhagen. If only he could get hold of Jacob Mesmer, it could still be possible to get home to Christianshavn before midnight and enjoy a well-deserved beer at The Sea Otter.

He slowed down as he approached Gethsemane and could see the long white wall in the distance. Soon after, he turned down a narrow dirt road on his right, following the uneven path through the high wheat. The suspension creaked on the bumpy road, and he slowed down even more. Four or five hundred metres further ahead, he stopped the car and got out. It was quiet, apart from the faint hum of a combine harvester in the distance. Not even the birds were singing. Clouds had gathered above, and the air stood still, as if the landscape itself were waiting for a thunderstorm that was on its way. Ravn stepped into the fields and waded through the wheat stalks that reached up to his waist. He could see the white wall around Gethsemane about three or four hundred metres ahead of him.

Ravn continued through the wheat field, approaching the rear perimeter of the farm. Ploughing his way through the soft terrain in his

Converse trainers wasn't easy, but he was certain that no one was going to let him through the front gate. Especially after Ejner had warned them about him. Nor was he inclined to meet the local copper again, even though—

A pheasant took flight right beside him, and Ravn got such a fright he nearly fell over his own feet. He cursed the bird to hell and took a swing to his left, giving the wall a wide berth so he wouldn't be caught on the surveillance cameras he'd spotted earlier. He noticed that the white brick wall tapered down into an old bastion of stone. Ravn emerged from the wheat and walked along the low stone wall. The acrid smell of urine and horseshit on the large manure heaps fortifying Gethsemane stung his nostrils. He stepped up onto the stone and jumped down on the other side, landing on the edge of the nearest heap. One foot disappeared into the stinking hay and mud, and he made two or three awkward hops to the side to get clear of the shit in a hurry. Once he'd reached relatively dry land, he brushed off his trousers and stamped most of the muck off his shoes. After literally stepping ankle-deep into the shit, he regretted not trying to scale the front gate after all.

The clouds rumbled above, and he continued along the man-high compost heaps. When he came round the last heap, the heavens opened, and the rain pelted down. Ravn flipped up the hood of his jacket and continued over the yard. A few metres ahead stood a little boy, staring at Ravn. His face was filthy, and he had dark rings under his eyes. He was barefoot, thin as a rake, his dirty blue overalls clung to his pointy shoulders. Ravn was about to say something to the boy, but he turned on his heel and dashed through the mud to the barracks at the end of the yard.

Ravn looked around, all at once aware of a sweet and nauseating smell that drowned out the stench of horseshit. He recognised the smell from his days on the force—when someone called the police, complaining about the strong smell coming from a neighbour whom they hadn't seen in a long time. It was the unmistakable smell of death.

44

Ravn continued over the muddy farmyard to the barracks that the boy had disappeared into. Halfway over the courtyard, he noticed a group of men repairing the roof of a garage building nearby. All the men were dressed in identical blue overalls, and their heads were shaved. The emaciated men took no notice of him as he came past, their eyes fixed on their work, and even though the rain was hammering on the tin roof, Ravn could hear them chanting: *The Lord is my shepherd . . . I shall not want . . . the Lord is my shepherd . . . I shall not want . . .*

As he passed the men, he caught sight of an old horn loudspeaker that was fixed to a high pole close to the garage. Looking around, he realised that similar loudspeakers were mounted by the barracks as well as along the gravel path that led towards a large production hall. Some of the poles also supported surveillance cameras, and Ravn thought that if someone was watching, they would have spotted him long ago. He headed for the main door of the first barracks. The windows were shuttered, and he couldn't see anyone inside. He knocked on the door and tried the handle, but it was locked. Behind him, two women ran over the yard. They too were dressed in worn blue overalls, their hair was cropped short under identical blue scarves, and they merely cast a glance in his direction as they headed for the large hall.

Ravn tried the door handle of the next barracks, but this was locked as well. A crackling sound came over the nearest loudspeaker, followed by the first few notes of an out-of-tune organ. "Brothers and sisters, the time has come for your salvation . . . your happiness on earth and in Heaven, blesséd is the Lord . . . Blesséd is His word, His Son, and the Holy Spirit. Serve the Lord and He will have mercy on your sins . . . and even though you walk through the valley of death, fear no evil, for the Lord is with you, His rod and His staff are your comfort. Remember these wise words . . . *The Lord is my shepherd . . . I shall not want . . . the Lord is my shepherd . . . I shall not want . . .*"

The preaching voice followed Ravn as he made his way up the steep path to the production hall. As he came closer, he could see that the hall was enormous, with a beautiful whitewash main building that graced the top of the hill. Just inside the open gates to the hall, numerous people in the same uniform were carting wheelbarrows back and forth, and again, nobody looked up at Ravn, as if everyone were steadfastly ignoring him on purpose, chanting the same phrase that sounded repeatedly from the loudspeakers.

After Ravn had stood watching them from the gate for a moment, he went into the production hall. Here too there was a strong smell of ammonia, and he covered his mouth and nose with the sleeve of his jacket so he could breathe. Armed with spades and rakes, one team of workers received and spread out the compost that was delivered to them by the men and women handling the wheelbarrows. Another team of workers with primitive aluminium tanks fastened to their backs sprayed the rows of compost with ammonia. At the far end of the hall, a third team of workers were sprinkling brilliant white chalk over the dark compost. *"The Lord is my shepherd . . . I shall not want . . . the Lord is my shepherd . . . I shall not want . . ."* the voice chanted in a monotone from the loudspeaker.

Ravn was shocked by the wretched living conditions at Gethsemane. To his mind, calling it a "reform" or "rehabilitation" camp was a huge understatement. Even though the farm was secluded, he was surprised that no one had uncovered this place, and that the authorities had not intervened. The place should have been closed long ago, and the people responsible—Jacob Mesmer in particular—held accountable. Ravn feared that what he had seen so far was merely the tip of the iceberg of the horrors that took place in Gethsemane.

"Hey! What are you doing here?!" a voice rang out through the hall.

Ravn started in surprise and stared at the small man who was heading directly towards him. Apart from the blue uniform, the man was wearing a red armband on his right arm and a pair of high black wellington boots, which made him look like a proprietor from bygone times. "Who are you? Who let you in?" The man glared at Ravn, waving the hardboard he had in his left hand. Despite his skeletal state, Ravn recognised him from the passport photo he had seen in his storeroom in the cellar on Lysefjordsgade.

"Benjamin? Benjamin Clausen?"

The man blinked rapidly, and his lower jaw dropped in an ugly grimace. "Yes . . . and? Who are you?"

Ravn presented himself and put out his hand.

Benjamin did not take it. "What do you want?"

"To find out if you're alive."

45

Benjamin looked at Ravn intensely, not moving a muscle for a moment. Then he brought a hand to his runny nose and wiped it dry. "Do we know each other?"

"No, we've never met," said Ravn.

"But . . . you said you have come to see . . . if I am alive?"

"Yes, because I've read about you."

"Me? I doubt that . . . Where?"

"Think, Benjamin," Ravn said.

Benjamin shook his head and looked around anxiously. "I don't know what you are talking about or who you are, but I'm asking you to leave. You are trespassing on private property. Come with me." He put a hand on Ravn's arm and tried to pull him away.

Ravn looked at the dirty hand on his sleeve and remained standing where he was. "I've read your report, Benjamin."

Benjamin snatched his hand back. "What . . . what report?"

"I doubt you've written so many reports of the kind that you don't know which one I mean."

Benjamin's cheeks flushed. "You . . . you need to leave. Right now."

"You seem nervous, Benjamin." Ravn looked around briefly. "I thought everyone around here already knows that you have worked for Ferdinand Mesmer . . . that you have reported their activities, including those of your Master, Jacob Mesmer . . ."

"What do you want?" Benjamin snarled.

"As I said before: to find out if you were alive. You disappeared without a trace. Even Ferdinand Mesmer was worried about you."

"Worried . . ." Benjamin scoffed. "That man is the Devil himself. I regret every single day that I had anything to do with him."

"Well, he's not exactly my cup of tea either."

"And yet, you are working for him . . . right? You are here at his request . . . you are a disciple of the Devil."

"Tone down the rhetoric for a moment, will you?" Ravn snapped back. "I am not here only on account of Ferdinand Mesmer—"

"Great. But if, as you say, you are concerned for my well-being," he said, casting his eyes down, "you can go now because, as you can see, I'm perfectly fine. Now would you be so kind as to leave the premises?"

"No. Not before I have spoken to Jacob Mesmer. Is that him preaching over the loudspeakers?" Ravn said, pointing to the closest one and shaking his head in disgust. "Personally, I prefer listening to the radio when I'm working, golden oldies . . ."

Benjamin turned to the first two workers and whistled. The men threw down their spades and ran over to Benjamin. He nodded towards Ravn and the men grabbed his arms.

"What the devil are you doing?" Ravn burst out.

"You can call for your master all you like, but you are leaving. Right now," said Benjamin.

Ravn let the two men haul him out of the hall and down the path towards the barracks. Benjamin followed on their heels.

"Benjamin, give it up, I've come to speak with Jacob Mesmer and I'm not leaving till I do."

"The Master does not want to be disturbed. His work is too important to bear interruption."

"I mean it," said Ravn firmly.

"So do I," said Benjamin. "The Master has much work to do. Devotes all his time to us, world peace, and the coming of God. The great Rebirth."

Ravn tried to wrench himself free. "I have a contract for him."

"From Ferdinand Mesmer?"

"Yes, so let me go." The two men tightened their grip on him.

"I won't let anything from that Satan fall on the Master's ears. Just like everyone else outside these walls, he has tried to sow evil amongst us, destroy everything we have tried to build over the years."

"Take a look around you, Benjamin. Look at how you live."

"I don't expect that someone like you would understand what it means to sacrifice yourself for the greater good. To understand what it means to live an ascetic life."

"*Ascetic?* This is not ascetic, Benjamin, this place is a crime. And it ought to be reported. There are children starving here because of your stupidity . . ."

Benjamin stared at Ravn. "You break in here, by order of a man who is the epitome of evil, and within two minutes of your trespassing, you think you can judge our church . . . I feel sorry for you . . . You are a small-minded human being . . ."

"Just let me bring Jacob this letter from his father. No more than that."

Benjamin laughed. "Are you so naïve?" He crossed himself. "I hope that you find a different path than the one Ferdinand Mesmer has laid out for you . . . Otherwise, you are truly forsaken."

Ravn was unceremoniously marched past the compost heaps and the garage buildings where the small group of men were still working furiously. When they reached the gate facing the forest, Benjamin took a key out of his pocket and opened it. The two men shoved Ravn out through the gate and Benjamin locked it hastily behind him.

"I bring greetings for you as well," said Ravn, meeting Benjamin's gaze.

"Ferdinand Mesmer can keep his greetings."

"They are not from Mesmer. From Lisa . . ."

Benjamin tried to seem unperturbed, but his hands were shaking as he put the bunch of keys back in his pocket. "When did you see her?"

"A few days ago."

"I see. How . . . how is she?"

"No better than the day you poured caustic soda down her throat."

Benjamin stared at Ravn in horror. His bottom lip trembled.

"I . . . I never did that."

"Well, somebody did, and if it wasn't you, it must have been Jacob. She didn't look so pretty after that little ritual he performed on her . . ."

"Get out! Leave!" Benjamin screamed at him. Then he spun on his heel and ran back up the hill.

Ravn watched him go. Then he fixed his attention on the surveillance camera that was mounted on the pole just inside the gate. He extracted the envelope from his belt and waved it at the camera.

If that didn't coax Jacob Mesmer out of his hiding place, he didn't know what it was going to take.

46

Ravn had been sitting at the window of his room for hours. He reckoned that if Jacob Mesmer or anyone from God's Chosen wished to contact him, they would do so through their faithful disciple Ejner. His white rabbits were hopping about on the lawn, and even though his car was parked in the yard, there was no sign of the man himself.

Ravn could not get the sight of the scrawny boy from the farm out of his mind, and regardless of how things played out or whether he was able to find Jacob at all, he was determined to report the appalling living conditions at Gethsemane to social services.

His mobile phone rang, and his guilty conscience immediately brought him to the present. By now, Victoria would be beside herself with worry over her beloved Wilma, but the caller on the display was anonymous. "Ravn," he said expectantly, but it was not the Mesmer he was hoping to hear from.

"What results can you report?" the old man barked into the receiver without preamble.

"Depends on how you define 'results,'" Ravn said.

"I would think that was obvious. Have you found my son and delivered the contract to him for his signature?"

"Yes—or rather, maybe to the first and no to the second."

"What's the hold-up?"

"I was thrown out—by Benjamin Clausen, incidentally—before I was able to meet your son in person."

"Well, at least you found Benjamin. How is he?"

"Stark raving mad—or fanatical if you like—but despite his miserable state, he appears to have embraced his role as the whip-lasher of Gethsemane."

"I'm not sure I understand."

"Yes, not surprisingly. You have to see this place with your own eyes to believe it," Ravn said. "The farm is surrounded by high walls and surveillance cameras that keep your son's disciples locked in. It looks like a bloody concentration camp—and there are children involved!"

"That sounds awful," Mesmer said in a flat tone.

"It's appalling, a crime," said Ravn. "I'm going to report the situation to social services myself, and—"

"Let's not get ahead of ourselves," said Mesmer evenly. "Did Benjamin say anything about my son?"

"No, he was more interested in painting a live portrait of *you* as the Great Satan."

"Can you confirm that Jacob is on the farm?"

"I heard his voice over loudspeakers installed about the place, but—"

"Loudspeakers?"

Through the window, Ravn spotted Ejner coming out onto the lawn. The rabbits hopped over to him, and he crouched down on his haunches and began feeding them carrots.

"Ravn, are you still there?" Mesmer said impatiently.

"Yes . . . they've mounted loudspeakers on poles at various points on the yard so everyone can hear his sermons while they work, which does indeed seem to motivate them, so it appears your son hasn't lost his studied leadership skills . . ."

"Ravn, it is essential that Jacob receives the contract immediately, and that you return it to me with his signature as soon as possible."

"I'm doing what I can, but your son might not actually be at the farm."

"What do you mean?"

"Jacob is not reporting the daily news. His voice could be a recording made ages ago."

"So find out if he's there or not—that's what I'm paying you for! The board members of SIALA are losing their patience. The deal is in jeopardy," Mesmer added with a tremor in his voice.

"I'm on it," Ravn said calmly. "But even if I do find him, what makes you so sure that Jacob will sign the contract?"

"Just give it to him. Quickly. The rest will fall into place, believe me."

Ravn sat in the dilapidated armchair with his mobile phone in his hand. Mesmer senior sounded desperate. But only with respect to closing his deal with SIALA. That bastard couldn't give a shit about anything else, including whatever atrocities were committed against innocent people at Gethsemane.

On the lawn before the main house, Ejner pushed himself to his feet with one of the rabbits in his arms. He stroked its ears a few times. Then one hand closed around the animal's neck while the other gripped its hind legs and yanked down hard a couple of times till the neck broke. Dangling the dead rabbit by its ears, Ejner stepped over the low fence and hurried over the yard.

If the rabbit killer didn't bring him a message from Jacob soon, he would make another attempt to get over the fence of Gethsemane early the next morning, Ravn thought, watching Ejner with renewed disgust. And this time, he'd make straight for the main building where the Master of God's Chosen would probably be hiding. Benjamin seemed flummoxed and upset when he had mentioned Lisa. Perhaps he had nothing to do with her disfigurement? But he probably knew how it happened. In that case, he was sure he could get the truth out of him. And, if necessary, persuade Benjamin to testify against whoever was responsible.

Ravn could feel his old hunting instinct returning to his bones—followed by an aching hunger and, not least, a thirst for a pint of the local beer that he'd had the pleasure of tasting the night before. But he wouldn't leave his room tonight. He would sit here at the window and wait, keeping a watchful eye on the rabbit killer until he got a sign from Jacob.

47

Ravn started in his chair by the window as a car door slammed out in the yard. The blue evening sky had been replaced by darkness, so he must have been dozing for a long time. He stood up and cupped his hands against the pane, peering into the dark outside. At first, he'd assumed that Ejner was leaving the yard, but now he could make out three tall figures milling about Victoria's Volvo. One of them opened the boot and climbed inside. He was damned if he was going to let some thief pinch Victoria's prize possession! Ravn thought as he rushed outside onto the yard.

"Is there something I can help you with?" Ravn said amiably, striding up to the closest figure in the yard.

"Is this your car?"

The man was a head taller than he was. Crew cut, khaki camouflage trousers, and a dark T-shirt that strained over his muscular chest and biceps. *This could be trouble*, Ravn thought. "Well, it certainly isn't *yours*," he said. "And would you kindly ask your pal to get out, right now?" Ravn held the man's gaze and merely jerked his thumb at Wilma's boot.

"Where is it?" asked the muscular man in front of him.

"Where is *what*?" said Ravn.

A sinister smile appeared on the man's face, and Ravn tensed his muscles instinctively, ready for whatever might come next.

"The envelope you had in your hand earlier today," the muscle-man said. "At the farm. I want you to give it me. *Now.* Is it in the car, or do you have to fetch it inside?"

"Did Jacob Mesmer send you guys?" Ravn asked the muscleman, who appeared to be the guy in charge of this little operation.

"There's nothing in the car," the muscleman's sidekick said as he scrambled out of the Volvo. The moment the first sidekick posted himself on Ravn's left, his mate appeared on Ravn's right. Out of the corner of his eye, Ravn sized them up. Similar to their leader, the two sidekicks were muscular men with crew cuts and identical camouflage clothing. Ravn decided he'd go for the leader first. He was fairly sure he could floor the guy, but whatever happened after that probably wouldn't go in his favour. Then again, it was not the first time he'd been outnumbered in a fight.

"Is it inside?"

Ravn didn't blink. "I asked you if your master sent you."

"All you got to do is fetch the envelope and give it to me."

"That's not going to happen. I've been asked to deliver it to Jacob Mesmer only. You can tell him that from me."

The leader nodded at one of his sidekicks, who immediately set off across the yard and went into the annex.

"Is Jacob at Gethsemane?"

None of the musclemen replied.

"I would really like to meet with him so we can put an end to this matter."

Still, the two men remained silent, glaring at Ravn. Soon after, their pal returned. Empty-handed.

"It's not there, Patrick."

"Why don't you just give us the envelope?" the guy called Patrick said, and immediately lunged at Ravn's stomach.

Ravn saw the punch coming a mile off, feinted, and head-butted Patrick soundly on the bridge of his nose. Patrick hit the ground hard, and his two sidekicks shoved Ravn against the Volvo. He fought them off but eventually caved and fell to the ground, where their boots took over the beating until he heard a voice yelling at them to stop.

Patrick sat down on his haunches.

A bloody nose and jaw appeared before Ravn's face. "I'm only going to ask you this one more time: Where is the envelope?"

"You . . . can ask me as many times as you like . . ." Ravn said through gritted teeth. "But . . . I will only deliver the envelope to Jacob Mesmer in person . . ."

Patrick spat a glob of blood and snot onto the cobblestones and stood up unsteadily.

Ravn looked up. The sidekicks towered over him, fists clenched and ready for another round. Just a few metres behind them, Patrick was talking into his phone. After a few seconds, he came over. "Nine o'clock tomorrow morning at Gethsemane. And make sure you bring the envelope with you," he said, glaring at Ravn. Moments later, the three men retreated over the yard, got back into their pickup truck, and sped away.

Leaning on the mudguard of the Volvo, Ravn pulled himself up to his feet. He'd taken quite a beating, but nothing seemed to be broken. It was nothing a few ibuprofen and a line of shots couldn't cure. Unfortunately, neither were within reach. And he still had Mesmer's unsigned contract floating in the cistern of the annex communal toilet, tightly sealed in a Netto supermarket plastic bag.

When he finally met Jacob tomorrow, it would feel like a victory. But right now, he felt sore, grumpy, and woefully underpaid.

48

Søllested's main road seemed to loll in the heat as Ravn drove through town the next morning. When he drove past the petrol station at the supermarket, he spotted the local policeman filling the tank of his four-wheel drive. Ravn slowed down and waved out the window. It took a moment for the policeman to recognise him and return the greeting. He considered making a pit stop and informing the local police about the living conditions on the farm but thought it might just complicate matters. Besides, Jacob probably wouldn't talk if he pitched up with the police in tow, so he picked up speed again till he came to the crossroads and took a left to Gethsemane.

The manila envelope containing the contract rested on the passenger seat. No doubt Ferdinand Mesmer would offer his son a handsome price to give up his share of the business, but that aspect of the case was of no interest to Ravn.

Ten minutes later, Ravn pulled up in front of the gate to Gethsemane. He was about to get out and ring the buzzer, but the gate opened automatically. As he approached the buildings, he saw two of the men who had paid him a visit the night before. Patrick had a splint on his nose that was held in place by plasters across both cheeks. He glared at Ravn, who gave him a mock salute with two fingers to his brow before turning up the narrow gravel path to the main building.

A group of people were waiting for him on the broad stairs before the entrance, several of them soldiers in camouflage clothing. But he noticed a man and two women dressed in identical grey uniforms with a collar, which lent them a secular appearance. Ravn parked next to two black Audis. The moment he climbed out of the Volvo, the gathering on the stairs set in motion and came down to meet him. Unfortunately, Jacob was not a member of the welcoming committee.

The man in the grey uniform smiled and extended his hand to Ravn. "Samuel," he said in greeting and fixed his penetrating eyes on Ravn, who introduced himself in kind. The two middle-aged women presented themselves as Åse and Birgitte, respectively. In the unflattering grey uniform, which was two sizes too small, Åse looked like an inflated toad, and Birgitte was an almost comical portrait of Åse's exact opposite with long limbs and a horse-like face. Ravn remembered the names of these Elders from Benjamin's report.

"Welcome to Gethsemane," said Samuel, taking the lead.

"Thank you."

"If you would be so kind as to follow us."

Ravn did as he was asked, and a handful of the crew cuts brought up the rear. Samuel led them past the main entrance and around to the back of the house. Ravn looked up at the pompous building, which was a stark contrast to the menial barracks he'd seen the day before. "Your headquarters are impressive," he said to Samuel.

The dignified-looking man nodded. "Thank you," he said. "We are very grateful for what the Lord has bestowed upon us."

"It couldn't have been cheap."

"Is that for the Master?" Åse intervened, pointing at the manila envelope in Ravn's hand.

"Yep."

"Shall I give it to him?" she said, extending her hand.

"Thanks, Åse, that's very kind," Ravn said, "but I'll hang on to it a little longer. Where is Jacob?"

"This way," said Samuel, leading their procession further down the gravel path, and Ravn caught a glimpse of the large production hall at the end. He wondered whether the soldiers would lead him all the way down to the compost heaps and steal the envelope from him. But the next moment, Samuel turned off the path and headed for a white low-slung building surrounded by trees and a beautifully mowed lawn. The front door was wide open, and Ravn could see several rows of empty chairs. Inside, the cool room smelt of fresh paint. There was a low stage in front of the chairs and two microphone stands. A large wooden cross painted black hung on the end wall. Two men in blue threadbare overalls were dusting off the chairs with a cloth. Samuel clapped his hands briskly, and they immediately stopped, hurried over to the rear entrance, and disappeared out the door. "If you would wait here, the Master will receive you," Samuel said at last, turning to Ravn.

"We're not wasting each other's time here, are we, Samuel?" Ravn said, taking a step closer. Out of the corner of his eye, he noticed their escort on guard.

"I . . . I'm not sure I understand."

"I will be extremely . . . disappointed if you're playing me for the fool, and Jacob is not here . . ."

"I can assure you that the Master is here. And that he will soon welcome you to Gethsemane in person."

"If that is the case, why am I standing here talking to you and not Jacob? He is the one who determined that we should meet at nine o'clock. It's quarter past nine now . . ."

"The Master is preparing his sermon for the Bible meeting this evening," Åse said. "It's an important occasion with many outside guests. You are also welcome to join."

"Thank you, Åse, but the sooner I meet with Jacob, the sooner I can be on my way again."

"As soon as the Master has completed his sermon, he will receive you. Why don't you take a seat while you wait?" Åse said, pointing to the nearest chair.

"Thank you, but I'd prefer to stand."

"Bless you," said Samuel. Then he turned and made for the door.

Åse and Birgitte nodded in parting and followed on Samuel's heels with their escort bringing up the rear once more, leaving Ravn alone in the room.

* * *

It seemed that the cultivation of mushrooms—or whatever it was God's Chosen did to earn their money—must be going well if they were able to fund an establishment of this size. On the other hand, it was easy to make a profit if you treated your employees like slaves without pay. Ravn wondered how many people were being held at Gethsemane. If you included the men, women, and children he had seen around the barracks and the production hall yesterday, he reckoned it could be about forty to fifty people. Plus the grey-uniformed Elders; there must be more than the three who were part of the welcoming committee. And the posse of crew cuts in camouflage clothing. The latter seemed to function as Jacob Mesmer's private army, his own kind of Swiss Guard, as if he were the pope. Ravn had noticed that many of Jacob's soldiers had the coat of arms of the Royal Danish Lifeguards tattooed on their arms. And he remembered from Benjamin's report that Patrick was a veteran who had attempted suicide but found refuge in God's Chosen instead. These soldiers were dangerous, men who had pledged their loyalty to the cause. They were the members of the congregation who were called to take up arms when war was declared.

After he had been made to wait for more than an hour without any sign of the Master, Ravn knew what the game plan was: The waiting was designed to wear him down. A method not unlike the one he and Mikkel had used when they interrogated suspects. Every interrogator knows that it's the waiting time in the cell—not the questions in the interrogation room—that subdues a suspect. It saps their energy, making them passive and willing to talk, even the aggressive types. It helps to give the interrogator the edge, the initiative, and the power *before* the actual interrogation begins.

So Ravn resisted the temptation to ask the guards for news of Jacob's arrival. If waiting was the Master's strategy, it revealed something important: Jacob wasn't only interested in the contents of the envelope; he wanted to pump Ravn for information and get as much use out of him as possible.

A chair scraped near the entrance and a man in a blue uniform entered the room. It was Benjamin. Before Ravn could react, the emaciated detective pulled him aside into the shadows. "The others were right. You have returned!" he hissed into Ravn's face.

Ravn snatched his arm back. "Take a step back, Benjamin, or you'll regret it!"

Benjamin shook his head. "You should never have come back!"

"I had to. You didn't let me see Jacob yesterday."

"No, *you* don't understand what evil you've let loose upon our heads, Ravn."

49

Benjamin seemed even more forlorn than when they'd met the day before. His hollow cheeks called to mind a prisoner in a concentration camp. And when Benjamin spoke, Ravn noticed that several teeth were missing in his upper jaw. "Let me deliver the envelope, at least," Benjamin pleaded, pointing a filthy index finger at Ravn's hand.

"No, Benjamin. As I told you yesterday: I have to deliver it personally."

"Because Ferdinand Mesmer demands it?"

"No, because I gave Ferdinand Mesmer my word; that's all," Ravn said firmly. But the sight of Benjamin's dirty blue uniform made him feel sorry for his colleague. "What have they done to you, Benjamin? You look like hell."

"At least I'm not forlorn—like you are."

"Really? How so?"

"You . . . you don't understand our rules. Knowing the truth demands a willingness to sacrifice . . ."

"I understand what I see, Benjamin: You and the others in blue are kept like slaves, while the folks in grey live a privileged life in the castle on the hill."

"I don't envy anyone. The mark of Cain is not mine. But I don't expect an outsider to understand our ways."

"So, you're saying that you're doing all this of your own free will?"

"Of course!" Benjamin said, and smiled at Ravn. "Everything we do is done in gratitude for the Master's praise of the Lord."

"Hallelujah," said Ravn. "If that is so, why is the farm surrounded by a high wall and barbed wire? Why are guards patrolling the grounds?"

"The soldiers are here for our protection. They guard against all the evil coming from the outside that would wash over us. They shield us from Satan and everything else we have fled from. The guards are on par with all other members of our congregation."

"Really?"

"Yes. Many of them have returned from horrible wars. They have scars on their souls, but the Master has taken them in . . . shown them the light and the road to God."

"A moving story, Benjamin, but I don't buy it. What about the children?"

". . . *Let the children come to me, said Jesus* . . . they are simply following their parents . . ."

"No, Benjamin. The children are abused. I've seen it myself."

"What you have seen is people in need. Believe me, they were much worse off *before* they knocked on our door. At Gethsemane, we take in everyone—the people who have been rejected from society—men, women, and children who no one wants to touch. *We* are the ones who gather up the rubbish that society throws away . . ."

"But you hold them captive like slaves."

Benjamin shook his head. "You don't understand. It's all part of the cleansing process, the extermination of evil. It's entirely natural. We all have to go through it."

"You mean like what happened to Lisa?"

Benjamin leaned on the back of the nearest chair. "If . . . if I tell you what happened to Lisa, will you leave?"

"No. I'll find out what happened one way or another. And if you have anything to do with it, I'm coming for you, do you understand?"

"You . . . you talk like a policeman. You . . . did serve on the force?" Benjamin said with a note of respect.

"Yes. I took my turn."

"I applied once . . . many years ago. But . . ." Benjamin looked away, and his eyes drifted to some unidentifiable object in the middle distance.

"What happened to Lisa, Benjamin?"

"Okay . . . I'll tell you," Benjamin said, swallowing hard. "We were living at Belgiensgade . . . with other members of the congregation, and—"

"I've read as much in your report. You described how you dragged her into the cellar and began performing your ritual on her," Ravn said, deliberately harsh.

"No, noo . . . it wasn't like that at all," Benjamin said with desperation in his voice. "Lisa was possessed, and we tried to help her—free her from the grip of evil . . ."

"And Jacob took the lead, am I right? He was the one who decided she was possessed?"

"Possession is not something you can *decide*, but yes, the Master is the one with the clearest vision. He can see the demon before anyone else."

"Did you feed her the caustic soda in the cellar? Is that how you intended to *cleanse* her?"

"No, no, not at all. Nobody laid a hand on her. I swear on—"

"But you did tie Lisa down, Benjamin. That's what you wrote in your report."

"Yes, but only because we had to . . . so that the demon wouldn't make her hurt herself. The demon was going to kill her, but the Master saved her life. He drove it away . . ."

"Are you saying that Lisa became well after that night?"

"Yes," Benjamin said with a nod. "We were all so happy and praised the Lord for His power over evil. But—"

"But what?"

"Even if we didn't know it ourselves at the time, we were arrogant and vain. We did not wish to take the Lord's gift for granted. But a few days later, when we were gathered in the garden, Lisa suddenly became unwell. I thought it was because of the heat, so I told her to go inside and lie down in the lounge, where it is cool," Benjamin said, staring into the distance again. "She gave me a hug before she left and whispered something I did not understand in my ear—she was talking in tongues, and soon after, it was clear that it was the demon talking . . ."

"I see. So who decided to give the demon caustic soda?"

Benjamin seemed oblivious to the irony in Ravn's tone and smiled at him. "So you *do* understand? It was Lisa. She took it herself. So that she would be free . . . She knew that the demon would never relent . . . that it would always live inside of her."

"So, no one helped her take the caustic soda?"

Benjamin shook his head. "She was so brave. She found it in the kitchen cupboard while we were outside. She drank it. But she was screaming in pain. And when we came into the kitchen, she was lying on the floor while the soda burnt away her skin. Even though she was in excruciating pain, we could all see the gratitude shining in her eyes. She was free."

"No, Benjamin. She was admitted to a psychiatric hospital," Ravn said, and swallowed the lump in his throat.

"Only her body was there, Ravn. Her soul is with the Lord."

"Benjamin, you are ill. You need help," Ravn said.

"You need to go now. I have told you everything I know."

"I'm not leaving until I have met with Jacob. Why are you so afraid for me to meet him?"

"I'm not afraid," Benjamin said, blinking his eyes rapidly.

"What has he done to you? What happened after Lisa drank the caustic soda?"

"Despite all my failings, the Master took mercy on me."

"By treating you like a slave?"

"How many times do I have to say it: We are *not* slaves."

"You showed Jacob your report. How did he react?"

Benjamin's gaze dropped to the floor.

"Did Jacob ever ask about his father?"

"He doesn't want anything to do with that Satan. Nor with you!" Benjamin looked up triumphantly.

"You don't think he wants to meet with me?"

"Well, you're in good shape." Benjamin smiled at him mockingly. "So you'll probably get to meet him eventually. But try not to provoke his anger."

"He has a temper?"

"Let's just say a righteous anger against sinners."

"Who set fire to the church on Belgiensgade?"

"No one. The fire was a divine intervention that showed us the way to Gethsemane . . ."

They heard footsteps approaching and Benjamin looked up in fright at the open door. Ravn went towards the doorway to take a look.

Åse was coming up the path with a tray that bore a carafe and a single glass. Casting a glance over his shoulder, Ravn saw Benjamin weaving his way through the chairs, making haste towards the rear door.

"A man died in that fire, Benjamin. There will be an investigation into his death."

Benjamin shrugged. "The Lord giveth, the Lord taketh away . . ."

"Was the fire a message to Jacob's father?"

"The Lord giveth, the Lord taketh away . . ." Benjamin repeated before disappearing out the rear door.

Åse came into the room and put the tray next to the Bibles on the sideboard just inside the door. "I thought you might be thirsty," she said, pouring some water into the glass.

"Yes, thank you. Is Jacob on his way?"

"The Master is still hard at work, but I don't think you will have to wait much longer. He is looking forward to meeting you." She handed Ravn the glass and left the room again.

Ravn drank the water in the doorway, watching Åse descend the narrow path. She had a few words with the guards at the bottom and then made her way towards the barracks. The guards looked up at him, and Ravn had the distinct impression that he was no longer free to leave Gethsemane of his own accord.

50

The sticky heat presaged yet another thunderstorm, but for now, the rain was kept at bay. Ravn was seated on one of the chairs near the back of the temple. He had developed a searing headache. It might have been a symptom of the change in weather, or the overwhelming hunger in his belly—he couldn't tell which. It was now three thirty in the afternoon and he'd been waiting for Jacob for almost six hours, which didn't beat his own record for keeping a suspect waiting, but it was close. Not moving an inch the entire time, the two guards in front of the door had been vigilant. Ravn had long since checked the rear exit where Benjamin had disappeared, but Patrick and one of his sidekicks were posted there, and when he had tried the door, Patrick had kindly but firmly asked him to stay inside and wait for Jacob. Ravn said he'd waited long enough, but neither guard chose to comment.

A crackle of static emitted from the loudspeakers mounted just below the ceiling in the corners, followed by the distorted chords of an organ. It was the same music he had heard the day before, albeit without the accompaniment of Jacob's monotone preaching. Soon after, the sound of mumbled voices from outside rose above the music. Ravn stood up stiffly and went over to the doorway.

A congregation of about twenty people dressed in grey uniforms were making their way up the path. Their heads were bowed, their hands folded in prayer before them. When the first person reached the entrance, the mumbling stopped, and the group filed past Ravn in silence. He noticed that neither Samuel, Åse, nor Birgitte were amongst them.

The congregation took their seats in the first few rows of chairs. Soon a lesser representation of the camouflage-clad guards came into the room. Patrick was amongst them, and there was more scraping of chairs as the guards took their seats in the rows just behind the members dressed in grey. A few minutes later, Samuel and Åse arrived side by side, followed by six other people who were not in uniform. Catching sight of Ejner bringing up the rear, Ravn reckoned they were outsiders. Ejner avoided his gaze and hurried to take his seat.

"Samuel?" Ravn said, catching the Elder's attention as he came past.

"Yes?" Samuel said, as if surprised at being addressed directly in the church.

"When can I meet with Jacob?"

"In just a moment . . . when we begin . . ."

"I would really like to talk to him before you do. I have waited a long time."

"That we all have," said Samuel gravely. "Fortunately, for something good . . . I believe you will have an enlightened experience."

Ravn gripped Samuel's sleeve, holding him back. "I have not come for the sake of any kind of experience provided by Jacob. I have an important document for him."

Samuel took a deep breath and sighed heavily. "We all believe that the world revolves around ourselves. This is how we forget the Lord."

"I need to talk to Jacob. Now."

"I know you want to talk to him. And I will let you know when that is possible. For now, I kindly ask you to take a seat," Samuel said with a cool smile, nodding at a chair in the back row. Then he continued up the aisle to join his brethren at the front.

Watching the docile congregation, Ravn wondered whether Jacob would ever make his appearance. Was the Master at Gethsemane at all? The next moment, he heard stamping feet approaching the entrance, and then the flock of workers dressed in blue uniforms came into the church at a slow run. There were plenty of free seats at the back, but the blue-uniformed members of the congregation filed into the back of the room and stood against the wall with their heads bowed.

Led by Samuel playing the guitar and Åse at an electronic organ on the stage, the congregation began to sing their praises to the Lord. It seemed to be a homegrown hymn, whose only content proclaimed that God was great and almighty, and that they were grateful to serve Him. The chorus was repeated for about ten minutes, but Ravn felt as if it were an eternity. When the music finally stopped and they had all recited the credo of God's Chosen, Åse played a few chords on the organ. As if on cue, the rear door opened and Birgitte entered with a corpulent man in cream-coloured trousers and a large, free-flowing calico shirt that was stained with sweat at the armpits. The fat man was panting in the stifling heat and mopped his sweaty brow with a handkerchief. The congregation rose to their feet and began to clap in unison. Ravn found himself on his feet as well—not out of respect, but pure curiosity at the spectacle of the Master, who had finally made his appearance.

Jacob leaned heavily on the cane in his right hand and shuffled onto the scene with obvious difficulty. Ravn recognised him from the author picture on the front flap of his book on exorcism. When he reached the middle of the stage, he slumped heavily into the chair that had been provided for him. Jacob made a limp-wristed wave at the gathering, whose applause erupted in response. Birgitte turned to face the congregation and asked everyone to take their seats. Ravn deliberately waited till everyone else had sat down before he did the same, so that Jacob would see him in the crowd, but he wasn't sure if his ploy was successful.

Samuel began to preach. In contrast to Jacob, who was slouching in his chair, Samuel was energetic and passionate in his delivery. But, more interested in watching Jacob's every move, Ravn was only half-listening to Samuel's sermon. The Jacob Mesmer he saw before him had nothing of the charismatic leader that Benjamin had described in his report. In fact, more than anything else, it seemed as if the Master had been hauled onto the stage for show, as if he were an ageing pope forced to remain in office till death, regardless of ill health. Jacob couldn't have been more than a couple of years older than he was, but Ravn thought he looked like an old man long past his prime.

The congregation burst into song once more. The words were different, but the content was the same. In the rows in front of him, people raised their arms in the air, others rose to their feet and swayed to the melody. Even the crew cut clan seemed swept up in the music. Ravn turned his head and cast a glance at the members in blue overalls. Everyone was singing along feverishly with their eyes closed. Benjamin was standing near the far corner, his arms raised in the air, as if to embrace the heavens.

Ravn could not remember when he had last felt so utterly out of place.

After about an hour of Samuel's preaching and communal hymn singing, Samuel asked the congregation if anyone had anything they wished to confess. A sea of hands went up. One after the other, without regard to their place in the hierarchy, the members who had raised their hands were summoned to the stage.

Samuel listened to the troubles of each and every one, repeating out loud what they said to him so that the congregation could share their burden. It seemed to Ravn as if the ceremony was equal parts healing and confessional, especially because the members shared both their physical pains and psychological woes. The latter were consistently diagnosed as possessed by a demon . And according to Samuel, several demons were present that evening. Fortunately, every demon could be driven away. In every case, the relevant member kneeled before Jacob, who rested a hand on their heads and mumbled a prayer. As the evening wore on, the hand he placed on his disciples' heads seemed at once heavy and limp, as if the entire proceeding tired their Master.

Once the confessional was over, Samuel respectfully asked the Master if he wished to say a few words. Birgitte brought him a microphone and a glass of water, and then Jacob addressed his congregation at last. Ravn was surprised at the frailty of his voice, but the import of his words was anything but faint. He accused the congregation of weakness and wavering faith. They were sinners—each and every one of them—who had succumbed to demonic lust, laziness, greed, arrogance, envy, and, not least, gluttony, which threatened to destroy the church. Therefore he challenged everyone to submit to the Lord and beg for His forgiveness. When his outburst was over, Jacob threw down the microphone, which boomed like thunder through the loudspeakers when it hit the wooden floorboards.

Ravn doubted very much that Jacob had spent much time on writing his speech for that evening. It seemed as if the waiting had all been for the sake of intimidating him. He had to admit he was exhausted, and he was looking forward to getting this case over and done with so he could get the hell out of there.

"Let's assemble in groups," said Samuel.

The congregation rose on his command and cleared the chairs to the sides. Ravn was the last to stand up, and his chair was immediately removed. All around him, the members dispersed into groups of about ten people, regardless of hierarchy. With their hands resting on each other's shoulders, they began to pray and talk in tongues.

Ravn felt a hand rest on his shoulder and turned his head. Birgitte stared into his eyes and gave him a stiff smile. "The Master would like to speak to you now."

Ravn looked up to where Jacob sat on his throne. With four fat little fingers, he summoned Ravn onto the stage.

51

Birgitte bowed to Jacob, who was lounging in his chair, and he looked up at Ravn lazily.

"This is the man I told you about, Master," said Birgitte. "His name is Thomas Ravnsholdt, and he would like to speak with you."

"Just call me Ravn."

Jacob took his hand reluctantly, and the handshake was limp, as if Jacob's limbs were made of dough.

"I've been here before to deliver this to you," Ravn said, holding the envelope out to Jacob. "But it seems your people take care not to disturb you under any circumstances."

Jacob accepted the envelope and laid it in his lap. "I've heard about you. Seen events that concerned you."

"Is that so? From where?" said Ravn.

Jacob pointed up at the ceiling. "*He* shows me everything."

"*He's* a good connection to have," Ravn replied with a smile.

"You are not a believer, I see," Jacob observed wanly. "*He* has already told me that."

"There are different ways to believe."

"White lies are the device chosen by sinners and infidels."

Ravn chose not to reply. He was not about to get into a theological discussion with this man.

Jacob looked at the envelope in his lap. "I don't need a prompt from God to know who this is from. How did you find me?"

"I followed the breadcrumbs. Good old-fashioned detective work."

The corners of Jacob's mouth curved into a smirk. "Then you must be a very good detective," he said sarcastically. "But you are not the first man my father has sent."

"I wouldn't know anything about that."

"So, the one secret agent knows nothing of the other, even though they have the same master?" Jacob scoffed. "I find that hard to believe." His gaze appeared to drift past Ravn and settle on the people assembled behind him. "What is *your* motive, then? Have you also come to spy on us?"

"I've come to deliver that document. No more than that," Ravn said, nodding at the envelope.

"You don't seem like the kind of man who is content to play the messenger only," Jacob said coldly. "You seem more like the kind who seeks to . . . attain a goal?"

Jacob pointed at something over Ravn's shoulder, and Ravn turned to see what it was. In the group nearest to them, Samuel immediately slapped Benjamin on the back, and Benjamin stepped out of the huddle, which quickly closed again. Samuel led Benjamin up to the edge of the stage, where the latter remained standing with his head bowed and his hands clasped behind his back.

"Do you know this man, Benjamin?" Jacob asked.

"No, Master."

"You haven't even looked at him, Benjamin. Take a good look and give me an honest answer."

Benjamin glanced at Ravn and quickly shook his head.

"Are you lying to me? Don't you know that he is a spy, just like you?"

Benjamin kept his eyes fixed on the ground.

"I haven't come here to spy on you," said Ravn. "And I've never seen this man before."

"Neither one of you is telling the truth," Jacob said with a shrug. "The Lord sees everything. Whereas the rest of us have to rely on surveillance cameras," he added, smiling to himself.

"I . . . tried to get him to leave. I kicked him off the property so he wouldn't disturb you, Master," said Benjamin, close to tears.

"You see?" Jacob said, pointing at Benjamin. "This man cannot help lying. The demon is in his mouth, speaks with his tongue."

Ravn shrugged. "I didn't recognise him. And I'm sure he has his reasons for saying what he did. Either way, he has nothing to do with the document that I have brought to you."

Jacob ignored him and kept his gaze on Benjamin. "There is very little truth in what has been said here today. You never learn, do you, Benjamin? You abuse every morsel of trust that is bestowed upon you. It's in your nature."

"I'm sorry, Master. I regret my sins."

Jacob wiped his mouth with his broad hand. "Go back to your group, sinner."

"Yes, Master."

"But leave the armband here. You won't be needing it anymore."

The tears brimmed in Benjamin's eyes as he slowly unfastened the red band from his arm. He folded it neatly and put it on the edge of the stage. He remained standing there, as if rooted to the spot, until his Master dismissed him with a flick of his fat wrist.

Jacob yawned and looked at Ravn. "They're like little children. You have to watch them like a hawk."

Ravn didn't reply, and Jacob glanced at the envelope in his lap. "Do you know what's inside it?"

"It's a contract concerning Mesmer Resources, but I don't know the details."

Jacob looked at Ravn in surprise. "Mesmer Resources belongs to my father. I have nothing to do with it. What did he tell you?"

"That you were the one who designed the Mesmogramme."

Jacob writhed in his seat. "That was a lifetime ago. A completely different place . . . What does he want?" he said irritably.

"As far as I understand it, Mesmer Resources is about to merge with another company, but he would like to buy you out first. But take a look at the document yourself."

"So, my father wishes to disseminate his empty promises to even more people, and create even more godless souls in this world?"

"You would know the contents of the Mesmogramme much better than anyone else," Ravn replied evenly.

"What are his conditions?"

"I have no idea. As I said, I'm simply here to deliver the contract. If you would like to sign it now, I'd be happy to take it back with me. Or you can post it," Ravn suggested.

"What has he told you about me?" Jacob said, and started to rip open the envelope.

"Not much. There was no need for that. He simply asked me to find you."

"I know him and what he is capable of—and he would never miss a chance to undermine me. Am I right?"

"No."

"Are you saying my father actually had something nice to say about me?" Jacob snorted in disbelief.

Ravn shrugged. "To be honest, I believe he regrets what happened, regardless of the reasons you parted on bad terms."

Jacob leafed through the many pages of the contract. "Did he say anything about our past?"

"He spoke about your work together, and his concern for you when you started your . . . movement." Ravn almost said "sect" but caught himself in time.

"The concerned father," Jacob scoffed. "He sent his spy, Benjamin, after me."

"Who you were able to convert, it appears," Ravn pointed out.

Jacob looked up from the contract. "How do you fit into this whole scenario? What do you stand to gain?"

"Nothing. It's a job like any other."

"How much is my father paying you?"

Ravn cast a glance around the room. "Right now, it doesn't feel like nearly enough."

Jacob returned his attention to the contract, reading the last page with particular interest. Then he put back the pages in the envelope, and Ravn thought he probably wouldn't be able to return with a signed document.

"Did you notice his hand?"

"Whose hand? Your father's?"

Jacob nodded.

"Did he have something to do with the fire at Belgiensgade?"

"Ah, so you know about that as well? You've been a clever little spy, haven't you? But no, it was an accident. The insurance company that paid the compensation was convinced of that."

Ravn didn't know what to believe, but he still wasn't buying Benjamin's claim that it was some kind of "divine intervention." "If he didn't burn his hand in the fire on Belgiensgade, when did your father sustain the injury?"

Jacob laughed and tried to get out of the chair without help. Birgitte sprang to his aid and gave him the cane. He whispered something in her ear that seemed to surprise her. She stared at him for a moment, and he gave her a nudge in the ribs with his elbow to get her going. The next moment, the organ music started up once more, and the congregation stopped muttering immediately. The groups disbanded, and everyone made for the door—the people in blue at a run.

"May I give you a tour of the grounds? Our own garden of Gethsemane?" Jacob said.

"Thank you, but I have a long trip back to Copenhagen."

"Copenhagen can wait. And I'm sure you'd like to return that contract signed?"

"I don't care whether you sign it or not, Jacob. And to be honest, I've seen more than enough of your establishment."

"You don't look happy."

Ravn shrugged.

"You are doing us a disservice. Let me show you what we have achieved. Afterwards, I'll sign the contract, so you can get the praise you deserve from your master. Perhaps even a bonus—a fine bone to chew on," he added with a hollow laugh.

"All right," Ravn said with a sigh. He was already regretting it.

52

Ravn followed Jacob out the rear door, escorted by Patrick and two of his men. Dusk had fallen, and Gethsemane basked in shadows. After the constant chanting for hours on end, the silence was overwhelming, and the farm was as eerie as a ghost town. Jacob led the way along the path to the large production hall, but just before they reached it, he veered to the left and went round the back to a lesser building with a blue metal door. Patrick sprang ahead and opened the door for his Master. A cacophony of machinery escaped from the dark inside. Jacob edged his bulky form through the narrow doorway with Ravn and the guards at his heels.

"This is where we ferment the fertiliser," Jacob yelled over the noise. An elderly man in a grey uniform was posted at the control panel, keeping an eye on the temperature gauge. He only noticed their arrival once they were standing right next to him, and the moment he saw Jacob, he bowed several times. His Master extended his hand, and the man kissed it in gratitude. The sight of the servile man watching the gauge gave Ravn the creeps, not least the self-satisfied expression that was spread over Jacob's face, as if he were a mafia boss or a cardinal.

"William is our fermentation expert. He monitors the ventilation and pasteurisation process to create fertiliser of the finest quality to nourish our dear mushrooms, God's hallowed microorganisms."

"Yes, I saw your people in the production hall shovelling manure and spraying chemicals over the lot," said Ravn in a chilly tone. "Looks like a toxic process to me."

"Ah, in that case, you must know all there is to know about the preparation of manure," Jacob said with biting sarcasm. "You ought to join our movement."

"Thanks, but no thanks."

William bowed obsequiously once more as they came past and continued under the massive heating pipes running above the corridor to the far door. The next hall they entered was cool and dark with a mild smell of soil. Six rows of cultivation boxes in four tiers stretched over the length of the hall, which must have been about thirty to forty metres long, Ravn reckoned.

Jacob walked over to the nearest row and dug his fat fingers into the soil of the second-tier mushroom bed. The clump of soil in his hand revealed a filigree network of white threads. "Look," said Jacob. "It's called mycelium: a fungus with a multitude of branching hyphae. Beautiful, isn't it? Each cultivation box contains its own complex network that keeps branching out."

"It seems you have green fingers," Ravn remarked drily.

Jacob returned the clump of mycelia to the bed and patted the soil down with his palm. "Not at all. Contrary to a gardener or a farmer in the fields, we're not interested in making things grow. We break everything down in order to recreate nature's own process of decomposition. The mushrooms feed on the rotting threads so they can develop and grow."

"Is that what you do with your congregation?"

"Do what?"

"Break them down so you can build them up again."

"You're not shy about expressing your opinion," said Jacob. "Perhaps that's one way of looking at it. We have a system that is designed to teach our members humility on their journey to true faith. But I wouldn't call it 'breaking them down,' as you say."

"Your methods don't seem particularly dignified. Especially the way you treat the people in blue uniforms."

"In every society, it is important that each individual understands that their actions, their words, even their thoughts have a consequence. And that consequence can either be a reward, when the individual puts the congregation's interests above their own, or sanctions, when they act against the community's best interests. They must learn that there are . . . regulations for negative behaviour."

"You mean punishment?"

"Reform."

"So you humiliate those who don't toe the line. Is that your 'system'?"

"No one is humiliated. We educate them. In my experience, I have learned that benediction and penance are equally useful tools to drive the flock to Paradise. Darkness and light, just as the Lord created it."

"Do these principles of yours apply to children as well?"

"I don't understand what you're talking about."

"I've seen children in blue uniforms amongst those whom you wish to 'reform.'"

"Naturally, the children stay with their parents. Are you suggesting we ought to separate them? That would be inhumane."

"So children are also punished here?"

"As I pointed out before: No one is being punished," Jacob said. "Everyone is being educated in the teachings of God, albeit in diverse ways. The children at Gethsemane are free and happy. They are free to play wherever they please—and their parents are free from worrying about them. How many children in the city can say the same? Out there, children are subject to abuse, not here," he added, resting a heavy hand on Ravn's shoulder. "Did you know that mushrooms are in a class of their own? They belong neither to the animal nor the plant kingdom. They belong to a world of their own."

"No, I did not," Ravn said tersely.

"If you study mushrooms more closely, as I have, you will discover that they are a . . . nexus between the two kingdoms: half plant, half animal. Mushrooms can hold the two worlds together, even as they keep them distinct. It is an organism that lives in total darkness and feeds on the dead. They live their existence either as a parasite, or in symbiosis with their host."

Jacob led Ravn through the hall and on to the next cultivation hall, which was an extension of the first. In here, the process was in a more advanced stage. The cultivation boxes were arranged in four long rows, and the beds were filled with thousands of white button mushrooms that shone in the black soil. At the far end, four women were picking the mushrooms and packing them into cardboard trays that were stacked on a cart alongside them.

"*Agaricus bisporus*," Jacob said, carefully extracting a large mushroom from the cultivation box in front of him. He held it against the light and observed its delicate light-brown lamella. "What lay people call mushrooms is only its fruit body that serves to disperse the spores. We can cultivate a fruit body four times before its function is spent."

"Sounds like a profitable business, everything taken into account."

"Taking what into account?" Jacob snapped moodily.

"Your property, the expensive cars parked outside, and . . . free labour."

Jacob shook his head. "You insist on misunderstanding our operation. We have many mouths to feed, and new members arriving all the time. The prejudice and lies fabricated in the outside world have been damaging to our operation. But . . . we don't complain. We still take in the people rejected by your world. Those people no one else wants to help. The poor. The mentally ill. Alcoholics. Drug addicts. Thieves. Murderers. War veterans. We do not judge people for their past because we know they have a future here, irrespective of who they are. Communities before ours have been condemned, entire segments of society destroyed. But the Lord shields us from harm . . . Let me show you something," he added, casting the mushroom aside.

Jacob showed him the way past the rows of mushroom beds to a narrow corridor that led into the packing hall. In here, members in grey as well as blue uniforms were standing at a long conveyor belt, packing the filled mushroom trays into wooden crates. The trays appeared to bear the Danish flag logo that he recognised from his local supermarket in Christianshavn, but he wasn't sure if they were identical. He followed Jacob through the hall and past the conveyor belt to a metal door at the other end. Jacob opened another door and flipped the light switch on the wall inside. The fluorescent pipes flickered and eventually lit a small room before them.

"Over the years, we have made some important discoveries in this laboratory," Jacob said proudly, sweeping his cane into the room. "This is our scientific centre."

Ravn peered around the windowless room. It might have been an abandoned physics lab at a public high school, he thought. Little more than a cramped room, it had a single metal table with three workstations and a microscope each. A thick layer of dust had settled on every surface. Used test tubes and toppled glass lab jars littered the space between the old microscope stands. Two defunct refrigerators with open doors were placed against the far wall. Apart from three jugs containing an unidentifiable rotting mass, the shelves just above the fridges were empty.

"Mushroom cultivation is the financial engine of our operation, but scientific research is actually our main area of business. It is here we wish to discover God's miracles and bring the fruits of His creation to society. Duly patented, of course." For the first time since their little tour began, Jacob's smile was genuine. Ravn was utterly baffled. *How could this man be so blind to the miserable state of the laboratory?* He seemed genuinely proud of his operation.

"It is a scientific area with enormous potential," Jacob went on enthusiastically. "Think of discoveries like penicillin, enzymes for washing powder, pesticides to combat rodents, or fermentation agents for the food industry. God's miracle in microorganism form," he said, smiling again.

"Why did you discontinue your research?"

Jacob frowned. "Who said we had stopped?"

Ravn shrugged. "It doesn't look as if this room has been used for a long time."

"We have been fully operational in various areas . . . even though the persecution of the outside world has had a negative impact on our research facility. It isn't easy to attract the right employees and investors for such a complex project. But the Lord rewards the patient," Jacob said emphatically. "And therefore, hard physical labour, knowledge, and, not least, faith go hand in hand at Gethsemane," he added, banging on a bronze fermentation holder nearby to underscore his point with a metallic ring. "Our goal is to be self-providing in body and spirit."

In that moment, static sounded from Patrick's walkie-talkie just behind them, and he took the call.

"*We have a situation at the barracks . . . Are you with the Master? Over,*" a voice on the other end said.

"Yes, what has happened?" Patrick said.

"*We need the Master immediately! Over.*"

Jacob snatched the walkie-talkie from Patrick and brought it to his mouth. "What's the problem, then?"

There was a great deal of static before the voice returned. "*It's Benjamin, sir . . . It's bad . . . He is . . . possessed!*"

53

Ravn was escorted back to the barracks by Jacob and his guards, and by the time they arrived, a large group had Benjamin surrounded. Like a trapped animal, he was crouched on his haunches against a corner in the dark. Everyone kept their distance, obviously fearful of the hissing creature in front of them. Samuel was the only one who had ventured a few steps closer, holding a wooden crucifix before him as he mumbled words of prayer. Benjamin reacted with a snarl and a gurgling sound in his throat. His face was ashen and twisted into a pained grimace.

Jacob elbowed his way through the crowd towards Samuel. "I'll take it from here," he said.

"He seems to have quietened down a bit," said Samuel. "I actually think the mercy of God has been bestowed on him now."

"You *think*?" Jacob lifted his cane and poked Benjamin in the chest.

Benjamin growled and smacked the cane away with his right hand. The congregation behind Jacob cried out in fright, many of them making the sign of the cross before their chests.

"And so we meet again, Beelzebub!" Jacob yelled at Benjamin. "And again I will drive away your evil with the power of the Lord!" He jabbed the cane into Benjamin's chest so hard he slammed into the barracks wall behind him. "Leave the body of this poor man, you Satan!"

Benjamin quickly resumed his crouching position, ready to pounce. Frothing at the mouth, he snarled at Jacob and spat at him.

Unperturbed, Jacob raised his cane and took another swipe at Benjamin. "Satan, I command you, in the name of the Lord, leave this body and this mind."

All the while screaming and hissing at Jacob, Benjamin dodged the blows.

After a few more minutes, Jacob paused to catch his breath. "Listen to the Words of God, Beelzebub!" he yelled, and dabbed the sweat from his brow with his shirtsleeve. "*Then Jesus asked him: 'What is your name?' . . . And he said: 'Legion, for we are many.'* But Jesus drove them out of the man, one after another, just as I will drive you out of this man today. Flee to your kingdom of darkness, Satan!"

Benjamin doubled over in pain and clutched his stomach with one hand. Digging into the earth with the other, he cast small stones and grit at Jacob. "Leeee . . . gioon, Leeee . . . giooon," a deep voice inside him said.

"Leave this man!" Jacob yelled again.

Ravn observed the scene unfolding before him as the congregation began to pray for Benjamin in unison. Jacob's posturing and the crowd's chanting seemed rehearsed, even farcical, but their fear and Benjamin's anguish seemed to be authentic. He didn't believe that Benjamin was actually possessed by a demon, but something awful had definitely happened to him, and Ravn had to admit that witnessing the scene in the dark with a crowd of fanatics was quite terrifying.

"Hold him down!" commanded Jacob. "Help me to expel Satan's demon from this man!"

Patrick and one of his sidekicks went over to Benjamin, who immediately began to thrash his arms about wildly. But he was no match for the two guards. Quickly, they pinned Benjamin's arms behind his back. He struggled to free himself, but they overpowered him easily, and finally he simply gave up the fight.

"Holy water!" yelled Jacob. "Bring me holy water!"

Birgitte came forward at once with a carafe of water. "We forsake the Devil and all his actions," said Jacob as he approached Benjamin with the water.

Frothing at the mouth, Benjamin began to speak in tongues. Patrick grabbed him by the hair and forced his head back. Benjamin struggled again, snorting and spitting snot at the men, but Jacob was relentless. "We believe in Jesus Christ, His only Son, our master, who was conceived by the Holy Ghost, borne of the Virgin Mary, tortured by Pontius Pilates, crucified, buried, and duly departed to the kingdom of the dead . . ." he chanted as he carefully began to pour the water over Benjamin's face.

Benjamin screamed and tried to move his head, but they held him fast. Then Patrick took hold of Benjamin's jaw and forced his mouth open.

"Noooooo," Benjamin squealed.

Jacob began pouring water down Benjamin's throat. "We believe in the Holy Ghost, the sacred church, the hallowed society, the forgiveness of our sins . . . the resurrection of the flesh and eternal life . . . AMEN."

The carafe of water was empty. Jacob moved away and the two guards let go of Benjamin. He slid down onto the ground and lay still.

"Dear Lord in Heaven, we ask You to forgive this man's sin," Jacob began, raising his arms and the cane to the sky. "We beg You to have mercy and cast the demon out of his spirit. Repel the demon from our church so that it cannot inhabit another weak and innocent soul . . ."

Benjamin groaned and vomited a slimy green substance onto the ground.

A hush went through the crowd. People began to pray, thanking the Lord for the miracle they had just witnessed.

Jacob lowered his arms to his sides and regarded his congregation with satisfaction. "The power of the Lord is eternal. Amen." He turned to fix his gaze on Benjamin. "I hope you are grateful for His mercy. I hope you appreciate how great His power is over life and death. Know that He has tested you. He allowed the demon to demonstrate your weakness."

"Grate . . . ful," Benjamin gasped.

With that, the exorcism was over. Ravn could not fathom what had happened to Benjamin, but despite his weakened state, he seemed to be okay again. Samuel sat on his haunches next to Benjamin and uttered a few calming words as he dabbed away the vomit from the poor man's mouth and chin.

"'How did this demon find its way into our midst?' you might ask yourselves," Jacob said, letting his gaze wander over the congregation.

The murmuring and prayers stopped at once.

"Which one of you contaminated Benjamin with this impurity and sin?! For the demon's name was Sin!" Jacob yelled at them.

Everyone tried to avoid their Master's wrath.

"I know that you consider yourselves pure. But remember that in God's eyes, we are all sinners!"

"AMEN!" the congregation chimed in chorus.

"But this time, we cannot point a finger at anyone in our church. The harbinger of evil is not one of us . . . but he is right behind you!" Jacob pointed his cane over their heads.

The people gathered before Jacob turned their heads and stared at Ravn, the fear shining in their eyes.

Ravn swallowed hard.

"In good faith, we welcomed him into our midst, and even though we have prayed for him this evening, Satan has not left that man's side. *He* is the Demon Bringer," Jacob yelled, pointing at Ravn.

"Yield, Satan!" a woman in the crowd screamed at Ravn.

Ravn involuntarily took a few steps back. He could see that the fear in their eyes had transformed into something else. Bloodlust. The communal surge of hate against the outsider.

Samuel rose to his feet next to Benjamin. "Master, we cannot be certain that he is the one who brought the demon to our house."

Jacob scowled at Samuel. "Has the Lord spoken to *you*, Samuel?" he said.

"No, of course not. The Lord only speaks to *you* . . . Master."

There was a shuffle of feet as members of the congregation turned to face Jacob once more.

"I would simply like to point out that we cannot be sure that *he* is the harbinger of evil. What did the Lord say to you, Master?"

"Are you doubting me, brother Samuel?"

"No, not at all, Master. I just want us to be sure not to . . . throw stones, in such cases."

Everyone's eyes rested on Jacob. Some nodded in agreement with Samuel.

"Naturally, brother Samuel," Jacob said irritably. "But the actions alone of this man have exposed him as the Demon Bringer because he gave me this," he added, waving the manila envelope Ravn had brought with him, and his disciples stared at the envelope in terror, as if it were a handful of snakes.

"Yes, my brothers and sisters, not only did the Demon Bringer try to possess Benjamin, but first he tried to taint *me* with evil!"

A hush went through the room.

"The Demon Bringer brought this decree from the Supreme Satan . . . We all know who he is . . ." Jacob thundered. "Once again, this evil man is spreading lies about us. He is determined to destroy our house, our beloved church! He has sent another secret agent, a spy—just like he sent Benjamin—to poison our community." He pointed to the place where Benjamin had collapsed on the ground, but he was gone. "Where did he go?!" Jacob yelled.

Confusion erupted in the gathering as everyone looked around frantically for Benjamin.

"There!" Åse yelled moments later. "He's up there!" She pointed to the mounds of manure on the edge of the field.

Benjamin was standing on top of the first one, looking down at them. He shook his head, and the tears were streaming down his cheeks. "It's happening again . . . I can't take it anymore . . . no more . . . no . . . go away," he said, thrashing out with his arms.

"The demon has taken him again," said Jacob. "Why didn't you stay with him, Samuel?"

Benjamin began to slap himself in the face. "I don't want to do this anymore . . . I can't anymore . . . do you understand, Lisa . . . forgive me . . . forgive me for not saving you . . ." he wailed. "Now I understand what you went through . . . I will wait for you at the gates of Heaven . . ." All at once, he stopped crying, hopped down from the manure heap, and made his way along the embankment alongside it.

"Shall we go after him, Master?" Patrick asked.

Jacob did not reply at once. All eyes were on Benjamin as he ran through the wheat field, which billowed in the gleam of the moon. "No,

Patrick," he said at last. "Benjamin has chosen his own path to meet his maker."

Ravn was not sure what Jacob meant. But then he noticed that Benjamin was running towards a combine harvester in the field. "We have to stop him, Jacob," he said.

Jacob made no reply, and nobody moved. Everyone just stared after Benjamin as he weaved his way through the high stalks of wheat.

Ravn pushed his way through the crowd, but before he could reach the field, Patrick's hand closed over his throat from behind, holding him back. "You stay here," Patrick hissed in his ear. Moments later, two more guards grabbed his arms.

Out in the field, Benjamin approached the combine harvester from the side, and when he was right next to its path, he jumped in front of the projector lights with his arms raised to the sky. The whirring blades of the harvester mowed down the wheat before Benjamin and slashed through his body, sending a purple cloud into the night. The brakes of the combine harvester screeched, but it was much too late.

The combine harvester came to a halt in the swaying, blood-spattered wheat in its headlights. For a few moments, there was silence. Then the gathering at Gethsemane could hear shouts coming from the field. Ravn turned his head and glanced at Jacob, who had not said a word. His face was tranquil, as if he were satisfied with the conclusion of their evening ritual.

A fist smashed into Ravn's jaw. He hit the ground hard, immediately swallowed by complete darkness.

54

Ravn was woken by the pitter-patter of rain on the glass roof of the greenhouse. The moment he moved, he felt the plastic strip around his neck, keeping him fastened to a stake behind his back. He tried to stay still, afraid the strip might tighten even more and strangle him.

He remembered what had happened now. Patrick and his men had dragged him in here, beaten him to a pulp, and left him tied to one of the bearing poles of the greenhouse. His neck, feet, and hands were fastened with plastic strips that cut into his flesh.

Ravn ran his tongue over his teeth. As far as he could tell, nothing was broken, but his upper lip had a deep gash, and he could still taste blood in his mouth. He inhaled the cool morning air. The rain intensified the smell of rot that permeated the greenhouse. Glancing around as best he could without moving his head, he saw a multitude of mushrooms planted in low, square cultivation boxes. The plants came in all sizes and forms, many in bright rainbow colours of violet, purple, orange, and scarlet red. He could hear something rummaging in the dark, but he couldn't turn his head far enough to see what it was. The sound came closer, and the next moment, a boy in blue overalls stood in front of him, looking at him curiously. His nose was snotty, and he sniffed loudly. Ravn recognised the boy from the first day he came to the farm. Looking at his telltale features more closely, he suspected the boy had Down syndrome.

"Have you been bad?" the boy asked him with a grin.

"N-no," Ravn said with difficulty. His throat felt like sandpaper.

"Why are you sitting here, then? This place is for people who've been bad."

"I-I don't think I've been bad."

"Yes. Sometimes accidents happen. Before you know it."

"You're right about that. What's your name?"

"Ke-Ke-Kevin," he stammered. "What's yours?"

"Ravn. You know, just like the bird."

The boy laughed. "That's a funny name."

"Yes, I guess it is. Kevin, do you think you could help untie me?"

Kevin looked at him suspiciously. "Are you a demon?"

"Nope, not me."

"Because if you are a demon . . . I can't help you. Then it's . . . your fault that you're . . . t-t-t-tied up."

"I promise you that I'm not a demon, Kevin. Can you see those shards of glass over there?" Ravn said, trying to nod at the pile of shards he'd seen next to the mushroom bed in front of him.

Kevin's gaze didn't leave Ravn's face for a second. He stretched out his hand, and with one dirty index finger, he poked the swelling around Ravn's eye. "They hit you a lot. Your face is ugly."

"Yes, they beat me good and proper this time."

"*Good and proper,*" Kevin aped Ravn, and laughed. "Who tied you up, then?"

"The soldiers, you know, the guys with the short hair and beady eyes."

Kevin folded his arms over his chest. "I don't like *those* guys."

"Me neither. Why don't *you* like them?"

"They . . . t-t-t-tease me . . . And they hit. They're not nice."

"No, they're not. Kevin, can you bring me one of those glass shards over there? I want to get away before they come back and hit me again."

"I . . . could get in trouble."

"I promise I won't tell anyone, Kevin. And I'll make sure they don't tease you anymore. Or hit you . . ."

Kevin grinned at him. "Okay." He went over to the glass shards and picked up the largest one. Holding it outstretched between his thumb and forefinger, he returned to Ravn.

Footsteps sounded on the gravel outside. Kevin dropped the shard in fright and backed away from Ravn.

"Don't get too close to the demon, my boy," Jacob said as he entered the greenhouse.

55

Kevin stared at the Master in fear as Jacob shuffled over to Ravn. "What are you doing in here with this demon, Kevin?"

"He . . . he said he was no d-d-demon, Master."

Jacob stroked Kevin's hair. "You're one of God's lost little lambs, Kevin," he said. "You know you're not supposed to be in here, right?"

"Yes, Master. B-b-but I needed to p-p-p-pee."

Jacob laughed. "If you gotta go, you gotta go," he said. "But run along now. And I don't want to see you down here again, understood?" he said, patting the leather belt he had around his large waist for good measure.

Kevin's eyes lingered on the belt. Then he nodded energetically. "Understood, Master."

The boy spun on his heel, ran along the rows of mushrooms, and disappeared out the rear door of the greenhouse.

"Sweet kid, isn't he?" Jacob said to Ravn. "He joined us with his mother about six months ago. She fled from an alcoholic husband who abused her. There are so many evil people in this world . . . and you have woken up, I see, albeit it not from the sleep of the Innocent, Demon Bringer."

"Why didn't you stop Benjamin from going into the field?"

"Benjamin wanted to meet his maker in that field."

"You could have stopped him if you wanted to, Jacob."

"You give me too much credit. In fact, what happened to Benjamin was *your* fault."

"What do you mean?"

"You came here as the messenger of the Supreme Satan himself and tainted Benjamin with impure thoughts." Jacob smiled to himself. "I tried to save him, but it was your presence that sent him running into the rotating mouth of the combine harvester," he added, rotating his fat index fingers around one another to underscore his point. "You bear the responsibility for his death."

"Your bullshit might work on your disciples, Jacob, but not me," Ravn said flatly. "We both know that you used Benjamin, just like you're using me to demonstrate your power over them. Tell me, is Samuel the next contender for your job?"

"Don't confuse me with my father. Everyone here follows me of their own free will. Manipulation is my father's speciality. Just look at the situation he has put you in . . ."

"*You* are the one who had me brought in here, Jacob. You do realise that holding another person against their will is a crime punishable with eight years' imprisonment."

"Ah, the savvy private dick who knows the Criminal Procedure Act. Impressive. A former policeman?" Jacob came a step closer. "I wonder what made you leave the force. Was it the terrible pay? The long hours at the office? An unpleasant experience on the job? Something that scared you? A tragedy?" Jacob combed his face with a perception that was worthy of his father. "Hmm . . . you don't look like a man who scares easily . . . You're much too unintelligent for that . . . nothing but a blunt instrument . . . You are a cop."

"I don't give a shit what you think of me. Why don't you just let me go and we can go our separate ways."

"It's a bit late for that, don't you think?"

"Not if we can agree that the reason I'm sitting here is because I picked a fight with one of your men. Then you put me in here to let things cool off. It doesn't have to be any more than that. What do you say?"

Jacob looked at him for what felt like a full minute, then he burst out laughing. "I misjudged you before. You're not any old copper; you're a damn good one. I can see why my father chose you for this job. You must be one of his prized employees . . ."

"I'm doing just this one job for your father, no more. And if you really need to know: Yes, I am a former cop, and yes, the pay wasn't great, therefore the change. Your father definitely pays a whole lot better than the Copenhagen police."

Jacob brought a hand up to his mouth and regarded Ravn thoughtfully. "No, I don't buy it. Money is not the reason you changed jobs. My father manipulated you, just like he manipulates everyone else around him."

"Why would I lie?" Ravn said. "To me, this is a job like any other. And the sooner I can be done with it, the better. Now, are you going to cut these strips or not?" he said with as much nonchalance as he could muster.

"Did he tell you about the coffee test?"

"I don't remember."

"Yes, he did. I can see it in your face," Jacob said with satisfaction. "He told you about it, all right, and it got you to understand his business and make him seem harmless. I'll bet the story made such an impression on you that you tried it out on your friends, didn't you?"

Ravn made no reply, and this only seemed to animate Jacob even more.

"You see? If it's any consolation, he fooled me as well. And *I* was the one who came up with the coffee test—we raked in the clients with that one!" he laughed, shaking his head. "All you gotta do is give your business a human face, create a little empathy—and bam!—you've got them!" He snapped his fingers, as if he were a used-car salesman rather than a preacher.

"Congratulations, Jacob, you win. I *was* manipulated by your father. And now that we've established that, why don't you just sign the contract and score whatever money there is to be had? I'm sure it will be more than enough to run the farm. You can turn things around for yourself and your . . . movement . . . maybe even resume your research?"

A sad smile appeared on Jacob's lips. With a sinking feeling, Ravn realised that Jacob had no intention of signing the contract, never mind letting him go home. "Like every other animal on a leash, you don't understand the bigger picture. There is so much more to my operation than you could ever imagine, and we are not dependent on handouts from the Supreme Satan himself. With God's help, we'll be just fine." Jacob shifted his weight onto his cane and made to leave.

"Jacob, don't you understand that people will come to look for me? And Benjamin's death will be investigated."

"You are welcome in the House of God. You look thirsty. Are you thirsty?"

"What do you think?" Ravn said, trying to swallow the spit in his parched throat.

"Forgive me for being such a bad host." He patted his pocket and brought out a plastic bottle. "Perhaps I'm just forgetful, because I came down here to give you this water." He unscrewed the cap and put the bottle to Ravn's lips.

Ravn drank the lukewarm water greedily. Jacob withdrew it slightly so that Ravn had to stretch his neck to reach it. The strip cut into his throat as he tried to drink as much of the water as possible.

Jacob laughed. "Like an untrained puppy, you are."

When the bottle was empty, Jacob screwed the cap back on and returned it to his pocket. He wiped his sweaty brow with the back of his hand and dried his fingers on his shirt. "Which demons live in your soul, I wonder? Hate? Desire? Envy? Fear? Revenge?"

Despite the water, Ravn's throat felt dry. He had a bitter aftertaste in his mouth, and it felt as if his tongue was swelling up. He started to cough uncontrollably.

"Ah, yes . . . and there it is. The demon is on its way. But which one? Which demon has Beelzebub sent to embrace you?"

Jacob's voice seemed to come from afar, and when Ravn looked at him, he seemed unnaturally tall. "What . . . what have you given me?"

"Just a little holy water. To show you the demon . . ."

"You . . . swine," Ravn heard his voice say from somewhere far away. He was slowly beginning to understand Jacob's plan. "You . . . you poison your disciples . . ."

"My mushrooms show the way, to some more clearly than to others."

"You poisoned Lisa too. That's why she hurt herself."

"I am not responsible for Lisa's relapse. She was in a safe environment when we showed her the demon. She thanked us. No one could have predicted that she would lose her mind. It was God's will. God's punishment of a sinner, I think."

"Did you give Benjamin the same poison? Is that why you gave me the tour of the grounds? So that the poison had time to kick in . . .?"

"I don't poison anyone, Ravn. I merely help the demon along its way with holy water. So that it can come to the fore. God created the demons so people could learn from their mistakes. It is written in black and white in His Word."

"But . . . why let Benjamin die? Why keep me here? You know it will not end well for you . . ."

"Yup, you definitely do not understand the bigger picture, so you'll have to be content with the small one." Jacob appeared to bend forward towards him, and Ravn jerked his head away. The strip cut painfully into his throat, and he could not breathe.

"I hope you survive meeting your demon. Not everyone in our congregation has been that lucky, and now they fertilise our soil. Demons can be as strong as the mushrooms that invoke them. But if you survive, you are welcome in our church. You will be welcome amongst God's Chosen, Ravn."

Ravn's head lolled onto his chest. He was dimly aware that he was wearing blue overalls. He could not tell if the hallucinations had already started, but he had a horrible feeling that this nightmare had only just begun.

56

Ravn closed his eyes and tried to push aside the fear. He was fever-ish and hot, his clothing soaked in sweat, and although his eyes were clamped shut, a bright purple light penetrated his eyelids. In spite of himself, Ravn could feel the panic rising. It was all he could do to concentrate on breathing *in* through his nose, and *out* through his mouth, as slowly as he could.

Images of Lisa's disfigured face whirled uncontrollably in his mind. He saw Benjamin fleeing through the wheat field, his body sliced by the rotating blades of the combine harvester, a purple cloud of blood in the moonlit sky, the same purpura colour that burned into his retina—*stop!* The shard of glass lay inches from his right leg. He could cut himself, bleed to death . . . *Don't think!* It was just a rush, nothing else. *It's not real, it's not real, it's not real* . . . he told himself.

Open your eyes.

He could not tell if the voice was in his head.

Open your eyes to what will happen before you.

He obeyed. Blinked his eyes rapidly. He was alone in the greenhouse. Daylight shone through the dirty panes, but there was another flashing strobe light before his eyes that made it impossible for him to focus. As he breathed in and out, the ceiling and walls of the greenhouse appeared to pulse, expanding and contracting accordingly. If he held his breath, the movement stopped, but the moment he breathed, the pulsing set in, and his surroundings constantly changed form and colour. And then the chorus of voices began . . .

He was terrified now, and he closed his eyes, but it was as if he were staring helplessly through his eyelids. *Come with us . . . come with us . . . come with us . . .* the voices chanted.

Above his head, the clouds flitted across the sky at a furious pace, daylight turning into darkness, and darkness becoming daylight, as if time itself were shooting past. Weeks dissolved in a split second, months and years rushed past him, time was spooled forwards with increasing speed, until Eva stood right before him, and then he realised that he was wrong: Time had in fact been spinning *backwards.*

He was back to that fateful morning three years ago. He said goodbye to her without an inkling that it was the last time he would see her. Their last moments alive together. A hurried morning routine with coffee and half a bread roll with cheese that was eaten standing at the kitchen counter as they made to rush out the door. A quick glance, a fleeting kiss on their way out the door, both of them distant and preoccupied with what the day at work would bring . . .

He started to cry the moment he saw Eva standing before him . . . blood on her shirt. She was facing him, but he knew that the back of her head was smashed. She was dead. This was the Eva he had tried to bring back to life countless times—in his mind, day and night. He tried to reach out towards her, but the plastic strips held him fast. He tried to say something, but no words came out of his mouth. He could hear Eva's voice, but her lips were not moving. She asked him if he had forgotten her. She told him that this was the worst fate of the dead. They were bound to a place that was cold and grey and forgotten. *All alone.*

He pleaded with her, told her that he had not forgotten her—he would never forget her! She said she didn't believe him, but it was okay, she understood how hard it was for him to hold on . . . and he kept telling her that he would always love her.

You promised to find the man who killed me. It was not an accusation, simply a statement of fact.

"I tried, Eva. I did everything I could to find him. You have to believe me . . ."

You promised to look after me.

"I know."

The image of Eva faded out. He made no attempt to hold on to her. He was too riddled with shame, and the tears poured down his face.

Ravn opened his eyes. He didn't know how much time had passed. He looked around. He was sitting in the greenhouse, bound to the stake. The brilliant multicoloured mushroom beds before him. Everything seemed normal. It was quiet. The voices were gone. His hands were free, and he rubbed his sore wrists where the plastic had cut into his skin. Then he saw the shard of glass and picked it up.

Free yourself . . . you can *be free . . . you* can *be the master of your salvation.*

It sounded so simple. The only escape. Logical. An obvious truth that rises to the surface of your mind. He shook his head at his own stupidity and started to cut himself. First, along the large veins on the underside of his arms, then across his bare chest, the blood like warm milk flowing from the open sores, as if he were christening himself in his own blood . . . *free of the past, sanctioning his own guilt . . . He was free at last.*

57

Ravn screamed and opened his eyes. His heart was hammering in his chest. He gasped for breath and tried to look down. The strip around his throat limited his movement, but he managed to glance at his breast: no blood, no cut wounds. But his jeans were smeared in vomit, he realised, as a sharp stench of stomach acid filled his nostrils. It felt as if his head were about to burst, and a fire was burning in his belly, the flames reaching up into his chest and throat. Ravn feared that the psychological effects of the poison might have abated, but the physical effects were just getting started . . .

He heard a car approaching outside. Soon after, it stopped on the gravel nearby. A car door slammed. It sounded very close to him, so the main building and front yard where he had parked the Volvo could not be far off. He wondered whether someone had come to look for him.

He looked around for the glass shard and spotted it beside his right knee. His legs were still bound at the ankles, but with extreme difficulty, he managed to bend his knees and give the shard a shunt with the heel of his shoe. It landed a few inches short of his bound hands. Straining against the strip around his neck made it cut deep into his flesh, and he desperately manoeuvred his body in an attempt to reach the shard. At last, the strip snapped and he propelled the shard within reach of his fingertips. He began filing away at the strip that bound his wrists. Finally, the strip broke, and he looked down at his bloody hands for a moment, reliving the nightmare of slitting the veins in his own arms. Then he cut the strip fastening his ankles.

Ravn's legs could barely hold his weight and he leaned heavily against the pole. The greenhouse walls were spinning around him. At the end of the rows of cultivation boxes, someone had left the rear door open. Peering through the trees outside, he caught sight of the yard. A dark four-wheel drive with police written on the side door was parked in the drive, but he couldn't see the local policeman anywhere.

Before he could take a step forward, his body was wracked by a coughing fit, and the pain in his stomach was increasing steadily. He clung to the pole and spat blood onto the ground. He stared at the globule in horror. He had heard of severe internal damage caused by the intake of toxic mushrooms. Worst-case scenario, all bodily functions ground to a halt, a slow and painful death. But he had no intention of ending his days as fertiliser for Jacob Mesmer's mushrooms. He steadied himself against the pole and began to limp down the lane between the first two rows of cultivation boxes.

From the doorway, he could hear voices coming from the front yard. In his haste to find the policeman in time, he tripped over the threshold and tumbled over onto the grass in front of the greenhouse. He tried to get up again, but his legs were not responding. Craning his neck on the grass, he caught a glimpse of the policeman standing in the yard, talking to Samuel, Jacob, and two guards. Jacob shook his head at something the policeman said. After a few moments' rest, Ravn pushed to his feet and took a couple of unsteady steps and slumped against the nearest tree trunk. He tried to call out to the policeman, but little more than a rasping sound came from his throat. Ravn lunged at the next tree. The policeman took a few steps away from the others, twenty metres tops, he reckoned, and he'd be able to throw himself into the yard in front of the local copper's feet.

The policeman was standing in front of Victoria's Volvo, which was still parked between the two black Audis he had seen before. The policeman pointed at Wilma and said something to Jacob, but Ravn was still out of earshot to hear Jacob's reply. Ravn staggered towards the row of trees bordering the front garden. With a frown on his face, the policeman took a few steps back towards Jacob.

". . . I don't believe you because . . ." Ravn heard the policeman say, but he couldn't make out the rest. Something about a search, and the member of God's Chosen who had died in the wheat field.

"Believe whatever you want!" Jacob yelled at the policeman.

"Help," Ravn said desperately, in a gasp that was no more than a whisper.

All at once, a loud bang reverberated over the yard and people ducked instinctively. Patrick was standing at the top of the stairs that led up to the main building, a double-barrelled hunting rifle resting on his shoulder. He cocked and aimed at the policeman but fired the next round at his car instead, shattering the windscreen.

The policeman ran for cover behind his car.

Jacob raised his cane over his head. "Can you feel the coming of Judgement Day, you filthy devil-monger?!"

Patrick reloaded his rifle and fired at the nearest front tyre of the police car. The policeman threw himself into the driver's seat and took cover behind the steering wheel.

Samuel grabbed Jacob's arm. "Stop this madness, Jacob, make it stop!" he pleaded.

Jacob gave Samuel a hard shove in the chest, sending him over backwards onto the gravel. "There is space in Hell for you, old man!" He raised his cane and pointed at the police car. "Patrick, send that Satan on his way with gunfire that will show him the almighty power of God."

Patrick aimed and fired a round into the bonnet of the car.

The policeman had managed to get the car into reverse and stepped on the accelerator. The car swerved down the gravel drive and sped towards the gate. Minutes later, the enormous four-wheel drive burst through the gates and veered out of sight.

Utterly exhausted, Ravn rolled over onto his back and rested his head on the cold gravel. In the distance, he could hear the screeching tyres of the police car disappearing down the country road.

"Good work, Patrick," Jacob said. "It's just as I foretold, my faithful brothers and sisters: Satan's agents will come to us. And now there is no way back. We are at war."

The soldiers gathered around their Master and nodded, and Patrick reloaded his rifle.

Ravn felt something poking his side and he opened his eyes. Jacob was standing over him, jabbing his side with the cane. "Are you still alive, Demon Bringer? You are a tough little bastard, aren't you?" He wiped the sweat from his brow and shook his fingers in Ravn's face. "Yup, you'll soon descend to Hell yourself, no doubt about that."

Ravn was just beginning to understand the extent of Jacob's fanatical plan.

58

Patrick cocked the hammer of his rifle and pointed the double barrel at Ravn. He held his breath. If Patrick pulled the trigger now, his head and torso would be pulverised. "Just say the word, Master," Patrick said to Jacob, who was standing beside him.

Samuel came up behind them. "Master, you cannot do this. Killing this man in cold blood goes against everything we stand for—and believe in."

"Nonsense. *Eye for eye, tooth for tooth, hand for hand, foot for foot, burning for burning, wound for wound . . .*" Jacob said. "Don't you remember the Scriptures at all, Samuel?"

"But he's just the messenger. He has done no wrong."

Jacob glared at Ravn. "I still don't like him. But spare your ammunition, my son," he said, resting a hand on Patrick's shoulder. "God's mushrooms will do the work. Look how the Demon Bringer is shaking already . . ."

Patrick lowered the rifle and smiled. "Shall we throw him on the compost heap, Master?"

Jacob shook his head. "You'd better bring the spy along, Patrick."

The Elders climbed the stairs to the main entrance and Patrick and one of his sidekicks pulled Ravn to his feet. He was very weak. If they hadn't been holding him up, he would've fainted again. They dragged Ravn up the stairs and followed the others inside. Ravn was sufficiently conscious to take a look round. He was surprised to see that the interior was undergoing an extensive renovation. The intermediate ceiling and dividing walls had been removed, creating one large room, so it resembled a theatre.

Ravn was hauled along to the far end and deposited at the base of a bearing pillar that he was fastened to with his hands behind his back. He leaned against the cold steel, breathing heavily. Ravn felt as if he was about to lose consciousness again. The room danced before his eyes, and he was struggling to concentrate. In a daze, he registered that Jacob and the others had sat down next to one another at a long table. They were watching grainy video footage on an old monitor, which appeared to be gathering images from the cameras installed at strategic points round the property. Organ music and Jacob's chanting voice came from a small loudspeaker placed on the table. *"The Lord is my shepherd; I shall not want . . . the Lord is my shepherd; I shall not want . . ."*

"They're all running around like headless chickens," Jacob said, rubbing his chin. "A couple of gunshots ring out, and they're completely rattled. Interesting."

"Naturally, our brothers and sisters are afraid," said Samuel, who sounded rather shaken himself. "Perhaps you should give them a few words of comfort, Master. Make sure that the situation does not escalate out of control."

"We cannot yield to Satan. *He* was the one who attacked us first."

"The policeman merely wanted to know if Benjamin was one of us. Why this aggression, Jacob? From the very beginning, we have never condoned violence."

"You seem to forget that I was the one who founded God's Chosen, Samuel. You only joined the movement later."

"No, I have not forgotten . . . Master," Samuel said.

"From the very beginning, we have prepared to defend ourselves against Satan."

"Yes. By means of worship, prayer, and hymns—"

"By whatever means the Lord has put at our disposal. Do not fall prey to doubt, Samuel," Jacob said, looking at him gravely. "Least of all now, when we have chased the demons out of our gates, so we can live in peace and in accordance with the Word of God once more. Do not doubt, Samuel."

Samuel cast his eyes to the ground. "I do not doubt the message of God. I just don't understand your confrontational approach, Jacob." He glanced anxiously at Patrick and his mates. "We do not preach violence. On the contrary."

"He's doing it in order to create chaos," Ravn intoned in a hoarse voice.

Everyone at the table turned their head and stared at him.

"You are simply making matters worse for yourselves," Ravn went on. "It is only a matter of time . . . before the police return with reinforcements."

"And we will welcome their return. Isn't that right, Patrick?" Jacob said, turning to his loyal disciple.

Patrick nodded. "Let them come, Master. We have fought and beaten Satan's demons before."

Jacob smiled at him warmly. "I know, my brave son. You are our crusaders. Our army of angels. Our true protectors."

"Samuel . . . stop them before innocent people get killed," Ravn stammered. The pain in his stomach was unbearable.

Åse crossed herself. "The demon is poisoning you with his evil tongue, Samuel."

"Don't listen to him, Samuel," Birgitte added.

Samuel said nothing. As if turned to stone, he stared at Ravn.

Jacob turned to Samuel, put an arm around his shoulder, and hugged him close. "Samuel, my old friend. We all know where this is going. We have talked about this so many times before, prepared ourselves for the inevitable, and there is no reason to relent now. We must stand together and be strong in our faith."

"It's not your decision, Jacob . . . Master . . . nor is it up to the Elders to decide . . . It is the *congregation's* decision. You must call everyone together and explain the situation. Support them. Let *them* choose."

"Of course." Jacob withdrew his arm from Samuel and turned to Birgitte. "Could you assemble the congregation for us, sister?"

Birgitte leaned forwards and turned off the video. She selected another tape from the shelf and loaded it into the player. Moments later, a howling siren blared from the loudspeakers outside.

"Patrick, my son," said Jacob. "Will you and your holy warriors ensure that our meeting is not disturbed, and, if necessary, defend your brothers and sisters from demons who wish to enter our grounds?" he added with a smile, as if he had asked Patrick to wash the dirty dishes in the sink.

"Of course, Master."

"May you be blessed by the Lord, my son. Go and prepare yourselves, then."

Ravn watched Patrick and his men open a hatch in the floor and descend down a stairway. A few minutes later, they returned carrying heavy ammunition crates and machine guns slung over their shoulders. Ravn recognised the weapons: M95 automatic rifles, which were typically used by the army and were probably stolen. They had enough weapons to start a mini civil war, and he had no doubt that Patrick and his army were prepared to use them. Ravn feared the worst for the women and children who could be caught in the crossfire. This could turn into a bloodbath.

59

Murmuring voices woke Ravn from a feverish sleep. He was extremely thirsty and tried to swallow a few times to produce spit in his mouth, but his throat was bone dry. His symptoms had intensified; the initial pain in his stomach had now spread into his limbs. And he was feeling apathetic, as if the gravity and danger of his situation no longer mattered, as if he had resigned himself to the inevitability of his fate.

A large congregation had assembled in the cave-like room, their attention trained on Jacob, who stood before them. Patrick's men—the holy warriors of God's Chosen, as their Master had called them—surrounded them, keeping guard. Ravn thought he had heard a helicopter as well as troops approaching, but he could not tell if it was real or just another hallucination. Kevin stood in the middle of the group wearing the blue uniform, holding the hand of an emaciated woman as he stared at Ravn. The moment their eyes met, Kevin's face lit up in a huge grin and he waved enthusiastically at Ravn. "Raven . . . it's the Raven, Mamma!"

Ravn tried to return the greeting with a smile, biting back the pain.

Kevin's mother yanked the boy's arm and told him not to wave at the demon. Kevin obeyed reluctantly and cast his eyes to the ground.

Ravn noticed a further ten children amongst the congregation's members—some appeared to be even younger than Kevin. Three of them were wearing the grey uniform, and the rest were dressed in blue. With the exception of Kevin, all the children seemed afraid or intimidated by the grave proceedings around them. Through a haze of fever, Ravn caught snippets of Jacob's sermon . . . "The Demon Bringer over there . . ."

Some members of the congregation turned their heads and stared at Ravn. Judging by the expressions on their faces, they no longer seemed to fear him. Perhaps he looked harmless in his weakened state, or perhaps he was the least of their concerns at that moment.

". . . he brought this declaration of war from the Supreme Satan, my earthly father, and a horde of demons have infiltrated our church ever since . . ." Jacob went on. "I say to you, my brothers and sisters, that these spies are amongst us right now." He pointed the manila envelope at the crowd. "You know who you are—you forlorn sinners—those who have cast off the Word of the Lord, preferring to cling to the evil of Satan instead . . ."

A murmur ran through the congregation.

"This pack of lies," Jacob said, waving the envelope again, "was written to destroy our blessed community, and alienate us from our Heavenly Father. I am deeply distressed that it has come this far . . ."

"Can we not defend ourselves against these lies as we have done before, Master?" an elderly man dressed in grey in the first row asked. A few of his peers standing nearby nodded at him in encouragement.

"I wish that were true, my friend," Jacob said, looking at the man with a troubled expression moulded on his face. "But *these* lies will embroil us in a lengthy legal battle, which will drain the life from our veins. We will win in the end, of course, but our righteous victory will come too late . . . and ultimately, Satan will prevail."

The sound of moans and crying erupted amongst his disciples.

"What kind of lies does that document contain, Master? Can you read from it for us?" the man asked.

"No," replied Jacob in a mournful tone. "I neither can nor will read from this wicked decree because the lies it contains will annihilate your souls. Possess your thoughts for eternity. Even *I* was only able to read the first few diabolical pages—with God's help."

"Can we not fight these lies with goodness?" Kevin's mother asked. "We could declare and stand firm in the Word of God."

All eyes in the congregation turned to her, and she lowered her gaze immediately, clearly uncomfortable being the centre of attention.

"We have so many brave souls amongst us," answered Jacob, extending his arms towards his congregation, as if to embrace them in a paternal hug. "May you be blessed by the Lord, sister. But I'm afraid it's too late for that since the agents of Satan have surrounded our walls . . . demonstrating once again the power of evil . . ." His voice broke. "I'm so sorry . . . that it has come to this . . . I . . . I'm so sorry that I have failed you . . ."

"Don't cry, Master, this is not your fault," said the elderly man who had stepped up before. "We thank you for your guidance. For everything you have done for us."

"Amen," the congregation murmured. "Amen."

Jacob dried his eyes and smiled gratefully. Ravn still didn't understand why he stubbornly refused to accept his father's offer. Surely, the money would be sufficient to keep the farm running so that Jacob could continue to preside over his holy kingdom. Why was he lying to his congregation instead? Was a martyr's death more important to Jacob than anything else?

"We are all in agreement with you, Master," said Samuel, who was standing next to Jacob. "But we must have other alternatives. Why don't we surrender and pray for the sinners out there? They can never take our faith from us, after all."

"Surrender to Satan?!" Jacob said so viciously that he sprayed spittle in Samuel's face. "And abandon God? Is *that* what you're suggesting, Samuel? Isn't that Judas-talk I hear?"

Samuel flinched. "Perhaps we could flee, Master, just like the old Israelites did?" he said with a tremor in his voice. He looked out over the congregation, searching for support. "Perhaps we can apply for amnesty? Or hide . . . flee to our German brothers and sisters across the border?"

Murmuring erupted in the hall. It seemed as if everyone began to talk at once. Some people suggested they flee to the forests in northern Sweden. Others talked of the island that the community had always dreamed of buying off the Norwegian coast. Another man suggested they could flee to the Orthodox sister congregations in the east. At last, Jacob broke up the menagerie by banging his cane on the ground.

"Be still, brothers and sisters!" Jacob said. "I know that the seriousness of our situation can give rise to desperate thoughts. But we are surrounded; we cannot flee. And even if we could, where would we go? We have no money. The outsiders' and infidels' lies have ruined us. This was supposed to have been God's House, but they have taken it from us."

"But what are we to do, Master?" the Elder in the first row pleaded.

"We will embrace God," said Jacob firmly. "The road to Paradise is not paved with property and gold. We will return to God."

"AMEN!" the congregation chanted in unison.

"Will you follow me to Paradise?" Jacob said.

"AMEN!"

"What exactly do you mean by that, Master?" Samuel said quietly.

"Have I not been clear?" Jacob snapped at Samuel. "Do you know of *more* than one Paradise than the Kingdom of God, Samuel?" he scoffed.

A scattering of nervous laughter came from the assembly before him.

"We have prepared ourselves for this for a long time, my dear friends," Jacob went on. "The road to Paradise will not be difficult; I promise you that. Let us go to the temple together now. Åse and Birgitte have prepared everything for us. We will sing and pray together, in the name of the Lord—"

Jacob's preaching was interrupted by the sound of a helicopter above. He took the walkie-talkie out of his pocket and spoke into it. Moments later, gunfire erupted outside. The congregation started in fright and looked up at Jacob.

"It's all right, take it easy, my friends," Jacob said. "Everything is under control."

The sound of the helicopter faded, and Jacob talked into his walkie-talkie again. Then he smiled at the assembly. "Everything is in perfect order now," he said. "Our holy crusaders have chased away the flying demons. Let us go on to the temple."

On Jacob's command, the congregation were ushered towards the door, and everyone began to sing one of their homegrown hymns.

Ravn was left alone in the main building. He glanced towards the monitors on the table. On the centre screen, he could see Jacob leading his disciples up the gravel path to the temple. On three of the other monitors, he could see the guards posted along the walls and the broken-down front gate. Three police vehicles had barricaded the road leading into Gethsemane.

Ravn pulled on the plastic strips bound round his wrists, but it was useless. He was much too weak to break free.

60

A cool sensation on his lips woke him up. Water, a plastic bottle pressed to his lips, Ravn realised. He drank the water greedily, and it splashed over his face, blinding him. He stopped drinking and lowered his head, gasping for breath as he tried to focus on the frail figure that had brought him the water. "Have the police stormed the temple? How many people are injured?"

The figure made no reply and Ravn lifted his gaze.

Kevin was standing in front of him with tears in his eyes. His body was shaking so much he was spilling the water. "I . . . I . . . d-d-don't want to meet Jesus," he said.

"Kev-Kevin, can you do me a favour and give me a little more water?"

Kevin lifted the bottle and carefully put it to Ravn's lips. This time, he didn't spill quite as much. Ravn emptied its contents and thanked the boy. Then he turned his head and looked at the monitors on the table. There was no sign of the police and Jacob's men were still guarding the entrance. Nothing seemed to have changed in the interim.

"I-I'm sorry I didn't come to free you earlier," said Kevin.

"That's okay. Do you think you could help me find something to cut myself free?"

Kevin nodded. "I was afraid . . . That's why I didn't come sooner . . . It's hard to help someone when you're scared."

"I know what you mean. But you came back. That's really brave of you, Kevin, thank you."

"That's all right."

"Can you take a look over there on the table, see if there's something sharp we can use on these strips of mine?"

"Yup," Kevin said. He dropped the plastic bottle on the floor and scampered over to the table. "There's nothing here, Raven." Kevin stuck his hand in his pocket and brough out a rusty nail. "But maybe we can use this? It jabs okay, but I'm not sure it can cut . . ."

"It's perfect," said Ravn. "Come over here and I'll show you what we can do."

Kevin came over to Ravn and sat on his haunches in front of him.

"Put it between my hands and the plastic strip, and then turn it as hard as you can, okay?"

Kevin did as he was told and started to rotate the nail. The plastic strip tightened, cutting into Ravn's wrists.

"Doesn't it hurt?" Kevin asked, looking at him curiously.

"Not much," said Ravn through gritted teeth. Moments later, the strip snapped. Ravn brought his hands to his lap. "Thank you, Kevin. You did really good," he said, rubbing his aching wrists.

Kevin smiled. "Can we fetch my mum now?"

Ravn supported himself on the pillar and pushed to his feet gingerly. He doubled over in pain as his stomach cramped and he vomited the water onto the floor. He took a moment to recover and wiped his mouth with the back of his hand.

Kevn wrinkled his nose. "You're not feeling so good, are you?"

"Well, I've been better. Do you have any more water?"

Kevin shook his head. "Can we go fetch my mum now?"

"Where is she?"

"She's in the temple with the others."

"Hmm . . . that won't be easy, Kevin," Ravn said, looking around. "Do you know where we can get hold of a mobile phone?"

Kevin shook his head again. "We're not allowed to have phones. Only the Master has one. He's in the temple too. And the sol-soldiers. Some of them have phones. Who do you want to call? Your mum?"

"Er . . . no. We need to call the police, Kevin. They can get us out of here."

"I want to take my mum with us."

"Of course. The police can get her out as well," Ravn said, catching sight of the hatch in the floor. "Do you think you could help me walk over there?" Kevin came closer and Ravn leaned on his shoulder. The frail boy sank to his knees under Ravn's weight, and they nearly toppled over. But then he caught his balance and helped Ravn limp over to the hatch.

Ravn sat down and peered into the cellar. A naked bulb in the ceiling was the only light. "Wait here," he said, and carefully climbed down the narrow steps.

"You're coming back, right, Raven?"

"Sure I am, but I need you to stay up here, okay?" Ravn continued down the steps and took a look round in the cellar. It was a long, low-ceilinged room that might have been a military barracks from the looks of the rows of bunkbeds, separated by tall metal lockers. Ravn limped down the narrow corridor between the bunkbeds. At the far end of the room, the corridor forked into two. The left fork led to a bathing area and toilets, and the other fork led into a large kitchen. He went into the kitchen, where four long rows of tables created a common dining area. He went over to the sink and filled a cup with water from the tap.

"RAVEN!" Kevin yelled from above.

Ravn sipped the water carefully, afraid he might throw up again.

"RAVEN!" Kevin yelled again.

Ravn put down the cup and rummaged through the top kitchen drawers. In between kitchen utensils, he found a vegetable chopping knife and a lighter, which he put in his pocket. Unfortunately, he didn't find any other kind of weapon to defend himself with, but the knife was better than nothing. He hurried back upstairs, afraid that the boy would inadvertently attract attention.

"I thought you'd gone, Raven," said Kevin the moment he returned.

Ravn could see that the boy had been crying and he stroked his head. "I said I was coming back, didn't I?"

"Can we fetch my mum now?"

"How did you get into the house?" Ravn asked.

Kevin pointed to the window that faced the garden between the main house and the large production hall. "I just hopped in through there."

"Come with me," Ravn said. He'd recovered somewhat and could walk to the window without leaning on the boy. The garden was silent and deserted, cloaked in darkness, but he could hear the helicopter blades whirring high up above. Kevin slipped out the window and Ravn followed after. "We have to be quiet as mice so no one sees us, okay?" he whispered, taking Kevin's hand to hold him back.

The boy looked at him with eyes like saucers. "Quiet as . . . mice," Kevin whispered with a nod.

"Do you know where the soldiers are posted?"

"Post-ted?"

"Where they're standing guard."

"Oh, sure." Kevin smiled. "They're *every*where."

"What about over by the compost heaps? Do you think we can get over the wall there?"

Kevin shook his head. "The soldiers are hiding down there, Raven . . . keeping watch."

"Are you sure?"

"Yep . . . they threw stones at me when I came past earlier. Can we fetch my mum now, Raven? I don't think she wants to meet Jesus either."

Ravn doubled over in pain as his stomach cramped again. He squeezed the boy's hand so hard he snatched it back. In the distance, a megaphone crackled with static and then a voice sounded into the night, appealing to the congregation to contact the police: *If anyone needs help, please proceed to the gates immediately.* Then the unit leader announced a telephone number that people could call if they were unable to come to the gate at this time.

The police action was proceeding according to the book, Ravn thought in frustration. He knew the police would appeal to everyone to remain calm and come forward of their own free will, but the unit leader would simultaneously be preparing a strategy for attack. He'd taken part in similar routine police operations countless times. Ravn reckoned that the police wouldn't take any chances in the current situation. For as long as they could, they would negotiate and appeal to Jacob Mesmer to surrender.

"Come on, Raven, we have to fetch my mum now," Kevin said, pulling on Ravn's arm.

"We need to find a telephone, Kevin, that's the most important thing right now. I can't help your mum all on my own, you understand?"

Kevin nodded. "Of course, I'm not stupid. We'll find a telephone in the temple—I'll find one for you, Raven."

Ravn had no idea how Kevin meant to find a phone in the temple, but it was worth a shot. Besides, he needed to get an overview of the situation on the ground. His only solace was the knowledge that as long as the congregation remained gathered in the temple, there was less risk of innocent people getting caught in the crossfire when the police went into battle with Patrick's soldiers.

Ravn took the boy's hand, and they snuck down the dark gravel path leading to the temple. He paused by the trees just before the lawn. The door was open, and light spilled onto the grass. Kevin pulled impatiently on his hand, but Ravn held the boy back and put a finger to his lips. "Take it easy, Kevin," he whispered. "Let's see if we can sneak in through the back."

Kevin nodded and they continued round the side of the building. Ravn could hear people praying, somewhere crying, the occasional sob, a woman groaning. Kevin looked up at Ravn and clung to his hand tight. Ravn put a finger to his lips again, desperately hoping the boy would stay quiet. Soon after, they reached the back door. Ravn let go of Kevin's hand and took the kitchen knife out of his pocket. Ever so carefully, he opened the door, and they crept inside.

The sound of murmuring and people crying rose as Ravn and the boy silently made their way down the narrow corridor behind the stage curtain. Ravn caught sight of Jacob. His upper body bare, his arms raised in the air, and his head thrown back, the Master was standing on the stage, his sweaty torso swaying from side to side, as if he were in a trance.

"Can we fetch my mum now, Raven?" Kevin said, pointing at the stage.

Ravn made no reply as he stared at the spectacle on the stage. Two metres from Jacob's feet, Kevin's mother was lying on her back next to three other members of the congregation, frothing at the mouth, as she stared blindly at the black wooden cross on the wall behind her Master.

"Can we fetch my mum now, Raven?"

61

A long line of people were waiting in a queue that stretched throughout the temple and led up to the stage. Most members were holding hands, crying, and mumbling prayers to themselves. Åse and Birgitte were standing behind a folding table at the edge of the stage, handing out disposable plastic cups to the members who filed past. Birgitte tapped a clear liquid into the cups from a thermos that stood on the table, and Åse was the one handing out the cups to the members individually.

Jacob was holding a microphone to his lips. "*. . . and Jesus answered: 'You do not know what you are asking. Are you able to drink the cup that I am about to drink?' And they said to him: 'We are able.'* We are also able, my brothers and sisters, we will also drink from the Heavenly Son's chalice so we can join the Lord's Heavenly crowd. Come closer, my friends, join these faithful brothers and sisters before me who are already on their way to meet Jesus."

"Do not falter," Jacob said to a young couple clutching hands just in front of him. "Believe in the Lord."

"I can't do it, Master," sobbed the man, lowering the cup in his free hand.

Jacob frowned and looked at the man with obvious disdain. "Your resistance is futile," he said. "The evil people on this earth have already won. We must return to our Heavenly Father. That is all there is to be done. If you resist and stay here on earth, you will end in Purgatory, you understand? It's over. We must do this so we can start over, find our salvation as redeemed sinners . . ."

"But . . . there must be something we can do."

"You can drink the holy water in your chalice. Don't let the demons waiting at the gates win," Jacob said, pointing at the front door. He cast a glance over his congregation, smiled, and went on. "Don't let them throw you in prison with murderers and rapists. You deserve better than that. The outsiders want to turn us against one another. Break up families. Take your little children away from you and give them up for adoption where they will be brought up by sinners. Trained to become prostitutes and drug addicts. Is *that* what you want? Let the children come to Jesus. Let them grow up in God's Kingdom. Amongst God's Chosen. Have mercy on the little children and let them drink from the holy chalice." Jacob pointed at the plastic cup in the man's hand.

Looking around desperately, Ravn caught sight of Samuel standing with a group of soldiers between the first two rows. Samuel was trying to persuade a reluctant group of members to join the queue. An elderly woman had refused to step into line. Jacob had noticed her as well. He stepped down from the stage and intervened. "Do not abandon your faith in Jesus now, sister," he said. "Do not betray your brothers and sisters. They deserve better. Do not let the Devil beguile you, sister. The Devil will not lead you to Paradise. He does not want you to sit at God's table . . . I am asking you to turn away from the Devil, sister."

With tears pouring down her cheeks, the elderly woman got to her feet. "But I'm afraid, Master."

"Do not be afraid," Jacob said. "That is the Devil talking. We will go to sleep and wake up in God's Kingdom together. I have told you this so many times before. Do not frighten your children. Do not be a sinner. I know that your heart is pure, sister." He pointed at two little girls who were standing in the queue with their parents with tear-stained cheeks. "Look how brave these girls are. Look how happy they are that they will meet Jesus. Take your example from *them*," he added. "I am asking you to be brave and have faith in Jesus. Believe in the power of God."

"I'm sorry, Master, forgive me," the elderly woman said. Wiping away her tears, she let Samuel put his arm around her shoulders and lead her to the queue.

Ravn stared at the scene before him in horror. He could not believe his eyes. In all his years at the force, he had never seen anything like this. He felt utterly powerless to stop them. He was hopelessly outnumbered, and Jacob had complete control over the members of his congregation. On the stage, another couple fell to the ground, frothing at the mouth. He looked at the empty plastic cups littered about and reckoned that the poison the others had been given was much stronger than the dose he'd received from Birgitte.

"Kev-Kevin," a weak voice on the stage said. His mother turned her head to the side and reached out an arm to the boy.

"M-m-um—" Ravn put a hand over the boy's mouth before he could say any more.

In his weakened state, Ravn held on to the struggling boy as best he could. "Shhh, Kevin," he whispered, drawing the boy back down the corridor to the rear door. When Ravn reached out for the handle to open it, the boy broke free. "Kevin, stop!" Ravn said, but it was too late.

The boy ran down the corridor and burst onto the stage. Ravn could hear him calling to his mother, but his voice was drowned out by Jacob's on the loudspeaker. "Praise the Lord! Kevin, our lost little lamb, has returned to the flock . . . now he too can drink from the holy chalice . . ."

Ravn threw himself into the bushes on the edge of the lawn, flattening himself against the ground. He gasped for breath. It felt as if his belly were on fire. The next moment, the back door of the temple opened, and a soldier stuck his head out. He lit a torch and shone its beam over the lawn, but there was nothing to be seen. Ravn peered through the bushes at the low building. He was still having a hard time believing what was going on in there with the police right outside the gates. The mass murder was well organised, and Ravn reckoned that this must have been Jacob's plan all along. He simply used Benjamin's death as a convenient platform to generate an imminent threat from the outside.

Ravn was desperate for a plan to help the innocent people—men, women, and children, including Kevin—in the temple. He had to get help from the police. Right now. But he had no idea how he could convince the unit leader to go off script and order his men to storm the farm immediately. He didn't have a phone, not even a torch to signal a Morse code of distress—anything that could help him communicate with the police. One way or another, he was going to make Jacob pay for this. He had a mind to return to the temple and cut that psychopath's throat with the kitchen knife, but he told himself that this wouldn't help save Kevin and the others. *Perhaps he should confront the soldiers at the gate?* If Jacob's warriors started shooting at him, the police might intervene, return fire . . . but that wasn't enough. He needed the entire force to enter the grounds and get the people out of the temple.

If the unit leader played this by the book, he would wait as long as possible, hoping to tire out Jacob's men. But if he let that happen, everyone in the temple would die before the police arrived. It would be a massacre. *How was he going to force their hand and provoke an attack?* Ravn wondered. If the unit leader knew that civilian lives were in danger, he would attack now, regardless of the resistance and firepower he would meet from Patrick's men. He had to attract attention to the catastrophe. And then it struck him. Perhaps that was it: create a catastrophe . . .

A madcap idea was forming in his head. Ravn had no idea if it would work—never mind if he could pull it off without getting himself killed. But if he could do it, he had no doubt the police would be provoked to storm Gethsemane.

62

Ravn kept in the shadows of trees that lined the gravel path to the production hall and the barracks. The farm grounds seemed deserted, and he reckoned it was likely that Jacob's warriors were posted along the outer walls and the entrance, ready to take on the battle with the police if they tried to breach Gethsemane. For now, it seemed he would be able to move around unseen until he found what he was looking for. Jacob's plan for a martyr's death left no room for survivors. That much was clear. But he wasn't so sure that Patrick and his men were prepared to die with the others in the temple.

The pain in his belly brought him to his knees. And he felt the left side of his body going numb. He slapped his left thigh with his right hand until the feeling returned to his leg. This seemed to help a little and, moments later, he limped further along the path to the production hall.

Above him, the police helicopter was still circling the farm, but apart from that, everything was quiet. He peeked inside the deserted production hall where the white chalk spray rested like a sprinkling of fresh winter snow over the compost. An overpowering stench of ammonia filled his nostrils. Near the closest row of cultivation boxes, the primitive spraying equipment he had seen earlier lay abandoned on the ground. The compost was sprayed with a diluted ammonia solution, and this is what had fostered his plan: He had to find out where they kept their reserve tank of undiluted liquid ammonia.

Logically, the tank would be relatively close to the production hall. *Perhaps it was stored in one of the low buildings he had seen between the hall and the barracks?* He went round the back of the production hall and continued to the ramshackle building straight ahead. When he came past the garage, he knew he was close to the outer perimeter of Gethsemane, and Jacob's warriors would be keeping watch nearby. When he reached the first door of the low building, he looked round quickly. No one was about. He leaned his shoulder against the metal door and pushed it open. It squeaked on its hinges, and he scurried inside.

He peered round in the dark. It appeared to be a toolshed of sorts. Along the wall to his left, he could make out the shape of a workbench, and the opposite wall was lined with metal shelves filled with boxes and spare parts. At the foot of the shelves, he saw the outline of four metal jerrycans. He walked over to the cans and picked them up in turn. All were empty except for the last one. He screwed off the cap and brought it to his nose. *Diesel oil.*

Ravn staggered out into the night once more, the half-full jerrycan of diesel in his hand. He was running on empty. *He had to find that tank of ammonia. Now.* After a few steps, he had to stop. He sank to his knees and rested for a moment, leaning on the can with his head bowed. He regretted not going back for Kevin instead. *Perhaps if he'd cut Jacob's throat, he could have created enough chaos to stop the massacre?* But it might have sped up Jacob's plans instead. *He just didn't know.*

When he reached the adjacent shed, he leaned against the door and toppled over backwards into the dark room. He lay on the ground for a moment, catching his breath. The smell of ammonia filled his nostrils. He almost smiled. This had to be where they kept the undiluted tank of ammonia. He rolled over. At the far end of the shed, he could see the contours of the tank. He pushed to his feet and hauled himself slowly along the wall. The oval tank was peppered with rust. It looked like a bomb dating from the Second World War, which was not far from what he had been hoping for. If he could open the tap and release ammonia vapours into the air, he could create an explosion. During his time on the force, he'd heard stories about ammonia explosions that could annihilate entire buildings. On its own, liquid ammonia wasn't flammable, but the vapours it released were another matter.

Ravn found the tap just below the pressure gauge, but a large metal lock prevented him from turning the screw. He looked round in vain for something that could break the lock. Instead, he picked up the jerrycan and brought it down hard on the thin pipe connecting the tank and the pressure gauge. He kept hammering on the pipe as hard as he could. At last it broke, and a stream of ammonia vapour hissed out the end.

Ravn dropped the jerrycan and stared at the pipe, utterly exhausted. The vapours made him cough, and he held his sleeve up to his mouth. He reckoned it wouldn't take long before the entire room filled with the explosive gas. Picking up the jerrycan again, he stumbled over to the other side of the room and poured the contents over the table, wooden bench, and adjacent wall. Then he cast it aside and took the lighter out of his pocket.

He could hear the ammonia gas hissing from the other end the room. He paused with his thumb on top of the lighter. He had no idea what concentration of gas was required to create an explosion, and in spite of himself, he was afraid that if he flicked the lighter on now, the room would blow up spontaneously. He gave himself a moment to consider his alternatives, but none came to mind. And he was damned if he was going to let Kevin die, especially after the courage the boy had shown by coming to look for help and free him single-handedly.

Holding his breath, he flicked the lighter. A thin flame ignited, and Ravn set alight the pool of diesel on the table. The oil caught fire and immediately licked up the wall. He was about to open the door when he heard voices approaching outside. He took out his knife and listened. The moment the door handle moved, he threw himself at the door and just registered Patrick's surprised expression before they both crashed onto the ground.

"Fire!" yelled one of the soldiers.

Ravn felt Patrick's hand around his throat, and he jabbed the knife blindly at him. Patrick howled in pain, and Ravn scrambled away from him.

"Get him!" yelled Patrick.

Casting a look over his shoulder, Ravn saw Patrick's men standing in the doorway, staring at the flames in horror. Patrick staggered to his feet, blood seeping from the knife wound on his shoulder, raised his machine gun, and aimed. *So this is how it ends*, Ravn thought in a split second. And then the shed seemed to lift, shudder, and flip over backwards simultaneously as it exploded, and Patrick disappeared in a sea of flames that swallowed the trees between them. The shock wave from the explosion threw Ravn through the air, and he came down hard on the ground about fifteen or twenty metres further down the path.

Ravn rolled instinctively when he hit the ground. He gasped for breath, dimly aware of a searing pain in his leg. Looking down, he noticed that his left trouser leg was on fire. He kicked out frantically and covered his leg with soil, which soon smothered the flames.

Ravn was momentarily deaf with a high-pitched ringing in his ears. He watched the silent spectacle unfold before him, the flames rapidly spreading to the adjacent buildings. Several more explosions erupted, sending tongues of fire into the night sky. An arsenal of gas containers shot like missiles into the sky, and Ravn sought refuge amongst the trees. His hearing began to return, and above the ringing in his ears, he heard a volley of gunshots from the road. The next moment, the projector lights of the helicopter swept over the farm.

The police had finally stormed Gethsemane, but Ravn was terrified they were too late.

63

Grenades lit up the sky as the special forces unit stormed from their respective flanks. Leaned up against a pillar by the rearmost mushroom bed, Ravn followed the battle going on outside. He'd intended to crawl back to the temple, but he only got as far as the greenhouse, taking refuge amongst the multicoloured mushrooms, and at long last stilled his thirst with water from a tap. In a daze, he listened to the gunfire. Jacob's army had M95 rifles that made a deep throbbing sound, whereas the police used MP5 rifles that fired with a higher pitch like a crack. At first the throbbing gunfire dominated the battle, then the cracking took over, and he hoped this meant the police were gaining the upper hand.

Ravn heard a clatter by the door, and the next moment, it crashed open, splintering the panes. A pale figure, naked from the waist up, limped out of the shadows: Jacob Mesmer.

Jacob had a wound on his right side that was bleeding heavily. His cane in one hand and the manila envelope in the other, he staggered down the centre aisle between the mushroom beds. Then he stopped, sat down on his haunches with obvious difficulty, and buried the envelope in the dark soil in front of him.

Ravn fumbled for the knife next to him and clasped its shaft as hard as he could. He grabbed onto the tap beside him and tried to get up, but a jab from Jacob's cane in his chest sent him toppling over backwards, and the knife slipped out of his hand.

"Well, well, well . . . the Demon Bringer lives . . ." Jacob said, pointing the cane at him.

"Have . . . have you killed them all?" Ravn said through gritted teeth.

Jacob sat down heavily opposite him. The rolls of fat on his chest shuddered under his movements as his hand crept to the bleeding wound in his side.

Ravn's fingers felt for the knife on the tiles, but the point of Jacob's cane shunted it away from him.

"No need for unpleasantries, Demon Bringer," said Jacob. "Let's enjoy the silence." A rally of gunfire erupted outside. "Well, as long as it lasts . . ."

"Where is Kevin? Did you kill him as well?"

Jacob burst out laughing. "Your concern for our little lamb is touching, but Kevin and his mother are sleeping peacefully with the angels of the Lord. Amen."

Ravn shook his head. "You . . . you . . . but you don't have the balls to take the poison yourself . . ."

"Our ceremony was interrupted. The police stormed our temple after a massive explosion—you don't happen to know anything about that, do you?" Jacob said, cocking his head.

"I wish it had taken you with it to kingdom come," Ravn said bitterly. "Kind regards from Patrick—he looked surprised, seconds before he burnt to death . . ."

Jacob nodded with a satisfied expression on his face. "I'm sure Patrick would be happy. Sounds like you gave him the honourable soldier's death that he's been thirsting for ever since he returned from Afghanistan . . ."

The beam of the helicopter's projector light swept through the greenhouse, blinding them, and both Jacob and Ravn shielded their eyes with their hands. When the light moved away, Jacob tightened his grip on his cane and made to get to his feet.

"Why, Jacob? Why did all those people have to die?" Ravn asked. "Do you hate your father that much?" he added, trying to keep Jacob back.

"Is that what he told you? That I hate him?"

"If that isn't the case, why didn't you just sign the damn contract and take the money? You didn't have to murder all those people to make a point!"

"I didn't murder anyone. I merely showed God's Chosen the way to Paradise. They deserved the grace and kindness of God, nothing more. It is God's command that they return to Him . . . He has acknowledged that our love for Him is true, therefore we may join Him in Heaven today . . ."

"You seriously expect me to believe that God talks to *you*?"

"He has always spoken to me. From the day I asked for His help . . . from the day I realised that the Mesmogramme would only lead to perdition and poverty—"

"What the hell are you talking about?"

"I told him . . . I confronted my earthly father with my Heavenly Father's message, but he didn't understand. He wouldn't listen to the reality of the situation, even though it was written—"

"And what reality is that?"

"That we were indoctrinating our clients with the Mesmogramme . . . doing the Devil's work."

"The *Devil's* work?"

Jacob nodded, deadly serious. "We were selling a patented philosophy with clever abbreviations, a language that only a select few—those who attended our seminars and bought our books—could understand. We were creating a flock of godless people who would sell their souls to earn a ticket to the upper echelons of management . . . Always start with the top. Once you have convinced top management, the host of middle-tier management will come running . . ."

"You're deluded, Jacob," said Ravn. "And it sounds like you brought your business philosophy with you when you founded your movement."

"How dare you make fun of the work of God!" Jacob snarled. His outburst resulted in a coughing fit and his hand sought out the wound in his side. "The Mesmogramme kills families," he went on once he'd recovered sufficiently. "The system poisons good Christian values with its pre-defined personality types, its unchristian indoctrination of employees from the moment they walk through the door. These companies have become the church of our times, and upper management is the high priest they obey."

Gunfire sounded just outside, and Jacob grabbed his cane and struggled to his feet. His trouser leg was soaked in blood.

"I find it interesting that you call it the *Devil's* work when you are the one behind the Mesmogramme."

"In God's eyes, we are all sinners," Jacob said laconically, and made the sign of the cross over his chest. "I admit that when I started working for my father, I was also impressed by all those clever leadership strategies that top consultants in the industry preached. I found it fascinating. So I distilled what our competitors were preaching and developed my own system. But then God showed Himself to me . . . showed me how far I had strayed from His path . . . I was ashamed and forsook all the evils I had done for the company. But it was imperative that I also expose the illusions that my predecessors had created. I began studying their methods in detail so I could tear down their false temples . . ."

"Is that so? And what did you find?"

"I don't expect an outsider to understand these things," Jacob said patronisingly. "But I will tell you the truth: First, I discovered that the most renowned leadership strategy that has been peddled to industries for decades was created by a man who developed heathen comic strips like *Wonder Woman*," Jacob spat out in disgust. "Second, it came to my attention that one of the most ubiquitous management systems in the business world was based on perverse Jungian theories—it was created by a swindler who practised the occult! And the greatest management organisation in the world is founded on no more than American housewives' scribbles at their kitchen tables—and meanwhile, their husbands worked with Oppenheimer to create the first atomic bomb, which pushed humanity one step closer to Hell," Jacob fumed. "Don't you get it? These people were charlatans. Each and every one of them are agents of Satan, just like my father."

"*You* are the one who has murdered your entire congregation, Jacob."

"I am simply trying to demonstrate my point."

"Which is?"

"That no one can compete with the Holy Scriptures. In a sea of worldly systems, God has *the* perfect irresistible product to offer mankind."

"And what is that?"

"Eternal life. Who can beat that?" Jacob said with a fat grin on his face.

A shot sounded—a cracking sound—and the next instant, Ravn heard commands yelled by the police outside. Jacob was leaning against a pillar, breathing heavily, and it didn't look as if he was going anywhere.

"How did your father injure his hand?" Ravn asked.

"What do you mean?"

"If he didn't injure it in the fire in Belgiensgade, when did the accident happen?"

"The accident? Okay, let's call it an accident," Jacob said, looking at the door. "It happened a long time ago. We should have died in the flames. Then none of this would have happened and we would be with God in Heaven now."

The masked men from the special unit came through the door with their machine guns raised. The lights from their headgear danced round in the dark. When the beams fell on Jacob and Ravn, the leader yelled at them to surrender.

"Yield, Satan!" Jacob screamed, pointing his cane at the police.

The cracking sound erupted immediately, and in a spray of bullets, Jacob dropped heavily to the ground at Ravn's feet. Moments later, a dark pool of blood spread over the tiles.

Ravn raised his hands in the air, his eyes fixed on Jacob's bloody and disfigured face, the bubbles of blood trickling from the corner of the preacher's mouth.

64

The wildfires at Gethsemane raged, lighting up the night sky, and ambulances had been called to the area. Two rescue workers brought Ravn out of the greenhouse on a gurney, a paramedic right on their heels. Ravn's nose and mouth were covered with an oxygen mask, but he was still conscious as they pushed him along the narrow path past the burning main building, where firefighters were trying to control the blaze. Two policemen stood over five of Patrick's men, who were lying face-down on the lawn with their hands tied behind their backs. Through the trees near the top of the path, Ravn caught a glimpse of the body bags lined up on the lawn outside the temple. And two men in white overalls were carrying another body bag out of the main building. Ravn clawed the oxygen mask off his face. "Is . . . are there any survivors?" he said to the paramedic following the gurney.

"Don't take this off," said the paramedic, trying to return the mask to his nose and mouth.

Ravn pushed her hand away. "Survivors?" he said again. "I asked you . . . if there were any, for fuck's sake."

The paramedic cast a glance over her shoulder, put his mask firmly back in place, and kept her hand on it this time. "I . . . I don't know, but it doesn't look good," she said, giving his shoulder a gentle squeeze as they continued down the drive. "You were lucky. Get some rest. Try to relax, it's going to be fine."

Ravn closed his eyes for a moment as they hurried along the drive and out through the front gate, through the crowd of police officers and rescue workers heading the other way. A sob escaped from his lips. He couldn't bear the thought. For the people in the temple, help had come much too late. He caught a glimpse of the local policeman's petrified face amongst the spectators who had gathered on the side of the road. The paramedics asked everyone to move aside and pushed the gurney over the road to the nearby field, where the military Merlin helicopter was waiting.

They lifted Ravn's stretcher into the helicopter and placed him next to the other survivors. Ravn lifted his head to look, but they were all wearing oxygen masks. Then he caught sight of the boy on the stretcher furthest away. Ravn grabbed the paramedic's arm. "Kevin? Is Kevin still alive?"

"Who?" the paramedic said.

"The boy at the end. Is he still alive?"

The paramedic glanced over her shoulder. "Yes, he's going to make it. He's a tough little boy, that one," she said with a smile.

Ravn dropped his head back onto the stretcher and closed his eyes in relief. He listened to the hum of the engine and the whirr of the blades as the helicopter started. Moments later, he felt them begin to rise into the air. He opened his eyes again. Through the side window, he saw that Gethsemane's main building was still ablaze. *Amen*, he thought, hoping it would burn to the ground.

Ravn felt a strange quiver in his stomach, as if the helicopter was losing altitude. Wondering whether they were going to crash, he looked around at the others, but the rescue workers were calmly going about their care of the survivors. It was quiet all around him. And then he knew it; he was the only one falling, deeper and deeper into an everlasting darkness.

The high-pitched monotone from an ECG drew the paramedic's immediate attention to Ravn. His head lay askew on the pillow. One arm had slipped to the side, his hand resting on the floor. On the ECG monitor above his head, the line was flat.

The paramedic sprang up from her seat and weaved her way through the other survivors to Ravn. Removing the oxygen mask, she noted that his lips were blue. She checked for a pulse and found none. "I need a defibrillator, *now!*" she yelled over her shoulder. When she ripped open his T-shirt, exposing his chest, she noticed a manila envelope underneath, which she thrust aside onto the floor. One of the men from the rescue team stepped up and attached the defibrillator's electrodes to Ravn's chest.

"Clear!" yelled the paramedic.

They both pulled back, and the paramedic activated the defib. Ravn's body jerked, but the line remained flat. "Again. Clear!" the paramedic yelled.

They tried three more times without any change.

"How long till we reach the hospital?" she asked.

"About six minutes," he said.

"Shit! He doesn't have that long! Give me the adrenaline."

The rescue worker took a syringe and an adrenaline ampoule from his bag. As he pierced the top of the ampoule and began drawing the liquid into the syringe, the helicopter dipped in a gust of wind, and he would have dropped the syringe had the paramedic not held him fast. He nodded his thanks and gave her the syringe. The wind picked up again, and the helicopter dipped once more.

"Bloody hell," said the paramedic in frustration.

"It's now or never," said the rescue worker. "Or we're going to lose him."

"I know . . . but I'm afraid I'll miss and puncture his lung . . ."

"We'll be at the hospital in two minutes," he said, pointing out the window. In the distance, they could see the blinking lights of the helipad on the roof of Rigshospitalet.

"He doesn't have two minutes," said the paramedic, straddling the stretcher. The rescue worker held her steady, and she pressed her back against the low ceiling of the helicopter. Closing one eye, she aimed the needle at Ravn's heart and, with a quick jab, planted the needle between his uppermost ribs and pushed the plunger home. "And?" she yelled at the rescue worker.

He looked up at the monitor. The line was flat. "Nothing."

"Shit . . . shit . . . shit!"

65

The media had a field day. Not only in Denmark, but all around the world, news of the tragedy on the island of Lolland had fuelled the headlines for weeks. Even Eduardo's newspaper, *Information*, which usually avoided sensationalism, had jumped on the bandwagon and written a series of articles on the incident. The media had dubbed the tragedy a "mass killing" and, as such, Jacob Mesmer's plans to beguile the world with the notion that the incident would be classified as a "mass suicide" were scuppered.

They suffered a total death toll of ninety-one people. Fourteen of these were killed in battle with the police. Three people were killed in the explosion that initiated the police's intervention. The forensic team recovered body parts, including an aluminium prosthetic leg, scattered on the scene. The remaining seventy-four members of God's Chosen died from poison that was distributed and imbibed in their temple. Apart from three members of the special unit with light injuries, the police did not suffer any casualties.

The investigative unit found the remains of a laboratory in the burnt-out warehouse on the farm, as well as a greenhouse where toxic mushrooms had been cultivated. Several of these fungi were hybrid clones of various *Amanita* and *Morchella*. The forensic team had not yet been able to discern exactly what kind of poison had been administered to the members of the sect. But initial autopsy reports revealed that the victims had ingested concentrations of cyanide, various amatoxins, and psilocybin. Based on the fact that the latter substance is a psychedelic drug compound, the authorities were currently investigating the theory that Jacob Mesmer had used the substance to manipulate his congregation, which led to their death.

The Forensics Unit also found numerous cadavers, in various stages of decomposition, in the manure heaps at Gethsemane, indicating that further murders may have occurred within Mesmer's organisation, and that the heaps served as a macabre burial ground. In an attempt to find out how many bodies may be hidden there, technicians were currently combing the compost for traces of DNA. In the meantime, the Danish Food and Agricultural Ministry had banned the sale of mushrooms cultivated at Gethsemane. Three large supermarket chains reported a marked decrease in the sale of edible mushrooms in general—not only those mushrooms that were produced in Denmark. Why Jacob Mesmer had chosen to take the lives of so many people remained a mystery. As yet, the investigative authorities had no theory on this point. The members of the sect's inner circle were all dead, and, according to the media, the answer to his question had been buried with Jacob Mesmer.

Eduardo had tears in his eyes and a bunch of white lilies in his arms. Møffe was on a leash at his feet, and Victoria stood at his side with an arm around his shoulders. Eduardo swallowed hard and tried to hold back his tears. "I should have gone with him. Then this would never have happened," he said.

"How would that have helped? If you'd gone along, you'd both be lying here now, Eduardo," Johnson said irritably.

"It would have been easier to bear," said Eduardo. "I'm never going to forgive myself."

"It's going to be all right, Eduardo," Victoria said, stroking his arm. "Ravn didn't ask you to come along. You know he liked to do things on his own."

"The two of you are talking about him as if he's already dead," Johnson said, shaking his head. He took a step closer to Ravn's hospital bed. He was asleep and looked so frail, so unlike himself with all those electrodes and tubes that hooked him up to various machines by his bedside. And a catheter was stuck in the large vein in his neck, attaching him to a dialysis machine. Johnson's face went pale when he looked at the blood running through the tube.

"You're not going to faint on us, are you, Johnson?" Victoria said.

"Of course not," Johnson said, looking away quickly. "In all my time as a boxer, I've seen a whole lot more blood than *that*," he scoffed.

"Yeah, mostly your own, I imagine," Ravn said faintly, his eyes still closed.

"Lazarus awakes from the dead," said Victoria. She let go of Eduardo and stepped up to Ravn's bed.

Ravn opened his eyes and tried to focus on the little party assembled at his bedside. A half-smile came to his lips. Eduardo almost dropped his bouquet of lilies as Møffe lurched forward and rested his head on the edge of the bed. "Hey, take it easy, Møffe," Eduardo said.

Ravn laid a limp hand on the sheet next to Møffe's head.

Møffe strained at the leash and grunted. Smacking his chops a few times, he wagged his tail and gave Ravn a particularly forlorn look.

"How do you feel?" Victoria asked, taking a seat on the edge of the bed.

"Better. They're taking good care of me."

"They say you almost croaked," said Johnson.

"The doctors say I was gone for a few minutes."

"You . . . you were *dead?*" Eduardo said, gaping at him.

"Only for a very short time, apparently."

"*Madre mia* . . . what was it like?"

Johnson gave Eduardo a hard stare. "How the hell should he know—the man just said that he was *dead.*"

"I know, I know, but did you see something? A light? Another universe?"

"I swear to God . . . the Spaniard is losing it," Johnson said, rolling his eyes.

"Johnson, for your information, lots of people have reported that after they were declared dead, they had left their bodies and were able to look down at themselves," Eduardo said indignantly.

"I didn't see anything," said Ravn. "Neither myself, nor anyone else. The last thing I remember, I was in the helicopter. And when I woke up, I was attached to all these damn machines."

"What do the doctors say?"

"That I was lucky. Apparently, Jacob didn't give me the same kind of poison that was distributed to the people in the temple. I think he gave me the same drug that he gave Benjamin. According to the doctors, it was a psilocybin and amatoxin cocktail . . ."

"Sounds unpleasant," said Johnson. "What . . . what's their prognosis?"

"I'm going to live."

Johnson nodded. "That's the main thing. I'll buy you a round when you get out of here."

"It will be a cheap one."

"Excuse me?"

"The doctor says that a single drink could send me to the grave. My liver is badly damaged. So are my kidneys. And even after the dialysis is complete, I have to go easy."

"That bloody *cabrón*, Jacob Mesmer. I hope he rots in hell," said Eduardo.

Johnson picked up a vial of pills from the bedside table. He turned it round in his hand and read the label. "Nitroglycerine?" he said, shaking his head. "Watch these don't blow you up."

"Do you have heart problems as well?" Victoria asked.

"Only if I forget to take those," said Ravn.

A tense silence fell over Ravn's get-well-soon party. His friends looked at him with grave concern.

"Do you know why Jacob did it? Why did he kill himself and all those people?" Victoria asked, trying not to think about Ravn's close call and obvious ill health as a consequence.

"Because he was a psychopath!" Johnson burst out.

"You're probably right about that, Johnson," Ravn replied. "Perhaps Jacob thought martyrdom was the best deal he was going to get."

"What about the contract you had to deliver? Did you get a chance to read it?" asked Eduardo.

"No," Ravn said, closing his eyes. The dialysis made him nauseous. Or maybe it was all the drugs they were pumping into his system. Either way, he was overpowered by exhaustion and slipped out of consciousness.

66

A few days after his friends came to the hospital, the staff nurse announced to Ravn that two police officers had come to see him. Ravn had hoped that one of them might be Mikkel, but it turned out to be two officers from the team investigating the massacre on Lolland. He didn't recognise either of the guys from before, but they'd clearly done their research and were kind enough to treat him like a colleague, congratulating him for his good work.

"It must have taken balls to start that explosion," said the younger of the two, whose name was Niels.

The officers said they needed to clarify the circumstances leading up to the massacre so they could build a strong case against the people responsible, namely, the group of surviving soldiers whom the police had arrested.

Ravn answered their questions as best he could. "How many people other than the soldiers survived?" he asked when the officers had completed their interview.

"Eight adults and six children," said the senior officer, whose name was Gregers. Ravn couldn't help noticing that his bald head was shaped like an egg. "They'll probably give you a medal for your efforts to save innocent civilians," Gregers said, wiping away the beads of sweat on his brow.

"I don't want a medal," said Ravn. "My only hope is that the case will make the police change protocol so they can intervene sooner next time."

Gregers buried his hands in the front pockets of his jeans. "I understand," he said. "I think we're about done here, Niels?" he added, turning to his colleague, who had taken a seat in the chair by the door.

Niels nodded. "One more question," he said, sweating even more than his colleague in the oppressive heat in Ravn's room.

"Shoot," said Ravn.

"What were you doing over there?"

"As I explained earlier: On behalf of a client, I had a meeting with Jacob Mesmer, but thanks for repeating the question."

"Yes, you said so. But what was the meeting about?"

"It's confidential. So is my client's name, by the way, before you ask."

"Give us a hand here, Ravn, we're on the same side," said Gregers.

Ravn made no reply.

Gregers looked round the room at all the flowers and cards from friends who wished him well. "My guess is that you were working for Jacob Mesmer's father, Ferdinand Mesmer. And that *he* was the one who sent you to Lolland."

"You can just nod your head, then we don't have to ask you any more questions," Niels suggested.

"You can ask as many times as you like. My answer remains the same."

"Why are you protecting him? Does he have more to do with this than you're telling us?"

"Who?"

"You know who. Why did Jacob Mesmer commit mass murder precisely when you arrived on the scene?"

"Are you trying to suggest it was *my* fault?" Ravn said with a hollow laugh.

"No. But maybe it had something to do with your client, Ferdinand Mesmer?" Niels asked.

"I've never met anyone by that name," Ravn said, holding Niels's gaze. "If you must know, I knew Benjamin Clausen, who was at Gethsemane, through a common acquaintance."

"Do you mean Advocate Lohman? The client you had both worked for?"

Ravn shrugged. *They've obviously done their homework*, he thought.

"We could have a chat with him instead."

"Of course," Ravn said. As far as he was concerned, they were welcome to talk to Lohman. Other than an earful in his stuffy office, they wouldn't get anything out of it.

"So . . . you don't have anything else to add?" said Niels.

"Only that my client and I were concerned about Benjamin's mental health."

"Did Benjamin's suicide have anything to do with what happened in the temple?"

"I have no idea. I'm not a psychologist."

"What was your impression of Jacob Mesmer?"

"My impression? The man was nuts."

"Define 'nuts,'" said Gregers.

"Tally up his victims and you'll understand what I mean."

The two officers wished him a speedy recovery and left him in peace.

When Ravn was certain that they were gone, he turned on his side with great difficulty, opened the drawer of his bedside table, and rummaged through the stack of get-well-soon cards, letters of thanks from the victims' bereaved, and the drawing of the helicopter that Kevin had made for him. Ravn knew that Kevin was now living with a foster family on Fyn. As soon as they released him from the hospital, he was determined to send him something. *What can you send a boy who has just lost his mother?* he wondered. *Maybe a toy helicopter, or something else that could distract him?* His fingers fumbled in the bottom of the drawer where he had hidden the manila envelope.

After the officers in the greenhouse had verified Ravn's identity, they immediately set about calling for paramedics to the scene. Ravn had used the opportunity to recover the envelope from the mushroom bed where he had seen Jacob bury it.

During his recovery at the hospital, he had read its contents several times. Ferdinand Mesmer had offered his son a huge sum of money. Jacob had about twenty million good reasons to sign the contract and waive all rights to the Mesmogramme. In the event that this was not sufficient incentive, however, Ferdinand Mesmer had included another document: a letter from the past.

Ravn could not fathom the contents of the letter. But he was damn sure Ferdinand Mesmer had included it purely for the purpose of putting pressure on Jacob, some kind of blackmail that might have tipped his son's hand, which resulted in mass murder at Gethsemane.

67

Ravn was hospitalised for thirty-three days. When he finally returned to Christianshavn, it felt liberating to once again be able to smell the combination of sea breeze and fried foods from the cafés along the canal. Some might consider it noise, but he revelled in the shouts of neighbours, the call of hawkers, the traffic on the roads. It gave him a sense of security. Still unsteady on his feet, he felt like a sailor who had returned after a long, arduous journey at sea, clinging to all the old familiar things of his home port.

The only things he took with him from the hospital were the arsenal of prescribed pills, Kevin's drawing, and the manila envelope. He had bought Kevin the largest toy fire engine he could find and sent it to him in Fyn with a letter, thanking him for the drawing and wishing him all the best for the future. The toy reminded him of Victoria's Volvo, which played on his guilty conscience, most of all because she'd had the decency not to mention her car—even though he knew she missed Wilma every single day. He had rung his contacts in the police and found out that the car had been impounded by the police on West Zealand, as well as Jacob Mesmer's Audis, which were being searched for prints and evidence in the case. They had promised him to expedite the process if possible and get someone to deliver the Volvo to Christianshavn as soon as they were done.

"What?" Ravn realised that Eduardo had said something to him. They were grocery shopping at Brugsen on Christianshavn Square.

"We should get you some fruit as well," said Eduardo as he pushed the trolley down the aisle. The trolley was already full. "What kind of fruit do you prefer?" he asked, checking out the fresh fruit display.

"I hate fruit," said Ravn, breathing hard even though he was leaning heavily on the edge of the trolley. "What the hell am I going to do with all this food?"

Eduardo was filling a plastic bag with various fruits that he selected with great care. "You have to ensure that you get all the nutrients you need, Ravn," Eduardo replied. "I've received a list and dietary advice from the hospital."

"When did the two of us move in together?"

Eduardo ignored the comment as he tied a knot in the plastic bag. "I mean it, Ravn. It's time you took your health seriously."

"I am. I do," said Ravn. "But I have a twelve-litre fridge on board, Eduardo. I don't have space for all this stuff."

"Then we'll put some of it in *my* fridge," Eduardo said. "Digestive biscuits are supposed to keep you regular," he added, heading for the next aisle.

"I've never been more regular in my life."

Ten minutes later, Ravn and Eduardo were back on Christianshavn Square. Now that Eduardo was weighed down by three full shopping bags, Ravn no longer had any difficulty keeping up with his friend's pace. The morning sun was high, and the square was buzzing with life. "Hi there," said a young girl who stopped in front of Ravn. She was dressed in cut-off jeans and an orange vest top. "Here you go," she said, handing Ravn a colourful pamphlet.

"Um . . . thank you," said Ravn, taken off guard.

The girl ran a hand through her wild, knotted hair. "We are a small group called The Children of Light," she said. "If you'd like to meditate with us or join us for a hot meal, you are welcome to visit our centre on Bådmandsstræde. It doesn't cost anything," she added with a smile.

Ravn nodded his thanks and put the pamphlet in his pocket.

"I hope to see you soon," said the girl. "May you have a wonderful day."

Ravn made no reply. He merely stared after the girl as she made her way back to the small group of people who were dealing out pamphlets on the square. Many of them were singing along with a young man who was sitting on a low wall, playing the guitar.

"Do you think that's how it always starts, with singing, dancing, and a common wish for everlasting happiness?" said Eduardo.

Ravn shrugged. "I don't know how it starts. But I've seen how it can end. Let's go."

They kept walking and made their way down the embankment on Overgaden Oven Vandet.

"Did he actually sign it?" asked Eduardo.

"What do you mean?"

"The contract. Did Jacob actually sign on the dotted line?"

"Why do you ask?"

"No reason. It's just that I saw a press release that Mesmer Resources will merge with SIALA as expected. There is some speculation as to whether the new conglomerate will register on the stock market."

"I have no intention of buying any shares."

"Well, they might be very valuable," Eduardo joked, hitching up the shopping bags. "I assume that irrespective of whether Jacob signed that contract or not, Ferdinand Mesmer now holds all the rights to the company?"

"It's none of my business. What's your point?"

"No point. I'm just talking here."

"Well, take a break."

Eduardo looked at him. "I'm sorry if I said something that—"

"Forget it. I'm just tired . . . that's all. I'm sorry, Eduardo," Ravn said with a wave of his hand.

They walked the rest of the way home in silence, and Møffe was waiting for them when they got back on board *Bianca*. Ravn knew that Ferdinand Mesmer had used him. He was played like a hand in poker. But he couldn't figure out how. And it was bothering him like hell.

68

Ravn sat on the rear deck with Møffe on his lap, looking at the dark water in the canal. It was ten p.m., the sun had just gone down, and the air was still warm. That evening, Eduardo had made a delicious dinner for him, but he had no appetite. Fretting over him as always, Eduardo said he would cancel his date, but Ravn insisted he was being ridiculous and eventually persuaded him to go as planned. Ravn appreciated his concern, but it was starting to get on his nerves. He was looking forward to the day their relationship would go back to normal, but his shift from beer to Earl Grey tea told him clear as day that things would probably never be like before.

"The wounded warrior has returned home."

Ravn half-turned in his chair and greeted Katrine, who was standing up on the quay, looking down at him, and Møffe grunted at the interruption.

"Would you like to come on board?"

Bianca rocked gently as Katrine stepped down onto the rear deck. Møffe hopped off his lap and padded over to Katrine. She took a dog biscuit out of her pocket and gave it to him. Møffe licked his chops and let her scratch him behind the ears. Then he returned to his basket by the cabin door.

"Have you come to check up on me?"

She sat down in the chair opposite Ravn. "I'm sorry I didn't come to see you in the hospital."

"That's all right. I got the flowers . . . from Ferdinand Mesmer."

"He sends his regards. He's very grateful for everything you've done."

"I can imagine. I hear the merger is good to go?"

"Almost, yes. But his gratitude was rather with respect to those people whose lives you saved."

"I see. Does he even care?" He looked at her sceptically.

"He's a good man . . . deep down."

"I don't have anything other than tea to offer you, so—"

Katrine shook her head. "I don't need anything, thanks." She leaned back in the chair and extracted a white envelope from the inner pocket of her blazer. "We need to settle your bill for the last part of your assignment," she said, giving him the envelope.

"I should probably send you an invoice first."

"There's a little more in there than you'd add up from your time slips," she said with a smile.

Ravn took the envelope and peeked inside. Without counting the bills, he could see that it was a hefty sum of money. "This is a lot more than we agreed. Why?"

"The assignment became a lot more complicated than we anticipated. Besides, there are also the personal consequences to take into account."

"So this is for pain and suffering?"

"What you went through could not have been easy."

Ravn closed the envelope and laid it beside him on the deck. "So I shouldn't read anything more into it than that?"

She looked out over the canal. "I assume the police have interviewed you?"

"We've had a little chat, yes."

"Did you tell them why you went to Gethsemane?"

"I said nothing about Ferdinand Mesmer. He can rest assured about that."

"Thank you. He appreciates your discretion."

"I figured as much."

"Something else entirely . . ." She turned to look at him.

"The contract. That's what you want to know?"

She nodded. "Did you get the chance to give it to Jacob?"

"Isn't it obvious?" He stared back at her, trying to gauge her reaction.

She shook her head. "No, I don't think it is."

"Jacob received the contract."

"Do you know what happened to it?"

"I have no idea. Either the police have it, or it's lying buried somewhere at Gethsemane."

She nodded and looked down at the deck.

"Isn't it irrelevant, now that the merger is going ahead?"

"Of course. It's more a question of discretion. We don't want confidential information to get into the wrong hands."

"Do you know what's in the envelope?"

"No, do you?" She smiled back at him, but her expression was calculating.

"There wasn't time for that," he said, deadpan.

Judging from her smile, he thought she bought it. Katrine stood up and he followed suit with difficulty.

"We're holding a reception for Mesmer & SIALA on Thursday. You are welcome to join us."

"Thank you, but I don't think there's anything to celebrate."

Katrine shrugged. "Look after yourself, Ravn."

"You too."

Katrine leaned forward and kissed him. Her lips were hard and cold, and strangely this turned him on. He returned her kiss, and their bodies locked together as their kiss became deep and heated. At last, Katrine pulled free from his embrace, and Ravn brought a hand to his lips, which were throbbing.

"I . . . I'd better go," she said.

"Why? You don't seem like the kind of person who doesn't finish what she's started."

She smiled. "That might be the worst compliment I've ever received," she said, poking him gently in the ribs. "It's just that I don't want to . . . put your life in jeopardy. You're still sick, after all."

"I'm not *that* sick," he said, returning her smile. He fumbled in his pocket and jiggled his vial of pills in the air. "And don't worry if it looks like I'm gonna have a heart attack, I've got nitroglycerine and EPO handy."

"Okay, that's definitely the worst pickup line I've ever heard," she said, laughing heartily for the first time.

Ravn took her hand and led her through the open cabin door and into his bedroom at the bow.

Her skin was warm, and it felt damn good to touch her, taste her, hear her moaning, feel her pulse and her muscles working under him, the sweat between them, the contours of her arching body, and the rush in his head as he finally let go. *So full of life*, he murmured into her hair, not quite understanding his own words but aware of the feeling behind them. Afterwards, they lay close; he felt her warm breath tickling the side of his neck, where the catheter had been. He listened to the creaking ropes that tethered *Bianca* to the quay. Then he pulled her closer and fell into a deep sleep.

When Ravn woke again, it was dark. He was alone in the bed and could hear her rummaging in the cabin. He saw her silhouette moving as she was going through his things, which he let her do, because it didn't surprise him and it suited her character: searching, suspicious, and always at work. But most of all because he knew in advance that she wouldn't find what she was looking for. Soon after, she gave up and sneaked off the boat.

He would have liked to talk to her for a while, find out where she came from. He wanted to know what unit she used to work for, about her experience. And then again, it seemed like none of them wanted to talk about their past. Their relationship was a fleeting experience that was already over. And he was okay with that.

The next morning, a fine film of mist had settled on the deck. Ravn wrapped his duvet around himself and drank a cup of Earl Grey with a bread roll for breakfast. The neighbouring boats were shrouded in the mist and rain. The door to Eduardo's ketch was closed, and he reckoned that his friend had probably spent the night at his date's place—yet another in a long line of women, but Eduardo always seemed to believe that this was going to be the *one*, until the next one came along . . .

Ravn padded over to Møffe, who was lying in his basket. The dog grunted when he stroked his head gently. Then he stuck his hand under the dog's blanket and extracted the manila envelope. He wasn't interested in rereading the contract, only the note that Mesmer had attached to it.

The suicide note.

69

Ravn had turned his chair to face the embankment so that no one could catch him unawares as he reread the note. Ferdinand Mesmer had not made any comment, merely attached the note to the contract as if it were some kind of addendum, which indicated that its cryptic contents were a private communication between father and son. Judging from the mediocre quality of the frayed piece of paper, Ravn reckoned it had been torn out of a cheap notepad. The note itself was handwritten in curling letters, but it bore neither a date nor a signature.

I cannot delay it any longer.
The fiasco repeats itself on a daily basis.
Our life. Our world. Our choice. My choice.
Is a hopeless construction that is doomed to fail.
Now and in all eternity.
I have been damned to perdition.
The flames are my only redemption.
The definitive end to yet another project that I should never have begun.

The third-last line had caught Ravn's attention the moment he read it. Every time he read the line, the image of Mesmer's disfigured hand came to mind. And Jacob had mentioned the injury. It was as if he were about to reveal something about his past, just before he died in a rain of bullets. The only information Ravn had on Jacob's childhood was not reliable because it had been provided by his father. Apart from that, he had the testimony of the rector of the Bible Institute. Poul had described Jacob as empathetic and hard-working, a leader who was always ready and willing to help others in his class.

The suicide note contained no indication or explanation for Jacob's actions. And yet Ravn was certain that his father used it to turn the screws on his son and make him sign the contract. The question that haunted Ravn most was whether Ferdinand Mesmer had indirectly provoked Jacob to commit mass murder. Did he know in advance that the note would push his son over the edge? If he did, this case was far from over. But he needed to understand the context within which it was written.

I have been damned to perdition.

He knew the feeling. But he was none the wiser for it.

Exhausted is what he was. Perhaps this conundrum wasn't his problem to solve.

It was time to take another ration of pills.

70

"It's damn good to see you, Ravn," Mikkel said for the third time within the space of fifteen minutes. They were sitting at a café on Halmtorvet. Mikkel had called him up the day before and suggested they meet for a chat at the café. He probably just felt guilty for not visiting him in the hospital, Ravn thought. He had hoped that Mikkel might have some news about Eva's case, but as yet, Mikkel hadn't mentioned a word on Kaminsky.

The waiter arrived with their order. Mikkel glanced at the soda water that the waiter had placed before Ravn. "Have you given up beer?" he joked.

To Mikkel's surprise, Ravn nodded.

"Turning over a new leaf?"

"Something like that."

Mikkel raised his latte in a toast. "We had more guts in the good ol' days . . ." He took a sip of his coffee and put it down on the table. "That was quite a stunt you pulled over on Lolland. The guys back at the station can't stop talking about it," he said, jerking his thumb over his shoulder.

"Ninety-one people died that day, Mikkel."

"You should concentrate on the number of people you saved, Ravn. Not to mention the three *bandits* you put out of action with that explosion. That's three arseholes less who could've put a bullet in one of our guys . . ."

Ravn nodded and took a sip of his soda water.

"The chief would like you to pop in. You know, give you a reward while the press takes a couple of snaps for the papers."

"Is that why you called?"

"No, of course not!" Mikkel said indignantly. "I'm not his messenger boy."

"Oh yeah, since when?" Ravn said, winking at him. "What about you, back on full time?"

"Sure thing. Melby and I are working the streets. We're looking for weapons now, rather than drugs. The boys at the top are not happy about the latest developments out there—far too many guns out there, *bandits* shooting at each other . . ."

"How's your injury doing? Healing okay?"

"Well, I can still feel it playing up once in a while," Mikkel said, moving his arm slowly. "It's as if the tendons aren't properly attached to my shoulder."

"What about Kaminsky?"

The mere mention of the name brought a twitch to the corner of Mikkel's left eye. "What about him?"

"How is the case against him progressing?"

"You mean cases. The queue of people who want to interview him is not getting any shorter. And he's causing a bit of a ruckus in detention, I hear."

"What have you heard?"

Mikkel looked round to make sure no one nearby was listening. "The man is a psychopath," he said in a lowered voice. "First, he attacked the state legal counsel assigned to him—stabbed the poor guy in the eye with a pen. After that, they were treating him as extremely hostile. He's under maximum guard, only interviewed in handcuffs and shackles. The last I heard, he attacked one of the guards and bit off half the guy's ear. So now they fetch him in full gear and helmets."

"I would've bashed out his teeth instead," Ravn said.

"Yup, and that's why I miss you," Mikkel said, leaning back in his chair.

"I was hoping you'd have some news for me on Eva's case."

"I know. That's the reason I called."

"Okay. Spit it out."

"I've finally managed to get access to the stolen goods we found during the search of Kaminsky's place. They're keeping the goods at the compound at Copenhagen police headquarters." Mikkel glanced at his watch. "I thought we could pop in and take a look."

Ravn stared at him in silence.

"I thought you'd be happy."

"Of course, I am, I really appreciate your help with this, Mikkel, but . . . what are the chances we'll find something that was stolen more than three years ago?"

Mikkel shrugged. "The chances are minimal, but it's worth a shot."

"Okay, let's go, then," Ravn said, hailing the waiter for the bill.

Moments later, they got into Mikkel's black Golf that was parked in front of Station City. With Mikkel seated behind the wheel, the tyres of the Golf thundered over the cobblestones on Halmtorvet, reminding Ravn of the good ol' days when they used to go on patrol together. Mikkel *always* drove hell for leather, whether they were chasing a suspect or not. *Nothing had changed, apparently.*

They tore down Tietgensgade and towards the intersection with Bernstorffsgade, where Mikkel slammed on the brakes. Ravn's gaze settled on the iconic neoclassical arches of Copenhagen police headquarters. "So, Kaminsky is sitting up there?" he said.

"Yep," said Mikkel.

So close, yet so far, thought Ravn.

Mikkel put his foot down on the accelerator and spun the car round in the intersection. They drove down the road until they came to Mitchellsgade. The duty officer nodded at Mikkel and let them pass through the gates. Mikkel cruised past the police garage and continued to the end of the drive where three large containers stood lined next to one another. A blue-shirted police officer with grey hair was standing by the third, unlocking the seal of the container.

"Why are they storing the containers here?" Ravn asked.

"Good question," said Mikkel. "I guess it's part of the strict security concerning the Kaminsky case."

"It couldn't have been easy for you to gain access to the containers."

"Blue-shirts help one another, don't we?"

They got out of the car and greeted the police officer. He asked them to make it quick so he could seal the containers again before anyone found out what they were up to. Ravn peeked inside the first container. It was filled with exclusive brands, Bose electronic devices, B&O flatscreens.

"Shall we take a look?" Mikkel asked.

Ravn shook his head. "The thief didn't steal our old television or electronic equipment other than Eva's laptop, so I don't think it makes sense to look here." He continued to the next container. In this one, the stolen goods were packed on shelves. Mobile phones, tablets, and other electronic devices. Laptop computers were stored on the bottom shelves, and Ravn went down on his haunches to study the goods more closely.

Eva's work laptop was a black IBM. She'd had the foresight to engrave the name of the law office on the lid. And it had a Snoopy sticker by the touchpad. He'd teased her about the sticker, told her it wasn't very lawyer-like to put dog stickers on her office computer. *Why are you the only one who gets to have a dog?* she said.

After a few minutes, Ravn had finished searching the shelf of stolen computers, without finding Snoopy. He stood up slowly and turned to Mikkel. "Shall we take a look in the last one?"

"This is where we keep the trinkets," said the police officer, who was trailing on their heels. "Jewellery, cuff links, watches, that kind of thing." The goods were stored in metal lockers, which the officer opened for them. "There must be several millions' worth in here." Ravn pulled out a few of the drawers and looked inside. He felt like he was in a Tiffany for criminals.

The thief had stolen Eva's Rolex. It had a jubilee arm strap and a date engraved on the back of the dial, the date Eva passed her bar exams. It was a gift to herself for completing half a lifetime of law studies.

Ravn went through one drawer after another without finding anything that resembled Eva's Rolex. It was hot and stuffy in the container, he felt faint, and his heart was hammering in his chest.

"Are you okay, Ravn?" Mikkel said, noticing the pallor of his face.

Ravn nodded, but he could feel the beads of perspiration breaking out on his forehead. He tried to speed up the process, which only made him feel worse.

"Shall we take a break?"

"No, why would we do that?" He tried to sound enthusiastic. He ought to have taken his pills hours ago, but he wasn't going to pop pills in front of Mikkel and his colleague, as if he were some kind of junkie. He knew he was being ridiculous—neither one of them would judge him for it, least of all Mikkel. He was just being vain, but he didn't need anyone's pity. He blinked his eyes rapidly and pulled out the next drawer. It contained ten slender Rolex watches for women. He picked up one of them and turned it round, but his hands were shaking so much he couldn't read the inscription on the back. He put the watch back in the drawer so he wouldn't drop it.

"Tell me what we're looking for so I can help you," said Mikkel.

"I've got this," said Ravn.

"Of course," said Mikkel. He raised his arms in the air and took a step back.

Instead of picking up the watches individually, Ravn turned them backside up. The last watch in the line had an inscription made up of numbers. He picked up the watch and studied the date, which had almost been completely rubbed away. At that moment his left leg went into a spasm. He put the watch down hastily and grabbed onto the edge of the locker to steady himself. The locker tipped towards him under his weight, and Mikkel intervened just in time to stop it from crashing onto his head.

"Bloody hell, Ravn, are you sure you're okay?"

"I . . . I need some air."

Mikkel draped Ravn's arm over his shoulder and hauled him out of the container to get some fresh air.

"I'm okay now," said Ravn, extracting himself from Mikkel's grip.

"Was it her watch?"

Utterly exhausted, Ravn leaned back against the container and slid down onto the ground. "I . . . I don't think so, but can you just check the date on the back for me?"

"Sure thing," said Mikkel. The minute he was gone, Ravn fished his pills out of his pocket and took two of the nitroglycerine tablets. Mikkel was back in a flash.

"It's the 24th or 22nd of July, followed by the year 1989."

"Okay. Then it doesn't belong to Eva."

Mikkel turned to the police officer and thanked him for his help.

"You're right. It was worth a shot, Mikkel, thank you."

Mikkel sat on his haunches next to Ravn. "Just say the word when you're ready for me to drive you home."

"So I guess that's it, then?"

"What do you mean?"

"This isn't going to get us any closer to the truth, is it?"

Mikkel shook his head.

They sat there together for a while, just staring at the ground without saying a word. The hinges of the containers screeched as the police officer sealed them again.

"I know it sounds like a crock of shit, and I've said it before, but I'll say it again: It's time to move on, Ravn."

"I'm doing the best I can, Mikkel."

"Really?"

Ravn nodded and pushed to his feet slowly. He looked over at the police headquarters on the other side of the road and let his eyes wander to the top floors. This is where the most dangerous criminals in the country were incarcerated. These people had to be kept away from society, as well as the other detainees. If evil incarnate existed—the kind of evil described in Jacob Mesmer's hellfire sermons—then this was where you would find it. And Kaminsky was the worst of their kind.

"So close, yet so far," mumbled Ravn.

"Say what?"

"Nothing," said Ravn. He might not be able to meet the Satan incarcerated in Copenhagen police headquarters, but he had received an invitation to meet another of the same kind.

He would go to Mesmer's reception tomorrow. His victory celebration.

71

The large dark-green banners bearing the monogram of the new corporate conglomerate billowed in the wind over the bank between the company headquarters and the water. The 150 guests had been invited to the reception milled about on the square, drinking the champagne that waiters dressed in white served with canapés on silver trays. Ravn was standing on the fringes, watching the crowd, which had fixed its attention on the interim platform floating at the quay, where Ferdinand Mesmer was giving his welcome speech dressed in a black tuxedo. Reflected in the sharp sunlight, the platform and the surface of the water appeared as one, and it seemed as if Ferdinand Mesmer was standing—if not walking—on water. Indeed, this was exactly what he was able to do on a day like this one, surrounded by prominent guests who adored him and wished to celebrate the success of the merger with him. Reminding him all too vividly of Mesmer junior's sermon to his disciples who were sentenced to a gruesome death, the sight made Ravn feel sick to his stomach.

"Champagne?" The girl in a white uniform appeared out of nowhere, a glass in her hand.

"No, thank you."

The acoustics were appalling between the water and the steel-and-glass buildings and, from where he stood, Ravn could only catch snippets of Mesmer's speech. But he caught what was essential to Mesmer: a historic day, a new era . . . followed by something about beliefs and benchmarks and a series of catchphrases . . . blah, blah, blah . . . words that had the audience raising their glasses in a toast, but they meant nothing to Ravn. The audience applauded whenever Mesmer held an artistic pause, and when he concluded his speech, he stretched out his arms as if to embrace them all in a bear hug.

When Mesmer's speech was over, a frail little man joined him on the platform. The two men shook hands, and the audience applauded with renewed enthusiasm, accompanied by a burst of flashlights as photographers and press clamoured to capture the great moment. Ravn presumed the little grey man was the director of SIALA. The next instant, a brass band began to play and what seemed like at least a hundred green balloons were released into the sky.

Ravn watched Mesmer step up onto the quay. He was immediately surrounded by well-wishers, and Mesmer conversed with broad smiles and gesticulations. Ravn recognised some of the faces, which included members of parliament, several prominent business leaders about town, and—to Ravn's great surprise—Chief of Police Niels Vestergaard himself. Ravn had never met the Chief himself, but he knew that Vestergaard was a lawman who had come to the force directly from the prosecutor's office and had never set foot in a patrol car. Vestergaard was a man borne of the system and was more interested in rationalising than lending an ear to the cops on the street. Mesmer could certainly teach him a few tricks.

"So you chose to come after all," Katrine said, appearing at his side.

Ravn nodded and returned her smile.

"Can I get you something to drink?" she said.

"No, thank you. But perhaps you could get hold of Mesmer for me?"

She laughed. "He has a long guest list tonight, Ravn, but I'll be sure to give him your regards if I get a chance to talk to him myself."

Ravn extracted the manila envelope from his jacket. "You think this might shorten the queue?"

"So . . . you had it after all." She sounded disappointed. Probably because she hadn't been able to find it after searching his boat.

"Yep."

Ravn followed Katrine with his eyes as she made her way through the throng of guests till she reached Mesmer. He seemed irritated that she had interrupted his conversation with the mayor, but Ravn could gather from his gesticulations immediately after she whispered in his ear that he had made his excuses. Not long after, Mesmer was standing before Ravn, extending his hand in greeting. "I'm so pleased to see you. I'm honoured that you are able to join us today."

Ravn shook Mesmer's knotty, deformed hand.

"Shall we go inside and talk?" Mesmer said. "Just the two of us," he added, giving Katrine a look that made her stop in her tracks.

72

Ravn and Ferdinand Mesmer went into the large conference hall, which had a spectacular view of the water. Round tables were decked in white and silver for the gala dinner that evening, and on the dance floor at the far end, a few technicians were rigging sound equipment and loudspeakers.

"Please, take a seat," said Mesmer, pointing to a chair at the nearest table and sitting down himself. He took out his handkerchief and wiped his sweaty brow.

Ravn sat down and put the envelope in front of Mesmer. He resisted the temptation to look inside. "Katrine told me that you didn't have it anymore."

Ravn shrugged.

"Well, I really appreciate you returning it to me. Have you had a chance to read the contents?"

"*I cannot delay it any longer . . . The flames are my only redemption,*" Ravn said, citing the note.

Mesmer swallowed hard. "I assume you have come to collect a . . . finder's fee? How much?"

Ravn leaned back in his chair. "When I was a rookie, we were occasionally called out to some disturbed soul who had committed suicide," he said, regarding Mesmer with a cold stare. "As a rule, we would first ask the duty officer whether the victim was a man or a woman, mostly to protect ourselves. Only because men are always decisive when it comes to suicide; typically, men jump in front of a train, hang themselves, or blow their heads off with a hunting rifle. My commanding officer once told me that the reason for this was that when men attempt suicide, it's because they want to escape from a desperate situation, whereas for women, it is usually a desperate call for help. And therefore a woman's attempted suicide is a lot messier, less definitive; they try to drown themselves or take an overdose—or some other situation from which they might still be saved. Even when they cut their wrists, you will find many lesions along their arms—hesitation, half-hearted lesions made before they have the courage to make the decisive cut, which usually lie across the wrist, and you seldom die from that."

Mesmer cast a glance out the window. "That's all very interesting," he said impatiently, "but I don't understand where you're going with this."

"My point is that this . . . gender classification, if you will, is only the rule and there are always exceptions."

"I still don't see what this has to do with me," said Mesmer. "As I said before: I'm happy to pay you a reward for returning these documents, which must not come into the possession of anyone else—"

"Half-hearted lesions," Ravn said, cutting him off. He pointed at Mesmer's disfigured hand. "Like the pyromaniac who regrets the fire he has started, and now will do anything to put it out. Do you regret it? Do you regret your actions the night you tried to kill yourself and your son?"

Mesmer looked down at his hand, which looked like a knotty hoof. "I can assure you that I didn't hesitate a second that night. On the contrary."

"Really? But I still don't understand why your note could have such a decisive influence on Jacob so many years later."

"No, you don't understand. That note was supposed to remind Jacob that he still had a debt to repay."

"A debt for what? That you saved him from dying in a fire that you started yourself?"

"You've got this all backwards, Ravn. I never started that fire."

"But then why—"

"It was Jacob."

Ravn stared at Mesmer. "So the suicide note—"

"The note is Jacob's—*he* wrote it."

Ravn didn't know what to think. "I'm sick and tired of your lies, Mesmer," he said.

"I've never lied to you, Ravn. I merely held back information that I didn't think was relevant because I wished to protect the privacy of my family."

"So tell me this: Why did Jacob attempt suicide back then?"

"I honestly don't know. Perhaps it's like you said before: Men want to escape from a desperate situation they find themselves in."

"I didn't mention it to give you an excuse."

"That wasn't my intention. To this day, I cannot fathom why Jacob acted the way he did that day," Mesmer said, looking out over the water outside. "Finally everything was coming together: We had achieved excellent results with the Mesmogramme, and he was instrumental in that success. Our life's work was coming to fruition, large companies were standing in line to implement our system . . . we were making money like never before . . ."

"Perhaps Jacob had other priorities?"

"Jacob lived for his work; he *was* his work. He wasn't a family man, but he was content with what he had. He was a good father and husband who provided for his family."

"There is a difference between love and providing for other people's needs."

"I know that, but I have no reason to believe that he did not care about his family. That's why it all seems so absurd."

"Okay. So tell me what happened."

Mesmer took a deep breath. "I had noticed that Jacob had started to lose interest in the project," he began. "It was towards the end of the process when the development phase was over, and we were focussed on selling and implementing the system. He started arguing and contradicting colleagues in management, stopped attending meetings, and generally became increasingly introverted, but I thought it was just a phase he was going through." Mesmer looked up at Ravn, as if to implore for understanding. "I thought he needed time to adjust. Learn to enjoy the *fruits* of all his hard labour. But apparently this was impossible for him to do," he added bitterly.

"And the fire?"

Before he continued, Mesmer poured himself a glass of water from the jug on the table and took a sip. "I was working late that night and went into Jacob's office to fetch a report I needed. Jacob had gone home early, which wasn't unusual at that time. I was sitting at his desk, going through some files, when I noticed the notepad." Mesmer bowed his head. "It was pure luck that I saw his note."

"So what did you do?"

"I . . . I tried to call him, several times, but no one picked up the phone. So I drove to Virum, which is where they lived."

"If you thought they were in danger, why didn't you call the police?"

"I didn't take the note seriously—I didn't think he would do anything that stupid . . ."

"But he did?"

Mesmer nodded. "By the time I arrived, the house was in flames. The neighbours were standing out on the street, staring at it like terrified sheep. Luckily, someone had had the foresight to call the fire department, but they hadn't arrived yet."

"So you went in there yourself?"

"Yes, of course," Mesmer said. "The kitchen was in flames. I called their names, but no one answered. I was terrified that they were all dead, but I started searching the rooms . . . and I found them in the master bedroom, all three of them. Jacob was the only one still conscious. Elisabeth, his wife, and my grandson, Carl, were sleeping or unconscious— drugged, I later learned. Jacob was shocked to see me there. He began to cry hysterically, begging for forgiveness for what he had done, begging me to help him . . ."

"So what did you do?"

Mesmer looked Ravn square in the eye. "I pushed him aside and picked up my grandson," he said coldly. "I wasn't going to let Carl die because of his father's madness."

"Did the boy live?"

"Of course," Mesmer said indignantly. "I took him in. I looked after him. I got him safely out of the flames," he said, rubbing his hoof with his good hand.

"And after that . . . Jacob turned to religion?"

"Yes, but only after a lengthy period in a psychiatric hospital . . . He used his time there to simply delete from his mind everything that he'd done, everything that had happened, and cut all ties with his family. I think this was the only way he could move on: denial. He demonised his past and branded *me* as the Devil incarnate."

"What about the investigation into the fire? Were any charges laid?"

"Charges for what? It was an accident, a frying pan that overheated. A terrible tragedy in the suburbs. The case was closed—"

"Because you withheld important information—not least Jacob's suicide note."

"Everything I have done, I did for Carl's sake. To protect him. It's hard to grow up without your parents. I couldn't bear to burden him with the knowledge that his father had tried to kill him."

"So you've been taking care of the boy ever since?"

Mesmer nodded and looked out the window, his eyes searching the guests until his gaze fell on a young man in a blue suit and bright orange trainers. "Carl has just completed his psychology studies with distinction," he said with obvious pride. "Next year, he will go to INSEAD Business School in Fontainebleau."

"And I assume he stands to inherit your shop?" Ravn said, tapping a finger on the table.

"My *shop*, as you call it, needs new blood. New vision," Mesmer said curtly. "This merger builds a bridge between the private and public sector, a bridge across national borders. We are not just the people fuelling the machine in the steam room; we are *building* a new machine. You need specialists for that. With my guidance, Carl will take the helm."

"Just like his father did? Until he broke down?"

"I can hear an accusation in your tone, but I don't understand why."

"Because you're an unscrupulous, manipulating bastard who uses everyone around him."

"By all means, don't sugarcoat it," Mesmer remarked drily. "What you don't seem to understand is that there is a fine balance between appealing to a person's own moral code, their morals, ambitions, and personal needs, on the one hand, and applying physical or psychological pressure to elicit a reaction, on the other. The first is an art, the latter is the work of a psychopath."

"Save your sales pitch for the people out there on the dock," said Ravn. "Regardless of how you phrase it, I know perfectly well that the only thing you cared about was getting Jacob to waive his rights to the business. Even if it would cost him his life—not to mention the lives of his entire congregation. You knew exactly what button to push."

"I don't have that kind of power," Mesmer said. He appeared to be genuinely aghast by the accusation. "You're talking about a power that doesn't exist—it's contrary to nature . . . As Heisenberg puts it, indecision is an inherent part of human nature . . . not just an expression of human failure . . . or ignorance."

"I don't give a shit about Heisenberg or any other pseudo-academic bullshit you like to misquote, Mesmer. I hope you can live with your actions, and that you will be able to look your grandson in the eye one day, when the boy finally realises the truth: that you were to blame for his father's death, and the death of ninety-one innocent people."

Mesmer reached out for the envelope and opened it.

"Don't worry, the note is still in there. You can keep your dirty secret," Ravn said in disgust and stood up. His left leg was starting to cramp, and he swayed on his feet a little before he continued to the door.

"So what is it you want, Ravn? Just say—"

"Nothing that you can offer me," Ravn threw over his shoulder. "You and I are done."

73

A few days had passed since Ravn's meeting with Ferdinand Mesmer. He stood on *Bianca*'s aft deck with a hosepipe. It had taken him all morning to scrub the moss and dirt from the teakwood planks, and the sun was high. The rough physical labour had done him good, even if he needed to take a lot of breaks. Before Eva died, they had jogged together once a week, sometimes even twice. They usually ran along the embankment, following the path that led to Holmen. As a rule, they came back the same way, but once in a while, they'd run back along the canal and end up in one of the cafés for a cup of coffee. Good times. He'd take up running again, he thought, and clambered onto the quay to switch off the tap.

As he was winding up the hosepipe, his thoughts wandered to his meeting with Mesmer. A few papers had covered the merger, including some pictures from the reception. The picture of Mesmer with his grandson fascinated him. No matter how manipulating Ferdinand Mesmer was, he did not doubt the man's love for his grandson. Ravn's thoughts were interrupted by the loud snort from a lorry braking just behind him. He turned round and was surprised to recognise the dented truck from Lolland with Victoria's red Volvo loaded on the back.

"You're not easy to find," said Dan the Man, hopping out of the driver's seat. He grinned at Ravn and shook his hand heartily in greeting.

"It's good to see you," said Ravn.

"Well, it looks like that sect didn't kill you, eh? We followed the news in the papers," said Dan.

"Nope, I'm still here," said Ravn, slinging the hosepipe over the tap. "How are things going *downunder*, on Lolland?"

"Good, thanks," said Dan. "Apart from the invasion of tourists keen to see where it all happened." He rolled his eyes. "Even though there isn't much to see. Most of the farm burned down, you know. Is that where you live?" he said with a big smirk, nodding towards *Bianca*.

"Yup."

"And the Copenhageners call us *socially disadvantaged*?" he said, patting Ravn on the shoulder and laughing out loud. "But she's a beauty, no doubt about that."

"Thank you," said Ravn. "Should we unload the car, then?"

"Sure thing. But you haven't been particularly kind to the lovely ol' dame."

"What do you mean?" said Ravn, following round to the back of the tow truck.

"Well, first you cooked the radiator and now this . . ."

Ravn gaped at Victoria's Volvo in horror. The paint on the left side was blistered and black, exposing the bare chassis underneath, presumably from being too close to the inferno he'd caused on Gethsemane. All the windows were shattered, and the right rear tyre had melted and clung to the axle like a massive clot of dirty chewing gum.

"She still starts okay, but she's not pretty anymore. Shall we just put her down here?" said Dan, pointing to the free parking spot next to them on the bank.

"No!"

"No? Okay, so where would you like me to put her?"

"I can't return her looking like *that*," said Ravn, looking around frantically.

"Ah . . . is . . . did you borrow the car from someone else?"

Ravn nodded, wringing his hands as his brain raced, trying to figure out what to do.

"Hmm . . . no . . . the owner probably won't be thrilled about getting her back in this state."

"You think?!" Ravn dug out his mobile phone and opened his browser. "Come on," he said, moments later.

"Where are we going?" said Dan.

"I'll tell you along the way."

They jumped into the truck and the mechanic cruised down Overgaden Oven Vandet while Ravn searched for the nearest garage. He directed Dan the Man down Amagergade on the outskirts of the neighbourhood, so they wouldn't come too close to Victoria's bookshop. He shuddered to think what would happen if Victoria saw Wilma in her current condition.

Twenty minutes later, they pulled up in front of The Auto Body Shop on the outskirts of Kastrup. A young guy called Ali came out to greet them and looked over the damage.

"Can you fix it?" said Ravn.

"Well, everything can be fixed," said Ali. "The question is whether it's worth it."

"It is. Name your price," said Ravn.

Ali shook his head.

"I've got a real nice Passat for sale, a station wagon. I can give you a fair price."

"All right, mate. But it won't be cheap."

Ravn gave Ali his number, and Dan was kind enough to drive him back to *Bianca*.

"You're a good friend," Dan said in parting. "But honestly, I'd never let you borrow any car of mine."

After Dan had left, Ravn collapsed into his chair on the aft deck, and Møffe came over and lay down by the leg of his chair to offer some sympathy. Ravn scratched the dog behind the ears while he regarded his nicely scrubbed deck with satisfaction. Despite the upheaval with Wilma, he hadn't experienced any nausea, pounding heart, or muscle cramps, and he took that as a hopeful sign that he was on the mend.

In the evening it started to rain, and he went indoors. He even considered popping in at The Sea Otter, but the pub was less appealing now that he couldn't drink; he'd have to come up with a different hobby. He missed Eva. Her company.

He decided to get an early night.

In the early hours of the morning, Ravn woke up as *Bianca* dipped a few times suddenly, in the way she did when someone came aboard. He sat up in bed and looked out the open door of the cabin. Through the panes at the stern he could see two silhouettes moving in the dark. Møffe began to growl, which indicated that it wasn't Eduardo or someone the dog recognised.

Ravn crawled out of bed and grabbed a large torch that could serve as light as well as a makeshift weapon, although he doubted he had the strength to overpower a burglar. A figure appeared in the doorway, and he turned on the torch and shone it directly into the opening. Katrine shielded her eyes with one hand, while she fed Møffe a dog biscuit with the other. Møffe took the biscuit carefully and stopped growling. Behind Katrine, he noticed two other people, so he reckoned she hadn't come to spend the night.

"Put on some clothes, Ravn," she said.

"Where are we going?"

"Mr. Mesmer would like to talk to you. He's waiting outside," she said, pointing to the quay.

Ravn turned his head. Through the side pane, he saw the outline of the black Mercedes S idling on the embankment.

74

Ravn climbed up onto the quay and tried to smooth down the creased T-shirt he'd just pulled over his head. The street was deserted and had the metallic smell of rain on the cobblestones. He glanced at his watch. *Four o'clock in the goddamn morning*, he thought. As he bent down and laced up his trainers, he peered through the morning mist. Katrine had brought along two smartly trimmed young men in dark clothing. Athletic bodies, discreet, and watchful in their movements—probably former elite soldiers or secret service bodyguards, Ravn reckoned. He stood up and Katrine accompanied him to Mesmer's car.

"It was a lot more fun the last time you popped in," he said, trying to catch her eye, but she avoided him. "Any special reason for the back-up this morning?"

Katrine made no reply, merely opened the rear door of the Mercedes. Ravn couldn't fathom what Mesmer was doing there, or where this was going to end. He was keenly aware of the fact that he was the only one who knew about Jacob's suicide note, and that Mesmer was a man who needed to be in control. With this in mind, he got into the car beside Mesmer, and Katrine closed the door behind him.

It was relatively cool inside the car. Matte black carbon panels and grey leather seats. Mesmer gave him a measured look, and Ravn replied with a loud yawn. "What do you want, Mesmer?" he said.

Mesmer squirmed in his seat, making the leather creak in the still interior of the car. "I regret the way that we parted at the reception," he said. "I must have said something to offend you."

Ravn looked up at the glass roof of the Mercedes. A streetlamp cast an eerie light on them. "I'm tired of your company. It's four o'clock in the morning, and I'd like to go back to bed, so why don't you drop the small talk and fast-forward to where you tell me why you are here?"

"Very well," said Mesmer. "I'd like to conclude our business in an amiable manner."

"Why do you care what I think of you?"

"It is my wish to settle my debts equitably, so that no one feels cheated."

Ravn smiled. "You mean you're afraid I'm going to talk?"

"That's not the whole truth."

"No?" Ravn looked at Mesmer sceptically. "But rest assured, I'm not a snitch. It's not in my nature. And even if I were, the fact of the matter is that I don't give a shit about your business, your merger, least of all you and your family. Put in another way: Nothing about you is worth talking about. Is that clear enough for you?"

"Yes, perfectly clear."

"Great. And now I'd really like to go back to bed," Ravn said, gripping the door handle.

"What's the hurry? Is it just because you want to wake up refreshed for yet another day in your life that you hate?"

"No, in fact, I think I'm going to wake up to a beautiful day, as long as you don't show up."

"Always ready with a smart remark to cover up your pain, aren't you?"

"Save me your pseudo-psychoanalysis."

Mesmer shrugged. "I know your past, Ravn. I know about everything that pains you. I know why you quit your job with the police. Why you've been trying to drink yourself to death over the past three years. Why you agreed to take on cases for missing persons. It can all be boiled down to one word, right?"

"No, two words: fuck you."

Mesmer smiled. "Perhaps no more than one word, a name: Eva."

Ravn let go of the door handle and clenched his fists. "I don't know what you've heard, but this is not a subject you want to raise with me. Especially when you don't have your bodyguards to protect you."

"Take it easy, Ravn. There is no need for threats. All I want is to help you."

"I don't need your help, Mesmer."

"How can you turn down an offer that you haven't even heard?"

"Because I know that anything that comes from *you* is not worth having."

"Now you sound just like Jacob."

"Then perhaps he wasn't entirely nuts after all."

"I think we both know that has been proven beyond a doubt," Mesmer said gravely. "Why don't you take a deep breath and listen to what I have to say before your reptilian brain reacts blindly."

"Talk. Quickly."

Mesmer rubbed his deformed hand. "I can offer you what you have been hunting for the last six months. You have imposed upon your colleagues with no result. But I can help."

In spite of himself, Ravn could feel his heart hammering in his chest. "What exactly are you offering me?"

"Ten minutes."

"Excuse me? And who has been talking to you about me?"

"Why don't you try concentrating on my offer instead of breaking your head over how I collect my information. Just by looking at the people I surround myself with, you ought to know by now that I always get the information that I need. Half the police force knows that you can't let go of that case. And who can blame you? Family ties are often so strong it feels like they're strangling us . . ." Mesmer said with a devilish smile.

"Ten minutes," Mesmer repeated. "That is what I can offer you."

"I still don't understand."

"Ten minutes with Andrej Kaminsky."

Ravn's head snapped round to face Mesmer. "You're taking the piss."

"Nothing could be further from the truth."

"Are you trying to tell me that you have Kaminsky at your disposal? I don't see him here," Ravn spat out, looking round.

"According to my information, Kaminsky is being held in isolation in police headquarters. Cell number twelve. It's the cell at the very end of the isolation corridor."

"Are you saying you've got the keys?"

"I'm saying I have unhindered access to ten minutes with the prisoner, and I am offering this opportunity to you. Is Kaminsky not the man you want to talk to? Is he not the man you believe might have information about Eva's death?"

Ravn leaned back against the plush leather seat. "Am I supposed to believe that you can get me access to Kaminsky? I'm struggling to figure out what you hope to achieve with this charade."

"I'm trying to help you. Pay my debt to you," Mesmer said with a sigh. "You need to understand something: The world is controlled by people like me. We are the ones who make the rules that others have to follow. I'm not saying that we are above the law. All the power we have is a great responsibility, but it also gives us a free pass to do things that other people—people like you—could never dream of. I can even out the playing field. Call it a divine intervention if you like. This is what I am offering you: the loan of my free pass for ten minutes."

"So I can talk to Kaminsky at police headquarters?"

"Yes."

"And when would this happen?"

"Now."

Ravn regarded Mesmer evenly, trying to discern if he meant it. "I . . ." He shook his head. It felt wrong. All of it. This was not how he had imagined he would finally gain access to Kaminsky. What he really wanted was revenge. Kaminsky had been unattainable, a convenient target for his feelings.

"Shall we go?"

"I . . . I don't know."

Mesmer leaned towards him. "What's the matter, Ravn? Cat got your tongue for once in your life? Are you too scared to take your fate in your own hands?"

Ravn looked at him angrily. "Shut up, Mesmer, and call your driver."

75

The electric gate to police headquarters on Otto Mønsteds Gade slid open for the black Mercedes S, and they proceeded quietly through the neoclassical arches to the prison yard at the back. As soon as the car stopped, Katrine got out and opened the back door for Ravn. Mesmer turned towards him and shook his hand. "Farewell, Ravn. I hope you find what you're looking for."

Ravn nodded and got out of the car. He looked around the yard briefly. He had been there a few times many years ago, when he and the other members of a special unit investigating the first large-scale war between the various biker gangs commuted back and forth with prisoners. Four prison guards in black uniform were waiting for them at the entrance. Ravn and Katrine crossed the yard together. She greeted the lead guard, and he asked Ravn to follow him inside.

Katrine remained behind. "Ravn," she said.

Ravn glanced at her over his shoulder.

"Take care of yourself."

"Thank you," he mumbled, and continued up the stairs to the entrance.

The guards escorted Ravn up to the guards' locker room on the third floor. All four men were kitted out in full combat gear. The lead guard was a tall man with a full ginger beard. He walked over to a metal locker, took out another set of protective gear, and laid it out on the bench along with a helmet and an extra baton. "I suggest you put these on here, rather than wait until we get upstairs to the maximum security division."

"Is that really necessary?"

"To visit Kaminsky, yes."

The other guards were busy strapping on their helmets, goggles, and oxygen masks. One of them took a two-kilo container of tear gas out of his locker.

"Who are you going to gas?" asked Ravn.

"It's just a precaution," said the ginger-bearded guard.

"I think I'll give the combat gear a miss," said Ravn.

The guard gave him a tight-lipped smile. "It's my responsibility to get you in and out of his cell alive," he said.

"How many times has Kaminsky offered resistance?" Ravn asked.

"Every time we go in, without fail. We're not taking all these precautions for our own amusement."

"A zero-tolerance approach?"

"Exactly."

"Has it helped?"

"None of my men have been seriously injured to date, so yes, it's useful. But no, he isn't any less aggressive than the first day he arrived if that's what you mean."

"I'd like to try a different tactic. Shall we?" Ravn said, heading for the door without waiting for a reply, and the guards followed him reluctantly.

"Consider yourself warned," the guard mumbled.

Ravn and the guards took the stairs to the upper floors where the maximum security cells were located. When they reached the top floor, they continued down to the end of a corridor with red-painted metal doors and stopped in front of cell number twelve. The lead guard slid open the peephole and peered inside Kaminsky's cell.

"Is he awake?" Ravn asked.

"Kaminsky never sleeps," the guard replied in a metallic voice through his mask. "Kaminsky, we're coming in!" he yelled without further delay. "Please face the back wall with your arms up and your palms against the wall. Now, Kaminsky!"

"Piss off, you pig!" a gravelly voice called from inside the cell.

"You've got ten seconds before we gas you," the guard with the tear gas said. "Nine . . . eight . . . seven . . . six . . ."

"I'm on my way," Kaminsky said.

The lead guard stepped back from the peephole and unlocked the cell. On his signal, the second guard opened the door and the others filed into the cell in their full combat gear.

Kaminsky was standing with his back turned, facing the wall with his hands raised as requested. He was wearing a pair of red jogging bottoms and nothing else. His long black hair covered the top part of the large Orthodox cross that was tattooed on his back. Two guards approached the prisoner with a straitjacket while the other two covered them with batons raised. It took them less than a minute to strap Kaminsky into the jacket. "You can choose whether you want to put this on," the lead guard said to Kaminsky, holding up a muzzle.

Kaminsky looked at the guard lazily. "You look like shit. And as I don't eat shit, I'm not going to take a bite out of *you*," he said, and snapped his jaws viciously, making the guard jump back.

Kaminsky smiled. "Perhaps another time."

"Take him up to the kennel," said Ravn.

The ginger-bearded guard shook his head. "The deal was ten minutes. In *here*."

"I want to talk outside."

"That would be against the security protocol," the guard said. "The prisoner stays in his cell."

"We've already broken every rule in the book. It's no longer relevant to discuss proper procedure. Let's get him out, now, thank you."

The lead guard stared at Ravn for a moment, then nodded. Kaminsky looked at Ravn with curiosity. Then two guards hauled the prisoner into the corridor and up the stairs that led to the roof.

"Mind if I borrow this for a moment?" Ravn said, snatching the guard's baton before he could react.

76

The "kennel" was an eight-by-three-metre exercise quad on the roof of Copenhagen police headquarters. Leaning against the door to the stairwell, Ravn watched Kaminsky with a keen eye. He had shuffled to the middle of the quad and now looked up at the grey sky beyond the mesh-wire cage, filling his lungs with fresh morning air.

Kaminsky turned his head and regarded Ravn with a languid expression on his face. "Why did you wake me, pig?"

"They say you never sleep."

"I sleep, I wake up, I need coffee. Do you have any coffee?" he asked in Danish with a strong Slavic accent.

"No coffee. Just questions."

"You and about a million others ahead of you in the queue," Kaminsky said, cocking his head at Ravn. "But you're not like the others, are you? The others dress well. And they come to me in the daytime, not like a thief in the night. Are you one of the special forces pigs who attacked my business?"

"No."

"So it wasn't one of your friends I killed? Boom, boom, boom," he said, opening his eyes wide. In his straitjacket and with the mat of filthy black hair, Kaminsky looked every part the madman.

Ravn shook his head. "I didn't know him. He was new to the force. You shot a rookie."

"I've shot many people."

"Is that a confession?"

"Is that why you're here? To get a confession out of me? What are you going to do? Beat it out of me with your dick?" Kaminsky said, gyrating his hips. "You think I want to be your bitch?"

"Not at all. I'm not interested in what happened that day. Other people are handling that," Ravn said, leaning the baton up against the wall and taking a step away from it. "I have come to talk to you about a completely different case."

Kaminsky's eyes rested on the baton before fixing his gaze on Ravn, who had casually stuck his hands in the front pockets of his jeans. "You *are* a special forces man. Something tells me we've met before . . ."

"This is the first time I've ever clapped eyes on you," Ravn said, deadpan. "And hopefully the last," he added with a smile.

Kaminsky smiled in return. "I like you, little pig. What's your name?"

"My name is not important. I'm not here. And that means that the information that you give me cannot be used against you in a court of law."

"And why would I answer your questions? What do you take me for? A snitch? Do you know what happens to a snitch? I cut off his dick and feed it to him."

"Sounds unpleasant. But all I want from you is a little information on an old case so I can close the file."

"What do I get in return?"

"What would you like in return?"

"Let me hear what you want first, and then I'll name my price."

Ravn looked Kaminsky in the eye. He didn't sound convincing. More than anything else, it seemed as if he was simply drawing out the conversation so he could stay outside in the fresh air for as long as possible.

"I took a look at the stolen goods found at your premises," Ravn said. "Three containers full."

"Nothing to do with me."

"Give it a break, Kaminsky. Everybody knows that you've been storing stolen goods at your club on Colbjørnsensgade for years."

Kaminsky shook his head. "Are you trying to tell me that you've woken me to talk about . . . a few stolen flatscreens, little pig?" He laughed out loud. "You're pulling my leg. Who are you?"

"I wouldn't dream of pulling your leg, Kaminsky. And you know as well as I do that there's more than a couple of flatscreens in those containers. You've made good business over the years. All I want to know from you is this: Who delivered the goods?"

There was a loud bang on the metal door behind Ravn. "Three minutes!" yelled the guard.

Kaminsky gave him a cool smile. "Hmm. Sounds like you're running out of time, pig."

"You have a family, Kaminsky. A wife, three boys, and a little girl. I can make sure that they are given permission to come and visit you if that's what you want."

Kaminsky held his gaze. "Are you sure you have that kind of power?"

"I have enough power to be standing here right now. Judge for yourself."

"What exactly is it that you want to know?"

"I need to know who in your network was working the neighbourhoods about three years ago."

"I honestly can't remember, so many faces—"

"On Christianshavn. A break-in that went sideways. A young woman was killed. I need to know who the thief was."

Kaminsky cocked his head until his neck cracked. "Now I remember where I've seen you before . . . in the newspapers. It was *your* woman who was killed. You're that policeman whose girlfriend was killed while you were on the beat . . ."

"A name, Kaminsky. That's all I'm asking."

Kaminsky burst out laughing. "Man, God must really hate you," he said mockingly.

"Not as much as I hate him," Ravn said coldly. "A name, Kaminsky, in return for visitation rights for your family. Who was the perp, Kaminsky?"

"I'm not stupid, pig. You don't have that kind of power. I don't know how you got in here, but you can't offer me anything. You are a loser. What kind of policeman—what kind of *man*—can't even protect his own family?"

"Give me a name, Kaminsky."

"You're a pussy . . . a pussy-man—"

"A name!"

"Go fuck yourself."

Ravn took a step back and grabbed the baton. In that moment, Kaminsky charged at him headfirst like a bull. Ravn swung the baton and hit Kaminsky on the shoulder, sending him to the ground. He hammered into Kaminsky until his strength failed. "A name!" he yelled breathlessly.

Kaminsky looked up at him and spat. "You hit like a girl."

Ravn lifted the baton and aimed for Kaminsky's head. *This was useless*, he thought. Kaminsky would *never* talk. And his eternal silence meant there was no hope of solving Eva's case. He wanted it to stop. He wanted some peace. Kaminsky didn't kill Eva, but he had to pay for it—for all the blood he had on his hands.

"Your ten minutes are up," the ginger-bearded guard said behind him, grabbing the baton out of Ravn's hand.

"He doesn't know anything," said Ravn, looking down at Kaminsky. "You're going to rot in your cell, Kaminsky."

"I have more freedom than you'll ever have, pig," Kaminsky said, spitting a glob of blood at Ravn's feet. The other guards picked him up off the ground. "You've got to be the worst policeman that ever lived!" Kaminsky yelled at Ravn. "You must be fucking blind if you can't solve that case."

The lead guard nudged Ravn towards the door.

"You don't know shit!" Ravn snarled at Kaminsky over his shoulder.

"Ravn!" Kaminsky yelled.

Ravn turned round in the doorway, taken by surprise that Kaminsky knew his name after all. Either someone had given it to him, or he had read it in the papers. But there was clearly nothing wrong with his memory.

"I *know* that it wasn't a thief, Ravn. I *know* it."

Ravn held his gaze. *This guy was playing him, and he knew it.*

"You don't know shit, Kaminsky. Have a miserable life."

77

A sudden shift in the weather brought rain clouds over Christianshavn and the rest of the city of Copenhagen. Chasing the summer cheer away, the wind that followed the rain left the embankment wet and deserted. In multicoloured raincoats, the tourists crouched in the harbour tour boat that came past the misted-up windows of The Sea Otter, valiantly snapping pictures of the historic buildings with their cameras and mobile phones.

Ravn was propping up one end of the bar with Møffe curled up for a nap under his stool. It was a Tuesday morning, and apart from a couple of regulars seated at their tables by the window, the pub was empty.

"Would you like another cup of coffee?" Johnson said, holding the coffeepot in his hand.

"Just half a cup, thanks," said Ravn. Over the last hour, he had told Johnson about his bizarre meeting with Mesmer in the early hours of the morning, and his vigilante interview with Kaminsky at police headquarters thereafter. Johnson was not a man shy about weighing in with his opinion on just about anything, but this time, he listened quietly, simply plying Ravn with coffee until he had finished telling his story.

"It could've ended badly," Johnson said at last, lighting a cigarette.

"Yes. If the guard hadn't intervened, I could've crushed Kaminsky's skull."

"You shouldn't take everything so personally, Ravn."

"This is Eva we're talking about, Johnson."

"Exactly. And killing Kaminsky isn't going to bring her back."

"I know, I know," Ravn said, shaking his head.

"You don't want to end up like that detective you told me about, Bertil . . . Bernt—"

"Benjamin."

"Right, Benjamin. The guy chopped up by a beet hacker."

"It was a combine harvester, but no, I don't."

"You need to move on, my friend. Put all of this behind you. Be a professional," Johnson added for good measure with a strong Amager accent, and Ravn couldn't help smiling.

Ravn sipped his coffee. It tasted bitter, but he'd probably have to get used to it because Johnson had made it very clear that coffee and water was all he'd serve Ravn at the pub until his health improved.

"Kaminsky said that it wasn't a thief who killed Eva. He said I was too blind to see who it was."

Johnson stubbed out his cigarette in the ashtray. "Ravn, take it from an ex-boxer: You always psyche out your opponent before a match. He was playing you. The guy was desperate, for heaven's sake."

"I know that. I just wanted to tell you what he said."

"Forget that bastard Kaminsky. Forget all those arseholes."

Ravn nodded and slid off his barstool. "What do I owe you for the coffee?"

"It's on the house. As long as you don't order a latte or a cappuccino, or whatever folks call it nowadays . . ."

"I had no idea you served cappuccino."

"I don't. This is a pub, not a coffee shop. Where are you going?"

"To deliver Victoria's car."

"Well, it's about time. She's missed Wilma terribly."

"I know."

"I hope you've looked after it like gold," said Johnson, putting the coffeepot in the sink behind the bar.

An hour later, Ravn pulled over to the kerb in front of Victoria's bookshop in her shiny red Volvo. Ali was right. Yes, it *could* be fixed, and no, it *wasn't* cheap. Despite the sizable fee he had received from Mesmer, he only had a few thousand kroner left in his pocket. But he didn't care. What mattered was that Victoria was getting her beloved Wilma back in one piece.

Victoria was standing in the doorway when he climbed out of the car. Her eyes running over her car from bonnet to hatch, she puffed a cloud of blue smoke into the air. "So, finally you bring her back to me."

"I'm sorry it took such a long time, Victoria, but the police have only just released her," he said with a sheepish smile on his lips.

Victoria came over to Ravn and snatched the keys out of his hand. "Have you washed Wilma? She seems a lot shinier than usual."

"It was the least I could do."

Victoria sniffed loudly. "Is that wax I can smell? You didn't wax her, did you?"

"Of course not. If anything, it's elbow grease you can smell. I gave her a really good rubdown," he quipped.

Victoria took a tour round the car, examining it closely. Then she popped the keys into the breast pocket of her tweed suit. "It's good to see you, Ravn," she said, mollified. "I've just put a fresh pot of coffee on. Would you like a cup?"

"Thanks, but no thanks, Victoria. I've had more than enough coffee at The Sea Otter. And I've got a lot of things I need to do today."

"Oh yeah? Like what?" she said sceptically.

"I've been thinking about the suggestion you made when we went to visit Eva's grave."

"What part?"

"That I should start my own agency."

Victoria smiled. "I'll be damned. You really want to give it a try?"

"Yes. If the offer still stands to help me with the books and all that administrative crap."

"Of course I'll help you, Ravn. But what exactly are you going to do for clients?"

"I've received a stack of letters from all kinds of people who've read about my involvement in the Mesmer case, as well as the other two in Sweden and Germany. Folks who want me to investigate various things, but mostly missing persons. Some of the cases seem quite interesting."

Ravn noticed that Victoria was no longer listening. Something about the Volvo had caught her interest and she looked past him.

"What?" said Ravn as she slipped past him.

Victoria bent down and inspected the front fender. "Is . . . is that a . . . bullet hole?" She stuck her index finger through the little hole in the side.

Ravn damned Ali to hell for overlooking the hole. He tried to smile at Victoria. "Are you sure that hole wasn't there before?"

"One hundred per cent sure."

"Perhaps it's just rust, Victoria?"

"Rust?!"

Ravn nodded. "It's an old car, Victoria, so—"

"Wilma doesn't rust, Ravn!"

ABOUT THE AUTHOR

Michael Katz Krefeld (b. 1966) is one of the most-read Danish crime authors, and his critically acclaimed books have been awarded several fiction prizes. He is best known for his bestselling crime series featuring Detective Ravn, which has thrilled readers across the globe. Having begun his career as a screenwriter, Krefeld tends toward fast-paced and highly unpredictable thrillers. The fight against evil and personal sacrifices made for the greater good are typical recurring elements of his work.

Podium
DISCOVER
STORIES UNBOUND
PodiumAudio.com

www.ingramcontent.com/pod-product-compliance
Lightning Source LLC
Chambersburg PA
CBHW030934120726
47906CB00002B/572